I0746417

BAD CAT
GOOD WOLF

by

ERIC LITTLE

TABLE OF CONTENTS

Chapter 1—A COLD DAY IN PARADISE   3

Chapter 2—TREEHOUSE   10

Chapter 3—TIGER MOUNTAIN   17

Chapter 4—THE BOGACHIEL RIVER   21

Chapter 5—A CUTTING WIND   26

Chapter 6—BAD PACK TWO   31

Chapter 7—DRONES   36

Chapter 8—TIGER CATCHES MOUSE   41

Chapter 9—BOARDING PARTY   44

Chapter 10—STORIES   51

Chapter 11—WOOD STOVE AND WOLF-EARS   58

Chapter 12—CLOSE QUARTERS   64

Chapter 13—THE SKI LODGE   72

Chapter 14—THE BARGE   78

Chapter 15—THE INTERROGATION   82

Chapter 16—THE DROWNED FOREST   88

Chapter 17—BIRTH OF THE STONE MASONS   93

Chapter 18—SEALS AND NORSEMEN   98

Chapter 19—TIGER MOUNTAIN   104

Chapter 20—THE SARGASSO WIND   109

Chapter 21—STONE BY STONE   118

Chapter 22—THE VIKING DUDES   121

Chapter 23—BLOOD IN THE WATER   131

Chapter 24—SNOWBOARDS AND VIKING DUDES   138

Chapter 25—PRISONER   142

Chapter 26—RACHEL AND THE TIGER QUEEN   147

Chapter 27—BATTEN DOWN THE HATCHES   158

Chapter 28—MISSING   161

Chapter 29—THANK YOU, BUCKMINSTER FULLER   171

Chapter 30—TIGER TRAIL   174

Chapter 31—HOMEWARD BOUND   181

Chapter 32—IN THE QUEEN'S LAIR   188

Chapter 33—EVERYTHING LOOKS WHITE IN A BLIZZARD 192

Chapter 34—UNTO THE BREECH, ONCE AGAIN   203

Chapter 35—CAT FIGHT   208

Chapter 36—DOWNTOWN TIGERTOWN   215

Chapter 37—THE ART OF BATTLE   222

Chapter 38—WUDANG COMES TO TIGERTOWN   225

Chapter 39—THE WORLD IS BLEACHED AND I MUST SEE 231

Chapter 40—PEACE TALKS   240

Chapter 41—PLAYING IN THE MUD   250

Chapter 42—ON PATROL   261

Chapter 43—BAD DOG REDUX   269

Chapter 44—BLUE GLACIER   275

Chapter 45—THE INDIGO TOWER   286

Chapter 46—FOUND MY PARADISE   290

ABOUT THE AUTHOR

Chapter 1

A COLD DAY IN PARADISE

I awoke in warm pile of Wolves, shivering.

I turned my head to look up but couldn't see anything. We were covered by a thick layer of heavy snow. Pushing my way out from beneath the bear-hide blanket we all shared, I forced my way up until I freed my head and could look around. A white-gray alien landscape of shrieking wind and stinging ice crystals surrounded me. What had happened? Fumbling through the cobwebbed holes in my mind, I abruptly remembered.

The first snowstorm of winter wasn't due for five more days! Our newborn Nation of Wolves, a mixed colony of humans and Wolfkind, was on day two of forging a homeland in the Hoh Rain Forest, on the newly created island once known as the Olympic Peninsula. We were building a place where a former slave-Dog of the Commander's Navy could walk tall and not hide who they were. A place where we didn't have to shave our faces and arms to pass for human.

A land where nobody lies.

A haven for Wolves.

Wolf Haven.

I ducked back down out of the wind and nudged my second in command, Fitz, the Wolf formerly known as Five. He woke with a glare that I barely glimpsed before he lowered his eyes respectfully. It was my due, but only served to remind me of how badly he wanted my position as Alpha. Seems like it's always been that way, but I kept hoping for better between us.

"Fitz, let the cubs and everyone else sleep. Take Sigrid, Eddie, and Tinker. Your team needs to secure the camp's perimeter and the blind fisherman's boat. Ella, Theo, Ona, come with me. We're going to check on the humans. They're kind of fragile and we didn't expect this storm yet. Everyone meet there afterwards. Let's go!" I ordered. Snow burst in all directions, completely insignificant in the full fury of the blizzard.

My pack are too heavy to walk on top of the snow's crust, so we crunched as we waded through fresh snow, waist-high, forging a path through the howling ice storm. Wolves are single-minded in the pursuit of our goals. Humans usually call this 'stubborn' unless they have the same objective, and then it's called 'enthusiasm'.

We finally got to the big tent. A smoking stove pipe poked out the side, way up. The tent glowed a very dull orange despite the whirling snow. Light and heat! I breathed out and relaxed a little. The babble of cubs and too many people in one room confirmed my thoughts. I growled politely and began to unzip the tent's entrance. Small human hands quickly joined my larger but stubby paws and it opened onto a lot of humans.

They were glad to see us. Noisy, but very friendly. Not your usual humans, in my admittedly short experience—better than that, they were our new family, our tribe, and Wolves embrace their own. Even if they don't look like us.

Not all Wolves have fur.

A human might have found the crowded tent claustrophobic, but it didn't bother us. People scooted over to make an empty spot for me on the ground. I carefully sat down in the overheated room. Wolfkind are noticeably larger than humans, but we don't need as much personal space as they do. They talk a lot, too. We were beginning to get used to that, but still had a long way to go.

When the snowfall ended late that morning, I eagerly followed Sigrid, Eddie, and the blind fisherman so they could show me where they wanted us to build a snug winter home. The cubs tagged along, happy to be out in the fresh forest air and a part of what was going on.

I leaned back to examine the towering Incense Cedar they had selected. It was huge, with mammoth branches spreading wide and blotting out the sky. It was only one tree in a forest of millions, but this one smelled of serenity and calm strength. It was beautiful.

All three adults and the two cubs were watching me for a reaction. As the pack's Alpha, I was used to this.

An errant wind whipped by, bringing a hint of winter strong enough to ripple the fur on my arms. I considered the matter. This was too important to our survival to get wrong.

"I like being up high where we can see everything while we can't be seen from the ground, but the Fisher clan can't climb like us," I offered.

Rachel studied the mammoth tree as well, leaning so far back that most humans would have fallen over, but she wasn't exactly *most* humans. She was a Wolf in human clothing, a girl cub of nine winters. Just because she looked like a human on the outside didn't keep her from being a Wolf in my pack.

Eddied and Sigrid, on the other hand, looked exactly like what they were, Timber Wolves with lots of human genes mixed in here and there. We were all hybrids like that except for Bookworm and Rachel, the pack's cubs. They were rescues. Now they're important members of our family.

Pack.

There are no stronger ties.

"What if we make long rope ladders that get pulled up when not in use," suggested Lenny, as he joined us. He was one of the good humans, a member of the blind fisherman's clan. In my experience, good humans were pretty rare, but none of us remembered much from back in the day when we were elite soldiers, so maybe that didn't say much.

I wasn't excited about the ladder idea. It would be difficult for humans to use, and Wolves were too heavy for such things. There had to be a better way. Maybe we could raise and lower people somehow? I saved the idea in the back of my head and turned to look at Sigrid.

We don't call her Seven anymore.

"I think we could take apart the abandoned tourist buildings down by the parking lot and use the wood to build a den up high where no one looks. The construction will go fast because the pieces are already dried and cut," she explained.

"Sigrid, I like it. How long do we have until the big snowstorm hits?" I asked. Everyone turned to look at our main tech Wolf. She speaks machine. Sigrid pulled up a weather map on her iPad. A red light was blinking on the computer, but she ignored both it and us as she studied the screen.

"All those wooden pieces mean lots of holes where the wind gets in. We would need to find a way to plug all the holes. Underground would be better, easier to heat and defend in case of attack," I suggested as we waited for her response.

"The American weather service predicts the first significant snowfall in maybe five days. The big storm front coming off the Pacific should hit us in seven days at most, but they can shift unpredictably due to fluctuating high-and-low-pressure fronts. We're pretty far back in the mountain foothills, but we're still going to need shelter before the storms hit, Alpha," Sigrid reported.

Well, that settled that. There wasn't enough time to dig a waterproof underground den that would hold all twenty-eight of us, Wolves and humans alike.

"Treehouse," I decided.

"If we completely disassemble the buildings, will we have enough extra material to put up a smokehouse like the fisher folk want?" I added.

Sigrid nodded abstractly, her mind already building castles in the sky.

I nodded back and looked at Fitz, my second in command. "Send two hunting parties into the rain forest and bring back enough deer to last several days. Everyone not on guard duty is on lumber breakdown detail. Bring everything here, to the base of this tree. Let's do it!" I growled and Wolves scrambled everywhere.

I scrambled too.

We Wolfkind were born of suicidal special-forces volunteers, our blank-mind bodies regrown by the Commander's genetic scientists. The scientists were our cold mothers, creating us in the secret compounds beneath Indian Island, and the Commander was our deadly father. He called us Dogs, made us eat slop from rusty trenches, and wear terrible collars that shocked us into unconsciousness at best, and death at worst. We guarded the Navy's Special Weapons, and no one ever got past us.

But then I woke up.

I realized that we were Wolves, not Dogs. Dogs assume the good-Dog position when someone yells at them. Dogs fear the master.

Wolves don't.

We painfully taught ourselves how to walk upright like humans again, even though our modified bodies weren't exactly designed for it anymore. We practiced in secret and carefully watched our keepers, memorizing their ways and gate passcodes. Eventually, we escaped the Commander and his Naval base, by imitating humans.

The world turned out to be a far larger place than we had realized.

YouTube became our teacher, and our minds soaked up data thirstily, attempting to fill the holes in our heads where memories used to go. We learned how to shave our arms and upper faces, how to dress so that we could walk among the humans without detection. Our former military training and fighting skills had been too valuable for the Commander to suppress and our paws remember the instruments of violence, though we can't even recall our original names or who we once loved.

Finding a channel on YouTube featuring the Hoh Rain Forest on the Olympic Peninsula of Washington State was the turning point. It was a place conceived for Wolves, and we immediately named it our Promised Land. When it came time to run again, this time we ran *to*, instead of *away*.

We made it partway there before the world we'd studied so hard vanished.

When we finally reached our Promised Land after all that struggle and loss[1], it felt like a heavy log had dropped away from our shoulders, and we could stand tall. That was when we cast off the numbers we had been given as slave-Dogs and chose free names for ourselves.

---

[1] "Bad Dog, Good Wolf" Book One of the Good Wolf Series.

The Hoh Rain Forest is a place of surpassing beauty, filled with towering trees, brooks and rivers, and dense emerald ferns as high as a wolf stands. You somehow instinctively knew this was a place where a Wolf could be Wolfkind, instead of hiding his true self.

I just never thought much about what to do when we finally got here.

Now winter was bearing down on us like a freight train, and Ella—that's the name she chose instead of Eleven—was saying that all the online forecasts were moaning about weather pattern disruptions from the massive fault shifts and Mount St. Helen's reawaking, several weeks earlier when the world changed forever. The experts on the mainland were arguing about ice-age winters and maybe no spring or summer. It could be years before we actually saw the sun.

However, we have learned that humans frequently lie, so we don't put much faith in their predictions. It didn't matter anyway. We were here now, and <u>nothing</u> would drive us from our home.

By the time night fell on our second day, we had disassembled the tourist center maintenance building and the attached garage down to the foundation. We were just getting started on removing the roof of the main tourist center. Wooden beams and plywood panels were organized in growing piles beneath the soaring tree. I looked around at our progress, then snarled to get everyone's attention.

"Return to camp, we'll eat and sleep, and get up as soon as we can see our paws in the morning light. Fitz, set guard duty. Everyone, make sure you wash up in the river before dinner. Grandma's making something called venison stew. Let's go!" I said, before turning and trotting downhill to the Bogachiel River. I was actually pretty tired, but an alpha Wolf doesn't let that show.

The water was cold, but we had fur for a reason. Rachel and Bookworm had to change into dry clothes, though, and complained as usual that they didn't have any fur except on their heads. Puppy snarls with no bite. I hid my silent wolf laugh as usual. Our cubs complain about small things, easily fixed. Their pack never lets the larger things get to them. We cherish our young.

The campsite had a long fire pit filled with glowing coals that looked like rubies in the last bit of the day's golden sunset. The fire pit was hung with simmering pots that smelled delicious. Over in a nearby clearing, a large bonfire was being built for after dark. Night falls quickly in the mountain foothills, and it had been rainy off and on all day. When that happens, the darkness can be absolute.

Our people, be they Wolf or Human, had been gathering at the bonfire after dinner. Eventually, somebody usually starts singing and then the Fisher clan all joins in—even though there's no full moon! But the best was yet to come.

After a while, people began taking turns telling stories!

We Wolves love to hear stories, our minds immediately enriching the words with color and scent and texture as we gazed abstractly into the crackling fire. Such things become important when you don't have actual memories to fill the holes in your mind.

Fires have quickly become more than just a heat source for us. Some of us had lost their entire families to fire. (Some of us couldn't keep from poking at it with a sharp stick.) Fires push back the darkness and keep our ancient enemies at a distance, even if we can't remember what forms they take. And thoughts wander in strange neighborhoods after staring into the firelight for a while. There is a comfortable, quiet introspection that joins us all together around a blazing fire. And we needed all the help we could get to meld clan and pack, Humankind and Wolfkind, into a cohesive nation before the Commander came looking for us in the spring.

It was going to be a long winter.

Chapter 2

TREEHOUSE

The next morning, we built the fire back up as the sun rose. The cold fog hung over us everywhere, but our fur and the fire kept us warm. Soon the humans started burning things over the fire so they could eat again. They do that a lot.

Eating.

I looked around at my Wolves. The pack was of one impatient mind—it was time to get to work. I raised my snout and everyone immediately headed for the giant tree we had selected.

Digging the razor-sharp talons jutting out from my back paws into the rough bark of the towering tree, I tore paw-sized steps as I ascended. At the same time, my upper paws sank effortlessly into the tree trunk, allowing me to climb rapidly.

It was a long way up.

When I reached the sliced marker high up on the tree's trunk, I stepped out on a wide branch and turned to face Sigrid and Eddie (once known as Eight) as they climbed up behind me. I felt small next to the massive trunk of this beautiful Incense Cedar. The tree's needles perfumed the air around us in scents of juniper and mint. Sunlight poured down through the tree's upper branches in thick beams of gold, piercing the mid-canopy of the Hoh Rain Forest. Lots of sweet birdsong rained down around us, but no avian flocks were anywhere to be seen. It was utterly magical.

Sigrid had gouged out lines in the bark with her talons, so we would know where to cut into the massive trunk. We needed to cut beam-sized notches on all four sides to secure the main weight-bearing beams. I was impressed with her ability to visualize her creations in three-dimensional detail and organize our tribe to make them real.

My pack have always laid out escape routes wherever we stay, even for a night. The emergency routes were usually way up in the mid-canopy of a forest, so we tended to associate being out of sight, high up in the forest, with being safe. Nobody looks up when they should.

Besides, everyone knows dogs can't climb trees and Commander Elwha saw us as runaway, unchained slave-Dogs. Bad Dogs. I may have growled a little at the thought. We needed to be ready. He would be coming after us someday soon.

Even the Apocalypse wasn't going to change that.

My head was stuffed full of things to do in a hurry. But that's an Alpha's duty, protecting his pack. I suddenly sensed movement far below us and leaned out a little but couldn't see anything— usually a good thing, though not always convenient. Leaping to the branch four meters below, then to the trunk, I began descending at speed, my talons leaving dark holes in the bright green velvet moss.

I didn't sense any danger, so I took a good look at the crowd of humans below as I descended. Sigrid and Eddie were a few meters behind me the whole way. When I reached the forest floor, I walked over curiously to see what was happening.

Everyone in the camp was there, all the humans, carrying buckets and wearing tools on their belts. They were also loaded down with more rope than I'd ever seen.

"Well, you didn't expect to get this done quickly without us, did you? What were you going to do, climb the tree one handed while holding on to a wooden beam with the other hand?" Lenny asked, quietly baring his tiny teeth, his eyes sparkling in humor. Other human voices chimed in, sounding happy.

"That's exactly what we are going to do!" Rachel declared flatly, ever protective of her pack. The happy noises stopped. Everyone looked at me.

"I guess I'm used to thinking only of the Wolves," I admitted, "Thank you for coming to help." I glanced at Sigrid and shrugged.

She shrugged back, then picked up a wide beam with her right paw and climbed into the treetops at speed.

Maybe she was impatient.

I grabbed an armful of rope and followed her. Immediately, all of my pack followed suit and joined me in the tree's canopy with arms full of building supplies and several long ropes. Sigrid started organizing things, and soon the humans were being hoisted up the massive cedar to join us.

On the ground below us, the Fisher clan assembled a square wooden platform that had a rope at each corner, connecting to a cable above it. Tosh and her daughters held the anchor rope that kept the platform from spinning as it was raised to the building level of the tree. This "pulley" thing was very clever, and we were able to lift quite a bit of stuff at a time.

Sigrid was a boss Wolf in her element, as she efficiently directed different teams of humans and Wolves in their tasks as the initial framework of the Treehouse was secured into place. The first two main beams fit neatly into the parallel grooves we had chiseled along both sides of the massive tree trunk, about thirty meters up from the ground. Once the other two cross-beams were in place, a series of foundation beams were laid across them, distributing the weight evenly. Then the floor of the first level was nailed onto these foundation beams, moving clock-wise, until we had a hexagram shaped platform hugging the tree. Then we moved on up to the next level and started over.

We had decided on three floors: the bottom one for Wolves to sleep in, the top one for humans, and a common level between the two where we could cook, eat, work on projects, or just hang out. This was also where we were going to install the old wood stove we'd found in the park workshop. I hoped the cast-iron monster would be the indoor bonfire for us once it was too cold outside at night. Sigrid said there was a lot of talk about a very bad winter on her satellite computer link, so I wanted to be ready for hard times.

By midday, we had finished the second floor and were rotating out for 'lunch breaks'. Humans sure did spend a lot of time burning perfectly good meat and eating.

As soon as the first two levels were floored, Sigrid assigned half of us to the job of attaching wall struts around the perimeter of the floors and the other half to constructing the third level. It's a good thing we heal fast. Hammers can do a lot of damage when they strike your paw instead of the nail. We learned quickly.

We quit at sundown, because some of us couldn't see what we were doing anymore, but by that point we had a framed roof!

For dinner that night we singed elk steaks with fat, oddly shaped, orange roots cooked in the fire's ashes. The Fisher clan called them yams, and said they were strong in nutrients. I thought they were way too soft, almost like chewing colored water, but didn't say anything. Grandma was enthusiastic about the orange things, and I didn't want to make her feel bad. Her other stuff was pretty good, for human food.

At the bonfire that night, people started talking about the day's work, and what we wanted to do tomorrow. It was pretty clear by this time that humans loved talking about their day, but we didn't mind. My Wolves all found this to be very interesting, if a little odd at times.

We learn more by listening instead of talking all the time.

It turned out that the Fisher clan had a well-defined hierarchy just like us, with the blind fisherman and the youngest cub, Witboy, at the bottom. Maybe that was why we worked so well together. All of us knew each other's rank in the command hierarchy. That tended to make things simpler and more efficient.

"We need to seal all those gaps and small holes all over our new home, otherwise we'll freeze to death when the storms hit," I said. I remembered how easily the cold wind found ways in during our trip over the big mountains. Even a few icy drafts would make our den very cold, especially for our humans.

"If we could wrap the Treehouse in the sails from that wrecked sailboat down at the river, we wouldn't have to fix each hole. There must be thousands of openings," Bookworm said into the fire-lit quiet as everyone thought about the problem.

I straightened up on my log and patted our youngest cub on the back. It had taken him a while to speak again after he lost his mother. He still didn't talk much, but we'd all learned to listen when he did. He was surrounded by his pack now and felt secure. Maybe for the first time in his life.

"Good idea, cub!" I told him quietly, but of course everyone heard me. I'm the Alpha, and Wolves have very good hearing. The blind fisherman's people were learning to listen like Wolfkind as well. Bookworm straightened a little in posture and touched the small book in his pocket with his right hand.

"When I was in high school, I worked for a while building fiberglass boats," Lenny said. We all looked at him, his black beard shining bronze in the firelight. He had a daughter on one knee and Witboy leaning against the other. His wife, Tosh, was sitting to the right beside him on his log with a daughter under each arm, her blond hair gleaming in the firelight.

There were lots of teeth showing. This wasn't a bad thing for most humans. In fact, humans thought this was a friendly expression, kind of like tail wagging. It all seemed backwards to me, but I was learning.

"So, we took this rough cloth, some woven stuff made of glass fibers, and laid it over a form. Slathered resin on it, see?" Lenny explained, "Once it dried, it was waterproof, firm, and very strong. Layer after layer of it the same way. Sailcloth isn't as loosely woven, but I think maybe we could paint it with resin and seal it in the same way."

"Resin?" I asked.

"Like honey that hardens into a shell," Lenny said.

Huh. My eyes met Sigrid's and she gave me a chin up. I glanced at Fitz and Ella; they concurred.

"Sounds good. Where do we get this resin?" I asked, "Are the sails on that wreck big enough to wrap three stories of Treehouse? Where would we get more?"

The blind fisherman cleared his throat. Everybody looked at him and hushed. When Grandpa speaks, everyone pays attention.

"When we came inland past La Push, there wasn't much left of the town. The tsunami slammed right over everything like a steamroller, leaving only sand and scoured foundations behind it. The Pacific coastal towns didn't stand a chance. Over six hundred boats from the marinas and charters, all thrown inland by a half-mile-high monster wave in a bad mood. About a kilometer inland, Henry started seeing boats in trees, floating buildings, cars stuck in barn roofs—no barn, just roofs, all kinds of strange flotsam. It had been long enough since the event that everything living had made it out a while ago. That left only the dead," he paused, before continuing.

"I sent everyone below deck except Henry after La Push. The stink of rotting fish and flesh lay over the land like some terrible blanket. The buzzing of the flies was a loud drone, but it was the maddened cries of feeding seagulls and eagles that were the loudest. I hope to never hear that hopeless music again," the fisherman said.

We all looked at each other; nobody knew what to say to that.

He continued. "After several hours sailing inland through the new channel, we left most of the stench behind, but I can still smell it in my mind. Not particularly excited about going back there, but it looks like we need to. In the morning, I'll take the *Becky's Reward* back down river, and we'll salvage what we need from the hundreds of wrecked boats scattered along the river," the blind fisherman offered.

"We're coming, too. You never know when you'll need a Wolf or three," I offered back. The white-haired grandpa chuckled.

"You never know," he agreed.

I ruffled Rachel's hair and leaned forward into the bonfire's light. Ella leaned forward into the firelight as well, focusing on the discussion with laser intensity. She tends to be a little protective of her Alpha sometimes.

"We'll leave at dawn, hopefully be back before dark with everything we need. Lenny, we'll need your help," I said. Lenny nodded easily. "Eddie, Twist, Tinker, and Nina, come with us on the boat. Everyone else work on finishing the Treehouse roof and walls. Storm's coming. Sigrid, you're in charge of everything above ground. Fitz, you're in charge of everything on the ground, as well as all security. Watch over the cubs!" I ordered. I exchanged looks with Grandma and waited. Wolves understand how to work together on a gut level.

"Humans and Wolves both," she said. "We're all the same tribe here. Pack and clan together. There won't be any discipline problems while you're gone, Alpha. Also, I'm getting low on supplies. Please find me some more canned tomatoes, basil, and flour. Then I can make a lot more cioppino and baguettes, providing I can put together an oven of sorts. Any questions?" she finished, obviously not expecting any. There weren't any. Everyone listened closely to Grandma, I'd noticed.

My mouth may have watered a little at the thought of the spicy seafood stew. It was really tasty in spite of the charred fish.

Chapter 3

TIGER MOUNTAIN

The snowstorm crashed against the base of the major's mountain, which contained her newly dug command bunker and overlooked prime hunting territory. She stepped lithely out onto the small observation balcony overlooking the western mountain slopes, all the way to the Pacific Ocean, if you had really good eyes. She placed her razor-tipped claws on the balcony's rim; like everything else here, it was perfectly scaled for a Tigerkind almost three meters tall.

Major Malgato breathed in deeply, savoring the small life signs in all their fecund splendor, pushed upwind of the storm's approach. The snow already lay waist deep in the valley below. She gazed without focus over her western domain, lost in thought.

She was tired. Major Malgato and her Tigerkin, formerly of the People's Republic of China Army Special Forces, had worked tirelessly to dig out this comfortable bunker. It was big enough for everyone, but she craved solitude. The next item on her plate was to get the team digging each of her people's mountain dens. Then she'd finally have some room to breathe. She leaned forward, studying the mountainside.

From here, looking over the western mountains, the major ran her two-week old mountain kingdom. Behind her inside the bunker were the six surviving members of the original strike force; cutting-edge hybrids crafted from 'volunteer' elite Chinese soldiers crossed with Siberian Tiger genes.

Only six. She almost sighed. When she had first set foot on the gray sand beaches of this beautiful land, the major had commanded more than twice that many.

That was less than a month ago. These barbarians were deadly at times. The native humans in this magnificent place may have been referred to as mice by her kind, but she had lost more of her pride here than in all of their campaigns for the People's Republic of China combined.

Thankfully, the six remaining Tigerkind were sufficient for her plans. They were all females except for one: Timing. In the spring, they would all have kits, and begin building a fighting force like this world had never seen. No longer would fat humans send her Tigers to die while they feasted at banquets. At last, there would be a place in the world where a Tiger didn't have to bow to mice.

Like so many times before, her thoughts were dragged once again to her humiliating defeat at the hands of highly trained walrus's or something like that. "Seals!" her disloyal brain supplied. She growled low and rough, engulfed by the memory.

The plan had been ideal—it had worked for them dozens of times. Tibet, Taiwan, Ethiopia. All went off without a hitch. Then she came to this cold and beautiful land.

It lay torn open for them; the tectonic shifts, the massive earthquakes, the tsunamis had completely destroyed the coastal infrastructure and isolated the Olympic Peninsula, now a massive island. Their vindictive president had even abandoned them via Twitter.

The newborn Island of Olympia was anybody's prey.

The mission was to penetrate Kitsap-Bangor Naval base, surveille, and clean out any mice nests. Then plunder some of the Special Weapons vaults. The base was supposed to be abandoned, with only a handful of sailors left behind.

Intel didn't mention they were Navy SEALs. Or that railguns had been miniaturized to the point that a single human could wield one. Queen Malgato had to learn that the hard way. And it was an expensive lesson—she lost half her team.

That was when she encountered the most hateful rodent of all, the big human wielding the sci-fi weapon she'd only heard of in low voices. Him. Captain Marc Christensen. Sneering at the image in her mind, she turned back to enter her command bunker again and faced her team.

The six Tigerkind looked back.

Everyone was completely healed up from the fight, but their nanite repair tech had worked really hard, and was now dormant in a recharge state or had gone to bed for a really long nap. Either way, it was not a good time to get hurt. Tigerkind weren't used to being careful that way and found the whole thing quite annoying. Almost as annoying as being cooped up with five other Tigers all the time.

Tigers weren't much for cuddling.

Squad leader Timing stood over two and a half meters high and would never be mistaken for a human, even in the dimmest of light. His head was mostly tiger, with the only hint of his human heritage showing around the nose and eyes. His male, striped Siberian tiger fur rippled in the usual patterns, but he stood upright like a human, and his eyes held a keen intelligence that was frightening in a body like that.

In between the flexible web of ammo and weapons that covered his elongated torso, bursts of fur jutted out, some of them still dyed the dull maroon of dried blood. His long body and muscular thighs were counterbalanced by wide shoulders with assorted weapons peeking over them. Like all the others, he was carrying a small armory including a missile launcher, assault rifle, scatter-gun, grenade launcher, and a full-auto .772 machine gun. Then there were the side arms and blades, too many to count quickly.

Tigerkin are deadly warriors; resourceful and very strong. That's why they need so much meat to survive. And Tigers are pan-species carnivores. They'll eat just about anyone.

"Just as I promised you, one Tiger, one mountain, like in the old days," the major announced, "Unlike the old days, we will spend three days a week working together to construct home dens for each of you and fortifications. We will spend another two days each week on staggered patrol schedules to maintain a secure kingdom. The remaining two days of the week are your own. Once we have properly marked our borders, we will all be able to relax and spend a little more time exploring. There are so many deer and elk here that the land is out of balance. We will hunt and glory in the meat we take. The mountains will be in balance again. Tigerkind has come." She stretched and continued.

"Unfortunately, our old human masters aren't going to be content to let us die of old age. They'll be coming as soon as they locate us. We must be ready," she snarled. Her Tigers snarled along in support. Nobody liked those guys.

Their old bosses in Beijing were quite capable, but they weren't Tigers. They were mice, and the natural prey of Tigerkind. Fifty on one is no problem for a Tiger. But the People's Army of China outnumbered the major's team a half-million to one. And as life had so grimly shown recently, a powerful weapon doesn't care who wields it—mice or Tiger. It kills all the same.

"We were lacking significant intelligence on the weapon capacity of the Trident base. Kitsap-Bangor was supposed to be lightly defended, if at all. Nobody said anything about Navy SEALs armed with railguns," Major Malgato paused and extended her claws into the unfinished floor beneath them. It was soft and very unsatisfying.

"We need that weapon before Beijing comes calling. I also want to clean that nest of humans from the earth. But by spring, we will know what we're stepping into. This time it will be different," she spit with an angry lash of her tail before turning her back to them and padding over to a heap of mismatched components partially wired together on the raw-pine communications bench.

"Xi-Rong, report on this mess," The major snarled.

Xi-Rong cringed. It didn't matter that she hadn't been given sufficient time to make sense of the pile yet. When the major's claws were out like this, you had to move quickly and produce any kind of result you could. She delved into the mound of electronic components like it was a fresh kill and soon the major's attention moved on. Xi-Rong knew better than to relax though and kept working with a nervous determination bordering on fear.

Bad things could happen when Tigers were cooped up together for too long.

And this was definitely too long.

Chapter 4

THE BOGACHIEL RIVER

At dawn my team met at the blind fisherman's boat, the *Becky's Reward*. Henry was waiting for us when we got there. I wasn't sure what went on in his head sometimes; he seemed pretty intellectual most of the time, but he also walked with a fluid economy of movement that whispered of hidden strengths. Maybe that's why I liked him. He had not a little Wolf spirit, even if it was concealed beneath a deceptively harmless effect.

I patted the blind fisherman on the shoulder as I passed him coming aboard, and he immediately went to the wheelhouse and began guiding the proud *Becky* efficiently out into the water. The sun was rising behind us as we puttered down the Bogachiel River westward towards the Pacific Ocean.

We Wolves immediately moved out onto the forward deck, savoring the river wind's mélange of exotic scent pouring upwind in our faces. All the humans clutched cups of hot bean-water, sipping constantly until the sun fully rose behind us. They stayed on the bridge, declining the cold, divine wind in favor of a heated wheelhouse. Just as well. We took up a lot of room on the modest bow of the *Becky*.

We knew the captain and Lenny could still see through the windows just fine, because after a while the blind fisherman cut his engines, and slow-slid into a stationary position on the river's port shore, where a forty-foot two-masted sailboat lay crumpled and broken. Lenny and the blind fisherman joined us on the

Becky's forward deck, and we all studied the remains of the once proud sailboat.

Her sails were torn here and there, but for the most part intact, if tangled in serious knots around the crumpled masts. There were ropes everywhere, and a gaping hole in the sailboat's midsection beckoned us with promises of mysterious treasure. I turned to check with the blind fisherman, and he somehow knew, urging me on with a dusting flick of his right hand. I growled my intention and leapt forward onto the boat's broken deck in sync with my Wolves.

The sails were our first priority, followed by rope and the honey stuff Lenny called resin. We loaded up the first two, but Twist only found a small bucket of resin below decks. Lenny said we would need at least fifty times this amount. We were going to have to continue our voyage down the river.

We drained the fuel tanks and removed a water storage tank, as well as a small gas oven including propane for Grandma. We also took five boxes filled with fancy bottles from the yacht's extensive bar. Lenny said it would make good trading stock when we eventually ran into other people. Lenny, Henry, and the old fisherman sampled some of the amber bottles to make sure it wasn't spoiled. They seemed pretty happy after that, so it must have not been ruined. It all smelled terrible to me. I was glad they could tell the difference.

We investigated three other similar wrecks in the next few hours, but the last boat was different. Lenny said it had been a Coast Guard cutter. Military. We didn't care much for the way the Navy had treated us, and I said so. The blind fisherman said that not all military forces were the same, and that the Coast Guard was quite different from the Commander's Navy.

That remained to be seen.

I focused my attention on the silent ship before us. It was named the C. S. Lewis, out of San Diego. The ship smelled of partially dried blood, but when we boarded it was obvious that the steel deck under our paws had been chemical-wiped clean of any scent except the harsh chemicals someone used. I turned to look at Lenny and the blind fisherman waiting back on the *Becky*'s Reward. Then I raised my nose and drew in a deep breath.

Once you got beyond the cleaning stuff, the dominant scent was that of not too recently spilled human blood, urine, and burnt oil. It was apparently seeping up from the engine room below decks. I looked at my Wolves, and we were of one mind.

Something bad had happened here.

Now we were all on high alert, even though what had happened here was firmly in the past. The vague nuances of clotted blood, spilled bowels and overripe bodies said it all. I was glad I had left Rachel and Bookworm back at camp. I didn't want our cubs to see what was waiting for us below decks. I didn't want them to smell it, for that matter.

As far as we were concerned, this was a pack matter now because it had happened in our forest. I was suddenly glad I'd left the blind fisherman and Lenny behind with Nina the White Wolf to guard the *Becky's Reward*. It might be the only fully operational boat within hundreds of kilometers, and human predator-packs always needed to be mobile. They tended to use up places pretty fast.

The smashed wheelhouse door was ajar, inviting us into the dark with a dank sneer. Nothing spooky about that!

I raised my chin slightly and some of our pack growled deeply down where you could feel it more than hear it. We entered and after looking around, I nodded to Twist; he quickly pulled a small tool from his belt and got us through the locked hatch inside the wheelhouse leading belowdecks.

His paws may have looked clumsy when he stuck pieces of wire in the door's lock, but we were through in record time, and he stared at his paws for a moment in awe. I suspect certain old skills lay closer to the surface these days than the Commander had ever intended.

We followed the corridor to the next hatch, and then down into a moderate-sized room stuffed full of machinery and bodies.

Seventeen dead humans lay crumpled helplessly in the hard spaces between the masses of gray machinery. The males were bullet-ridden, their once white uniforms more red than blue. The females… I took a great nose in and studied the scent picture as I exhaled though my mouth.

Anger bloomed to life in my heart as I detected another scent. These feral human predators were always in rut, more animal than the Dogs they tried to make us into. We all shared looks, a wordless promise to avenge these young humans. They may have been sailors, but they were innocent of the blood of violence like this. They weren't Commander Elwha's Navy.

"We can't let this happen in our homeland, in our beautiful rain forest. We need to act now to avoid much worse later. Remember the Coast Guardians," I said. Everyone raised chin. The pack was of one mind.

Twist documented the massacre, taking cell phone pictures of the scene and pocketing jewelry and random tech from the dead as he went. He couldn't help himself—he simply did not think the victims had any further need for it, and we might. I sighed. Scavenging was part of a Wolf's survival instincts and had served us well on our journey to Wolf Haven, our home.

Today, for some reason, this left an off taste in my mouth. It felt wrong to disturb these poor kids any further. But I said nothing. Twist is a good Wolf, and he wouldn't understand these feelings when it was a matter of pack survival. I don't understand them either.

I could sense that I was slowly changing but couldn't point to anything in particular and say—that used to be different. We Wolves are young in the world, and I wanted us to become something better than we are, something I couldn't even picture, but I'd know it when we became it. I did know that we needed to become the kind of tribe that didn't allow these tragedies to happen. We were freed from being the Commander's killer-beasts, but that wasn't enough anymore. We needed to become more.

A polite growl broke into my thoughts.

Eddie had located the armory. The hatch was busted open, but the substantial room was only lightly picked over. We ended up taking everything left behind, half filling the forward hold of the *Becky's Reward* with weapons, ammo, comm-gear headsets, and nine metal buzzards the humans called drones, with three fancy helmets to control them. Sigrid and the Wolves back at camp were going to love these! Maybe they could patrol our forestlands stealthily without ever leaving the warmth and safety of the Treehouse?

We were definitely going to need to patrol our lands.

This shameful massacre had happened after the earthquakes and the tsunami tore up our world. The Coast Guardian pack had survived the Apocalypse only to be slaughtered by their own kind. I may have growled a little.

At least we Wolves had their scents now; all twenty-three of the human pack had left their scent on the boat. This was not something we were going to forget.

On the way out, we checked the paint locker and found the real treasure: fourteen fifty-five-gallon drums of resin. They were heavy. While we were emptying the paint locker, the blind fisherman and Lenny broke down the big gun on the Coast Guard Cutter's forward deck, complete with mounting legs and full ammo cases. They didn't have to say anything.

Next time we came this way, we were going to be prepared.

As we coasted into our home's makeshift dock, the brass beams of the sunset lit up the pile of sails atop our forward deck in bronze. I felt good. We had everything we needed and more. We now had the armament to be able to defend our lands far beyond the personal combat range. We had found what Sigrid needed to build her castle in the sky. And if I was any judge of human food, that was the scent of cioppino and fresh baked bread in the wind. Grandma's cooking was pretty good. My tail may have wagged.

Yes, it *was* cioppino, and these gentle people kept our Wolf-sized bowls full and a fresh baguette in our paws all evening. It was actually better than pretty good. *Burnt food* good? Maybe I was beginning to understand why humans spent so much time preparing and eating food.

On the other hand, chomping down on a fat thigh of fresh venison is much simpler, and very satisfying. You even get to chew the bone! No need to go and complicate it.

That used to be enough for me… I was changing, and not sure I liked it. But then I *was* a Wolf, and Wolves don't sweat the small stuff.

Chapter 5

A CUTTING WIND

"You need to see this, Alpha," said Fitz, poking his shaggy head in the door of the big tent.

I nodded my head and began picking my way through the seated humans across the crowded floor. Once outside in the storm, I pulled my floppy hat down tightly over my ears. I had stopped shaving my face and arms to pass for human when we reached the promised land, but I still didn't have enough fur up there to stay warm. Or anywhere. But at least my body's fur was thickening in response to the cold. I itched all over with the new growth, and ignored this mild discomfort, as always.

The freezing wind cut at us in bursts, but we just tucked our heads down and trudged through the thick drifts, our long coats fanned out behind us like ducktails as we waded through white snow. The snow drifts thinned as we reached the shelter of the old-growth forest and our coattails now rode where they were supposed to. Speeding up, we were soon at the great cedar. We climbed up quickly.

It was a sad sight.

Last night's storm had ripped the new sailcloth walls of the Treehouse to shreds and torn out about half of the exterior wall beams as well. I roared in frustration. Then I sighed. Better to deal with what we had, not what we'd lost. I sent Fitz to get the pack and meet us back at the big tent. I took one last hard look at what remained of our home in the sky before climbing down the huge tree and trotting in that direction as well. The trip back to the warmth of the human's canvas shelter was quicker because we weren't breaking new trail.

"Time for a new plan. The storm ripped the sailcloth walls apart, and this is only the first snow of a long winter," I said, then nodded to Sigrid.

"We need to find a lightweight flexible building material to replace the Treehouse's walls. Quickly. Any ideas, people?" Sigrid asked. To the point as always. Sigrid is always very efficient, though sometimes she finds it difficult to pick up on Wolf non-verbal cues. Forget human behavior. But give her a satellite phone or computer, and she's a world class artist. We're all a bit broken, but the bone that breaks grows back stronger than before. Wolves, too.

We needed a solution immediately if we were to keep our humans from freezing to death this winter. Maybe the Wolves, too. We certainly felt the cold, but Wolfkin are quite difficult to kill. Right now, all our tribe was stacked on top of each other in the big tent, brainstorming solutions. It was very noisy and stuffy. We weren't having much success until Tosh cleared her throat and spoke up. Everyone immediately focused on her, waiting to hear what she had to say.

"Last night, Lenny said you found a shipping container filled with pallets of compressed cardboard bound for recycling. What if we stapled layers of corrugated cardboard over everything after painting each layer with the resin? I think it would be strong enough to resist the wind with the resin protecting it from moisture and gluing it together. The tiny air pockets trapped between layers would help insulate it, too," she finished with bared teeth. They were tiny but very white.

Huh. I felt Ella come alert, and we both looked at Sigrid; she was almost vibrating with excitement.

"That could work! And reduce heat loss at the same time! In combination with our body heat, we would be capable of maintaining a consistent interior temperature, no matter how cold it gets. This would allow us to survive the winter!" our tech Wolf exclaimed. I nodded and looked at Lenny.

"Do you remember where this shipping container is?" I asked. Lenny nodded back 'yes'.

"Okay, now we just need to retrieve this cardboard stuff and rebuild the treehouse walls. No problem!" I said confidently. I resisted adding, *in the middle of a snowstorm*, but just barely. Alphas need to stay positive.

I turned to the blind fisherman. "Is that deck gun mounted yet? We may need it when we go downriver again. How far is it to our destination? Can we be back before sundown?" I asked the patriarch of the Fisher clan.

"Yes. Three hours each way. And I have a feeling we're going to need both Wolves and deck guns before this is over. We can be back before nightfall if we leave in the next, say, twenty minutes. Lenny, we'll need you. Alpha, I suggest you have some Wolves dug in by the dock when we return, ready to fight if we are pursued home. Men like the ones that butchered the Coast Guard cutter are not to be taken lightly. Protecting our families, our tribe, is of the highest priority," the blind fisherman stated. His quiet voice somehow carried quite a way.

I nodded, then I spoke up, in deference to the blind grandpa with silver fur. I didn't know if he had 'seen' my nod, but I think he had sensed it. "Same teams as yesterday. Strap up with the big guns. Leave in ten!" I ordered and both Wolves and humans jumped to it. I strapped up with more shotgun shells and concussion grenades than I considered necessary—you can never have too many backup weapons in a fight. Options expand survival odds; even cats knew that.

Once I ran out of pockets to stash ammo, I straightened up and spun to face the human waiting for me by the front door of the tent.

"You should put me on the deck gun, Alpha. I know the weapon well. I can fire it accurately. But, more importantly, I know when not to shoot," said Henry in his quiet voice. I straightened. I was beginning to like this somber warrior more and more.

"Good idea," I agreed, and his shoulders ever-so-slowly relaxed. A human might not have noticed, but Wolves don't miss that kind of body language. He seemed to be almost establishing his place in the pack hierarchy, despite not actually being a Wolf. Huh.

Well, I guess our definition of a Wolf is becoming less rigid by the day. Thoughts for another time. We had stuff to do.

It took a while to prepare the *Becky's Reward*, clearing her decks of snow and getting the cranky engine going but we eventually cast off and chugged down the now transformed river. The riverbanks had become lush white cushions of snow, with the forest a painting of beautiful green needles poking through the white wonderland disguise. The still waters mirrored the white banks in a strange, upside-down world. I couldn't remember ever seeing such pale beauty before. After a moment, we Wolves moved to our usual spots on the bow, large snowflakes falling silently down on us, each weightless and unique.

I leaned forward on the railing into the chilly, pungent breeze cascading up over the bow of the good ship *Becky's Reward*. Inhaling mightily, I let the air drench me in a scent-tapestry, rich and detailed, yet somehow still devoid of any hint of a living being larger than a raccoon.

The scent-ghosts of the dead were another matter.

The phantom olfactory onslaught was still rich in rotting meat and seafood. While I did not find it pleasurable, it was potent in scent nuance. I drew another deep breath through my nose and exhaled through my mouth.

Hints of rotting fish, overripe shellfish and dead pig dominated. Underneath those lay the acidic breakdown of bladders, the salty iodine of drying seaweed, and the tender smell of decaying cow flesh. My belly rumbled and Twist elbowed me before dropping a silent Wolf laugh on top of it all. I Wolf-laughed back while miming rubbing my tummy with my right paw. Then I turned back to the downriver view.

It's good to be pack.

The cold wind continued to carry the pungent ghost-smell of death across our bow all morning, well-seasoned with light snow—the kind of snow you couldn't trust to put your weight on lest you break through the crust and fall. Our passage down the waterway was hemmed in with fairytale snow castles, and hiding just behind them, towering walls of verdant fir and hemlock. The rubbish and flotsam we had seen piled randomly in drifts at minor bends of the Bogachiel the day before were now pure white, fluffy pillows.

I looked behind me at the big gun bolted to the forward deck. Henry stood in that relaxed stance that was only a blink from action, the one SEALs and special forces have before a fight. Both his hands loosely held the grips of the fifty-caliber machine gun. Only his eyes moved, scanning the shore ahead. I had a feeling very little escaped his notice.

Behind us, on the bridge of the *Becky's Reward*, the blind fisherman manned the helm, his head cocked to listen to the kind of things only Wolves would normally hear. Beside him, Lenny was studying a chart that had been heavily marked up with a black sharpie. He mumbled data to the patriarch of the fisher clan. The old fisherman abruptly showed his teeth to a world he couldn't see, at least not with his eyes.

He had once told me that his Fisher God had taken his eyes, but then had made him see. The whole thing confused me, but Wolves don't sweat the small stuff, so I didn't try to figure it out.

"Pull up over there to the starboard at that little bluff just ahead. If I'm not mistaken, that snowdrift is the top of the shipping container we've been looking for," Lenny said to the blind captain. Everyone was silent, as the commercial fishing boat drifted neatly to a stop exactly where it needed to be.

I exchanged a look with Henry. Our captain was a little spooky sometimes.

Twist's mysterious paws made short work of the padlock and chain loosely holding the container's entry doors closed. The doors swung open with a clank and we peered eagerly into the dark interior. Nina and Ella posted themselves atop the shipping container, scanning our immediate surroundings intently. There was a bad pack prowling out there somewhere. It was only a matter of time until we ran into them.

Chapter 6

BAD PACK TWO

The Commander pointed his control unit at Sixty-four, the disobedient alpha Dog of his pack. The bio-engineered guard unit stood glaring at the Commander holding the Shiny, refusing to fall to good-Dog position despite his command. The Commander just smiled cruelly and activated the electro-shock collar around Sixty-four's wide neck. Convulsing, the Dog bit off half his tongue as his powerful jaws clamped down and he fell over. Within seconds, his nanites were already trying to rebuild the tongue. The alpha Dog's hulking body lay knotted on the ground, clenched into a fetal position identical to many burn victims. He shook violently, blinded by a white light only he could see.

"No!" howled Fifty-seven, the second in command of the pack. The huge, bio-engineered slave-Dog gathered her powerful hindquarters to leap, but the Commander simply pointed his Shiny at Fifty-seven and she fell to the ground convulsing next to her alpha. Then the Commander waved the control unit across the remaining pack members for good measure, punishing his eight-million-dollar guard Dogs so they would remember their place and not this regrettable episode. His Dogs needed to know in their very bones that the Commander was their master. That's what it took with these brutes. He looked over the unconscious pack one last time and smiled. Then he turned his back on them and walked away with a small group of nervous officers. No one was safe when the Commander was in this kind of mood. He drank up their fear as if it were a smooth well-aged brandy.

The Dog keepers moved in behind him and began dragging the insensate Dogs back to their barrack cages. This was by no means the first time such a thing had happened, especially lately. The recently amped-up electroshock punishments blew apart the neural pathways of memories, leaving gaping holes in the Dogs' minds, which is why they remembered neither their last defiance nor its punishment. Tabula rasa, every time.

Sixty-four never remembered previous Awakenings, the return of self-awareness, but it kept happening every time he was punished. Every time it took him longer to recover.

"They've started falling into poor habits, acting like bad Dogs," the Commander explained to the man next to him, "My Dogs need a very firm hand, or it may get worse. First, Three's pack goes AWOL, and now Sixty-four is acting surly and challenging my authority. We may need to adjust the balance of timber-wolf versus human genes in the next generation. I'd hate to do that, though—they are at their most deadly as they are."

SEAL Team leader Marc Christensen grunted. He was a powerfully built officer that could have cleaned up at poker had he been so inclined. His face was a stone wall that gave nothing away. He was an extremely dangerous man—but the Commander scared even him.

Of course, you don't show fear to sociopaths or superior officers with nuclear weapons. The problem was that his commanding officer no longer had anyone capable of reining him in. Commander Elwha was a newly stamped military dictator running a small nation with big weapons. He controlled Trident submarines, naval destroyers, an aircraft carrier, and the immense armories of Kitsap-Bangor and Indian Island's magazines. His kingdom's borders were water on three sides and the Olympic Mountain range on the fourth. Currently, his fleet and manpower were concentrated on his northern border, where his ships were the only barrier between the Chinese PLAN Fast Attack fleet and his homeland.

When the PLAN (People's Liberation Army Navy) fleet first cruised into Burrard Inlet near Vancouver, BC on a "rescue mission to protect ethnic Chinese from rampaging white supremacists", the Commander had just finished seizing control of all of the surviving naval forces on Olympia Island. After being abandoned by an America he no longer recognized, the Commander turned his back on his former allegiances, and created his own country, the nation of Elwha. It was, as many births are, bloody.

Once the Commander had gained full control, he was in position to stop an invasion of his new island country. Unfortunately, it was already too late for neighboring Canada. Commander Elwha's fleet now straddled what had become one of the world's most dangerous borders, the Straits of Juan de Fuca. His forces were a steel wall between the Chinese fleet and Olympia Island. But he could only stand by and electronically watch as the PLAN fleet gutted the dockside warehouses and slowly bombed the city of Vancouver into submission, one street at a time.

His Canadian neighbors had been caught by surprise, their armed forces already fully deployed in rescue operations from the massive 10.8 magnitude quakes and tsunami. Some rescues simply had to be seen through. It took too long to organize a defense. By then, the enemy had established a sizable foothold on the mainland and were multiplying by the hour. The missiles rained down like hail, neighborhood by neighborhood across the ancient city of Vancouver's face. It had seemed hopeless.

The Canadians' politeness is sometimes mistaken for weakness. Nothing could be further from the truth. They go to war with a deadly practicality. You have to grind them into sausage to stop them from fighting the good fight. While the very young and old were being evacuated eastward to the mountains, high school students, chefs, and construction workers had laid down their lives without hesitation, until the invasion of Vancouver had been transformed into the siege of Vancouver and the non-combatants had finally reached safety.

"How well can you continue to defend Kitsap-Bangor with the minimal force you have now?" the Commander asked Captain Christensen as they walked towards the docks.

"We're stretched very thin and covering a lot of area. Those Tiger soldiers tore us up good, but we punished them until the survivors ran for the mountains. My team can handle most anything, but we sure could use some additional personnel so that my guys can catch a full night's sleep once in a while, sir," Christensen answered.

"I'll see what we can do. I wanted to show you my genetically engineered guard units—we call them 'Dogs', *but they're more than that*. Are you sure what you fought wasn't my runaway pack?" the Commander asked.

"I believe what we encountered was similar to your bioengineered guard-Dogs, but instead of a melding of human and timber wolf, it was human and tiger. They were much larger than your Dogs, and highly intelligent, disciplined soldiers. They walked upright and stood close to three meters tall. I'm very sure, Commander," the SEAL team captain replied.

"Damn! That means someone else out there has developed the ability to genetically rewrite adult human bodies. Tigers come from India and China, and India couldn't keep a secret, even if they had labs capable of something like this. It has to be the damn Maoists!" he ranted. Everyone around him became very quiet and careful in their movements. He was a little dangerous when he was in this kind of mood.

"The other reason I showed you my Dogs is that I want you to hunt down those miserable deserters and "Three", the pack alpha, in particular. Find them for me, drag them home, and I'll really show them what happens to bad Dogs," he demanded. He paused for a second, regulating his breathing and calming down before continuing.

"They're not in any territory we control and what remains of the mainland media hasn't made a peep," Commander Elwha said, "That only leaves west to the Pacific Ocean. They must be hiding in the mountains to the west, or in the coastal zone beyond it. Use unmanned aerial reconnaissance as much as possible to cover more ground." The Commander paused, then continued.

"I know, you'll need more men to run the base while you're out tracking down my missing Dogs. Rest assured, I'm going to detail a generous combination of support and fighting men to take some of the pressure off. I do expect you to devote a lot more time to your search now, though." Then the Commander stopped and turned to look at the SEAL with deadly intensity.

"Yes sir, we will maintain the integrity of the base and hunt for your missing Dogs. Was there anything else, Commander?" asked Captain Christensen.

"Oh, yes. I almost forgot. Prepare defenses for invasion from the south. The US plans to loot us when they have time. They want more support and supplies for the LA and Sacramento refugee camps. Guess they should have thought of that before abandoning us! You are to treat any US military approach as an attack by a foreign power. Defend the base's magazines. I'm also returning a Trident ballistic-missile submarine to your base, under your command. Do you understand, Captain?" asked the Commander.

"Yes, Sir. Treat any incoming as a possible enemy attack. Defend the base. We're being reinforced," answered the SEAL. His face was granite.

"Good! You are invited to the Officers' Club for dinner. Chef got his hands on sushi-grade yellow fin tuna and prime rib-eyes. Dismissed!" the Commander said, as he re-entered the passageway to his offices deep below. Marc looked down and noticed that his hands were clenched and immediately relaxed them. Orders to deny aid and fire on highly trained soldiers, good men that were his brothers-in-arms only a month ago... he was going to have to be very fast on his feet to avoid that. Nothing showed in his face, but if you watched his hands, you'd see it.

Captain Marc Christensen was pissed.

Chapter 7

DRONES

Henry Chin scanned the waterways in an unfocused gaze that picked up movement quickly, allowing him to then focus on it. Trouble would most likely come from the water, but he scanned everywhere, just to be sure. Keeping one hand on the machine gun's controls, he periodically turned to check out behind him. He kept his M-4 carbine leaning against his leg in case he needed it for fine work.

Henry was not a tall man, particularly when he stood beside one of the huge Wolfkind. His black hair had been cut so close to the scalp that it was more of a suggestion than a presence. His arms looked like bundles of finely wrapped wire instead of regular muscles. He had a very low body-fat index, and his gaunt features showed his lack of interest in food. This was quite unusual in a man who had been an almost-famous chef merely one month earlier. He no longer cared about food; now everything tasted like ashes. He had only one reason for eating at all. There was a mission to complete. Then he could finally rest.

Before the world had changed, he had had a wife he adored, Nin, and a four-year-old daughter named Lily. He had had a great life, a fine restaurant, and took pleasure in creating things people enjoyed. Life had been very good. Never had he been so happy.

Then, the People's Liberation Army Navy of China had shown up to "protect the one point four million ethnic Chinese from gangs of rioting white supremacists" in British Columbia in the aftermath of the massive earthquakes. No one had invited the Chinese Navy in, and the surviving media was unable to find any sign of rioting white supremacists, but that didn't matter.

When the scattered Canadian defense forces, already fully deployed on coastal rescue missions, didn't immediately surrender, the PLAN armada seized control of Vancouver's waters and harbor by force. They continued blaming drug gangs and white supremacists as they began firing ship-to-shore missiles into the nearest business district of Vancouver, all to soften up the enemy population. Initial casualties were in the thousands, including a little four-year old girl named Lily, and her mother.

Henry had gotten there too late. He had knelt in the debris of a once familiar street, clutching a little girl's shoe, seared forever in his mind. When he finally stood, he made a promise, a sacred oath that the vicious killers behind the murder of his family would be punished. He intended to personally put them down. This was not an empty threat. Henry Chin hadn't always been an almost-famous chef.

He was born a thirteenth-generation fighting man of Wudang Mountain, and his blood oath was not something to be taken lightly. Henry's uncle had begun training him in Xing Yi kung fu at the age of four. At fifteen, he began training in Bagua Zang. At eighteen, he joined the People's Liberation Army of China to learn about guns and explosives, forbidden fruit on Wudang Mountain. Eventually, he rose to lead one of his country's most respected special forces teams. He traveled far and saw many places quite different from home.

It was during the invasion of Taiwan that he had lost his way. Chinese killing Chinese in the name of China just didn't make sense anymore. He was tired of killing. After twelve years in the army, he resigned his commission, married his girlfriend, and immigrated to Vancouver, British Columbia. Henry was thirty when he started his new life there.

Henry blinked his eyes hard as he remembered his family. He thought of them hundreds of times a day. He still ached for the coming time when he could join them in death, but somedays life wasn't completely tasteless anymore.

While Henry's injuries from the siege of Vancouver were mostly healed by now. he still wasn't in condition to take on a battleship and her crew yet. But he could see light at the end of the tunnel. His last mission wasn't far off now.

Henry swallowed and turned his gaze on the two Wolfkin atop the shipping container, guarding their team with a surprising skill at arms. He found their height impressive, standing well over two meters tall, and they were quite hairy. Their arms were a little longer than most humans and their powerful legs were a little shorter. They were very muscular in a way that was cut and looked more than a little feral. *And those big noses*, he thought, *and teeth!* Very alive, almost vibrating with energy. They treated their two human kids like precious gems, and Henry fully approved of that.

The Wolfkind worked together with an unconscious coordination Henry had only seen before in long-established special forces teams and Imperial Theater troupes. There was something both noble and honest about the Wolves, yet he also felt they were incredibly dangerous.

His gaze was suddenly pulled to Trey, the pack's leader, who was staring at him. Henry dropped his eyes and nodded politely before turning back to the river. He had turned just in time; he had almost missed it.

A commercial drone came cruising over the tops of the snow-covered willows, moving in a standard search pattern that crossed back and forth across the river. Henry released the big gun and picked up his M-4 to track the buzzing drone. He didn't shoot because it wasn't close enough to discover them yet. He raised his right hand in a "hurry" gesture to Trey, never taking his eyes off the target. He could feel Trey's eyes on him and heard the thump of the Wolf dropping to the ground from the top of the shipping container. Scraping sounds followed as four Wolves and a human dragged a two-meter-high pallet of compressed cardboard in the direction of the boat. The frozen mud helped, allowing the heavy pallet to slide quicker than soft ground would have. It still took too long. The drone would discover them in less than a minute.

Lenny hurried aboard to operate the boat's big crane and had it in the right position when the Wolves dragged the pallet to the edge of the small bluff where the *Becky's Reward* was waiting.

Henry felt the rumble of the boat's engines come alive under the blind fisherman's control from his forward deck gun.

Twenty seconds. Henry focused on the drone until it became all he could see.

Ten seconds. His trigger finger caressed the carbine's trigger.

The flat *crack* was loud, unnatural in the early afternoon air. The drone tumbled clumsily into the middle of the river and immediately sank. Henry lowered his rifle and called to the Wolves and humans.

"We don't have much time. The enemy will know something happened to their spy, but, if we're lucky, not what. It will take a few minutes for them get organized and investigate. Good chance they'll send another drone ahead, but up high where it will be difficult to shoot it. Expect an enemy boat in about fifteen minutes at the earliest," Henry cautioned.

"We need four more pallets," said Trey, looking at his Wolves until they dropped their eyes and burst into motion. Twist skillfully snaked a rope through the pallet's muddy wood boards, then looped it back through the hook on the boat's crane, which Lenny was running. Twist nodded respectfully to his Alpha, then dashed back to the container with the other three wolves.

The small crane lifted the compressed cardboard pallet and swung inward over the *Becky's* main hold as if it were a particularly full net of fish. Once the load was lowered into place below-deck, Lenny unhooked it and returned the crane to the riverbank, awaiting the next load. This time each of the four Wolfkin hefted a corner and began carrying the four hundred kilo load over to where Lenny was waiting. Their paws sank into the now slushy mud almost calf deep with each step, but they kept moving forward.

Two down, three to go. The Wolves ran back to the shipping container. Meanwhile, Henry carefully watched the tree line, his M-4 carbine nestled loosely in his arms. He knew what was coming for them.

He was right. The larger drone came in as high as the big trees. But Henry knew where to look and was lucky. It was making a beeline for the last known position of the first drone, directly over the river. Henry quieted himself to a statue, and gentle stroked the trigger of his rifle. The enemy drone burst into flaming pieces. That bought them another five minutes if their luck continued.

It almost did.

The last pallet was safely in the forward hold, and everyone made haste casting off. The *Becky* began chugging back upriver at an agonizingly slow pace. Now they were heavier and going against the mild current, so progress was slower than the trip down had been. Henry was facing downriver, where the trouble had shown up. His fifty-caliber anti-aircraft line-of-fire barely cleared the wheelhouse, but it was sufficient.

Everyone could hear the pirates before they saw them, rounding the recently widened channel of the Bogachiel river behind them. There were two jet skis with dry-suit clad passengers, each with a pirate driving and a second fighter wielding an automatic weapon and spraying lead all over the place. One jet ski came up each side of the fleeing fishing boat, strafing the *Becky* with more noise than actual damage. The *Becky's Reward* may not be fast, but she was solidly built, and tough as nails.

"Those small craft didn't get all the way up here by themselves. The big boat will not be far behind them, and heavily manned," Henry said. All the Wolfkin growled in agreement. Henry smoothly spun the fifty-caliber machine gun to cover the jet ski on the port side and followed it until the two jet skis merged at the bow. Then he blew them all to hell.

It was another eight minutes before the pirate ship swung into view behind them. It was much faster than the *Becky's Reward* and began rapidly closing the gap between the two boats. Trey snarled and his team raised their weapons to sight on the incoming threat.

Chapter 8

TIGER CATCHES MOUSE

The former Major Malgato, now the Tiger Queen of a small mountain kingdom in Olympia Island, leaned her weight forward onto the balcony railing, searching the lowlands for something she thought she'd glimpsed. She calmly clamped her Tiger-sized binoculars to her eyes and started methodically following a spiral search pattern. Queen Malgato was sure that she'd seen smoke from a chimney or a small, hot fire.

Mice sign.

She studied the slopes of the descending mountains, as they gave way to the Hoh Rain Forest. It appeared that the great storm was pausing to catch its breath before pushing all that snow uphill. The visibility was greatly improved from earlier, but it was still snowing in some places.

There it was again! She couldn't be absolutely sure, but she was reasonably confident. The Queen strolled back inside and walked over to the primitive radio communications center tying all her Tigers together, and tapped the broadcast button with a single long, black claw.

"Tigers," she purred. "Probable mouse infestation downhill where the tree line begins. We need to investigate. Timing, take the north side. Fu Yin, you take the south scope. Bai Li, you watch over our eastern approach. I'm going down the center aisle as soon as you cut off their escape and push them my way. Don't kill them! I'm in the mood for a little entertainment before snacks!" the

Major announced before adding, "Acknowledge and let me know when you are in position."

There was no graceful way for a Tigerkin to wade through the snow, and it took too damn long to get places with their bioengineered bodies, tall but short-legged. Forcing their way relentlessly through the snow and ice, and around boulders as big as a house, it took the Tigers over twenty minutes to get into position. Then Queen Malgato coughed, and the team moved forward slowly until they were close enough to see their prey easily.

It was a single greasy human, grotesquely swollen with layers of mismatched winter clothing. He was lugging a gunnysack full of clanking cans and sundries over his shoulder and muttering to himself. He occasionally looked back the way he'd come, instead of where he was going. He seemed to be worried about being pursued.

Why would anyone chase this fearful smelly man? Perhaps it had something to do with the big bag of cans (food?) he was carrying. It may not belong to him, which made the Queen wonder if he was a thief. Tigers are very smart about these things. And her Tigers hated thieves. She slinked closer.

Now the thief was sprawled out between the roots of a huge fir tree. He lit a hand-rolled cigarette, poisoning the air for a hundred meters and languidly began drinking a foul-smelling liquid from an earthenware jug. He didn't look particularly happy, just resting a bit without any hurry to move on. The Major hoped he was as fat as he looked, but since he was bundled up in all those clothes, she just couldn't tell.

Easy solution. She nodded.

Queen Malgato watched her team drive the thief into her paws and it worked perfectly. He jumped awkwardly to his feet and began waddling uphill, away from the forest when two of her Tigers strolled casually into view. The Tiger Queen waited until the lumpy human turned back to look over his shoulder. Then she planted herself directly in his path. He turned back and jumped straight up in shock. Major Malgato reached out a claw-tipped paw and briefly stabilized the thief. The she began peeling him out of his layered clothing like a particularly juicy mango.

The naked man screeched as she took him by the neck and wiped his filthy body back and forth across the snow, attempting to get rid of some of the stink. He was nicely plump after all! But that smell! Her Tigers gathered around when she finally stopped cleaning the prisoner and set him back on his feet. She leaned down, moving her massive Tiger head closer to his.

"Who are you running from, Mouse?" the Major asked in English. The prisoner's tiny teeth were chattering, making it difficult to speak. The Major snarled loudly, and he suddenly found his tongue and lost his water at the same time.

"Those Wolf-men left their campground last night, so I kind of helped myself. They had plenty! I didn't hardly take any of their food!" he sputtered, shaking with the cold. The Major sneezed and her soldiers froze. Sneezing is never a good sign with Tigers; it signifies anger or frustration.

"What Wolf-men? Describe them," she uttered in a deceptively calm rumble.

"Tall hairy guys with big noses… and t-t-t-teeth!" he jabbered. The Tiger Queen leaned close enough to block out the light. Then she flashed tooth.

"Uhh... they move very quickly when they want to. Well-armed. Feral looking," the captive thief squealed.

"And…" the hulking Tigerkind snarled.

"Uh...there are some normal people with them too, and a fishing boat. Yeah! Maybe they're trying to build a hidden place to winter in. Piles of building supplies move around and disappear a lot. That's all I know, please let me go now," the hapless robber said, looking longingly at his sack of stolen goods before wincing as the Tiger growled next to his head.

"Oh, but that would be uncivilized! You must come back to our den with us for dinner! You're our first visitor and deserve to be welcomed properly! Now stop dragging your feet, time to go!" Queen Malgato declared. She snagged the plump human by the neck and dragged him with her as she began retracing her steps up into the new mountain kingdom of Tigerkind. Dinner and a show as well! The perfect thing to help take up a long snowy evening!

She hoped he was a screamer.

Chapter 9

BOARDING PARTY

"Let them catch us," I said.

Lenny shouted "What?" but the blind fisherman just nodded. Henry looked at me for a blink before he also nodded.

I looked back at Lenny. "We can't outrun them; they'll be on us in a few minutes anyway. We don't want to lead predators home to our den. Once they board us, they'll find that chasing Wolves is one thing, but catching them is another thing altogether," I explained for the human's sake. Lenny did a funny rolling thing with his eyes, but I had no idea what the gesture meant. He didn't look too happy, though.

This new world is a hard place for a gentle man.

I planned to change that in Wolf Haven. We were going to have room for brave souls of all species, regardless of their battle prowess. There are many ways of fighting. Just don't bring up Cats. The spooky bastards are always starting trouble and then disappearing.

"Pirates are the same all over the world—vicious, greedy, and without honor. The world is a better place without them," Henry offered in a grim voice. "Once they get a foothold, they're very hard to get rid of," he added. Even I could tell it wasn't his first encounter with this kind of trouble. I turned to face him.

"What should we expect?" I asked Henry. He sure seemed to know what he was talking about, at least once you got him to open his mouth. I had the feeling he'd dealt with pirates more than once.

"They won't see us as a threat at first," Henry explained, his calming voice at odds with his tense body posture. Lenny started to interject something but changed his mind as he watched Henry. There had to be a story there, but Lenny didn't seem sure he wanted to hear it, so he just made a funny face and waited for Henry to continue.

"To pirates, we're just sheep, money on the hoof. If we resist, they'll slaughter everyone and loot our corpses. Then, they'll track down our camp, looking for our women, children, and supplies." He glanced at each of us, clenching his fists. Some things didn't need to be spoken out loud. He released a deep breath and continued.

"It would be best if that didn't happen. The only ways to effectively stop them are either to make it too expensive in men and weapons for them to interact with us or kill them all. My preference is the latter. Regardless, we don't want them to look closely at any of us when they board. We'll have to pretend to be sheep. You Wolves stay out of sight until it's time *not to*," he finished.

Concise and to the point. I nodded my pack's agreement.

Then I growled again to get my Wolves' attention and ordered "Fall back! Twist, you slip over the side when we stop and swim to the pirate boat's stern. Once things start happening, sneak aboard. Remember how we whittled down Riley's gang behind the Fisher clan's old house? Like that," I ordered.

"Tinker, Ella, wait just inside the two side hatches. Nina, you and I will be hiding among the cardboard pallets in the open hold below decks. Henry, you secure the bridge, protect our humans, and we'll clear the decks when it's time. Captain, you do any talking with the predator pack. We will take over when it's time to stop talking," I said, as we watched our pursuer slowly closing on us.

We ran until they thought they had caught us. It was really the other way around, but the enemy didn't know that yet.

The pirate's boarding lines had long ropes with hooks on the ends, which sank into the tough wood gunnels of our sweet *Becky*. The pirates were very excited and loud as they poured across our pinned ship's side and onto the *Becky's* deck. I could barely see our humans through the wheelhouse windows. They were holding their arms up and watching the apparent capture of their ship with stone-cold faces that concealed banked fires.

One team of invaders headed for the engine room, while another moved toward the bridge. They would never make it.

I raised my chin to Nina and …I phase into Flux. The world around me slows down drastically as I speed up. The ability and desire to use language falls from me in a burst of brilliant light that never hurts my eyes. I feel as if I have all the time in the world, in this place between the heartbeats. Base reality. I drink in the world around me in unformatted gulps of raw data that I digest whole. Not having to filter my perception through ponderous language processors and convoluted forebrain-based logic chains, I instantly, intuitively know what to do next.

I place my left paw on the top of a pallet and use it to spring up and over the hold's open hatch to the main deck. I float down to land directly behind a particularly dirty human back. He hasn't seen me yet, mired in the cold molasses of mundane existence. I smoothly pull my Bowie knife from its sheath and slice his left neck's carotid artery in a single movement before he even realizes I'm behind him. He begins to list to port, sagging in glacially slow motion.

Nina, also in Flux, is already at the stern of the main deck. She wades through four pirates before anyone realizes she is in their midst. Nina spins and they fall to the deck in slow motion like dirty petals from an anemic flower. I can't see Twist or Ella. As Henry exits the wheelhouse, the other humans tucked safely behind him, I focus on him. Henry whips into motion… He is in Flux, as well, a little slower than a Wolfkin but much faster than normal humans.

Sliding across the deck and down the timeline with an impossible grace of movement, Henry whips around slowly to break two pirates' knees and a right elbow. Gliding forward, he holds his two forearms tightly together, moving upward while his hands are open palms, making a flower shape. Henry reaches the third pirate. His blossom fist strikes the jawbone and right ear of the deadly invader. His hands snap apart, and he circles away as the body slowly descends to the *Becky*'s deck, its head lolling with a fluidity that shows there isn't anyone home anymore.

I reach over my shoulder and pull out my bullpup shotgun with the drum magazine. Plenty of time to select targets in the space between heartbeats. I am surrounded on three sides by enemy creeping my way as fast as they can. The fourth side is water. I count at least twelve enemy within a few meters. Most of them stink unpleasantly of stale beer, cigarettes, and dirty underwear.

Two of the twelve also carry the scent of the Coast Guardian Cutter massacre.

Snarling from the bottom of my throat, I begin striding forward, blasting almost-frozen targets with 00 steel buckshot as I go, unstoppable in my charge, cutting through them like a hot knife through butter.

Every pack has an alpha. I recognize him immediately and close in. The remaining enemies fall before me, reeds in the storm. I finish two of them with a head shot as I stride past their prone bodies. My shotgun barrel is burning hot in my grasp by the time I reach the gang leader and his personal guard.

He stands almost as tall as Wolfkind and is very muscular with scrawny legs. His long, craggy face is framed by a thick braid of ebony hair loosely wrapped around his neck. His eyes are concealed by sunglasses, but his nose is sharp, a small neatly trimmed beard juts from his chin, and his hairline is receding. He is wearing a dark blue coat, open to show two automatic pistols strapped to his sides. He is relaxed as he turns to face me in slow motion, handling his weapon with casual skill. He wears boot knives like flamboyant jewelry and carries a submachine gun loosely in his arms. He also has a lumpy bag peeking out from his waist with grenade shaped bulges. Placed defensively around him, his gang keeps a fearful eye on the boss. Only the most ruthless could rule this crew.

The other Alpha looks at me without any expression as I begin to shoot him. A lot.

The pirate king tilts backwards, confused in his last moments. The sheep are turning out to be Wolves. The remaining pirates grind to a syrup stop, staring at their leader's raggedy corpse as it slowly tilts towards the deck. Then everyone's eyes turn to look at me. I stretch until my neck cracks, then snarling loudly, I continue cleansing my sector of bandit refuse.

The noise dies down as I run out of enemies. Then someone shoots me. It feels like being knocked down by a truck and hurts like hell. *Pain never lessens in base reality*, I think, so I drop out of Flux…

I sat up on the *Becky*'s deck and looked down, watching my nanites already regrowing the edges of the fifty-caliber hole in the right side of my chest. Then I raised my gaze to search for the enemy with the big gun. The bullet had gone straight through my vest, nicked my liver and come to rest snagged in the armor on my back. High angle. My flesh was already knitting back together rapidly, but the pain was intense. Then another bullet smashed my left collarbone but missed my head and neck.

I finally looked up and to the left. There he was, on top of the pirate yacht's flying bridge. I threw back my head and howled in fury, then I looked back at the shooter just in time to see him aiming at my head. I dropped to four legs in a charge, aimed directly at him. I am fast even when I'm not in Flux.

He kept blasting and missing. I reached the stern of the *Becky's Reward* and leapt high, coming down on the pirate yacht's forward deck as if I had practiced it hundreds of times. Another bound, and I climbed the bridge's front windows and kept moving.

I came hurtling over the flying bridge and slammed onto the small platform, knocking the shooter back into the pilot seat just as he tried to run for it. He suddenly had a lap full of angry Wolfkind and froze, afraid to look up into my eyes. I stripped his rifle from his left hand and dropped it overboard, then leaned down to place my head against his little trembling one. Then I growled. Getting shot hurts. I was angry.

So, I showed him my teeth!

I didn't mean it in a human, friendly manner, but he apparently thought I was human-smiling. This made him very upset for some reason. I probably shouldn't have done it, because he suddenly began wiggling, and then started shooting me again, this time with a little pistol that made popping sounds.

I bit his head off. Some people never learn.

Twist stepped out from the pirate's boat's bridge and raised chin. Then he lowered his head in deference. Not all language is loud. We now had full control of our enemies' boat. I clambered from the dead sniper's lap and leapt down a deck to land next to Twist.

"The marauders below deck are all dead," Twist explained. "Found some frightened little humans locked up down there. I opened the hatch and motioned for them to come with me, but they were scared, gibbering in some language I almost remember. Then three enemy came barreling in and tried to cut me up. I took away their tiny knives and broke their necks. Then the little humans loved me, hugging my legs and crying. It was really noisy."

"Little humans? Cubs?" I asked.

"No, skinny little humans, looks like they haven't eaten in weeks. Should I leave them? I don't know if they'd like that," Twist explained, almost whining.

I didn't smile on the outside.

"We keep acquiring humans, don't we? Can't leave them here, on a doomed boat with full winter coming. Take them over to the blind fisherman and introduce them to our Fisher clan. Stay with them so they won't worry," I said. Twist looked a little relieved.

There were eight small humans. They only came up to mid-waist on me, although they might have looked taller next to most humans. They were skin and bones, poorly clothed in tattered rags. Each one stopped to bow deeply to me as they passed on their way to our wheelhouse. Henry stepped forward and said something in a foreign language, then changed languages, and the little humans got all excited again. He motioned them onto the bridge and brought them over to introduce them to the blind fisherman and Lenny.

After everything quieted down, Henry and I walked back to the stern of our new boat. "They're simple country folk who lived in a tropical rain forest on the other side of the world," Henry said softly. "They were kidnapped and sold as slaves, ending up working the gang's fishing boats. Fishing, cooking, cleaning, with sparse food and no time off. It was not a good life. These people are resilient and have always lived in harmony with their tropical version of a rain forest. They need a new home now, and I think you need citizens for your new nation. There is a lot of rain forest out there, and not many Wolves."

"There will never be slaves in Wolf Haven," I growled. "The little guys are welcome to stay or free to go, as they please. I hope they decide to join us." I noticed he said 'you need citizens' instead of 'we' but didn't dwell on it.

Now our growing tiny country had new citizens and a navy, even if it was only a commercial fishing boat and a badly misused yacht. I guess every nation must start somewhere. We were definitely better off now than we were this morning, although we also had more mouths to feed…

Chapter 10

STORIES

We came into our snowdrift dock slowly, so our people wouldn't open fire on the strange boat behind us. I stood forward on the *Becky*'s bow to demonstrate that everything was alright.

It was nearly dark by the time we'd moored our new fighting boat in a dead-end tributary and concealed it with cut brush. For dinner we ate something called "chili" from bowls around the bonfire, the thick snow falling silently overhead on our tarps and sizzling in the blazing fire. Everyone sat close to each other, savoring the body heat as the cold nipped at our faces, even our new tropical friends; a quiet little bunch. We had off-loaded the cardboard pallets earlier and dragged them to the Treehouse, but by then it was too dark to get anything else done. The wind picked up as it got darker. As we waited for morning's light to finish building our refuge from the elements, people napped and told stories to keep the cold night at bay.

I leaned forward out of the darkness at our back, the firelight flickering across my furry arms and legs. I had an arm around Rachel, and Bookworm was sandwiched between Ella and me. Our pack crowded the damp log we were sitting on; there is warmth in numbers. I practiced stretching out my paws, the razor-sharp talons gleaming in the fire's light. My paws were stubby compared to humans', but I didn't mind. The stretching helped.

I didn't know when it would happen, but I was definitely waiting for the blind fisherman to tell his story around the bonfire. We were all curious about Grandpa's back story.

This wasn't the night. Instead, Witboy told us about his favorite memory. He was the man-cub of the blind fisherman's family. Like most cubs, he thought he was much older than he was, and in his own quiet way, was fearless.

"It was the day the pink salmon came home, and Grandpa took me with him. He even let me steer and navigate the *Becky's Reward*! Grandpa found a spot a ways out from shore that looked just like everywhere else out there and anchored. I searched the dark waters but didn't see a single fish jump anywhere. Grandpa did have a strange sense of humor, but I kept my mouth shut. You never know with Grandpa," he said, waving an arm in the direction of the blind fisherman. Friendly chuckles drifted out of the shadows into the firelight.

"We got our rods just right with the special flashers, because the pink salmon is picky and smart for a fish. When the sun popped up, I looked around the empty sea and waited. After a moment grandpa held up his finger and tilted his head just so. Then he said, 'Can you hear that?' and I listened hard but heard nothing. I made a face because he's blind, right? And couldn't see me. Last time I thought that!" Witboy declared, shaking his head dramatically before continuing. He had to speak up a little for the humans because of the increasing wind in the trees and the fire's rambunctious roar. There were a few snickers from some of the cubs as well, but he ignored those.

"Grandpa turned to face me and somehow looked at me. Then he reached out and finger-thumped me on the ear. That was when I heard it coming, too.

"The pinks rioted in a huge school, crowding the Fishdar on the sea bottom and jumping out of the water on top. I caught my limit and then started catch and release, because how often does a guy get the chance to catch all the salmon he wants? When we got home, Grandma stood in the kitchen doorway with her arms crossed and a big smile. Grandpa tried to pretend we didn't catch anything, but that never happens, so Grandma got after him with a wooden spoon. He quickly surrendered and we went back out to

bring in our amazing catch. We felt like heroes that night!" Witboy
finished. Everybody grunted or slapped their hands together or
growled friendly-like. Witboy's dad, Lenny, laughed and patted
him on the back.

"Your story is from before, but it hasn't changed like the rest
of the world. The pinks will run again next year, after spring. We'll
go fishing just like in your story!" Lenny said.

"Well, it's my favorite memory from before. Next year it will
be my favorite *after* story, too!" Witboy declared quietly. You
couldn't see his wide smile in the fire's shadow, but we could hear
it in his voice.

In the morning, the snow took a break, but the wind didn't. We
moved as fast as we could, considering the safety ropes we were
all wearing. Two Wolves held sheets of corrugated cardboard in
place while two others stapled the sheets to the newly repaired
frame of the Treehouse. Then another Wolf painted a thick layer
of resin over everything. The rest of us were busy moving the
building stuff up the tree to where it was needed. We traded out
positions regularly to keep everyone fresh.

Once the first layer was in place, we started all over again. The
resin was still tacky, and held on to the new cardboard, which
allowed us to move faster. The humans started moving up bundles
of cloth and food staples every time the tree-lift team got ahead.
The windward side of the Treehouse didn't stink too bad, but when
we got into the sheltered side, the fresh resin's smell was a
palpable thing. We tried to breathe through our mouths, but it
tasted horrible too. We moved very fast on that side!

By the time night fell, we had finished eight layers of the
Treehouse's exterior wall. We left a large opening on the bottom
story for moving in and so the wind would air out the resin's
stench. I don't know if it was just the right shape for a beehive
flute, but the Treehouse vibrated as the fresh air passed through.
We could hear it even from all the way up in the forest canopy and
listened to its resonate drone as the breeze hit different melodic
notes throughout the long cold night.

The humans all crowded into the big tent. We Wolves laid
down a waterproof tarp topped by sleeping bags outside, but
shoved up against the tent's rear wall where the stove was. We all

snuggled down under our bear blanket, with a few tarps thrown over that. The snow quickly blanketed us, improving our heat retention. The cubs were safely tucked into the center of our warm pile of Wolves. With the bearskin blanket and nearness to the tent's wood burning stove, we all felt toasty and comfortable, but not sleepy. Not with all that clamor next door.

The humans sure do like telling stories, and we Wolfkind find them fascinating. We have very good hearing and could hear every word spoken in the overstuffed tent. There were a lot of words.

Henry told part of his story for the first time around the iron stove. My ears pricked up, and I felt my Wolves focus as well. We were all curious about this quiet man who was more than he appeared.

"I grew up on Wudang Mountain in China, famous for being the place where the internal martial art called Tai Chi Chuan was born. I remember being eight years old and spending the mornings in class, learning to write and read Mandarin, how to think critically, and do math. I hated math. What I loved was my afternoon classes with my uncle. He was a fighting monk of Wudang Mountain, and my Sifu. I had studied Xing Yi for four years by now, and was finally being taught the real Tai Chi, the style of the emperor's imperial guard, back in the days when there were still emperors.

"My uncle was a strict man. He was very hard to satisfy. When his rare compliment was bestowed on me, I felt like I could fly, and was happy for days. Scarcity enhances value, but I have always believed that it is better to encourage students than frighten them.

"One day during class, my grandfather, a revered but distant master of the arts, came down out of his monastery to visit. He didn't say a word at first but bowed to uncle and then walked to the center of the outdoor classroom and stilled himself. Sifu smacked me on the back of my head and gestured for us to join him. I was still new to the nuances of chi-flow but thrilled to try to move in harmony with such a master. I did have a few moments of almost decent form, but seeing the real stuff made me feel clumsy and young, almost as if I were a toddler. I didn't know whether to be embarrassed or happy! Then my grandfather stroked his long white beard and spoke with my Sifu.

"He is not strong enough to excel. Send him to me at the rock quarry on the east side of the mountain at dawn. He will learn stone masonry. That will strengthen him," he said, looking at me with ice cold eyes. Then I knew what emotion to choose, and embarrassment was my dinner that evening.

"The next day, my mother hugged me and handed me a small pail with rice balls, a water jug, and pickled tea eggs. Then she gently pushed me in the direction of the stone quarry. The sun was just coming up and I was chilled in the moist dawn air, so I walked briskly to warm up. But I shouldn't have wasted the energy, because my first morning was hell. For two hours, I carried shoebox-sized carved stone blocks to a waiting cart, hefting them high enough to push the stones aboard, then walking the eighteen steps back to the rock pile so I could do it again. I had never been so tired. When it was time for school, I could barely walk and got in trouble for nodding off when I was supposed to be studying. The less said of my afternoon lessons with Sifu the better.

"The following day wasn't quite as bad, but I was so tired all I could think of was that I was going to have to do this again the next morning and I was going to die sweaty and weak before the week was out. But I didn't die. Instead, I found the stones weren't as heavy as they used to be. Maybe I was getting the hang of this stone masonry stuff! Then grandfather pointed at a big pile of larger stones. I thought I was going to die for sure. But I didn't.

"After a month, my intimidating grandfather took me to a different part of the quarry, where he worked. He had me watch him chisel a long groove in the hard stone. This would have been easy, except that I was holding a stone in each extended hand as he made me squat in a horse stance. It was very difficult to pay attention to a boring stone groove when your arms are trembling, and sweat is pouring down your head into your eyes. It turned out I could stand up and put the rocks down for a break once in a while, if I paid close enough attention to the stupid groove he was cutting in the virgin stone. I had no idea why this was important, but I kept quiet and did what I was told.

"One morning, once the groove had grown to the length of three men, he had me point out its deepest parts. Then he hammered a wooden wedge into those places. All my studying of the boring stone groove had paid off! When he sent me for a fresh pail of water, I thought it was for us to wash up, but he just carefully poured it over the wedges and into the stupid groove. I thought this was just plain crazy, but you don't disrespect a fighting monk of Wudang Mountain, so I just bowed and trudged off to school. I only grumbled a little when no one could hear me," Henry said. He was quiet for a moment before continuing.

"The following morning, I was shocked to find that the wooden pieces had swelled, expanding the groove, and splitting the stone all the way down its length. I was grinning and Grandfather was scowling, but I thought I saw a twinkle of amusement in his eyes. Maybe he didn't hate me after all!

"Then he chalked a line across the rectangular stone, separating its length into square blocks. Grandfather handed me a smaller version of his hammer and a heavy blunt chisel, then stepped back to observe.

"Chinese martial artists don't use words to teach so much as physically demonstrating the right way and discouraging the wrong way. Maybe this was like a martial art he was teaching me? Or maybe it was just his way—regardless, Grandfather communicated just fine. But it made me look at stone masonry in a whole new way.

"My early mornings continued without much change as the seasons slipped by. I grew stronger and began to take pride in my stonework. On my twelfth birthday, after a wonderful lunch, Grandfather came to our house and took me for a walk. We walked for a while, maybe about twenty minutes, and then we came to an historic building site. An ancient masonry bridge, and on our side of the bridge a tall stone defensive tower was being rebuilt. It was very old. It had originally been built during the Yuen dynasty. I later found out the tower had been destroyed in a terrible earthquake the year before I had been born. It had lost most of its hewn stone blocks to the gorge far below, but when I first saw it, it was three-quarters rebuilt.

"I thought it was beautiful. It had arrow-slit windows on each story and thick walls five stories high that tapered up to a roofed Observation deck. Grandfather led the way up to the entry. I don't think I realized how important my grandfather was until that moment, when I saw all those fighting monks of Wudang Mountain bow and show him great respect as we passed.

"Once inside, we climbed the square stairs that took up half of the tower. At each floor, there was an open doorway to a room in the other half of the building. When we got to the third floor, he led me inside and stroked a stone of the wall. "Look closely. Do you recognize your work?" he asked.

"And I did! I stared at the wall in awe, studying how all those different pieces of stone came together into one powerful wall, into this beautiful tower. And some of those were mine! That changed the way I saw the world forever.

"Great things are made of many small pieces and talents. Things may not make much sense in the beginning, but eventually when you see the whole picture, they usually do. That was the moment I learned to wait for the larger view," Henry finished.

Many human hands slapping together and exclamations of approval. There were even muted friendly growls from under our bearskin blanket. I tilted my head to the right and nudged Ella.

"Maybe that's how he understands the way a pack works?" I said softly. For a quiet man, he told one hell of a story.

"I like the tower part," Ella whispered back after a moment.

Chapter 11

WOOD STOVES AND WOLF-EARS

The large wood-burning stove was still hot when we first picked it up to move it to the Treehouse, but by the time we had carried it to the giant incense cedar and hoisted it up into the sky it was barely warm. Then Ella and Felix showed up with a dead Grendel's metal hood. "Grendel" was what we had named the four-wheeled monsters that used to roar up and down the highways, in the days after we first awakened at the Naval base on Indian Island.

Earlier, Ella and Felix had stripped the metal hood and pounded it with big hammers until they had a level platform strong enough to hold our cast iron stove six inches off the wooden floor. Then Theo screwed it into our plank floor so it wouldn't move. The stove fit just right atop the Grendel trophy, and we soon had a heat source gradually warming our new home in the sky. The gap underneath the stove not only avoided setting our new home on fire, but also circulated warm air efficiently throughout the entire middle floor. Firelight licked everyone in front of the stove in warmth and dull orange. I found it strangely beautiful and wanted to enjoy it, but the storm was picking up.

The piano came next and ended up on the middle floor on the opposite side of the tree from the stove. We continued our work sealing the hole we had originally left open for access and air, with more layers of cardboard and resin. Then we installed an entry door on the lowest level that we'd salvaged from the buildings we'd torn down. Anyone entering our home in the sky would now have to go through the Wolf den to reach the rest of our tribe.

There was a continuous stream of humans and Wolves lugging things into the Treehouse, piling things all along the walls on the middle level common area. So much stuff! Where did it all come from? We Wolves had only our bear-hide blanket, sleeping bags, and weapons; that pretty much did it for the Wolfkind quota of the move. What more does a good Wolf need?

The interior wall of our Treehouse was a creamy light brown. It was reflective and caught the light from our candles and kerosene lanterns. Our bottom floor had a wide corridor down the middle as things were transferred inside as fast as possible and then moved elsewhere by a second group. All our bedding got tossed onto a raised platform that was to be our Wolves' communal bed.

Most of the armory was stored in the area below our raised bed. We wanted our weapons close; weapons under our guard had never been breached, even when we were only slave-Dogs belonging to the Commander. We weren't about to allow a breach now!

On the second floor, the common level housing the stove and kitchen, the food stores were piled along the sides. All the soft bundles of clothing and bedding were tossed upstairs for later sorting. Soon there were big pots of fish soup and water for tea simmering on top of the stove. The coffee was all gone. Some of the humans really missed the stuff, despite the toxin-withdrawal effects. I decided it would be a good idea to keep an eye out for coffee the next time we went downriver. We finally stopped working when it was too dark outside to see, and quickly clustered around the back half of the stove to warm up. I had an icicle beard that turned to cold water and dripped down my coat.

The pungent scent of wet fur and damp human rolled out on waves of moisture that only dried when we approached the fire stove. Instead of being served at improvised log tables for dinner like we had become accustomed to, we made a pack line, carrying our soup bowls for the cooks to fill. There were long loaves of bread baked yesterday, still chewy, that made good sponges for the soup. The human adults actually sprinkled sweet wine over their soup bowls! I sneezed in disgust but didn't say anything. Silent wolf laughs rained down all over. We were warm and fed in a den of our own construction, while a wicked storm kicked and howled impotently outside. That night, I fell asleep in a warm, happy mound of Wolves and, for once, didn't have any bad dreams.

It was a good day.

In the morning, the dark amber walls of our three-story den still vibrated with the fury of the storm. Our citadel tree, a mammoth Incense Cedar, swayed in the winds to a sensuous beat only it could hear. Ella said the gentle movement of the tree felt soothing, kind of like being rocked in a giant lap. You forgot it was there after a bit, but it still felt good.

The humans and Wolves climbed up, (or down), to the treehouse's middle story, a communal space for all species, and more importantly—the location of our big wood-burning stove. It was pretty cold outside. Good smells seeped from the pots perpetually steaming atop the stove.

Each of the three stories of our Treehouse hugged the massive cedar's trunk high up in the middle canopy of the Hoh Rain Forest. Paw-sized, gouged out sections of its bark held small oil-based lamps reflecting golden in the fragrant amber wood of our citadel tree. Kerosene lamps were hung across the ceiling about every twelve meters. In the center of one part of the ring-around-the-tree stood the industrial cast-iron wood-burning stove the park rangers had once used to heat their garage and workshop. Now it kept my pack and tribe alive. Bonfires had become our evening ritual, and here, in our giant windowless beehive, it is always evening.

We were facing the glass window side of the stove, a mixed group of Wolves and adult humans lounging and quietly chatting in the firelight. There wasn't a lot to do inside on days like this. I was getting fidgety, so I looked around the hexagonal room wrapping the massive tree's trunk. I thought it looked like a giant beehive from the outside. We should have thought of windows. I sighed; another thing to add to my list.

I moved to the interior tree trunk and leaned my shoulder into it while slightly crouching and crossing my arms. It was what the human males tended to do when bored and I was trying to imitate the posture, adding it to my human silent vocabulary. I tried to relax into this position, but my body just wasn't built for it anymore. I raised my eyes to gaze across the next section of the second floor.

On the other side of the stove was a gathering of all the cubs of our tribe, listening to Grandma talk about ancient kingdoms. This was called 'school', and we Wolves found it very interesting, sometimes even relatable to our newly born nation of Wolves.

All the cubs looked restless to me, but Rachel, in particular, was getting frustrated. She simply didn't think Wolves like herself and Bookworm had anything to learn from 'humans that lie'. Everything she needed to know she'd learn from Wolves!

Rachel simply wasn't interested in learning the human practices and customs that had left her and her first family—her human family—to die. She was trying not to be rude, but her words were a little harsh anyway. I thought Grandma was very patient.

The problem with her attitude was that Wolves must learn from everything around us in this world to survive. And humans are capable of being both our greatest enemy and our closest blood-relatives. We simply can't afford to ignore learning about humans any more than we can ignore the art of the hunt or go without sleeping for long periods.

We all knew Rachel hadn't had the best of luck among humans before the pack took her in and made her one of us. Now she was a proud Wolf-cub. Maybe too proud? I wondered. Huh. Seemed like things just kept getting more complex.

I felt like I should have a word with Rachel, but for the moment I just stared at her sternly in warning, if only for a second.

Not all communication need be noisy. Some kids get it quickly enough to avoid the drama. Some never do. I was lucky; Rachel is as smart as she is stubborn. But she dropped her eyes in respect to her Alpha and directed her undivided attention to Tosh who was now taking her turn at teaching.

Tosh is the beaming mother to a small pack of blond-haired human cubs. Add in Rachel and Bookworm and you have an apparent class size of six pupils. I say apparent because Wolves have very good hearing and aren't used to sitting around. So, when you add in twelve grown eavesdropping Wolfkind the class size is more like eighteen. Wolves don't talk much, but we sure are avid listeners.

"Today, during craft time," Tosh began, "we are going to make small bags to carry stuff in. The bags can be square like this," she held up a rectangular piece of scrap cloth and folded it in half to demonstrate, "or we can make different shaped bags." She folded the cloth again, this time into a triangle. "Then we punch holes in the sides and thread string through them to close everything but the top," she explained, demonstrating again.

"Do we get to keep them?" asked Carmen, the littlest girl.

"The first one, yes. But we'll also be making some for the kitchen to use later. You can also decorate your bags however you like," Tosh explained with a smile.

"Everyone, sit down in a circle," she said. Cubs eagerly spread out in a circle that included the teacher and curiously watched her dump a large basket of leather scraps, pieces of old clothing, a few worn-out shoes, and other salvaged supplies in the middle of the circle. The noise level picked up as the cubs chattered. But no one reached for anything, waiting for the teacher's permission. I notice a rare small smile briefly appear on Henry's face as he watched from the sidelines with everyone else. Snow days inside are kind of boring and this was the most exciting thing happening.

"Now, help each other if you see someone needs a hand or an idea. Any more questions? No? Then let's begin," she said with a broad smile. She was sitting in the circle on crossed legs like the cubs.

Many small hands dove into the leather scrap and rag pile. I was delighted to watch Tosh encourage and subtly guide her class with finesse and smiles. It was very effective. And I wanted to learn more about how she could do that without giving direct orders.

Sitting in a circle is strange for a Wolf. It is a human thing to pretend everyone is equal in pack hierarchy. All Wolves may be equally loved or hated, but all Wolves are *not* equal. How would anyone get anything done? Wouldn't it be sheer anarchy? The whole idea was abhorrent to me. I looked over my pack to see who else was studying the circle with interest. Only Ella and Fitz. Good. Everyone else was watching the cubs and stretching their front paws as if they too, were working on making something from the scraps. I decided right then that we needed to get started on patrolling our borders, to get outside and do something. Anything.

I also noticed after a moment of thought, that our cubs Rachel and Bookworm were working hard on something, their heads bowed together conspiratorially. This was as it should be. Packmates work together as a team, that's how Wolves do things. I did wonder why my cub's bags were so small, though. What use is a bag nothing useful will fit in?

I found out when all the kids were showing everyone their creations. Our cubs had made leather 'Wolf' ears for themselves and were proudly wearing them and showing them off to their classmates and teachers. Tosh raised a right eyebrow for a moment, then decided to let it go. The others' reactions ranged from bemused to wide closed-mouth grins. Then Rachel paused and looked directly at me across the crowded room.

"Sometimes they forget that Bookworm and me are Wolves and not humans. This is just to help everybody remember we are pack, that we are Wolves, even if we don't have much fur," she whispered. Of course, all the pack heard her, even if the humans around her didn't. Rachel knew exactly how to pitch her voice. A warm feeling in my heart blossomed, that's the only way I can describe it. I think it might have been "pride".

Tails might have wagged.

Chapter 12

CLOSE QUARTERS

Wolves are not meant to sit around indoors—but we had no choice. Even up here in the mid-canopy of the Hoh rain forest, the ice-age winter storms showed us what true strength is. The world around us was a shrieking white-out that barely distinguished night from day. Outside, the constant razor wind dropped our body heat dangerously within minutes. We had no idea if the weather would calm down in the morning or a month from now! Hour after hour we restlessly sat around the woodburning stove that kept us alive, shoulder to shoulder with the rest of our tribe, the Fisher clan.

I think this bothered us Wolves less than the Fisher clan; Wolves need less personal space than humans, and we take comfort in the physical contact of pack. Humans take comfort in talking. We Wolves, not so much—but we are avid listeners. The stories and conversation around that glowing fire encased in iron and glass were both fascinating and instructive.

"Why don't you make snowshoes, like the Alaskan gold miners did?" asked Bookworm. We were tumbled comfortably across the curving room in the brassy light of the wood-burning stove. There were humans and Wolves scattered all over, dinner was finished, and nobody wanted to go to bed yet. Even wolves can only nap so long in our giant beehive castle in the sky.

"What are snowshoes?" asked Fitz. "Wolves don't need special shoes," he added. I stared at Fitz, and he abruptly dropped his eyes in respect. I looked back at Bookworm, leaning against

Ella's side, intently studying the firelight instead of looking at anybody. Yeah.

"Please explain about snowshoes," I asked our youngest cub. He looked up at me in silent thanks and I felt good or love, or something like that; I'm not exactly the most introspective of people.

"The reason Wolfkind, including cubs like Rachel and me," Bookworm said, "can't walk on top of the snow like birds or rabbits, is we are too heavy, and all our weight is concentrated in the small area of our paws. Snowshoes spread out the weight across a wider area, and then we can walk on top of the snow. They are flat and long and strap under our paws. Maybe you bigger Wolves will go even faster if you wear snowshoes on all fours; I don't know. I walk better on two so far," our youngest cub explained. He paused for a second, then raised his head with confidence and continued.

"More importantly, we can cover a lot more distance with snowshoes. And we can patrol Wolf Haven no matter how deep the snow is," he finished. I snuffled his head affectionately and he silent wolf-grinned. Good idea, but we needed to know more. And where does a Wolf turn to learn more?

"Sigrid, do you have a satellite link we can use to access YouTube and research snowshoes? How is your battery life?" I asked my tech wolf.

"Not good. Sun hasn't been out lately, and the *Becky's Reward* has been shut down and put to sleep. Without the ship's generators, we have maybe twenty minutes power at most, so I need to be quick about it and download footage before the battery dies," Sigrid explained.

Sigrid is a brilliant tech scientist, if occasionally unaware of her physical surroundings to a degree most Wolves would find abhorrent. She was also prone not to notice the social signals most Wolves recognize on a gut level.

Luckily, there's pack; you are never alone. No Wolf is ever left to flounder. None of us let Sigrid's occasional thoughtlessness bother us; she is building beautiful homes in the sky and doesn't look down very often. Now her sky castle protects us from the terrible storms, even if it looks more like a castle built by honeybees.

Sigrid's iPad died after sixteen minutes, but we got to watch some good content before it did. Everyone in the tribe, human and Wolf, were crowded together as we had been the last several days, watching intently over Sigrid's shoulders as she sat cross-legged on the floor in front of the glowing screen.

The intent fascination we felt watching YouTube reminded me of the first time we watched television, peering from the forest brush through the wrinkly cat-woman's front window. It was almost a thirst that I had no words for. The truth was, we were desperate for something to do but didn't recognize the feeling. In our short free lives, we'd had never had the chance to experience the inadequate visual and aural input state humans call boredom. I didn't care for it much.

We eagerly watched how snowshoes were made and used, and knew we could do that. But snowshoes weren't what got everyone excited. It was the clip with humans snowboarding. Now that looked like something a Wolf was born to do! I snarled to quiet the excited yapping and growling.

"We need to plan, to organize our days," I said. "We've never had to spend days on end without going outside or moving around. But that's what's happening. So, we have to focus on the things we need to accomplish survival and a future. A Wolf guards its territory, patrols it, hunts for food and protect the cubs and den. This is a Wolf at its most basic, but none of us are simple anymore.

"We are *more* now, and this also means maintaining our armory in peak condition and learning to use the drones we took from the Coast Guardians' boat," I said. I took a slow breath through my nose to gauge my tribe's feelings, then continued.

"A Wolf needs the proper tools to accomplish its mission. And this time, that means snowshoeing and snowboarding and protecting our forest nation any way we can." I paused again for a beat.

"We have powerful enemies. The Commander and his navy, the pirates downriver, and don't forget that those damned Tigerkin are sure to pop up and start trouble when we least expect it. We need to train, to build, and stay busy through this winter, no matter how long it lasts. This is Wolf Haven, our home, and nothing will ever drive us from it!" I declared. The room exploded in loud comradely growls and enthusiastic cheers from the humans. I waited for all the noise to settle down and turned back to Sigrid.

"How much power do we need to run everything, and how do we get it?" I asked.

"To keep our computers and both our satellite cell phones operational, keep the lights on, and run the drones, we need half a megawatt per day by spring. We need a modest power plant," she answered.

"Where do we get such a thing?" I asked. I had no idea. I wasn't sure I even knew what a power plant was. But if Sigrid needed it to keep the computers on, we'd find a way to get one.

"Maybe one of the small towns around here that survived would have a coal or natural gas burning one," Lenny offered, "but we would have to fight and take it in the middle of winter. The town's people wouldn't survive. We can't do that. We might find one in decent condition in one of the empty smaller towns, but where would we get enough fuel to run it?" It got kind of quiet until the blind fisherman spoke up.

"What about a wind generator? The kind that wind-farm had before the tsunami. One of those generators can produce up to two megawatts. Would that do?" he asked. "It was down the Oregon Coast just past the Columbia River, if I remember correctly".

It got kind of noisy for a while after that. Lots of talking. The humans sampled the whiskey offerings we'd salvaged and started showing their teeth more than normal. This also made them talk even more. Everyone got to bed late.

"I want to try something," Ella said the next morning as we watched the cubs eat breakfast. "I want to carve stone and build a tower, up on the ridge," she said confidently.

"Huh?" I responded brilliantly. I know; I'm not at my best early in the morning after a late night.

"We are beginning to attract attention. We need a visual center of power, a symbol of our new nation. Somewhere people will expect to find us that is strong and secure. We don't want anybody sniffing out the Treehouse where we sleep and raise our cubs," Ella said.

I raised chin for her to continue.

"I'm strong," she explained. "I know I can learn to cut stone and I've discovered that I like building things. Some of the other Wolves want to help too. Maybe we can even build a tower before the Commander finds us! I also think it would be a useful way to spend all this spare time we have on our paws now, my Alpha. Wolves aren't meant to sit around all day and do nothing." She was right about that! I thought for a moment.

"That sounds really good!" I said, and the pack got excited at the idea. "You have Henry put together a training program for you, three other wolves, and as many humans as wish to work on the tower. You will oversee building it but work with Henry and Sigrid on the design," I directed. I waited for everyone to calm down a bit before continuing.

"I will take another team of three wolves and travel with the blind fisherman and Lenny to the Oregon coast and that torn-up wind farm. We need power to thrive. And if there's one thing we are rich in, other than enemies, it's tall trees and wind," I said. I turned to my second-in-command.

"Fitz, you have the third team. Take charge of base security, arrange patrols, and make enough snowshoes and snowboards for all our Wolves and humans," I ordered, looking around at my mixed tribe to make sure everyone was with me so far. They were.

"We're going to operate in three teams of four wolves each. The stone masons under Ella and Henry, the wind-generator salvagers with me, and the security team under Fitz," I said, peripherally noticing the intent regard of our cubs, Rachel and Bookworm.

"All cubs will go to class during school hours, but they may choose to spend their free time helping any of the teams. Adult humans will join any team they wish, go fishing and trapping, or work on the everyday chores of survival here. I want everyone to meet back here midday to report progress. Let's do it!" I barked, and all my people scattered happily in different directions. It felt good to be doing something after being cooped up for so long.

It was cold on the water. We finished clearing the decks of the *Becky's Reward*, but the steady snow was methodically undoing all our work. At least the winds were behaving at these lower altitudes, and we didn't lose much body heat under our heavy coats and floppy hats.

Afterwards, we met in the snug canteen, where we ate our meals on the *Becky*. There were six of us; four wolves, the blind fisherman, and his first mate, Lenny. We barely fit. The humans were making tea, a coffee substitute from what I understood. It was just dirty water to me.

Grandpa had been explaining the parts we would be collecting, and I wasn't sure how to make it work. "Captain," I asked the old fisherman, "are the metal stems holding the generators out of the water short enough for us to carry on the *Becky*? How will we take them down?"

"No. They're the height of four *Becky*'s laid bow-to-stern. I suspect we won't have to worry about taking them down; the Tsunami will have taken care of that for us," the blind man explained. "The *Becky's Reward* is a powerful boat and can pull a barge through medium seas for days without a problem. However, first we need to find a barge."

I looked at Felix, but he was as lost as I was. "What's a barge, and how do we get one?" I asked.

"It's a salvaged water-tight boat hull," the captain answered. "With all the above-deck super-structure and all the heavy stuff below decks removed, it will be flat and light, which makes the barge very buoyant and able to carry a lot of weight. It won't need an engine compartment because we tow it. When we get to the offshore wind power farm, we'll pile all the stems and blades we can fit on top of the barge and secure the load tightly. But the generators concern me more than the stems and propellors." He paused to sip at his brown water.

"Let's hope we can find at least five functional generators from the more than three hundred they had a month ago. That would give us three generators to use and two for spare parts. A month in the salt never did anything mechanical any good, but these are built to withstand years of bad weather. I think there's room to put at least five generators in our rear hold. Once we've loaded the generators, the stems, and wind-blades on the barge, we'll make our way home towing our prizes behind us," exclaimed the blind fisherman.

"There will be hundreds of boat hulls for us to choose from along our journey downriver," he added.

Lenny groaned and covered his eyes. "He makes it sound easy, but I'm the one who's going to have to cut all that metal," he grumbled.

"Wolves make everything go faster," I offered. The blind captain started laughing until he fell into a coughing fit. Lenny stopped complaining and laughed, too. I had no idea why they were laughing, but it still made me feel kind of good. Must be my human side.

We loaded up for a two-week trip, with lots of protein shakes, Grandma's chili in sealed gallon jars, baskets of fresh cornbread, and a sizable portion of the armory. (You never know when you're going to need a shoulder-fired missile or a mortar). We were starting to use the ground camp again between the big snowstorms, so everybody met back there for lunch, and I wrestled a little with Rachel and Bookworm after they ate. Bookworm actually laughed out loud when I let the two cubs win and they worked together to tickle me. I nuzzled the cubs one last time and stood up, exchanging a look with Ella as I rose. Her eyes lingered on mine a moment longer than I expected. Hmm.

I turned to my second, Fitz. "Keep the com systems powered. In case of emergency, we are a call away, but it could take us two or three days to get back. Maintain a low profile. No singing at the moon until we get back. Guard the den and protect the cubs, all of our people, our tribe," I ordered.

Fitz growled, "Of course, Alpha," politely.

As we walked to the *Becky's Reward*, my team fell in around me. Felix, Nina, and Twist, plus the captain and his first mate. I didn't look back, but I could feel Rachel's wistful gaze on my back. Maybe next trip.

We stepped aboard the *Becky* and the blind fisherman steered us out into the middle of the Bogachiel river. Our fishing boat forged ahead through restless water more ice than liquid. The ice made the strangest tinkling sound against the *Becky*'s hull. Fat snowflakes swirled in spiral patterns and the banks were cotton candy drifts pierced with green needles. The upriver wind was cold and rich with exotic scent. I took hold of the anti-aircraft gun and checked to make sure everything worked properly. I don't recall learning to operate this weapon, but my paws remembered just fine. Felix took position to my left, one paw resting on my ammo box, the other cradling a grenade launcher. Twist had the stern, complete with mortar and incendiary shells. Nina perched cross-legged on the small roof of the wheelhouse; a fifty-caliber Robar C-50 anti-material sniper rifle cradled in her powerful arms.

I exhaled slowly, consciously relaxing my muscles despite the cold wind, studying the river and her banks as we navigated our way down the Bogachiel.

I was expecting pirates.

Chapter 13

THE SKI LODGE

Queen Malgato bared her teeth, her massive fangs gleaming in the faint, high-altitude sunlight trickling through the chalet's tall windows. She nodded minutely to her security team Lao Zi and Fu Yin, who immediately divided and glided along opposite sides of the enormous lodge's central area. Once they determined there were no threats, Lao Zi returned to face her former commanding officer. now Queen, Malgato, and bowed. The boss Tiger stretched leisurely and padded into the huge room surrounded by her Tigerkin.

"This will do nicely," she said, looking around the abandoned ski lodge's lobby with satisfaction. "I want that in my bunker," she said, pointing at an emerald-green couch at least twelve feet long. "And that," she added, pointing at a thick Persian carpet by the front desk. This place was large and full of useful stuff—her Tigers were going to be able to furnish everyone's bunkers now! She turned her attention to Bai Li, her surviving Com officer.

"We need to seriously upgrade our Com and surveillance equipment. A place this large requires a facilities center, power generator, a complex security system and maybe even a small armory. Track them all down and take a quick inventory. Report back in forty," the Queen ordered. Then she turned her massive head to stare at Xi-Rong and Bao-Tien Gong.

"Find the power room. See if the main electrical generators can be relocated to our base. Then look for smaller standalone units; a resort like this is sure to have a lot of outdoor events that would require mobile power. They probably have a number of diesel generators small enough to move around. Find fuel supplies for them as well. Report back in forty minutes," she ordered. Her tech Tigers moved out with feline grace, leaving their leader to check out the front desk area.

She examined her surroundings as only a Tiger can. No movement anywhere. She drew in a great breath through her nose and studied the scentscape. Mold and mildew mostly, but rodent droppings and raccoon musk were the only signs of life. Minor nuances of rotting citrus and potatoes. She snorted. There was a lot of polished wood, and three huge stone fireplaces taking up the center of the enormous room. The only windows she could see were up high, with just enough dusty light trickling down to see everything in twilight vision.

The Tiger Queen padded over to the front counter. There was a dead computer screen neatly fit into the ornate wood of the top of the desk, and several drawers below just begging to be dug through. The Queen delicately hooked a claw and tugged on the main drawer. It resisted until the simple lock snapped and then it slid open smoothly. Inside were a bunch of blank electronic room keys and a folded white pamphlet with a picture of the ski lodge on the front.

The Major spread out the paper document in the dubious light filtering in through the high windows above her. It appeared to be a map of the entire ski lodge and facilities. She studied the map closely. Apparently, there were additional areas of the complex that the Tigers had been unaware of. Something called a "ski hut" caught her eye. It seemed to represent a barn containing something capable of rapid movement over snow. She licked her chops at the thought of fresh meat.

The Major returned to studying the lodge's layout. After a moment, she folded the pamphlet back up and slipped it inside her body armor. She turned to examine the doors labeled "Offices" in small gold letters behind the front desk. There were sure to be plenty of interesting things in the manager's office and the ski lodge's main vault! She broke the door's lock and ducked to enter the small office complex.

You never knew what you'd find in these situations, but the Major and her team were well-drilled in surviving off the land in enemy territory. Tigers are born to thrive in survival scenarios and excelled at them. And now that she'd cut their ties to the People's Liberation Army of China, her team was completely on their own. Her newborn mountain kingdom was badly lacking in resources, so the Tigers were going to have to salvage everything they could to make it through the coming winter storms. It smelled like it was going to be a long winter, too.

The alternative was to find out if freezing to death came before their high-metabolism bodies self-cannibalized and they starved to death. The stakes were high, but the Major had faith in her team. Tigerkind are very smart.

The manager's door was unlocked, and she slipped into the room. It took less than five seconds to locate the big safe behind the bad art hanging on the wall. The lock was surprisingly sophisticated for such a remote backwater, and it took the Major longer than she expected to get the commercial vault open. After twelve minutes she eased open the steel door to look inside.

It had been worth the effort! Someone had stored an encrypted satellite phone that could reach anywhere in the world. She activated it and checked for connectivity. Not only did it have four bars, but unless she was mistaken, it had an untraceable Internet signal. Spy stuff. It even had a box of spare lithium batteries.

She briefly wondered which intelligence agency was responsible for her luck, but really, who knew? Intel said that this former US state territory had been riddled with foreign spies, including special agents of the Peoples Republic hunting a man called Salamander—no, it was Chameleon! She chuffed at the thought of giant lizards and tucked her new satellite cell phone into a thigh pocket before digging deeper into the safe.

There were a few manila envelopes stuffed with US paper currency, a surprisingly decadent selection of women's jewelry, and even two custom hunting rifles in a hard case. But the real find was an aluminum briefcase containing a gold-plated Desert Eagle hand cannon, three clips, and a massive suppressor that screwed on to the barrel. It was absolutely beautiful.

After admiring her find, she gathered the jewelry together and dumped it into a briefcase she had snapped open out of curiosity. It had turned out to be stuffed full of photos of a nuclear power plant that was still active (if the steam venting into the cold night air was any indicator), five memory sticks, and a Browning Hi-power nine-millimeter with four clips and two boxes of cop-killer bullets. She threw away the photos but kept the gun. It looked like a derringer in her enormous paw, but she could still fire it and it was easy to conceal. It never hurts to have backups for your backups.

After hesitating a moment, she added the American currency to the now-overstuffed briefcase. Who knows when the next time she would be able to use cash was? But everyone knew that some mice would do anything for gold. It could come in handy. A little more searching, and she found also packing tape by the printer, so she wrapped the briefcase in tape to keep it shut. It was very full.

The Major carefully tucked her gleaming new hand cannon into a battle-harness compartment on her left side where she could quickly reach it. She also transferred the clips and silencer to where she could get at them easily. Then she rolled her neck until it cracked and spun to reenter the main lounge precisely on time to receive her team's reports.

"There is enough Com and entertainment tech to outfit all of our bunkers and more," Bai Li reported, "We also found satellite TV stuff, but we still need to track down and salvage the dish receivers. Once we position everything properly, we should be able to link up the signal between our dens so everyone can access it. These country mice were decadently rich, but our new kingdom deserves the best we can find," her Communications officer finished.

The Queen nodded in satisfaction, turned, and lay her gaze heavily on Xi-Rong and Bao-Tien Gong. They both bowed and Xi-Rong spoke. "The main power generator is built into the foundation, and several has huge consoles, very hard to understand without a manual. And there is no manual. We did find a large back-up electrical generator, and it is very heavy, barely portable. We are going to need a large sled to move it back up into our mountains," Xi-Rong reported, sneezing nervously before continuing.

"Good news: We won't have to pull them ourselves! We found something called a 'snowmobile'. We wrecked the first two when we were learning how to use them, but there are lots more," Xi-Rong grinned, "They're like powerful motorcycles that drive on snow instead of pavement. We believe that several hooked up together can pull a big sled, one large enough to carry the big generator uphill to our dens," she explained.

Bao-Tien reported next. "It's hard to tell how much fuel is needed to return to base with a full load, but we found enough fuel in the depot to make a number of trips back and forth. There are also five diesel-fueled electrical generators in a back-storage room, but we don't know if they work. We found a large tank of diesel, maybe twelve-hundred liters or so, to fuel them. Problem is that the tanks are only half full." She stepped back one pace in respect and lowered her eyes to the ground.

Queen Malgato didn't need time to think about it at all.

"Power first. Bai Li, find me a sled large enough to carry the big generator," the Tiger Queen ordered before turning back to Xi-Rong and Bao-Tien.

"Pull the five smaller generators out of storage, fuel them, and see if they'll start. Move the ones that start to a staging area in the driveway of this place. Drag the fuel tank outside too, then report back," she ordered.

"Lao Zi, go with Xi-Rong and figure out how to drive these 'snowmobile' things without wrecking any more of them. Find tow ropes while you're at it.

"Fu Yin, with me. We're going to check out this 'ski hut'. What does this 'ski' mean, anyway? Tiny deer? I see those pictured a lot on signs. Move out, team!" the Major declared.

Tigers scattered everywhere on their missions. They all took an unconscious comfort in their well-defined command structure. Tigerkind needed a militaristic society, it was the only thing keeping them from descending into deadly power struggles and cruel games played on their own kind. Tiger killing Tiger! Madness! Queen Malgato snarled at the thought and shattered the glass door leading to the mysterious "ski hut" with one blow. Time to get to the bottom of this conundrum. She hoped that "skis" were tasty.

They were boards. Skis were flat boards. Admittedly they were very shiny and curved up at one end but finding them was a quite a let-down. The Major had really hoped "skis" were some kind of exotic deer. These were not even close! She studied the room.

After a moment her eyes focused on the huge wall photo of humans bundled in brightly colored textiles, sliding down mountains on skis. It looked like they were moving very fast! She blinked and sat down to study the picture. Maybe these skis weren't a complete disappointment after all!

Chapter 14

THE BARGE

The snow fell in gentle weight, dampening all sound and sight around us. We sailed down the icy river, perched on the bow of the *Becky's Reward*, looking for trouble and determined to find it before it found us. The wind was intoxicating, rich in scent nuance and pungent promise. I took another deep breath through my nose, the tabula shuffling through myriad scents, a complex tapestry of aroma the likes of which I had never experienced.

The cloud-obscured, mid-day sun crept overhead in the same direction we were going; west. The water downriver briefly sparkled like a strobe light, and the cold wind bathed us in velvet scent. I loosely held the anti-aircraft gun's handles the way Henry had, relaxed, but ready to burst into action when the time was right. As I scanned the area we were entering, the fisherman firmly held the helm behind me on the *Becky*'s bridge. Lenny was mumbling in the captain's ear, telling him what he couldn't see, which I didn't think was much. The captain had awfully good sight for a blind man.

The banks hereabouts were snow sculptured castles, hiding all manners of dead boats and treasure beneath their cold embrace. We needed the right kind of boat, so I asked Grandpa to help us find the right wreck to salvage.

"What about that one?" asked Lenny, pointing to a fat-bottomed boat almost twice as long as our sweet *Becky*. It was shoved halfway up a mud bank and almost completely covered with mounds of the purest white snow.

I turned to our captain. "What do you think?" I asked.

He just smiled quietly without showing his teeth. "Too deep a keel. Too narrow. Maybe the next one," he replied. I exchanged a look with Twist. How did he do that? Sometimes Grandpa got kind of spooky.

I shrugged and turned back to the bow of our ship, inhaling the symphony of scent pouring past us as we made our way down the Bogachiel river to La Push and the Pacific Ocean. It was wild and magnificent.

Yet it didn't smell right.

The up-river wind reeked of raw earth and torn plant life and recent flooding. Rot and old death and clean saltwater. But it was what it didn't contain that intrigued us. There was no scent of metal or gun oil, of scorched metal or artificial chemicals. In fact, there was no trace of humanity at all. None of my Wolves had ever experienced such an aromatic conundrum. Something so new to our palates was very exciting and there might have even been a little tail-wagging for a moment. But only for a moment.

Because it was also a world without Rachel and Bookworm. And I couldn't imagine such a world. Maybe that was why it simply didn't smell right—no humans. Huh. I guess for better or worse we are bonded to our human side and a world without them was never going to be right.

I'm fine with that. "Doesn't smell right without humans," I said.

My wolves growled supportively. It's good to be pack.

The sun had sunk far enough into the horizon to bleed dusty gold and purple. The wind was becoming colder already. We could scent a little salt in the upwind current, a tease of the Pacific Ocean. Lenny said we were forty-five minutes from La Push. Suddenly, our captain of the good ship *Becky's Reward* cut the throttle and began coasting closer to the southern, marshmallow shore.

There was a wealth of rain-shot snow drifts, but we seemed to be closing on a huge, whale-like snowbank that concealed something just short of enormous.

Our boat slowly came to a stop right beside the snowbank in question. I looked up and out, studying the hull curve of the hidden boat that was partially obscured by snow. Then I turned back, reacquiring my Wolves as I made my way to the bridge of the *Becky's Reward*.

"What's next?" I asked the captain.

"Well, Alpha, first we need to clear the hull of snow, so we know exactly what we've got to work with. If she's a keeper, then we need to patch up any holes in the hull, then right her and float her. All further work will be done as we tow her out to sea. Now, Lenny will lead several of you below decks for reconnaissance. Everyone else can finish clearing the hull of snow and debris," the captain ordered.

I inclined my head and nodded to Lenny to lead the way.

We Wolves followed Lenny onto the upside-down hull. It was metal and my paw talons made odd little clicking sounds when I walked on it. Lenny was not a large man, but he was surprisingly graceful. I somehow didn't expect him to have such good balance moving across the broken ship, but then, Lenny was full of quiet surprises. Maybe that was part of why everybody loved him.

I motioned to my Wolves and spoke. "Grab brooms and shovels. Let's start clearing this wreck so we can see what we have!" I ordered. We leapt into action eagerly. We'd been cooped up on the ship long enough. Wolves like to stay busy. Within fifteen minutes we had the hull cleared and had exposed openings in the area of the bow. I followed Lenny as he dropped a rope ladder and descended into the dark rectangular hatch we had uncovered. Since the ship was lying on its starboard side, we were entering at a weird angle.

We stopped going down after about ten meters and worked our way into the forward portion of the wreck. The metal around us was rough with rust and dried gunk. It was very dark. Lenny had his helmet spotlight on, and that supplied enough ambient light for all us Wolves to see. We stood on the starboard wall, which was surprisingly clear of obstacles for a boat this size. But the smells…

Our noses were assaulted with rotting potatoes and diesel fuel and something that had been dead for a long time. The pungent attack was already deadening our noses. If we stayed down here too long, we'd be completely nose-blind. Lenny quickly led us deeper into the ship as he noted bulkheads and engines and fuel tanks (empty?). Then we got to the engines. Lenny took a moment to spray a glowing pink paint on the power generator before moving on. He spray-painted "X"'s on the walls several times for reasons I was unsure of.

Ten minutes later we climbed the rope ladder back up into the snowing bleach-white world. We all squeezed onto the bridge and Lenny quickly wrapped his hands around the mug of fortified hot tea the captain handed him to warm up. It steamed profusely, pouring a not unpleasant acidic note into the room. Nina sneezed and Twist wrinkled his nose in distaste. Not all scents are agreeable to all Wolves.

"What do you think?" the captain asked Lenny.

"Bigger than I would have chosen," he said, "but it will be harder to sink, too, at least by the time I get finished with her. Engines are slag, but we were going to dump those anyway. Not too much superstructure to remove above decks, and six water-tight compartments below. Once we clean her up, she'll carry all the wind blades and towers you want," Lenny reported, pausing to sip his tea.

Then he added "Bonus! I found significant reserves of acetylene tanks and welding equipment aboard, much higher quality gear than we have on the *Becky*. This is going to take a while, but it's not as hard as I feared," Lenny finished. Then he blinked.

"Hey! Do you think any of your Wolves would like to learn how to cut apart a steel ship with a torch?" he asked, and we all froze for a second.

There was nothing I could think of that we would love *more* than wielding a flaming tool of destruction so hot it cuts through metal like butter. Twist, Nina, and Felix were trembling slightly in excitement, and I was standing rigid so as not to betray how much we wanted this, but Lenny was clueless in these manners and didn't notice a thing. The blind fisherman did, but only sipped his hot tea and said nothing.

"I think these four Wolves would like that very much," I answered.

Chapter 15

THE INTERROGATION

"There's someone in lockup waiting for interrogation, Captain. He'll only give his name as Riley. We caught him and his men looting Armory Four. They gave us a good fight for a minute, but now they're all dead or run off. Riley's the only one left intact. The prisoner is down this way," reported his sergeant. The captain nodded and followed him to the brig.

"I'm Captain Christensen," he said after he sat down across from the man called Riley. He laid his well-honed patient gaze on the prisoner and waited. This simple technique often worked because most people hate a long silence and feel compelled to fill it.

Not this time.

After a moment, the captain leaned forward to place his sizable forearms on the table and studied the man. Riley was not a tall or heavily muscled man. In fact, he was more of a well-dressed baling wire and rawhide type and could have easily passed for a pro bantam-weight boxer.

Riley had shown himself capable of quick decision-making, but the fact that he was still alive while his gang was not, spoke loudly of his priorities. Captain Christensen noted the cold intellect that glinted behind the criminal's eyes; the prisoner's survival strategy had proved effective, if flagrantly wasteful of human assets. Classic sociopathic reasoning. *With a little polish, this guy would have made a good CEO,* the captain chuckled to himself.

Riley's pale blond hair and sun-reddened face said he spent considerable time outside, while his calm demeanor despite being held prisoner in a military cell suggested a familiarity with incarceration. The captive's physical posture clearly stated "alpha predator". His clothing said he was successful, but not familiar with the fashion sense of those who are born to coin. Riley's perpetually red nose suggested he had a well-developed taste for the bottle. This was a weakness Marc shared, but neither gave any outward sign of recognition of their shared addiction.

After a moment Riley allowed his eyes to rise slowly from the table's surface to meet his interrogator's gaze. He grinned at the captain with the practiced skill of a good liar. It was an infectious smile, but Captain Marc Christensen was definitely immune. His granite face did not respond. After a moment, the prisoner shrugged in self-mocking defeat and sat up straighter.

"Seems like Kitsap-Bangor Naval base has seen better days," Riley said coolly, "Wasn't too long ago that thousands of civilian workers and Navy sailors filled these empty grounds with nonstop motion. Now there are only a handful of sailors remaining, greedily laying claim to far more territory than they need or are capable of protecting," Riley said bluntly, leaning slightly forward to bring his mocking face closer to the enemy across the metal table.

"Now, I'm guilty of a bit of greed here and there myself, so I'm pretty sure that's why you ambushed us when we were only engaged in the legitimate salvage of abandoned assets. Looks to me like you can't occupy everything you lay claim to, but you also don't want anyone else to have it either," Riley said sarcastically.

The prisoner studied his captor as he verbally prodded him, watching his eyes to see what kind of man he was. Captain Marc Christensen didn't blink or react, and Riley abruptly realized that this was a very deadly man in front of him, not some paper-pusher but a warrior who had successfully destroyed his enemy many times. Riley's sardonic grin faded. *Who would have the highest body count, him or me?* the prisoner wondered silently. After a moment he leaned back to focus on Captain Christensen and continued.

"This is a new world," he said, stretching then sitting up alertly, his eyes flashing. "There is enough to go around for everyone. Don't be greedy. Let me go, and in return I won't round up everyone I can find with a gun, then come back and burn down your house," the prisoner demanded. Then Riley relaxed, leaning back again before continuing in a more reasonable tone.

"All you need to do is turn over the western half of the base to me, and I'll not bother you further. You're not even using it! And I won't make you pay for the men I'll have to replace if you play nice," said the Irish American gangster earnestly.

After a pause to consider his words, the captain slowly leaned even closer to Riley, not stopping until their faces were less than twelve inches apart.

"You have a mob of drunken gangsters," began Captain Christensen, "armed with civilian hunting rifles and shotguns. I have a Trident missile attack sub, four Seahawk helicopters and an aircraft carrier loaded with fighter jets less than three minutes away. This Naval base is the property of Elwha Nation, and we fight for what is ours. Now, how did you come to be here? Why on earth did you think it was safe to raid a military base?" asked the captain. He leaned back to study the gangster as he waited for a response.

"Your Kitsap-Bangor base is only a fragment of my territory," the man known as Riley began. "I am a successful businessman who has adapted to this new world like a fish to water. My management style requires significant munitions and the teams to acquire and wield them. You should strongly consider not standing in my way. It could be a very profitable decision for you," he said. "Think about it, anyway," he added, watching the captain's granite face for any sign of what he was thinking.

Riley was a man who believed that superior firepower was the simple answer to many of life's little problems. And where do you find the finest weapons? In the naval magazines of Elwha nation, of course. The US mainland remained under martial law, its entire west coast laid waste, and British Columbia was under military occupation by the Chinese People's Republic fleet. Where else was he going to go? Dublin? Riley refrained from rolling his eyes.

"If you wish to make a legitimate purchase from our arsenal," Captain Marc began, "You need to contact Naval headquarters at Indian Island. If, instead, you are attempting to steal important national resources in a time of war, the penalty is simple. The Commander will send his best to deal with you. I'm the best. Time to deal. Why are you more valuable to me alive than dead?" asked Captain Christensen so coldly that he may have breathed out a little frost.

"Wow. Gloves come off fast around here," exclaimed Riley. "Okay. My people are scattered everywhere around Olympic Island. I know who the local players are, where most of the bodies are buried, and offer services and products that are in high demand. I have my fingers on the pulse of this new-born land; I can make things run smoothly, or roughly, for you and your sailors. Right now, your people cower in fortified underground bunkers, while I walk the land freely, making money as I go," Riley stated with confidence.

"What about your men? You know, the ones you led to their death on an ill-reputed raid for your personal profit. You have no men left that I can see," the captain observed.

Riley grinned. "Men and women of their type are always available for the right amount of money. I'll have a new team by tomorrow night. They're like cheap batteries in a demanding toy; they keep failing and I keep replacing them," he explained.

"Yeah, whatever," the captain responded. "So, you go everywhere and know everyone. Then maybe you can tell me about any 'unusual' fighting forces on the island since the world changed?" the captain asked, his eye never leaving Riley's face. Riley flinched slightly when he asked about 'unusual' forces. Captain Marc didn't let his smile show. He leaned back from the small table that separated them.

"Dogs or Tigers?" the captain asked, his gaze locked on his prisoner's face like an alligator deciding whether to have a bite or not.

Then Marc's eyes widened briefly. "Both! You must be deadlier than you appear, to survive contact with both Tigerkind and the Commander's runaway Dogs," he added softly, his eyes still locked on Riley's.

Riley smiled as only an Irish gangster does when caught in a lie, then lifted his eyes to the ceiling and kept them there while he considered what to tell and what to hold back. A grateful base Commander would be a very handy thing to have, but he wasn't going to give away the farm in exchange for gratitude. After a moment, he turned back to face Captain Christensen.

"What's for dinner? I haven't had lunch, and I'm feeling a bit peckish. Don't you guys have fancy chefs for the officers and bosses?" Riley asked, attempting to redirect the conversation elsewhere. The last thing he wanted to talk about was the Wolfmen and Tigers he'd fought. He'd barely gotten away with his life both times! But the captain didn't look like he was fooled one bit. Riley could tell it was going to be a long night.

By zero-four-hundred the next morning, Captain Christensen was satisfied he had gleaned everything he could without resorting to harsh interrogation, and after gathering his team, he called the Commander to report.

"I have word of both your runaway Dogs and the Tigers who attacked Kitsap-Bangor. A gangster we caught attempting to loot one of our armories has had encounters with both. I'm a little surprised he survived them, but gangs and cockroaches have always been hard to kill off. This Irish crime lord is ruthless, powerful and spends the lives of his men quite wastefully. Apparently, there are plenty of men these days willing to turn outlaw rather than starve or sweat for an honest day's work," Captain Marc Christiansen reported to his megalomaniac boss on the phone.

"Excellent! So, where are my missing mutts?" demanded the Commander, suddenly wide awake.

"The prisoner had a combat encounter weeks ago with your missing Dogs," the captain began, "and later, with the same Tigers that my team encountered at Bangor-Kitsap. When they fled, the Tigers were headed northwest into the mountains of the Olympic National Forest. Apparently, the gangsters encountered your Dogs just north of Shelton, on the west side of the Hood Canal. He believed that they were headed north and might be accompanied by some human fishermen. The prisoner states that both species showed a sophisticated grasp of tactics and misdirection, as well as incredible speed of attack. He didn't have any idea where they might be right now, and wasn't interested in finding out," the captain reported.

"Good hunting, Captain. Bring me my runaway mutts and I will show them what happens to bad Dogs. Report in by..." The Commander held his smart-watch closer to his eyes. "...seventeen-hundred tonight."

"My team will be in the air within twenty minutes. We will track down your runaways. I will report back in four hours, Commander. Kitsap/Bangor out," Captain Marc Christensen said and hung up. Then he turned to his team who were crowded into the control room around him, listening and focused on their leader with faith that he'd take good care of them, just as he always had.

"That was the last time I will ever speak with that man as a subordinate." His team watched him soberly, clearly ready for this. "It's go-bag time. We won't be coming back this way again. I <u>will</u> <u>not</u> allow us to be put into a position of choosing between firing on our former brother-in-arms or mutiny. And we are not the neighborhood dog catchers either—in fact I don't blame those slave-Dogs one bit for getting the hell out of there. Enough is enough! We are going to disappear into the storm and find someplace beautiful to make our home," the captain said, looking around at his team for any reactions.

"It's about time," declared one of his NCO's, "I was afraid we were all going to have to grow beards and smoke cigars like Fidel in Cuba! The Commander is a bully armed with nuclear weapons. I want no part of Elwha Nation!" Everyone cheered then quieted down quickly when the captain cleared his throat. His men and women met his eye and silence ruled the room.

"Go get your families and any last-minute essentials to the airfield. We'll fly in a long southern loop around the Olympic mountains, turn north, and head for the rendezvous above Lake Quinault," he said, looking around at his people. "Meet back here in twenty minutes." His troops scattered, moving with quiet efficiency. There was very little chatter. SEALs and their families don't screw around when it's time to go.

Chapter 16

THE DROWNED FOREST

I watched for the mouth of the river where it widened and opened into the Pacific Ocean. We were still passing through the place that had once been the seaport of La Push. All that remained of La Push were polished cement slabs, mud, hills of plastic rubbish that had settled in dirty drifts, and tree root dams. Everything else had been swept away by the terrible tsunami. Sand, mud, and rotting wood that stunk of death and decay. Once upon a time, La Push may have been beautiful, but it was not a pretty place anymore.

The fresh mountain water of the Bogachiel River ended in an aquamarine border that clearly defined its entry into the ocean. On the other side of the line, the Pacific was a translucent gray, rolling in gentle, meter-high waves to shore. Seagulls screamed and dived into a patch of water off the port bow, a few hundred meters away. The blind captain laughed into the sea wind and pointed accurately in the direction of the rioting seabirds.

"Nice school of fish down that way," he said. "Lenny, bait and drop some lines off the stern. Maybe we'll catch some outliers." Then the blind captain turned back to us.

"We're heading straight offshore, until we're out of sight of land. Then we'll turn port and cruise south down the Pacific coast until we get to the wind farm, somewhere off the northern Oregon coast. We should arrive late tomorrow or early the next morning, depending on conditions. Sharp eyes, everyone! Watch for pirates until we make it far enough offshore to be out of sight."

We saw no one at all, aside from a thousand birds and a pack of leaping dolphins. The dolphins seemed happy to see us and traveled beside us most of the way out to sea. I felt a sort of kinship with the creatures that I didn't understand, but it still made me feel good.

Once we swung south, out on the open sea, I took my Wolves across the cables back to the barge. We liked to stay busy and had most of a day on our hands. Felix suggested we build a couple of fortified sniper nests amidships, where the deck met the hull. We didn't know how much metal to use, so we ended up wrapping multiple layers of steel around a bulging blister with a horizontal slit big enough to stick any gun we had through and fire.

At that point, it wasn't even noon yet, so we moved to the starboard side and built another machine gun nest. Next, we started on yet another, larger, heavily fortified weapons station on the stern of the barge. By mid-afternoon, we had finished constructing all three. Now we stood amidships in the salt breeze, admiring our work, and drinking great drafts of water when Twist mentioned that he didn't have a safe and concealed place to fire our mortar from.

Well, it wasn't dinner time yet, so I asked Twist what he needed.

"An open-air pit with fortified sides and a blast shield would be perfect, but this is a small metal island, and we can't dig a hole," he said, shaking his shaggy head.

"But we could cut one!" I replied. "What if we slice out a rectangular section of the deck, leaving the deck below as a floor and firing position. Then, we could vertically weld back sections of the removed deck as new bulkheads."

I looked down to see my indistinct shadow stretching three-times my height across the barge's metal deck. Nightfall wasn't too far away.

I stretched my neck and turned back to Felix, Nina, and Twist. "Let's do it! I think we can finish this before dark. We will cut the deck piece out together, then Felix and Nina will slice the metal into smaller pieces while I start welding blast guards around the opening. Twist, you get the mortar and some shells and meet us in the firing hole. That way we can figure out where everything goes. Move, Wolves!" I barked.

Good times.

After the cloud-clad sun disappeared into the western sea we washed up and gathered in the galley. Lenny and the blind fisherman took turns at the helm, joining us one at a time. Grandma's three-day-old chili was still pretty good when you sopped it up with the stale cornbread. After dinner, the humans stayed up late talking, but sleep claimed us Wolves quickly.

The next morning dawn crept slowly out of the east, a sallow fog-light reaching up into the mist-obscured sky. I hoped we might actually see the sun today, but the cloud layers and mist didn't cooperate at all.

Just like every other winter day since the Apocalypse.

I ducked to enter the bridge of the *Becky's Reward* and nodded to Lenny. He raised the usual mug of hot dirty water in casual salute.

"When will we get there?" I asked the *Becky*'s captain.

The blind-man-who-saw smiled at me without showing his teeth. It was the kind of smile that makes you drop a silent wolf-laugh, so I did. His grin got even wider.

"If I'm right, we are about seven hours from the wind farm. From the bow, you should be able to see it before anyone else. Watch for tall skinny towers and unusual reflections in the water. Also be on the lookout for anything that doesn't look normal, Trey," he said.

I growled politely and returned to the bow with my team.

We stuck our noses into the glorious wind, enjoying our first respite in days. We delighted in the leaping dolphins that had rejoined us. It was a beautiful morning at sea. A kind of peacefulness I couldn't remember ever knowing surrounded us in the dawn world. It was wonderful.

But we Wolfkind have learned to never let our guards down. Never.

As the late afternoon sky began darkening with surprising speed, we spotted our objective.

A drowned forest of dark, limbless trees like spindly towers, loomed out of a rich palette of gray. Only a few of the wind-blades still attached to the turbines were slowly turning in the inshore wind. There were hundreds of small, jagged islands of debris and abandoned boats and junk surrounding the remaining towers, creating a watery maze that looked dangerous as can be.

"It looks creepy as hell" Nina muttered, and we all had to agree. Our alertness level increased automatically.

Then Lenny said, "These wind towers are smaller than the usual ones."

Well, I wasn't sure of that at all, it was hard to imagine wind towers taller than these, even though only a small number remained intact. This spooky place was tall indeed, if not to Hoh Rain Forest standard.

I looked to my right. The dark clouds grew ever closer, a wall of angry charcoal just waiting to have a temper tantrum. I suddenly found myself longing for our peaceful forest, but we had come here to scavenge for parts from the windfarm. This was important. The sooner we could accomplish our mission, the sooner we could return to our beloved rain forest.

The *Becky* slowed even more as we drew closer to the flotsam maze.

Suddenly, Felix growled real low, and we all snapped our heads to see what he was warning us about. Three fat attack-boats with heavy machine guns came roaring out from concealed positions within the drowned metal forest.

"Now!" I snarled and…

…I phase into Flux. The world around me slows dramatically as the moment between heartbeats expands until everything around me is moving at a snail's crawl. I reach down with my right paw and remove the safety on the fifty-cal deck gun, as Felix lifts the ammo chain so it flows more efficiently. We are balanced on the cusp of battle forever…

The attacking boats are still out of range, though. Our *Becky*'s approach is agonizingly slow. The Flux is not a thing to be expended wastefully, so I….

…I oscillate out of Flux, ignoring the mild headache, residue from the rapid transition. Combat was still to come and linear logic would suffice for the current situation. I shook my head to clear it.

"Nina," I growled, and a loud crack comes from atop the wheelhouse where the White Wolf crouches, cradling a Robar antimaterial rifle aimed at the foremost enemy craft. The center boat swerved briefly, almost brushing its starboard-side comrade. They immediately increased the space between them with a coordination that demonstrated that this wasn't their first time working together under fire.

Pirates.

Chapter 17

BIRTH OF THE STONE MASONS

Henry had always enjoyed teaching students martial arts, but this was the first time since he was a boy that he'd taught anyone stone masonry.

Back on Wudang Mountain in China, a fifteen-year-old Henry had taught several of his ten-year-old cousins how to split stone, and other basic techniques in the art of stone masonry. His young students grew to love Stone as he did over the next few years.

Now here he was, on the other side of the world, about to start teaching a small class of hulking Wolfkin and humans the Tao of Stone. He looked down at the hammer in his hand. It had been a long time, but some things you never forget. And these new students were motivated. They had sought him out—and that was a compliment few good teachers could turn down!

He looked over at Ella, who was patiently waiting for him to begin—not calmly, Wolfkind are so alive, almost vibrating with energy that he really couldn't call her *calm*—but patiently. He cleared his throat politely, and his class grew still.

The mixed group of humans and Wolves stood below and to the right of the ridge where the tower would eventually be built, up against the rock bluff. A light snow was whirling around them, but everyone ignored it. The wind wasn't bad. Henry put his left hand on the rock face and brushed the snow crust away, feeling the stone's grain and hardness with a touch born of uncounted hours working Stone.

"This is good Basaltic rock. Once it was glowing red lava, but that was a very long time ago," he began.

"Stone is one of the five basic elements that make up our world. Stonework both takes a long time to finish and lasts for a very long time. What we build endures, so we take the time to get it right. Stone can provide a home to protect your family from the elements and danger. It can give you a path across wild rivers, even keep your animals from running away." He paused and rubbed the bare rock again before continuing.

"But it can also kill you. A rock was the first weapon man used to kill man, back before we developed more sophisticated weapons like the club. That was long before the Middle Kingdom arose," Henry said, noting the blank look on his student's faces. Looks like he was going to need to teach a bit more than technique, but he didn't mind. Henry liked history.

"Stone injuries are often serious. If you are careless in your work and drop a block of stone on someone's foot, they may never walk right again. This element should be treated with respect and caution. Everyone understand so far?" Henry asked. His students nodded politely, their eyes glued to him. He tapped the exposed rock.

"This is an exposed seam of basalt. It is an excellent building material, but here the stone layer is too thin to be useful. I've been looking around for a more workable seam, and we're in luck, but back to this stone in front of us. Look closely," Henry said.

"This rock's outer layer has hardened from contact with air and water. Once we cut through that weather-hardened shell, everything goes faster," he explained.

"The thing to remember about carving stone is that while it takes much longer than sculpting wood, it is also less susceptible to mistakes. You can't ruin something with one mis-stroke. You have to work hard to ruin stone." Henry dropped his free hand to his side.

"All good things in life have a cadence, and I thoroughly enjoy the pace of stone masonry. I hope you will, too. Now, watch closely as I demonstrate the first step in cutting stone," Henry said.

He positioned the wide headed chisel horizontally, then with the iron hammer in his right hand he began tapping the chisel rhythmically, cutting a shallow but wide channel down the exposed raw stone. Once the channel stretched from the top of the seam to the bottom, Henry sat down his hammer and tucked his chisel into his left pocket out of habit. Then he raised his hand and pointed below the layer of stone he had exposed.

"I've chiseled down to clay deposits, which often sandwich this type of stone. Clay is good for pottery and bricks, but not for building a tower. We need a thicker layer, large enough to cut into building blocks," he said, raising his finger back to the narrow seam of basalt. Tosh and Witboy crowded close enough to see better; the four Wolves clustered around them.

"This is what we need. Feel it. Go ahead. Learn how to recognize basalt by touch. It is a good stone for building things, such as our tower," he said, standing back out of the way.

His students clumped together to rub paws or hands across the finely grained stone. It had a funny indigo glitter to it, but since Henry hadn't mentioned it, the Wolves just assumed everyone saw it and found it unremarkable.

When the last of the apprentice stone masons finished examining the stone, Henry led them along a steep slope filled with brush and difficult terrain, slipping lithely through the snow-blanketed undergrowth. After about ten minutes, Henry stopped, dropped the heavy bag he'd carried and waited for a few of his students to stop panting for breath. Once he had everyone's full attention, he distributed hand axes and compact shovels to them out of the bag, noticing the confused looks on a few of the humans. He didn't let his subtle smile show. At least they didn't demand immediate explanations.

"Here" he said pointing to a concealed short bluff a few meters away. "I found this earlier. This is where we'll cut into the seam and harvest the basalt. It's an even, meter-thick layer that runs back into the hill and out the other side. This is where we will carve our quarry. By cutting into the side of the hill like a mine instead of digging down, we will have shelter and can work all winter no matter how bad the storms get," Henry patiently explained.

His students looked at each other and back at Henry in confusion, but they remained quiet, afraid to say something stupid in front of the group. It was obvious that they had no idea how to build a quarry and harvest basalt on a steep hillside covered in brush and trees. Henry's eyes might have actually twinkled in humor before he stepped in to rescue his students, but only for a second.

"Those of you with the axes, clear all the brush and small trees there and there. Just chop them down and set them to the side. Those of you with shovels, start removing the mud and dirt from this rock wall. I only want two meters across of exposed cliff face. Don't cut down the thick bush further out, I don't want anyone or anything stumbling across our quarry unexpectedly."

He waited for a moment for that to soak in. "Well, do I need to show you how to use a shovel?" Henry asked when they still didn't move. Lifting his shovel, he began efficiently clearing the ground in front of him. That's all he had to do; his students were keen observers and immediately began mimicking his movements and pace. Soon, everyone was caught up in a flurry of chopping and digging, and if enthusiasm exceeded skill, that was okay. He'd take it. Skill would come, but he couldn't force that spark of get-up-and-go.

Henry was pleased but didn't show any sign of it. That would come later.

Night fell quickly. He led his students back to the Treehouse in the twilight, but it took longer than the outward trip had that morning. It was cold, paws were raw, and for all their energy, even the Wolves were tired. At least everyone seemed happy. Henry knew they were going to be sore that night, but the deep healing sleep that comes after a hard day's labor would make up for it. Henry was bone weary too, and while he couldn't remember the last time he had a good night's sleep, he suspected he would sleep very well tonight.

Of course, the trick was getting his students up and back working early the next day, despite their blisters and aching backs. But Henry was feeling optimistic. These Wolves liked staying busy, and Tosh and Witboy were too stubborn to give up.

You learn a lot about a person when you spend a long hard day working beside them. And Henry liked these students a lot.

Chapter 18

SEALS AND NORSEMEN

Captain Marc Christensen, late of Commander Elwha's Navy and a Tier One Special Missions SEAL, waited for his Seahawk helicopter to come to close enough to solid ground before disembarking. He smoothly launched himself off his Sikorsky SH-60 Seahawk and landed in a forward stride across the snow-dappled grasses of the small meadow. His ancient eyes saw shades of nuance in everything around him as he studied the old-growth forest lining the meadow, savoring the ancient trees taller than almost anywhere else on this tree-shorn continent. Marc absolutely loved this place. And he was determined to make it a good home for his people.

The enormous CH-53 Super Stallion and the other two smaller Seahawks had also landed by the time the captain finished walking across the small alpine meadow. He found himself on the edge of a great cliff adorned with loose rockfalls and struggling cedar trees growing horizontally out of the stone face below.

He studied the rock cliff approach, visualizing which routes he would climb if he were an attacker. He quickly came to the conclusion that it would take over thirty minutes for a team to reach this meadow. With proper security and a few drone patrols, any invaders would be spotted almost immediately.

Marc turned back to look across the meadow and up the slope of the Quinault Rain Forest. The Olympic mountains receded upwards into the rain and clouds, fading into the angry leaden sky.

Definitely don't want to go any higher than this today. He needed to establish a base camp where the families would be safe, warm, and above all else, hidden.

This was a different, far more dangerous world than before. The megalomanic dictator Commander Elwha not only controlled his small country and a heavily armed navy, but extensive arsenals as well, including nuclear options. Now that Marc was no longer there to function as an impediment to the Commander, there was nothing left to rein him in. His ex-boss could drop a predator drone on their campfire in less than half an hour—and the captain had little doubt that he would, at least once he realized that the SEALs had abandoned Kitsap-Bangor Naval base and gone AWOL like his runaway Dogs.

With the relatively small size of his fighting force compared to the Commander's, his choices were limited. But if no one could *find* you, they could not bomb or overwhelm your people.

While men of Marc's caliber are highly skilled at the art of camouflage and blending in, building a permanent well-concealed home for your families, high in an isolated coastal rain forest, was not a thing to take casually. Unfortunately, they didn't have a choice in the matter.

He turned to his right-hand-man, Sergeant Liam Redcap. "I want to establish a secure perimeter immediately. Then we need to roll our helicopters back under the cover of the trees at the western edge of this little meadow. Secure them to the ground and cover any part that doesn't fit under the trees with tarps," the captain ordered. "The snow will conceal them soon enough. String up more tarps in the forest and start campfires under them, a little uphill of each helicopter. Get mess preparations going for a hot meal. With ninety-four of us including children, we are going to have to eat in shifts, but let's get something hot in everyone's belly as soon as possible."

"We have about an hour until its dark and a lot to do, so let's get moving!" his sergeant barked, and his troops spread out efficiently. It wasn't long before there was no obvious sign that the free company of the world's most dangerous warriors—Navy SEALs, had ever been there.

His people efficiently established a perimeter dotted with self-launching mine clusters chained to the team's cell phones, as well as a wealth of tripwires hooked up to focused high-explosives. The three helicopters were the center of the defensive area along the edge of the meadow's tree line. Drone patrols were quickly launched to surveil the cliff approach path. Soon warm fires blazed beneath three large tarps under the soaring trees, latrines had been dug, and tents erected by the time darkness fell with a thud, as it always does in the mountains.

And then the night winds began to rise.

The cold night air seared your nostrils if you weren't used to it. The freezing sea wind came up over the cliff and tore across the meadow, slamming into the mammoth trees like a sledgehammer. They had to discontinue the drone patrol flights after losing one. Supplies of everything were extremely limited.

"We bunk in the tents and copters tonight, but we need to get out of the wind tomorrow when it's light enough to see where we're going. This damned weather steals body heat too quickly for us to be exposed to it for long," the captain said as the cooks started dishing out chicken-fried steaks and pasta in a marinara sauce with coleslaw. Travel food. It was plentiful, hot, and filling, and everyone was really hungry. Besides, it was the last of the beef; nobody knew when they'd have that again.

The wind shrieked as it lost itself in the endless trees of the forest. Everyone stopped talking as they chowed down, leaving the ever-present windstorm to its crazed monologue, drowning out all other sounds in the forest. Sleep that night did not come easily to many.

The next morning a washed-out sunrise slowly crept across the eastern sky. The Olympic mountains to the east were briefly bathed in faded Technicolor, then the anonymous gray of poorly blended rain and fog took over.

The morning campfires blazed sideways in the offshore wind, whipping everyone's clothing noisily and drowning out the quiet sounds of hungry soldiers chowing down by the fire. The captain stood by a massive mountain hemlock's trunk, going over an old-school topographical map of the area with his team leaders and Sergeant Redcap, discussing where to check out first. Because of the breeze, it took four of their hands to hold the map in place long enough for everyone to examine it properly. Marc met his sergeant's eyes and inclined his head slightly.

"What's this trail here going south to north? Looks close. Might be handy to set up someplace withing walking distance of it. Maybe a quick escape route? Anyway, we don't want to dig in too close to it. Although I doubt we'll come across any lost hikers," Sergeant Redcap said without expression. The captain nodded.

"Now, over here looks promising..." Captain Christensen observed.

By oh-nine-hundred that morning, the captain's teams had scouted and discarded three possible sites. It was the fourth one that looked good. A large cave.

From the west the opening to the cave looked like a huge cartoon grin carved into the side of a ravine. It was invisible from above and low enough on the slope of the ravine to avoid what remained of the salt wind from the sea. The Cave entrance was wide enough for fifteen men to enter side-by-side. Or at least would have been, if it weren't half-filled with boulders and rock fragments. The entrance was in the shape of an evil clown smile, one with really bad teeth.

It turned out to be a twelve-minute hike back to the meadow where the helicopters were hidden, and less than four minutes uphill to the maintained National Forest trail they had seen on the map. A stream gurgled down the middle of the deep ravine in front of the cavern, so there was water nearby to be had, and the only easy approach to the cave was from the north, higher up the ravine, along a single wide stone shelf. The captain was pleased, but they had a lot of work to do if they were going to live through the impending ice-age winter the Canadian and American broadcasts kept moaning about.

"Mess break! Kids have been fed, so hit the line. Back to work in thirty," the sergeant called. The line filled up quickly. Marc took the moment to look over their progress so far.

It appeared that there was a layer of debris around seven meters deep covering the bottom of the cavern. Rocks of all sizes cemented together with dried-mud that was going to have to be removed by hand, and the wide gapped entrance filled in enough to conserve heat and conceal their winter home. Marc couldn't help but smile in satisfaction.

All they needed now was hard work and direction. He had a wealth of that. His operational forces numbered seventy-three, not counting the twenty-one children. Thirty-eight of his team were active-duty SEALs, many of the rest were their partners, and retired Navy parents or grandparents. The combined knowledge base of his people was massive. And nobody was particularly shy about sharing their opinions either. It could get a little noisy on occasion.

"Send a Seahawk to cache number four, the one with all the explosives and cement. We'll need plenty of both. Meanwhile, we'll set up a temporary camp near the trail where we can eat and sleep out of the wind, not too far from the ravine. Right here," he ordered, pointing to a level spot on the map. Then he nodded and his team leaders evaporated, intent on communicating his orders efficiently. His sergeant saluted despite no longer being a part of the American or Elwha National armed forces. The captain returned the salute crisply and turned away to begin walking to the cave's entry, perfectly comfortable in the cold mountain air. Everything was getting squared away, and the families had been working as hard as anyone else. Navy families knew how to function in uncertain times.

They'd certainly had a lot of practice lately.

By twelve-hundred that day the explosives had been retrieved, and the first of a series of controlled detonations had already begun. After the dust (it was a relatively dry cave) settled enough to see, teams of his people, suitably masked, moved in to clear rubble and prepare the area for the next detonation. Operations settled into an efficient rhythm of blast and clear, continuing through the long afternoon. The removed debris was carefully slid down the side of the ravine to a choke-point, where they became the rough beginnings of a small freshwater dam. Then darkness fell with a crash, like it always does in these parts.

The Sergeant had portable lights set up, and the work on their new home would continue through the night.

The night winds rose, their frigid fingers searching through the forest for warm flesh to chill. The families and his SEALs were clustered around the fickle warmth of several huge bonfires in the new temporary camp just off the north-south trail. Dinner was starting to smell good, but things were still a good ten-minutes from suppertime.

Of course, that's when the Viking Dudes showed up.

Chapter 19

TIGER MOUNTAIN

Queen Malgato stretched her long neck as she stood at her Tiger-sized balcony overlooking her western mountain kingdom. It was late sunset, and dull colors bled from the sky in faint ruby streams draining into the horizon. This was the first evening in quite a while the weather had allowed them to see almost to the Pacific. The clouds were still there, down in the lowlands, but her western kingdom was almost clear from up here. She raised huge binoculars to her tiger eyes, searching the distant tree line for man-sign. Nothing so far.

The Queen relaxed her paws and lowered the binoculars to her long silky waist. The ever-present wind teased at her ears as she went back inside, shutting the balcony door behind her and securing it. Her command bunker was large enough to host her entire remaining team if the need arose, but the Major was delighted to finally be alone in her own home after so long.

Her underground home was at last both secure and quiet. Only the wind whistling through the fireplace and the sound of her own gentle foot pads crossing the room feathered the silken solitude of a well-padded den. It was delightful.

She dropped the heavy bar to lock her bunker's entrance hatch, added some wood to the fire and then curled up on her long green couch in a nest of soft pillows. When she finally positioned everything just right, she let her eyes close for a little bit and just savored the still night. After months of being cooped up twenty-four hours a day with six other Tigers it was heaven.

The silence quenched her unease like… what? Water to a thirsty cub or maybe food to a hungry Tiger? She nodded off abstractly considering analogies and awoke only twice to feed the fire. She dreamed of mountain tops and man-wolves who were as smart as humans, but not as smart as Tigers. Thank the gods she was reborn Tigerkind, and superior to all mice, no matter how clever. And clever man-wolves were even worse than mice, but she kept dreaming about them anyway.

In the morning, the storm was back and in a foul mood. The wind screamed like banshees, and unruly gusts rattled her doorway and balcony. Queen Malgato built the fire back up and left the room for morning ablutions. When she returned, she had a long drink of water and sat down, spreading out a topographical map from the days before the world changed. It was hand-corrected in felt-tip and ballpoint, but only in a few eastern areas. A firm hand, her own of course, had drawn in the perimeter of what was now Tiger Mountain, the heart of their domain.

It was a beginning.

According to the map, the Hoh Rain Forest began on the mountain just below her bunker and rippled all the way west to the Pacific Ocean. The plump thief had spoken of hairy creatures living in the rainforest far below her, so she had to assume the western front was infested with inferior predators—predators that sounded very much like the man-wolves who had cost her a Tiger. She snarled at the thought.

The Queen studied the map again. So much of it was unmarked, without corrections. The Major decided that she needed to set up patrols of their borders. Now that they knew how to ski (more or less), her Tigers could cover serious distance. And she had a good idea of where trouble was going to be coming from. The Hoh Rain Forest.

Those filthy man-wolves owed her a rematch.

She got up and strolled to a scratched metal door in the back of her warm underground den. The steel door opened into a cold larder room carved into the mountain's bedrock. The larder was full of hanging game carcasses, dry-aging the meat at low temperatures for flavor and tenderness.

She entered the cold storage room, filling her nose with the savory delight of curing meats. The Queen wandered around for a minute or two considering her many options, and eventually ripped a leg of venison off a deer carcass hanging from a rough-forged meat hook. Then she returned to her couch, casually tearing into the meat as she studied the map again.

After a little while she tossed a thoroughly-chewed deer femur precisely into the trash bin in the corner and rose to turn on the primitive den-to-den communications system with her Tigers. She ordered Bao Li and Xi-Rong out on an in-depth survey of the area of their domain that she suspected overlapped with Wolf territory. They were strictly to gather information only, not interact with the man-wolves. That would come later.

She returned to her long green couch and tuned into the satellite Discovery Channel on her plasma widescreen. It was almost time for "World's Most Dangerous Animals", which she always enjoyed, but this was Shark Week, which Queen Malgato found to be the oddest combination of comedy mixed with plenty of crude chomping and biting. No finesse at all, but plenty of action. Sharks weren't very smart, even compared to local mice. She settled back to watch.

Bao Li and Xi- ng made it back a little after sundown.

"We surveyed the area you specified and found a maintained trail. It contained man-sign," Bao Li reported.

"It's clear the man-wolves have been patrolling there as well," Xi-Rong explained.

"Their trail barely came above the tree line into our territory, where the trail crosses our land, before they continue on out of Tiger turf, no doubt returning to the Hoh rainforest by some other route," Bao Li added.

"We did not find any potential ambush sites that weren't seriously flawed, this close to the tree line where our border ends," Xing growled.

"This is where the trees thin out and become smaller until they fade out to low brush lands piled with snow," she said, pointing out a spot on the map. "But once we went downhill, deeper into the forest proper, we found a number of locations where there are many high, wide branches actually overhanging the trail! The man-wolves' track go right under some of them. We can wait up in the trees for our prey to come to us, just like in the good old days. Then we fall on them like deadly hail from the sky. They won't know what hit them," Bai Li concluded, then quietly waited for her new orders, should her Queen wish.

"I want to have some way to know when their next patrol is headed our way. Timing, you and Lao Zi scout some lookout posts in the morning. Find places where we can spot the man-Wolves early, long before they reach the ambush site we are preparing for them. Bai Li and Xi-Rong, I want you to establish two primary ambush sites with well-marked exit routes and good positions overhead in the trees," the Major ordered before signing off and returning to build the fire back up. The single generator outside only provided enough electricity for basic light and comms (including Satellite TV), but not heat. At this rate, they were going to need to go diesel fuel gathering in another few weeks. Maybe she'd force her captives to carry the spoils back up the mountain a few times before she was finished with them. By finished she meant "killed and eaten" but not necessarily in that order. Prey made such satisfying sounds as they realized they were dying. That was actually the Tiger Queen's favorite part!

By afternoon the next day, all her preparations were in order. The lookout was continually occupied and both ambush spots were ready to be sprung. The time for waiting had come—and Tigers are the most patient of hunters.

Queen Malgato had teams periodically rotating out from the warmth of an improvised outpost, to the forest ambush locations. It was surprisingly dry inside the shelter, and body-warmth plus fire maintained a friendly room temperature in the small dimensions of their forest hut. No one fretted about the close quarters, although such crowding was not normal to Tigerkin, and could get a little awkward at times.

The truth is that Tigerkind is built for the hunt. And once they submerge their minds into the Stream (a shared state of altered consciousness), Tigerkin become the ultimate predator. No human mouse comes close to matching their physical powers or speed, although a few, a very few humans, were quite clever for lessor beings of inferior blood.

Regardless, the bald bipeds were outmoded relics of the old world, from before everything changed. They were this age's Neanderthals.

But Tigers were created for this new world. A fresh world built on the ruined foundations of the old one. Tigerkind was literally genetically designed for this moment.

This is the dawn of the Age of Tiger.

Chapter 20

THE SARGASSO WIND

I stared at the pirate seacraft tearing our direction. There were three of them, and the boat in the middle was on a collision course with our sweet *Becky*. The other two high-speed boats were separating to each side, no doubt intending to strafe us as the main enemy boat played chicken with the *Becky*. It was a good tactic. For humans.

Wolfkind, however, have their own rules. I wrap my paws around the machine gun's handles and…

…phase into Flux, coming alive in that timeless moment of transition between assessing a situation and doing something about it. The world creeps down the time stream so slowly that movement is barely discernible. I lift the handles of the fifty-caliber full-auto machine gun slightly and squeeze both triggers. The fifty-cal machinegun begins to buck in my paws, and I intuitively guide the bullet stream that is just beginning to explode from the barrel, anxious to start tearing up things. I swing the machinegun eight degrees to my left and sight on the port-side attacking boat's windshield. It is just in range and getting closer.

Crimson splashes onto the cracked and pierced windshield of the port-side attacker. I lower my machine gun's angle a little and began blowing a hole in the pirate's hull at the waterline.

The center enemy craft is still closing on us and I intuitively know that he isn't going to veer off-course. Twist's and Nina's gunfire doesn't even slow it down. I continue blowing holes into the portside enemy boat until the last possible moment.

<u>That's</u> when I click my headset three times.

The blind captain has been waiting for my signal and immediately breaks starboard, lurching clumsily in the water as fast as our barge-towing fishing boat can maneuver, fleeing deep into the drowned metal forest under the cover of the breaking storm.

Just before we disappear from sight, the blasted-to-hell pirate boat swerves across the path of the center incoming enemy boat. The crafts don't actually crash, but by the time they get their wits about them we have vanished into the freezing rain, black clouds, and murky turbulence swirling through a spindly dead forest that had once been a wind farm.

I return to mundane reality, dropping out of Flux and experienced the usual momentary wave of exhaustion that is the price we willingly pay for base reality. After a moment, I raised my head to look around me on the *Becky*'s deck.

The sky has darkened even more, and a sea storm is announcing itself with billowing ebony clouds that tear across the sky out of the west. Ice needles are beginning to whip the decks and wheelhouse. Myriad shades of gray fog and drizzle darkened everything around us as we gingerly forge through shadows deep.

According to the captain, this spooky broken forest used to feed cable television and air conditioning to thousands of humans up and down the coast.

Now it has become a dangerous shallow-water maze of smashed metal towers, trashed turbines, and huge sections of sharp, broken fan blades longer than the *Becky*. Countless derelict small craft and shipping containers have wedged against the broken tower bases, creating flotsam islands trailing long drifts of buoyant jetsam and debris. I think that before the tsunamis there was plenty of space between the wind towers to maneuver easily.

Not anymore.

Now it is the last place any sane sailor would willingly go. But then, the blind captain of the *Becky's Reward* is unusually generous in his definition of 'sane'. And being blind didn't slow him down a bit because *nobody* could see through all this mess.

Anyway, everybody knows blind guys are always better in the dark than the sighted. And when you take into account that the captain's Fisher God has made him "see", well, you gotta trust the blind man when it's dark outside.

I click once on my headset. Five different tones clicked reply. Good. All of my crew were standing by ready and waiting for their orders.

We'd been charging our new headsets since yesterday, using the modest excess electrical current the fishing boat produced while towing a barge at sea. Now they were fully charged and already beginning to prove their value. Communications are key, and this technology brought things to a whole new level for us.

The odd thing was that while this afternoon was the first time we'd worn the headsets we salvaged from the plundered Coast Guardian cutter, it already felt like I was donning an old and valued piece of battle gear. Felt like this wasn't even close to the first day I'd used the tech, but rather the thousandth time that I'd worn such a headset. On days like this, I found the holes in my head where memories used to be very irritating. I shook my head in frustration and droplets of saltwater flew everywhere.

"Captain, pass as close as you can to a few of the more-intact wind towers," I requested, then looked at Nina.

"Nina, you and I will jump to the tower's bases, then climb our way up the structures and find concealed positions. We'll perch in wait until the pirate boats come through looking for us. Make sure you have a position overlooking the channel's water. We need to be in place to drop down onto the pirate boat's deck as they pass by on our trail," I ordered. Nina and I immediately positioned ourselves on either side of the *Becky*'s bow in preparation for disembarking without the need for discussion. Wolves don't talk much, not like humans.

The *Becky's Reward* slowed even more and began a careful zigzag course, navigating the metal forest with skill. Lenny and Felix drastically shortened the tow lines for control in the tight quarters and the barge bobbed obediently in our wake. By now, the seas had risen considerably and the wind was spinning the few still-working rotors at a frenzied pace. Visibility had dropped to less than ten meters in the hard rain.

"Nina," I growled softly, and the white wolf sprang from the *Becky*'s forward deck onto one of the tall metallic towers that had broken off about twenty meters up. Her talons were sharp enough to pierce the sides of the metal tower for traction, making climbing easy. I watched her quickly fade upwards into a black sky well-saturated with fog and rain.

"There," Nina announced, letting the rest of us know that she had found a good place to perch. I didn't need to see her to know what she was doing now, checking her ammo again and settling in with her beloved Robar antimaterial sniper rifle. Our white wolf is a methodical and patient hunter.

The wind really began to howl. The stinging rain was mostly flying sideways now, and the waves were whiter than they were midnight-blue.

"Twist, set up in the barge's mortar pit and then climb halfway up the ladder so you can see out. Wedge yourself in good and wait for orders. Make sure you have a pair of binoculars and a good pile of incendiary shells ready to fire," I said into my headset.

"Felix, you remain on the *Becky* with the captain and Lenny. Your job is to protect our human teammates and our ship," I ordered, watching our passage closely as we came within six meters of a snapped-off wind-tower leaning out from a mangled mess of metal.

It bobbed and dipped crazily in the water but with a well-timed jump, I landed on a wet tangle of struts, a few uprooted trees, and several buckled shipping containers smashed together. The wood was slimy, slick, and unreliable. I managed to make my way to the broken tower base without falling. There I found a sealed hatch door with a round wheel-locking mechanism that took up most of one side of the tower. The wheel resisted at first, but… Wolf. Once I pried the hatch open, I climbed inside and propped it open behind me. A wide metal ladder led upwards so that's where I went. About twenty meters up, the passageway crumpled into an unpassable knot. This was as far as I could ascend from within.

There was, however, a rent in the tower's side back down a few meters. I retraced my progress and saw it was almost wide enough to climb through. With the judicious use of my talons, I was able to enlarge the hole until I could squeeze through. The Sargasso wind shrieked in anger and almost pulled me loose from my precarious position on the side of the tower. I wiggled halfway back inside and tried to find the least uncomfortable waiting position. I found it somewhere between being sucked out into the maelstrom and playing cork to an unhappy bottle of wine the size of a small elevator shaft. I've had better days. The ice needles of the incoming storm lashed me relentlessly, punishing me like a really bad Dog. My body armor and fur kept the worst of it at bay, but I lost my favorite floppy hat and was utterly soaked in freezing water. I remained nearly motionless though, patiently waiting to ambush an enemy that thought they were chasing *us* down.

The *Becky* gradually receded deeper into the drowned forest, moving through the dark debris maze until she was no longer visible from where Nina and I waited. All I could see was the back of our empty barge bobbing away from me. Then I couldn't even see that.

I checked my battle harness for the sixth time to make sure my throwing knives and fighting blades were secure but loose enough for quick access. My shotgun was freezing cold to the touch, but everything was where it was supposed to be.

Wolves like me tend to be a bit restless before the action starts.

Suddenly, Nina clicked twice in alert and spoke. "Incoming, two boats," she reported softly, "The third boat that Trey blew a hole in is nowhere to be seen. These two are moving slowly, using powerful spotlights to look for us. They never look up. They're about forty meters apart. First enemy will pass within ambush range in another two minutes, Alpha."

I cracked my neck and squeezed my way out a little further, so that I could leap successfully when the moment came.

"Nina, wait until the first one finishes passing under you, then put that Robar RC-50 to good use on the forward boat's spotlight operator. Take out the light too. The enemy will rush to the bow to investigate. Then when the boat passes under my position, I'll drop down onto the unguarded stern," I said.

"When the second boat passes under you, all the pirate's attention should still be forward on the first one where all the ruckus is happening. Quietly drop down onto the enemy's stern and secure the back of the second boat. Then work your way forward, removing threats as you go. Try to take control of their forward deck gun before they spot me and start shooting," I suggested. Wolves heal rapidly but getting shot hurts like hell.

"Got it, Alpha," came softly over my headset.

"Twist, be ready to drop a few incendiary shells on the bow of the second boat if Nina hasn't seized control of the deck gun in time," I ordered. I stretched my shoulders and eased my upper torso out of sight behind the metal tower's curve, waiting for the loud crack of a single fifty-caliber shot. When it came, it was almost hidden in the storm's tantrum, but Wolves have very good hearing. And the sound of a Robar sniper rifle is truly unmistakable.

The pirates reacted violently to the death of their forward gunner, with lots of chaotic gunfire spraying and ricocheting all over the place. I actually took a little damage, but the ricochets had stolen the round's inertia and my nanites immediately spit it back out with contempt. I growled anyway and leaned back around the spindly tower to take a good look at what was going on. Some of the fur on my head was beginning to freeze into jagged dreads but I ignored the unpleasant sensations. The plan was working.

The White Wolf is a creature of deadly beauty in battle.

Nina landed smoothly on the stern of the second enemy craft and began stalking three oblivious pirates peering forward and talking. The white-furred, two-meter tall Wolfkin slipped across the storm-lashed deck without notice amid all the sound and fury of the storm. The first pirate she took was a classic indoctrination kill—bloody, just the way the Commander liked it.

We are terrible enemies to face in battle, but we're better than we once were. Come a long way from our dark beginnings. We are evolving, but still have a way to go.

The first faux-orthodox kill was an illusion. Nina's pirate concerto in three parts was just getting started. She took the second enemy from behind, simply snapping the human scum's neck, a death he surely didn't deserve. Pirates are the worst parts of us made real. They walk the earth leaving death and destruction in their wake. But the hulking Wolf gently released him into death's embrace, and he never even suffered like his uncounted victims. Nina froze for a long second in physical punctuation to her clockwork kill, then released his body to slow-tumble to the deck.

Then the White Wolf flowed into the third movement of her lethal masterpiece, the part filled with emotion. The one that recognized the evil of this human predator and got bloody righteous on him. The hard rain hid the terrible sounds, but it couldn't wash the deck clear of red. Nina's movements were so rapid that they were only sketched and it was hard to catch it all.

My turn.

The first boat began to pass under me, only a little bit to the left of my uncomfortable perch. The boat's pirates were focusing another handheld spotlight in front of them but never aimed it upwards in my direction. I waited until the moment was right and…

…phase into Flux, as the world around me slows to a snail's crawl. I feel as if I have all the time in the world in this space between heartbeats. My coiled leg muscles lift me forward and down in a majestic slow float. The wind-driven needles of frozen water slowly poke me like a thousand sharp pins as I drift downward towards the pirate craft's deck. My left paw touches my throwing knives and pulls three from my battle harness. I am six meters from the deck. Two of the pirates appear to be arguing a short distance from where I will land.

They have no idea what's coming for them.

I throw an untempered steel knife at the short one's right kidney. The storm wind abruptly gusts, the target shifts, and the knife misses. My landing spot is three meters away. I launch the remaining two blades at the other one's neck as he begins turning his head to see where the first flying knife came from. He is tall and lean with a wispy mustache. I curl my long body, so that I will roll as I land. One of my thrown blades briefly sticks in his collarbone, the other knife slices away a patch of long hair from the side of his head. The tall pirate raises his eyes to try to focus on me. He is capable of operating at a very fast speed to even be able catch my movement.

I touch the wet deck and slow-roll, coming to my feet and moving forward in one continuous movement. The big one's eyes widen. He slow-motion startles and begins pulling out a machine pistol as fast as he can because he wants to live. Very fast, but not Wolf fast. Not Flux fast.

I reach out and snap the short one's neck as I pass, using his clumsy body to shield my movement. The tall one has gotten his weapon out by now and begins firing it in my general direction. Somebody up top thinks this is a great idea and begins spraying bullets at the stern deck as well. I roll sideways, dragging the pirate corpse behind me to soak up lead. I am able to reach the relative shelter of some cargo crates without taking too much damage.

But now I find myself pinned down by fresh gunfire from an increasing number of cut-throat killers syrup-pouring out of the side hatches of this enemy craft. The sheer mass of furious pirates is beginning to make things difficult even for a Wolf in Flux. I can hear them shouting as they gradually come closer, even over the roar of the storm and a heavy-metal soundtrack sung by lead slugs in copper jackets. I can also feel the boat slowing in the storm-driven water and realize that I have drawn everyone onboard the boat's attention. Not the plan!

Where is Nina?

I look back to her boat in time to see the White Wolf throw a pirate overboard into the stormy sea and seize control of the deck gun on the second enemy boat. She unleashes the heavy machinegun's full fury on the pirate scum pinning me down. I burrow between two of the cargo crates as splinters and bits of flesh and shrapnel fill the air in wild abandon. The terrible onslaught of fifty-cal death rips everything to pieces without ceasing. The silence when it finally stops firing is almost painful.

Rising to a crouch, I peek over the cargo crates that have shielded me from most of the deadly metal storm. The tall pirate peers back at me from a boat's interior hatchway heaped thigh-high with his crewmate's bodies. I am focused with hawk-like intensity on him as I bear down on him. He senses me closing on him and slow-motion hurls a huge grenade in my direction. I continue moving toward him, pulling my shotgun over my shoulder and swinging it down to his height.

I stride forward across the deck diagonally, studying the incoming grenade in its gelatinous flight. At just the right moment, I raise my left paw to catch the small death creeping my way, and throw it back as if it were a rock on a string. The grenade slow-dances back across the deck as I spin and dive for the nearest cover, the cargo crates I had left a split-second before. Explosions are even faster than the Flux. Get too close and no one's nanites can fix that kind of damage.

I am within a meter of shelter when the world lights up.

Chapter 21

STONE BY STONE

Ella let her breath out slowly, arms outstretched, standing motionless in the snow in a Wolf's version of hollow man posture. Then she slowly inhaled through her nose, savoring the unique scent of the Hoh Rain Forest. Her whiskers were glazed with ice crystals from the moisture of her breath when she exhaled into the freezing air. She didn't let it affect the rhythm of her breathing. Teacher Henry had taught all his students that breathing properly was centering. Calming.

And it was.

She cracked her lids and peeked out through slitted eyes into the early morning light. The buttery hint of dawn filled the eastern sky, but the air was still frozen, and dawn's first blush wasn't all it was reputed to be. She slowly inhaled again, while listening to Teacher's indrawn breath in order to match his pattern. This kind of physical syncing seemed to come naturally to Wolves. The human part of Ella that sometimes felt the need to chatter chilled out and a peaceful waking state took center stage. Her Wolf side felt curiously satisfied as well.

The morning fog on the ridge was peeling back from the mountainsides and retreating downhill, following the rivers and low places in the foothills. It hadn't snowed in two days, but the sun was still hidden in the volcanic ash-tainted clouds as they slow-boiled menacingly across the sky.

Ella tried to remember how long it'd been since she felt the sun's golden warmth on her fur. Back before the world changed, anyway. Seemed like a long time. Then she remembered that she was supposed to be meditating instead of thinking of the past. This meditation stuff was harder than she realized, but Wolves had never been afraid of a little work. Ella just needed to un-focus her thoughts and sense what was in front of her instead of daydreaming about the old days.

The crisp air tasted of spruce, incense cedar, and damp moss. It smelled like… home. Now that they had fought so hard to get here, she never wanted to leave their rain forest again. After a few more breaths, she successfully lost herself in the simple rhythm of circular breathing.

She heard the teacher's breathing change and opened her eyes fully to see Henry begin stretching his neck and legs. His students followed suit, then followed him back to the quarry cave. It was finally time to work with stone.

Ella had been aching to lay her chisel and hammer into a quarried stone block for a while. Pulling on her work coveralls and tool belt, she added a floppy hat with one tall pointy wolf ear sneaking out and the other obscured by the hat's fashionable tilt. Then she led the small group of neophyte stonemasons over to where they'd exposed the basalt layer that they were harvesting for the Tower's building material.

A three-meter-wide hole was hewn into the mountainside where they had removed the first fourteen blocks of raw stone. A meter-thick dome of exposed stone roofed the newly-dug baby cavern, and any hint of the clay remaining behind was inadvertent. The basalt layer being worked was well-exposed now, with the open top and bottom sections allowing plenty of room for everybody to access and cut it into stone blocks. Ella looked around. They almost had enough building material for the first level of their tower!

Henry clapped once, and everyone quickly lined up and gave their attention to their teacher.

"Today, you are going to divide up among different tasks and I will move between your groups, coaching you. Tinker and Theo: you are going to work on cleaning up the latest cut stone blocks by chiseling away their bumps and irregularities. They all need to be shaped to fit neatly together, then move each finished one to just inside our quarry's entrance.

"Sigrid and Tosh, you two will work on chiseling deep straight grooves in the virgin stone slab in preparation for splitting off more blocks. This afternoon we'll be working with the wood wedges and water.

"Ella and Witboy will come with me. We're going to prepare the building site," Henry said. "First, we'll clear the plant life and then the soil. This takes hard work, especially when the ground is frozen, but we need to see the bedrock before we can begin leveling it. We have a way to go before we will be ready to lay the foundation. Grab some shovels and hand axes." He nodded in encouragement to the apprentice stone masons as they left the stone cavern.

After exiting the quarry, the unlikely trio began climbing the crooked path up to the ridge. A hulking Wolf in a fashionable floppy hat, a Fisher clan boy, and a chef-warrior of Wudang Mountain didn't seem the least bit strange to anyone.

Family is family.

Chapter 22

THE VIKING DUDES

The first sign of incoming strangers was when the drone monitors chimed and began to transmit the rhythmic whap of synchronized electric guitar, rolling straight downhill to their small temporary camp. It was not long before everyone in camp could hear them too, even over the rising wind.

It was not that the strangers were stumbling or clumsy—quite the opposite—the gang of hairy tattooed Vikings moved through the forest with the grace of leopards. The bass-driven reggae blasting over portable Bluetooth speakers coordinated their movements, creased their stride. It was startling and announced their presence with the rhythmic beat of Stick Figure's "Sound of the Sea".

You could certainly hear them coming from a long way off. *Which was probably the point*, Marc observed. Nice, polite way of saying 'hi' without getting shot. He was looking forward to meeting and assessing these people. At least they had good taste in music.

A sophisticated bass melody preceding them, the strange group moved down off the main trail and casually strolled up to the SEAL's newly constructed sentry post at the entrance to their camp.

The hairy strangers all wore snow suits and head gear with body armor peeking out here and there. All the men had beards to mid-chest, and everyone had long battle braids spilling from under their furry hats. They were properly armed for a fully hostile environment. And dressed for it too.

The Viking Dudes kind of reminded Marc of some of the NATO soldiers from the Nordic countries he'd worked with back in the Finland border conflicts. That one started small but had quickly gotten serious once NATO started actively discouraging Russian private armies from straying across the border and setting up shop. Marc sighed internally. The past never stays where it's supposed to be. He returned his attention to the present, studying the visitors. There was a lot to study.

First thing he noted was that this small band completely ignored the deadly drones shadowing them from above, which isn't as easy as it sounds. Once you've seen what a drone can do to people, its anti-intuitive to take your eyes off of them. And the way these guys moved betrayed their former status as soldiers. All modern soldiers know what a drone is capable of.

The way they dressed shouted they were not following some fat cat's orders anymore. No uniforms, but similar style. When Marc studied the females, he suddenly understood what the old stories were talking about when they described Valkyries. These female warriors looked even more dangerous than the men.

He didn't look away in time. One of them suddenly grinned at him with a careless air.

Several of the other females chuckled and then focused their wicked grins at Pete, the guardian of the gate. Pete knew he did not stand a chance against wild-haired tattooed bad girls, and immediately began whispering succinctly into his headset as he un-safetied his M4. All the strangers grinned for a second, then returned their attention to Captain Marc Christianson.

Captain Marc Christensen never took his eyes off of the Viking dudes.

He was quickly joined by Sergeant Redcap and a dozen SEALs aggressively staring in the traditional old-as-man dominance exchange. That was a lot of concentrated staring, but the strangers did not seem even a little intimidated.

The big one just kept grinning at Marc, coolly unconcerned with the post-apocalyptic hostile possibilities that come of two armed fighting forces running into each other in the middle of nowhere after dark. The SEALs, however, were carefully pointing a lot of firepower at the ground between them. And none of them were smiling back.

Captain Christensen looked the strange group over again, noting that all of them carried well-cared for assault rifles, several side arms, and blades tucked here and there. At least four of them carried battle axes strapped to their huge backpacks.

They all moved in sync like a well-trained squad that had worked together for a long time. Their piercings and grooming were such that no modern army would tolerate, and some of the men even braided their beards with leather and shiny beads. Their body armor looked pretty state of the art, and they moved well in the snow despite their enormous backpacks.

Marc was sure they were former military, but they were still in really good shape, so maybe mercenaries? They didn't have the grumpy attitude of US militia men, so he ruled that out. Skin too white to come out of South America. That suggested overseas, European military of some kind. They were confident but not aggressively so. Therefore, not French or German. Talked too much to be Swiss. Too smiley to be former eastern bloc. That pretty much left Norway or Sweden.

He'd known a few Norwegians, and these guys had that feel—so relaxed it seemed as if they lived outdoors in the snow and mountains all the time. As if this was their natural habitat, not some overheated human hive of polluted air and water like so much of humanity existed in.

Well, at least before the Apocalypse. Things were really messed up out there now, so who knew? Maybe cities were no longer the future of human culture. Living in hidden caves deep in the rain forest screamed 'past' more than 'future', but Marc was good with that.

It was the 'living' part he liked.

"Captain, you're the first people we've come across in over a week. We're hiking north on the Cross Pacific Trail, on our way up to my cousin's house in La Push," the large barrel-chested stranger observed. "Hey, that smells pretty good!" he added.

Marc stepped closer to the Viking dude who spoke. The Stranger could obviously read Naval insignia and had called Marc by his correct rank. This did not lessen the captain's distrust one bit, of course.

He looked emotionlessly into Thorsten

's eyes. But all the stranger did was smile and politely waited for the captain to speak. Stole Marc's favorite technique and used it on him! He glared at the man. The Viking dude just stood there silently as if he could do this all night.

After a moment, the captain snorted and made a motion to his people to lower their weapons, which had been creeping upwards ever since he stepped in front of the stranger. He didn't smile at the stranger, but his demeanor became noticeably less forbidding. The stranger just grinned back.

"I'm Thorsten. This is my crew," he said easily. "We got out of Poulsbo just in time and have been making our way west and then north to La Push ever since. Kind of nice to see people who aren't trying to kill us," Thorsten said, briefly glancing at the armed SEALs and away.

Captain Marc swallowed a smile. What did this guy expect, walking up to their camp after dark? He studied the man for a second and found himself believing the words. They struck him as capable, like straight shooters who knew what they were doing, but weren't looking for trouble. They also made a point of not surprising Marc's people, even if it was an unorthodox manner of doing so. He came to a decision.

"Why don't you guys join us for mess and later we'll hear about your travels. These are perilous times, I'm sure you will understand that we need to disarm you," the captain said, walking over to prop his M-4 against a large log. Your rifles will remain within sight here and you can pick them up to leave anytime you wish. But when's the last time you had a hot meal and cold beer seated at an actual table?" Captain Marc Christiansen asked.

"It's been a while! Thank you. We accept," Thorsten answered. Bearded smiles blazed at Captain Christensen from some of the Vikings. Marc nodded and his men stepped forward to politely search each Viking dude before waving them forward into the camp dining spot under another tarp by one of the bonfires. The log table acquired a surprising number of weapons.

In this new Wolf Haven any information on threats, neighbors, terrain, and hostile forces was worth its weight in platinum. Intel gained by beer and food has always been valued highly, since it bypassed the unreliable results that come from coercion or pain.

So, it certainly wasn't chance that the Viking dudes had a number of friendly dining companions at the table as they ate and drank. Particularly drank. This was a strange new world, and the more the captain's force knew about their surroundings, the better they'd succeed. And they needed every advantage they could find. Every single one.

Captain Christensen didn't regret his decision to lead his people into the wilderness of the Olympic mountains. To stay was to lose their souls. Anything was better than serving in the Commander's Navy and being forced to fire on your former brothers-in-arms. To play survival politics under a megalomaniac dictator with a huge chip on his shoulder, to have to witness how he treated his poor 'Dogs' or anyone he considered disloyal.

And then to have to stay silent? Marc simply refused to be a part of it anymore.

The captain consciously unclenched his hands. They could never return to the US, but his people were going to build a new home here in the Quinault rain forest, a refuge that wasn't under the iron-fisted control of a psychopath with a chip on his shoulder. A place where they could live their lives in peace and grow old watching their grandchildren run and play. It was going to be difficult at first, but SEALs are no strangers to hardship and the prize was well worth it. This was something they could pull off; the captain was sure of it. So sure that he bet his life and the lives of his team on it. He prayed that it turned out to be a good bet.

Marc watched in awe as the Viking Dudes tucked into dinner like hungry bears storing fat for the winter. They sat side by side at several of the collapsible picnic tables, spread out enough to have free movement with both arms, joking softly as they methodically demolished platters of meatballs and pasta in marinara sauce. Coleslaw, too! The captain had been waiting for them to slow down before he questioned them, but it had been some time since he finished dinner, and these guys were still going!

He eventually tired of waiting.

"So, Thorsten, how did you end up in the middle of the Quinault Rain Forest on a Tuesday night?" Captain Marc Christiansen asked.

Thorsten looked up to meet his eyes.

"Didn't know it was Tuesday," he said, draining his mug. "In our brewery back in Poulsbo that lager would have been rejected and distilled into hand sanitizer." He smacked his lips. "But tonight, it was simply delicious," he said, wiping his mouth greedily with the back of his hand. "Environment flavors everything." Thorsten snap-grinned and then dug back into his dinner with a devotion that bordered on religious.

Marc noticed his fist was beginning to clench and took a deep breath. "Yep," he responded calmly. "Nineteen-hundred hours on Tuesday," he added.

"Okay," Thorsten said, straightening up and wiping his mouth politely with a napkin. He pushed his polished plate across the picnic table. Then, rotating to face the captain, he began to speak.

"We're a group of former military teammates and our families," he explained with a gesture indicating a few of the Viking dudes with less of a military posture and something more like MMA fighters, before continuing. "We all served together, and were good as a team, so after leaving the Norwegian special forces we naturally stayed together. Ended up traveling quite a bit, fought a few small wars, liberated a few hostages. The usual," Thorsten said.

"After a few years of adventuring, we got the hell out while we were still alive, and migrated to Poulsbo Washington, of all places. It was very much like home. Within a few months we had all started small businesses in town and often gave each other a hand when one of us needed it. Life was good, surprisingly peaceful. But we never forget who we are, and where we come from," Thorsten explained.

"Twice a year we go camping for two weeks in the mountains. That's because we all grew up in the fjords and mountains of Scandinavia and have *friluftsliv*, a deep bond with northern wilds that goes back thousands of years. Even though we're now thousands of miles east of the land of ice and mead, these northern mountains are still our slumbering gods. Well, that and Thor," he explained.

"This year we were planning to explore the relatively unknown southern slopes of the Olympic National Forest. It's not always convenient to take the time away from our small businesses and busy lives to go camping together, but we've always managed. It's a side of us that keeps the rest of our lives in balance. This is important," the Viking Dude said. He accepted another mug of lackluster lager with a big smile, took a great swallow, and continued.

"We set out as usual, in a caravan of off-road trucks. We always set our phones to silent once we leave the highway and enter the forest. It's not a real vacation if you have to take work calls, but we still stream music, of course. We're not barbarians." He grinned widely. Marc nodded slightly.

These guys were old-world warriors from the land of ice and snow, you know—northern barbarians! He leaned forward to place his crossed arms on the picnic tabletop. Maybe some of them might even be the fabled berserkers the old stories told of? He waited for Thorsten to continue.

"We left Poulsbo at five am and made it to our first campsite reservation several hours before dark. We set up camp across three campsites efficiently, and Tore dragged out a beer keg of his special IPA our craft brewery only sells in the tasting room. It was our first night, so we still had store-bought rib-eyes. Great dinner. The only problem was the RV party several campsites over, with at least thirty people having a really good time. Loudly. With rifles. And their music sucked," Thorsten complained.

The rest of the Viking dudes all grunted or nodded in agreement. "Once you hear Stick Figure, you can't go back to ordinary music," a brunette female Viking dude added, hefting a mug of beer and quenching her thirst. More grunts of approval from her team.

"We packed up and moved out early the next morning, our off-road vehicles leaving the highway after about an hour. We drove up a winding mountainside logging road. Google maps showed a nice little alpine meadow with a stream twenty-three miles away. Only took a wrong turn once, and we were able to reach it sometime just after noon. We were one long day from home when the Ferris Wolf set off Ragnarök," he said to the puzzled sailors at his table. "You know, the Apocalypse!" he added to sudden expressions of comprehension. He paused to drain the last of his beer and then leaned forward to face Marc.

"Finally got to sleep sometime after ten that first night and woke to the rose glaze of dawn five hours later. Built the fire back up and started frying a bunch of Tore's wild boar sausage from last spring. I had just started making amaranth pancakes for everyone in another cast iron skillet when the first big one hit," Thorsten explained.

"I thought the entire mountain was falling. Got bounced into the fire and received a surprise beard trim. The earthquake seemed to last forever, throwing us around on a land gone wild. We all got bruised up and some of us had a few bones broken as well, but at least we didn't lose any of our people. We quickly pulled ourselves back to our feet once the first tremors stopped and took stock."

"We only lost one tent, but two of our vehicles couldn't be repaired with the tools we had on hand. We all sat down for a quick smoke and talk, then reallocated the loads among the remaining three vehicles. We had a hell-ride back home in those overstuffed off-road trucks. It took seven hours to get there, but we were too late. Home wasn't there anymore," Thorsten said starkly, the horror plain in his pale face.

"There was nothing left of our small town. The lower lying neighborhoods of Poulsbo were flattened and drowned. The only intact building we saw was the big red brick Safeway store up on a hill, but everything lower was underwater. There were floating islands of rubbish everywhere and random piles of masonry sticking up out of the filthy water where buildings used to go. And the forested hilltop neighborhoods ordinary folk couldn't afford – they were on fire. It was a scene straight out of hell" he said. It had become very quiet, and some of his Viking dudes were staring off into space, reliving the nightmare with him. Everyone had a horror story about the day the world changed, but not everyone was ready to talk much about it yet.

"We tried to get closer, but a massive wall of flame blocked the only intact road we could find and we were forced to come to a halt. The firestorm was closing on us so fast! There were loud, sharp cracks and a terrible roar of greedy flames devouring everything in its path. We had to turn around and run for our lives to the chaotic report of thousands vaporized tree sap explosions. It sounded like the whole world was shooting at us," he said softly. Then he gave his head a little shake and straightened up.

"Our small caravan paralleled the highway back through the trees as they were catching on fire behind us. The highway itself was a fractured mess of abandoned cars and jagged concrete, with periodic gunfire that said enough for anyone wanting to know. Don't go up there.

"So, we didn't. We kept driving west alongside Highway 101, until we got close to Ocean Shores. That was where the real trouble started. Some kind of Malay pirates had violently taken over the little resort town there, and they weren't very neat about it. Whole town smelled like death. We barely got out of there with our lives. Our vehicles weren't so lucky, so we eventually had to abandon them. Our only real option was to started hiking the CPT trail north. Try to get to my aunt's place in La Push," the Viking explained, stopping to whet his thirst on a cold pint in one single draught.

Thorsten neatly placed the empty mug on the table, stood up, and raised an eyebrow at Captain Marc Christensen. Marc pointed in the direction of the improvised latrine and turned back to lay his gaze upon the remaining Vikings in the room. They were still eating and drinking. Slowly, leisurely, draining pints and emptying plates. They showed no sign of getting full and slowing down.

That's when it hit Marc. Instead of eating every bite, their guests were quietly stashing bits of food in their ample clothing. Marc's granite face didn't show any emotion as he thought about it. It wasn't stealing after all; the SEALs *had* invited them to dine. He decided he didn't mind feeding hungry soldiers, even if they had a habit of tucking away a little something for later. His people were going to need all the friends they could get in this new world.

But he had a feeling that it was going to be a long night.

Chapter 23

BLOOD IN THE WATER

I stretch my body forward trying to out-race what is coming as the enemy's hatchway bursts into blinding chrome light and heat. My body is mostly shielded by the crates. The ear-shredding clap of the explosion follows, and I am suddenly deaf, warm blood trickling out of my right ear. My head is ringing loudly and shaking my head doesn't make the church bells go away. Moving forward, I make for the hatchway to get a closer look inside the boat.

The White Wolf's Robar C-50 claps go unheard; I only see a pirate slow-motion tumble from the upper deck with a gaping hole through his chest. It is large enough that you can see completely through the wound. The world around me is wrapped in wet cotton towels through which only faint murmurs pass—and those are drowned out by the angry bells in my head. Everything smells burnt to my nose. But I just snarl and lower my head to focus on the fight. I don't need to hear or smell to kill the enemy. Shaking my pounding head again, I automatically check to make sure there is a fresh shell in my twelve-gage's chamber before crossing the shattered hatchway and making my way into the silent interior of the enemy craft.

It seems to me like the other Wolves should hear the deafening bronze-cast bells too, but no one seems to. I am lightheaded but I am Alpha. My will is stronger than these distractions. Pushing aside my weakness, I focus on the steep staircase to the bridge that runs up the centerline of the boat. I seize the left handrail and flow upwards. Just before the bridge comes into sight, I pause to brace my shotgun to shoulder, then take the last few steps to raise my head just over the edge of the bridge's deck. I duck back down. My brief glimpse confirms that the boat's bridge is a target-rich environment.

Three fighters on the port side, two pirate bosses at the helm, and two more reavers to the starboard. I release a breath and rise up to fire three shotgun blasts through the syrup world of base reality before ducking back down out of sight. I reload. Port-side pirates eliminated. Four hostiles remaining.

I slide across the steep stairs to the starboard railing and glance back at the stairwell above and behind me. The brass sparks and the vibrations I can feel through the railing testify to the silent hail of projectiles sprayed in my direction. These bastards can always be counted on to over-react. Several ricochets slap me in my armored parts, but it is nothing but loud talk, and about as dangerous. I hold my right paw against the railing until the little vibrations almost cease.

Slipping up the starboard side of the stairwell with my shotgun glued to my shoulder, I blast the two enemies to my right full of holes. I watch as the pilot and captain in the center of the room begin gelatin-swinging the muzzles of two AK-47's in my direction. In the place between heartbeats, there is time to do anything and do it with precision.

I ooze back down the stairs and back over to the other side of the stairwell. Without pausing I play Wolf-in-the-Box, rising to blast 00 steel buckshot into the captain's first officer and leaving the boat's commanding officer the last pirate standing. I sink back down out of sight before he can even finish turning in my direction.

I can feel his furious return fire's impact-vibrations against the handrail and stairs with my paws and feet. An AK only holds so many rounds, and he runs out of bullets. I remain mostly untouched. And now the pirates' captain is alone.

With me.

I need to capture him alive for intel purposes, so I slip my bullpup over my shoulder and pull out two large fighting knives, one for each paw. He finishes reloading and then lights up the stairwell above my head with more silent sparks and flashes. I wait for him to run down again with a Wolf's patience. He quickly does.

That is when I flow up the stairs, pushing off the top step in a portside loop that will end at the helm in the center of the bridge. I am halfway there before a silent hail of metal raises colored flashes and streaks in front of the stairwell I just left. The spark shower gradually veers in my direction.

I bounce off the portside window rim, my haunches pushing me forward in a great twisting leap.

I hit him hard, smashing into his left side, knocking the pirate captain over and riding him down onto the slippery deck. When we come to a stop, I flip him onto his belly and sit on him, holding both his arms in a lock with one of mine. My other paw holds a large blade a few centimeters from his left eye. Leaning forward, I bring my over-sized head down next to his and…

…phase out of Flux. The bone-weary exhaustion hit immediately, but I needed my verbal skills to question him. Panting for a moment, I adjusted to the mundane world. Then I brought my exposed teeth close to his face.

"How many are you, pirate?" I growled. I could see his mouth move, but I couldn't hear his reply. I forgot my ears weren't working! This was so frustrating! My attention was suddenly diverted as I sensed someone approaching on the stairs I had just come up. I watched the staircase until dark greasy hair came into view. The newcomer immediately began firing an ancient AK-M from prehistory at me. I spun my prisoner behind me to protect him from the inaccurate spray of steel-jacketed projectiles—the captive has no nanites.

I do.

Wolves are tough and regenerate rapidly; even a deaf one is never helpless or weak. I threw my left fighting knife deep into the attacker's right eye socket and the pirate froze before slowly falling backwards down the stairs. I knew he wasn't going to come back up.

I rose to my paws and leaned over to hit the all-stop on the boat's control section of the helm. Then I turned and began retracing my steps to the outside deck, dragging my prisoner with me by one leg. Everything around me still smelled burnt, but I could tell that he smelled terrible anyway. But it was nothing compared to the full olfactory onslaught of deck's abattoir when I stepped outside.

I clicked twice on my headset and said, "Nina," into my headset, discovering it was hard to talk when you can't hear yourself. I just hoped they understood my words.

"I'm completely deaf right now, have been ever since that explosion. This boat is now under my control. Come aboard. *Becky's Reward*, join us. Bring drinking water. Let me be clear. I can't hear your answers or questions. Alpha out." I felt very thirsty but didn't trust anything on this pirate ship. I began visually searching the deck, my lower left paw resting firmly on the pirate captain's neck. He wasn't very smart because he suddenly started wiggling wildly again. I growled real low. There were too many other things to do for me to be babysitting a captive human monster with attitude.

So, my lower paw may have squeezed his neck a little. At any rate, he stopped wiggling and became very quiet. I released my grip. So far being deaf hadn't slowed me down at all.

Looking around me on the shot-to-hell deck, nothing looked very promising. We were taking on water. Streams of crimson were running off the port deck amidships and the boat was beginning to list to the lee side. I looked down at myself. My body was covered with debris, blood, and bits of flesh, as well as a couple of burn spots. There was filth matted into my fur everywhere. Looking down at my prisoner, it was obvious that he was quietly dozing on the deck. Looking back up, I could see the *Becky's Reward* slowly chugging my way. There might be time to get cleaned up before they came aboard.

I walked over to the port side and set my shotgun and ammo bags down on the deck. I could just make out Lenny waving frantically at me from the deck of the *Becky* and shouting something but of course my ears weren't currently working. Didn't he get my message? That thought reminded me to take off my headset too. Setting it atop the ammo bags, I waved my arm back at him, then jumped into the cold saltwater of the Pacific Ocean.

It felt glorious! I dove deep. It was dark down there, but Wolves have good eyesight so I could actually see further underwater than in all that rain and fog upstairs.

There was a jumble of long, broken wind turbine blades on my right. A little to my left in the middle of the channel, three big fish with triangular fins were fighting each other and getting all worked up. Then some of their friends showed up. I swam back up to the restless surface and treaded water while trying to scrub away the filth on my fur and battle armor. After a moment, I dove again—the water around me was taking on a pink tone and I could smell blood everywhere.

Coming to a stop about four meters down, I turned to check the big fish again. There were a lot more of them now, and they were all circling and staring at me with big empty eyes. The circle around me was shrinking, and they were coming closer and closer.

I waited for them. Maybe they tasted good—I was very hungry. By now some of the big fishes were close enough for me to see horrendous white scars on some of them.

Then a big one darted at me, hitting my thigh with a sandpaper nose. I twisted and dug a big paw-full of fish meat out of its tail as it passed. Then I swam to the surface again, and examined the firm flesh in my paw. I took an experimental bite. Not bad! Skin was pretty tough though. Didn't fish have scales, not skin? I treaded water for a moment, scrubbing my fur and armor some more. The *Becky* was tying up to the other pirate boat Nina had captured. Lenny was still very excited and pointing at the water. I politely waved back and dove down again.

There were a lot more of the big fish now and they were all darting at each other and fighting. They were eating the one had I tasted in huge chomps. They had more teeth than a Tiger!

Suddenly, I became the center of attention. Hanging in the saltwater and turning back and forth, it was possible to keep an eye on the most aggressive ones circling me. It wasn't long before a particularly large fish made up his mind and decided to veer at me and try a bite.

I waited until he was close enough, and bit off his nose.

When he shook wildly and turned to flee, I grabbed his tail and swam for the surface. Nina and Lenny were now on our new boat's deck, staring worriedly into the water when I surfaced.

I tossed my still-writhing catch up onto the deck where the White Wolf casually shot it in the head a few times. The other big fish had followed me to the surface and were trying to bite my legs off. They may have gotten in a few tastes of Wolf, but I managed to catch two more of the enormous gray fish for us. Finally climbing aboard, I sat down next to my catch and tried not to let on how tired I was.

My body was almost fully healed up by the time we had everything battened down and lots of anchors holding the *Becky's Reward* and our two new boats in the dubious shelter of the metal forest. Being on the deck was like being sprayed with a cold firehose out there! But finally, we were inside, warm, dry, and snug in the galley while the maelstrom howled around us. The seating was snug, and the small room smelled strongly of wet fur, but it is renewing for pack to share dinner.

Grilled shark isn't bad, though I preferred Lenny's shark sushi, at least without the green hot paste. Lenny says that you get a taste for it if you keep eating it. "Why would anyone want to do that?" Twist muttered, low enough that only the Wolves heard him. I don't get it either. Humans don't always make sense.

That's okay. Wolves are honest and think everyone else is too, and Tigers are downright treacherous. Nobody's perfect.

After dinner the humans sipped their warm cups of their mountain brew with alcohol wafting out with the steam. They were smiling more than usual and talkative. More talkative than usual, I mean.

"We're going to need hand, uh, paw protection like heavy gloves to handle the wind-blades we'll be salvaging once the storm dies down. We'll locate them underwater, winch them up with the *Becky*'s loading crane from underwater, and then move each blade to the barge, where we'll lash them down. They're huge, and the sea wind has honed them to a razor's edge. Drop one on a foot and you won't have a foot anymore… unless you're a Wolf with nanites I guess. Hey, could you regrow a foot?" Lenny enthused.

The blind captain shook his head minutely while simultaneously poking Lenny under the table. We Wolves pretended not to notice. Lenny sat up straighter and stopped smiling for a moment.

"Why can't we just move the crane to the barge for the trip," I asked into the quiet, "We can raise the wind-blades directly up onto the barge. It will come in handy to unload when we get home, too!"

After a moment, the blind fisherman started laughing, a slow, low one that made you feel like joining in, so we all tried it out. Laughing together feels kind of like pack singing to the full moon, but happier.

"Truth is," the captain said, "I never thought in terms of stripping equipment off the *Becky* to use somewhere else. Blind spot born of protective feelings for our lady of the sea, I think. Yes, let's do it! This will cut our salvage operation's time by close to a third!" Lenny just stared at me, then exchanged his brew for a glass of the real stuff.

I dropped a silent Wolf smile on them and left the table. I had first watch upstairs on the bridge. Wolves can't afford to take any chances, especially in strange waters. Once there, I stood at the helm looking out into the dark fury of the storm and found myself missing our beautiful rainforest.

It's good to have a home.

Chapter 24

SNOWBOARDS AND VIKING DUDES

Fitz unburied himself from the compacted snow pile he'd ended up in during yet another attempt to 'snowboard' like the pics in the magazines. His frustration turned to anger when laughter rang overhead on the mountain side. Human laughter! He shot to his feet and began wading angrily uphill to join his Wolves on the trail.

Eddie and Sami were frozen with weapons drawn, peering up at eight or nine bulky humans, who apparently had been traveling on another trail some fifteen feet above them.

The hairy humans all waved a hand back and forth casually and motioned Fitz up to join them. Fitz had never seen humans groomed or dressed like this, but they were obviously members of the same pack. He didn't care; they had laughed at him, at his misfortune! He determined that he needed to immediately establish dominance, and then make these mocking Humans regret their laughter. They didn't know who they were dealing with!

Fitz stepped up through the snow onto the PCT trail with carefully controlled movements. He didn't want to spook them and have to chase them down. Things got messy sometimes when he got excited on the chase. And then it would be over before he realized it. He didn't want that.

Fitz wanted respect.

He wanted to be the alpha. He wanted people to see what happened when they disrespected him, or any pack member. Fitz was Wolfkind, a living bioengineered weapon originally designed for only one thing: killing. And while Wolfkind have risen far above their ugly childhood, sometimes you needed to make an exception.

He'd been a slave-Dog last time a human laughed at him, but he was a ranking Wolf now. A Wolf that had just been disrespected in front of his pack by a stranger, a Human.

He felt anger running through his veins like some powerful stimulant. Unlike last time however, there was no shock-collar to punish him for biting back.

The sight of an approaching angry Wolfkind—a two-meter-plus Wolf built like an especially-hairy Hipster Bruce Lee with pointy ears and large carnivore teeth—should be something to scare the hell out of a person. It should make them stop and re-evaluate their situation. Especially when the monster is glaring at them in a dominance stare, closing in with a deliberate pace. Closing to ripping range. It was terrifying.

Well, that was the way it was supposed to work, anyway.

Not this time.

Two of the chuckling human males were as tall as Fitz. They were all powerfully built, with big, wavy beards and long, coarse hair that looked like it had to be braided to control it. The females had long, flowing tresses as well, but no beards. Everyone had lots of tattoos. They all wore plenty of cold weather gear and body armor, mostly covered by black leather jackets that were accessorized with a bunch of well-kept assault rifles. The word "Vikings" was etched into the leather and on some of the gear. The dudes had more knives than anyone had time to count. Fitz could see little hammers on leather thongs around their necks.

Suddenly one of the brawnier males threw his arm around Fitz and hugged him! Fitz was about to bite him, but then the Viking dude said, "I did the same thing when I was learning to ride," and Fitz just stood there instead.

"Except I didn't do it nearly as gracefully as you, dude. Come on, let's see what we're working with gear-wise and then how 'bout I show you how to get your groove on," the hairy Viking dude said.

Immediately, all the other hairy strangers shrugged out of their huge backpacks and sat down on logs on the side of the trail.

Three of them lit up funny looking cigars that smelled different from tobacco. They were all digging roughly in their packs and comparing strange things, without all the usual chatter most humans insist on. This whole time these odd humans were passing the smoking brands from person to person in almost unbroken motion and breathing out huge clouds of whitish smoke. The mountain wind shredded the fragrant clouds almost immediately. They just made more.

Fitz stood there in utter shock. What had just happened? Weren't they going to fight? Why wasn't he mad anymore? He looked at Eddie in confusion, but Eddie just shrugged and let one of them measure his feet. He looked at Sami, but only got more shrugs. Then Fitz found himself being urged to inhale the burning twist—which he wanted no part of—and the straps on his lower paws being adjusted. He decided that he kind of enjoyed these unusual hairy humans. Fitz had never met anyone quite like them before.

In no time, most everyone was smoked, geared, and goggled up, then they were riding newly custom-fitted snow boards down the brilliant white slope like wild Wolves on rockets. It was very noisy, and all the humans were snowboarding downslope to the river around the wolves in startling leaps and supportive howls of "Dude!" and "You got this!" at Fitz and his pack.

It was the most fun Fitz had ever had! These snowboarding Viking dudes were awesome! The repetitive climbs back up the slope to the trail were slow going but Wolves never get tired when they're having fun like this. The climb added a restorative measure to the thrill of rocketing down white slopes balanced on a small piece of shiny wood.

Afterward, Fitz invited his new friends back to the ground camp with him, although he had no intention of exposing the home den, the Treehouse itself, to danger. But the Vikings could stay in the base camp, though! If they departed now, Fitz still had enough time to get everyone back to base before dark.

Now Fitz had his *own* story to tell at the campfire, and everyone would see what a great alpha he would make! He would be running things in no time. He was sure of it.

Fitz was young and the world was still a place of black and white, of obvious wrong and right. The world is always a simpler place when there is no gray. And while he was not a Wolf much given to introspection, he did finally recognize one thing.

He was happy.

Chapter 25

PRISONER

Eighteen hard hours later we strapped down the last of our salvaged equipment on the barge and turned north. Our Robar antimaterial rifle had damaged my captured pirate boat's engines, but Nina's was still in decent shape.

First Twist, Lenny and Old Fisher had stripped the sinking boat of anything we might need, including fuel, while the rest of us Wolves were working hard to cut free the least-damaged wind generator engines with our acetylene torches. We lost the first turbine we cut free—it broke the ropes wrapped around it and disappeared down into the murky jungle of submerged blades and underwater wind farm debris. They were much heavier than we had realized. We switched to using the shot-up boat's anchor chains and were eventually able to salvage twelve wind generators, although it took all of us just to move each one aboard. Lenny said we might not be able to restore all of them, but we could still use the rest for spare parts.

Tossing down protein shakes and shark sushi every four hours, we never had to stop for a human-style meal. Once we finished salvaging the wind turbines, we switched over to cutting up tower sections and moving them to the barge as well.

Meanwhile, Lenny and Old Fisher had moved over to the pirate boat Nina had captured and begun getting it seaworthy for the journey home.

Once we had recovered enough tower segments, we switched to salvaging the wind blades, and surprisingly, the underwater ones were in better shape. We hoisted them up one by one onto the barge's deck, switching out who was in the water regularly so nobody got too cold. I was catching my breath on the deck of the barge after working in the freezing saltwater when I looked over to check on our newest boat.

I couldn't help but drop a Wolf smile when I realized that our infant navy just doubled in size! We now had two fighting boats, a fishing boat, and a fortified barge. Now we just needed more Wolves to 'man' them!

Eventually the barge was as full of wind blades and tower sections as we could pile on, our newest boat was running, and the electricity-generating wind turbines were safely stashed away below decks. Our headsets were recharging now, so I entered the bridge of our sweet *Becky* and patted Old Fisher's back in greeting.

"We're going to have to drag the floundering pirate boat out of our path so we can get out of this dangerous sargasso sea," the captain said. "We need a team to go back out there and get a line on the hull of that sinking boat. Then we pull it out of the main channel so the *Becky* can get by and head for home on the open sea," he explained. I turned to my team, who by now had joined me on the bridge of the *Becky's Reward*.

"Felix, you and Twist go forward and secure a line onto the derelict boat. I'll get the towing chain myself and bring it to you. One of us may have to board the vessel to secure the line," I said. But the grapple worked just fine, and we were eventually able to move it out of our way without too much trouble, despite the storm and heavy seas. I toweled off my shaggy head once back inside and declared, "Let's go home, Captain!"

Then I went below decks with Twist and Tinker, leaving Nina on the bridge to keep an eye on things. We had a prisoner to interrogate. The close air belowdecks reeked of salt and wet wolf, and we were all plum worn out from the last twenty-four hours, but this was something we could do with our eyes half-shut.

The prisoner was awake but said nothing as we joined him on the metal deck of the aft hold. I leaned back against the bulkhead in the human body-language for bored and let my eyes slowly drink in our captive. He studied me back coldly before dropping his eyes. Yeah. Not an Alpha. Maybe that was why he dressed unnecessarily flamboyantly? Humans are weird.

He was decked out in tight black wool slacks, a loose cobalt silk shirt covered with an elegant short coat, and lots of gold jewelry everywhere it could be squeezed in. His body was tattooed colorfully on every centimeter of exposed skin I could see, except for the palms of his hands and his face.

His eyes looked like Henry's and his ebony hair was worn in a long braid down his back. There was a small dagger blade worked into the tail of his braid. He had a narrow chin-beard that almost made it to his chest, and powerful forearms and hands. He wore his flashy boot daggers on the outside of his boots, more as jewelry than weapons of last resort. Maybe they were a sign of his rank? Did captains in this pirate fleet always wear 'hidden' weapons where everyone could see them? I stepped closer to him, close enough to touch, and showed him my teeth.

"Who's in charge of your pirate fleet? How many boats do your people have?" I demanded. The defeated captain didn't say anything. He wasn't tied up; he knew by now he couldn't outrun Wolves. And where would he go, anyway? I nodded to Twist. He had thoroughly searched the pirate and had unearthed a mound of stuff; items now piled on an anonymous shipping crate.

There were three firearms, from a tiny derringer that had been concealed in a sleeve, to a single-shot custom twelve gage that had been strapped to his lower right leg. He'd also carried a machine pistol tucked under his armpit and several knives balanced for throwing in his jacket. There had even been two garrotes braided into his hair. Who was this joker trying to impress? What if he fell in the water—that much metal would pull a human under! Was this how pirates normally dressed? I snorted in contempt.

I looked back down at the pile. Twist had also found a satellite phone, two spare batteries, and a Bluetooth headset connected to the iPad in the prisoner's side coat pocket. I walked back over to the pirate and suddenly ripped away his jacket and shirt away in one sweeping movement. He twitched, but that was it. Almost impressive.

Or stupid.

I leaned closer to the bare-chested prisoner and took a deep whiff. His boots smelled of beeswax and salt, of tobacco, tar, and leather. He stank of sweat, blood, and death all wrapped up in creased gun-oil-stained wool trousers and inked sea-serpents crawling all over his chest. He didn't say a word and wouldn't meet my eyes.

After a moment, I abruptly moved very close to his head and snarled real low. "We don't have the time for the usual tactics human interrogators use to get information, and Wolves are not that cruel anyway. So, here's what I'm going to do. I'm going to ask you a few questions, and you will do your best to answer them. Or I'll simply rip you to bloody shreds and move on," I explained. He went completely still for the first time since we captured the pirate. I had his attention.

"Now. Where is the third boat I damaged when you jumped us?" I demanded. His shoulders slumped a little, and his eyes still wouldn't meet mine, but he did answer me.

"Uhh… the Taipan is hobbling back to base. Her communications are down, but when she is finally able to reach our base, she will definitely summon reinforcements. Significant reinforcements. You don't stand a chance once that happens," the captured captain said in a low voice. He sure didn't sound defeated. Why would he be so confident? I shared a look with Twist. I needed to know more. Maybe it was time to shift emphasis and figure out what was going on. I thought for a second and decided to ease into it.

"How did you end up a part of this gang, anyway? Have you always been a pirate?" I asked. He exhaled suddenly but I couldn't tell if it was anger or laughter. Maybe something else? After a few seconds he started to speak.

"I used to be a small-time smuggler on the Shanghai-Hong Kong route. When I moved up, I took over the Hong Kong-Vancouver loop. Much bigger. Within a few years, I had seven boats working for me and took a chance on investing in human smuggling ships, big ones. By the time The People's Republic of China took over Taiwan, I owned three commercial transports and had enough business to need three more. The money rolled in like a monsoon in a bad year.

"Unfortunately, I was beginning to attract the wrong kind of attention, and in the flush of the moment, I didn't pay enough attention to my surroundings. The rich investors who were going to take over and let me retire in luxury turned out to be the Tongs," he explained.

"Somehow, I ended up working for them. Nobody argues with the Tongs. Besides, independents are anybody's meat. But the Tongs take care of you so that you take care of them. I went from being my own boss to being powerful but following other's bosses' orders. We began moving quite a lot of product between Hong Kong, the People's Republic mainland and British Columbia. I worked quite hard and was paid obscenely well, but it wasn't the kind of job you could take a vacation from or quit. You wait for the day that you can enjoy some of the fruits of your hard labor. Then one day the world changed forever," he mumbled sadly. Then he stood up straighter and continued the story.

"The Tongs survived under Mao and lived through the Cultural Revolution. It takes more than just an apocalypse to put a stop to them. In this new world, we own the new San Diego-Portland-Victoria coastal run, and we take tribute, looting and despoiling our way down the coast as we wish. These days there's nobody left who can oppose us! We are a small division of a very powerful global organization that has absolutely no sense of humor. Maybe if you let me go right now, they won't hunt you down and slaughter everyone you care about. Maybe," he said, before muttering, "probably not," under his rancid breath.

I growled real low; couldn't help myself. You simply don't threaten my pack and family. Without thought I phased briefly into Flux and suddenly held the pirate's throat in my jaws. I could feel his heartbeat as the big veins of his throat flexed through my teeth, but I didn't relax into primal instinct and sever his head. I let him live. We released him to swim to shore once we were close enough. We gave him a chance, which was more than he gave his uncounted victims.

It wasn't justice, but it was enough for today.

Chapter 26

RACHEL AND THE TIGER QUEEN

The next morning, Fitz and the rest of the pack remaining in the Treehouse climbed the ladder upstairs taking Rachel and Bookworm to the second-story kitchen for their breakfast. Grandma insisted that even Wolves who are genetically part-human need to eat more than once a day and gave him that …look. The one that made him feel like a misbehaving new-born pup. Fitz didn't like feeling that way one bit.

Anyway, he knew he didn't want to take any chances with the pack's young. Wolves cherish their cubs. Besides, the Alpha had been quite clear about priorities and Fitz had always been able to tell which way the wind blew.

So early every morning, the home team of Fitz, Eddie, Ona, and Sami, the Stonemason Wolves including Ella, Sigrid, Theo, and Tinker, and the cubs un-piled from their bearskin blanketed bed and prepared to face the day together. Once everyone was dressed and ready, the pack climbed the ladder upstairs to keep the cubs company while they ate burned food with the humans.

The adult Wolves just hung out, stretching, or cleaning their guns and sharpening knives, enjoying the moment before the demands of a new day descended upon them.

That restful moment stretched into several and Fitz was dealing, no problem. Fortunately, Wolves are very patient; but when the inactivity starts itching, and the clock was ticking on a new day… Fitz scratched himself behind the ears ferociously. He knew he wasn't good at not letting these things show. How did the Alpha pull that off? What was that ticking sound? Oh. Fitz stopped clicking his paw talons on the floor and looked around to see if anyone was paying attention. Nobody was staring at him. He was good.

Fitz was trying to let the slightly-irritating buzz of quiet (for humans) speech flow past him when suddenly he focused on a conversation the cubs were having.

"I like learning by doing things. I like reading books. But I don't like this school thing very much. I've never been to school before. Do all of them keep students from leaving when they want to?" Bookworm confided in Rachel as they ate.

She raised chin in agreement. "They do. I don't like that either. This morning, I want to go out into the forest and taste fresh air. The air in here is so thick and drenched in human scent. I want to move around like a Wolf should!" Rachel said. After a pause she spoke again. "I'm going to ask if we can both go out with the pack today. Okay?" she said quietly. Bookworm dropped a silent wolf-laugh and nodded several times. By now, all the pack were focusing on the conversation in curiosity. There are no secrets in a pack. Wolves hear everything.

Rachel turned her attention to the ranking Wolf in the room, as was proper. "Fitz, this school thing day after day is boring, and Wolves aren't supposed to sit in one place and do nothing. That's what the Alpha said. Trey ordered you to watch over and protect us. I think you could do that better if we were close to you. Like on patrol. Cubs need to learn about the world. You said that yourself. I think we need to learn about snowboarding today. In my opinion you would best follow the directions of our Alpha by taking us with you on patrol this morning. When do we leave?" asked Rachel sweetly.

Fitz almost choked. What? Huh? For a female pup who didn't usually talk much, she sure did pack a wallop when she opened her mouth. Humm… It was true that the Alpha said to guard the cubs. And they were easier to protect when he could see them, so… maybe he should take them? What would his alpha do? *Protect the cubs.* That's what was most important. But there were risks outside as well, like snowboarding pile-ups or bears. Bookworm was smaller and more breakable, so he should stay in the Treehouse.

But if Rachel was right, *she* would be safer within his protective reach. Fitz certainly didn't want to screw this mission up; it was his first big chance to let his own alpha qualities shine.

After a moment he raised chin. Grandma was watching him closely from across the stove where she reigned as a sort of human alpha over all burning of food. She also had very good hearing for a human. But she didn't say anything to Fitz, and she didn't unleash that *look* on him either—she knew this was not Fisher clan business. Not that she was hesitant to speak her mind when necessary, but this was internal pack stuff, not clan. Grandma looked away as if her attention was somewhere else, but her human ears were intently focused on the pack's cubs.

Fitz turned his gaze back to Rachel. "Bookworm is going to stay in the Treehouse today with Ona and the other cubs and go to school. Rachel, I'm going to let you come along with us on patrol. You must follow the exact directions given to you by your pack. You are young and ignorant. We are not. Be a good Wolf cub today, Rachel. Okay?" Fitz asked. Then he let his alpha-style peek through as he regarded his pack's oldest cub. She respectfully lowered her eyes, and after a moment he looked away.

Rachel let a long breath out instead of dropping a silent wolf-smile where everyone could see. At last! A chance to get back outside where a Wolf belonged! She was going to go crazy if she had to spend one more day in this giant beehive rubbing shoulders with humans insistent on teaching her boring stuff a Wolf doesn't need. At last!

Of course, the humans still had to complicate everything, fussing over her, and insisting on making sure Rachel was dressed warmly enough. They had her wrapped in the new white fur coat Tosh had sewn for her. Double socks and scarf too! Quietly clipping her wolf ears to the soft fur hood of her coat—they would make her look more like a Wolf—she considered the sewing lesson the day before. Could she learn to sew well enough to make a Wolf suit?

Grandma hugged her and slipped a packet containing something warm that smelled delicious into her coat pocket. Then she lifted Rachel into the harness Fitz had strapped on and buckled her in.

Rachel blinked back tears; she had missed this so much. Her second life was born riding in her alpha's back-rig. Night after night, as the pack fought its way across the Olympic Peninsula in search of a homeland, she had peered over Trey's furry shoulder and felt safe for the first time since the bad men and the fires had crushed her world. She had been left with nothing, until the pack had adopted her and given her a family again. It was a powerful memory and Rachel felt so much love for her pack that it oozed out her arms as she rode Fitz's harness. She gritted her teeth, grinning into the frigid winter wind and tucking her chin into the Wolfkin's furry neck.

After a moment, Rachel impulsively reached forward and hugged Fitz. His head came back to nuzzle her briefly and then they were through the exterior door. Leaping high, Fitz exuberantly bounded through the freezing air and falling snow to land a third of the way across the rough-planked bridge between mammoth trees. His leaps were slightly different than Trey's; he was shorter, and Rachel noticed the minor changes because she knew her alpha's pace like she knew her own. It felt wonderful anyway.

A few days earlier, Rachel had helped build the sky-bridge over to the massive Sitka fir with fresh-split pine and lots of ropes. It was safer to descend down into the forest from someplace other than the treehouse—you have to protect the den. Even cubs knew that. Besides, Sigrid said it was not good to have outhouses too close to the den, so the other tree's platform served multiple purposes. The home team had just finished constructing small huts there the day before, to conserve heat as well as modesty. Humans were kind of fussy about some things. And it <u>was</u> very cold.

After bounding the rest of the way across the swinging sky-bridge to the mammoth fir, Fitz and the other Wolves methodically checked each other's gear. Then Fitz hooked his harness to a thick wire pulled tight overhead. "Ready?" he growled to Rachel.

Ready for what? This was new! "Sure," she said, politely. Who says Wolf cubs don't have manners? Grandma's face appeared in her mind, then Fitz stepped off the platform and they began zipping down through the trees faster than she'd ever gone.

"Yahoo!" Rachel yelled, but the fierce wind ripped the sound right out of her mouth. Fitz nudged her to make sure she wasn't in any pain. But this was the opposite of pain! This was great! The massive tree trunks whipping by slowed until they finally came to a stop on the snowy forest floor. She could still feel the wind on her face even though they weren't moving now. The exposed skin on her cheeks felt cold as ice, but it wasn't really unpleasant. She suddenly grinned, to the best of her frozen face's ability.

"Let's do that again!" Rachel shouted, but Fitz turned and began leading the Wolves up a well beaten trail to the ridge. After a few minutes, a path branched off from the main trail, leading to the stone cutter's quarry. Ella and the other apprentice stonemasons brushed by Rachel and split off. Fitz stood still long enough for each Wolf to briefly touch the cubs' arm in parting.

She was so excited! This was turning into a fantastic day! Now, if only the sun would come out. But it didn't, just like the day before and the day before that. Despite missing the sun though, the day was almost magical as they padded quietly through the gently falling snow. It was midmorning, and dark-gray clouds were roiling up the rain forest's slope as they came off the Pacific Ocean. The daylight was muted and the sounds around them were curiously muffled, lending a dreamlike air to the day. They continued to climb into the foothills and Rachel never got even a little bit bored. This was how a Wolf was meant to live!

"The Viking dudes call this path the Cross-Pacific Trail. They hiked all the way over the Olympic Mountain Range from Ocean Shores. That's the place where the pirates are camped out," Fitz explained. "We're going to continue on the trail for another two kilometers, up to where the trees stop growing. You can see all the way to the ocean, if the clouds clear a bit," he continued. "Then we'll snowboard most of the way home! It will be great!" Fitz stated confidently.

After twenty minutes, Fitz announced that they weren't far from their destination. The Hoh Rain Forest was still thick here, though, and the trees soared high into the sky. What they could see of it was wreathed in snow and dark clouds. Rachel couldn't wait to see the ocean from up above. She hoped the clouds would clear in time.

Fitz called a break at the foot of a truly enormous Sitka fir, so Rachel unbuckled herself and jumped down to the snow-covered pine needles. She stretched with the unconscious grace of a Wolf and began looking around herself in joyful freedom. The Wolves hydrated from their Yeti water bottles, unpacked some of the snowboard stuff they'd brought for her, and Sami checked Rachel's feet again to make sure the boots they'd brought for her would fit properly.

Sami liked being sure about things. She wasn't very high on the pack hierarchy, so she didn't want to make mistakes. Rachel was patient with the repeated fittings—she was too happy to be outdoors to be irritated by the quiet Wolf. Sami only wanted her to be comfortable, anyway. Rachel looked over at Fitz, who hadn't sat down with the rest of them and stood motionless with his big nose raised and quivering.

"I smell Cat!" Fitz growled suddenly, and all the Wolves froze, lifting nose to air. Then everyone jumped to their paws, growling way down in the sub-woofer range.

That was when two massive Tigerkin stepped into view from behind a tree downhill from them. The Tigers stood almost two-and-a-half meters tall, casually holding full-auto machine guns as if they were toys and not deadly twenty-kilo hunks of metal. The weapons were aimed at the Wolves, but they didn't open fire.

A fraction of a second later, all three adult Wolves were pointing M-4s back at the two Tigers. No one pulled a trigger because that would start something that might end with a dead cub, and of course, three dead Wolves as well. Fitz studied the two Tigers.

Who knew what those expressionless faces were thinking? *Nothing good.* Fitz was sure of that. He made a snap decision and tossed Rachel over his back into the harness, snarled loudly, and began bounding downhill at the Tiger on the left. He could feel Rachel belt in and press her head into the back of his neck. Eddie and Sami closed rank in the short charge with him. The Wolves felt invincible for a brief moment.

That was when a third, even larger Tiger abruptly appeared behind them and roared. She held a grenade launcher in one paw and a Chinese assault rifle in the other. Then four more Tigerkin descended from the trees around them on black ropes. The rappelling Tigers held their rifles steadily pointed at the Wolves, slipping down the ropes as if they were greased. Once they reached the ground, the Tigers sprang forward without a pause. The circle had closed and the bad guys were moving in. Fitz looked around. The enemy now outnumbered the Wolves seven to three. But that wasn't what concerned Fitz.

What worried the hell out of him was that all the approaching enemies' weapons were aimed at Rachel… not the angry Wolves pointing rifles back at them. Bastards!

Fitz glanced quickly at his Wolves. They concurred. Time to change tactics. Reluctantly lowering their weapons, they slowed to a complete stop, until only the vibration of their growling suggested that they weren't statues. The weight of their hostile stares was heavy as the Wolves glared at those who would threaten their cub.

The Tigers were unconcerned with the anger of Wolves and quickly surrounded Fitz's team without stepping into their comrades' field of fire. This is not something that happens by accident, Fitz realized. These were well-trained enemies. He growled louder but didn't move.

The biggest Tiger with the RPG padded closer, focusing intently on the pack's cub. This was completely unacceptable, and Fitz began trembling in fury as he crouched in preparation to leap at the Tiger's throat.

Rachel was afraid some of her pack would die if that happened, so she grabbed both of Fitz's ears and pulled back. *Let the Tiger see her.* That wouldn't kill anyone. "It's okay," she whispered to Fitz. "Don't attack," she added in case he was too angry to understand.

Fitz slowly rose out of his crouch, still trembling with unreleased fury. He smoldered at the approaching Tiger, but stayed right where he was. Sami and Eddie drew closer to him, flanking Fitz tightly in an unconscious desire to protect their cub. They were very upset, too, but followed Fitz's lead and allowed the huge Tiger to come closer.

The Tiger padded to within a meter of Rachel and stopped; her penetrating gaze locked on the little girl. Rachel looked back up into the Tiger's large eyes without fear.

"Are you the Tiger that killed my pack-brother, Ten?" Rachel bellowed at the towering Tigerkind. She hadn't intended to shout, but her anger just took over. Rachel hoped she hadn't initiated what she was trying to avoid but decided to bluff it out. She even threw in a good glare. It wasn't hard.

Queen Malgato chuffed in both surprise and delight. *What a delightful kitten, she thought, utterly fearless and confident of her place in the world despite being surrounded by Tigers!*

Of course, many kittens start out that way, she decided. But this little budding warrior was a female too—like the Queen. She was intrigued and leaned closer, towering over the small group of Wolves.

"What is your name, child?" she asked. "Why have you crossed into my kingdom?"

Queen Malgato remained motionless, so as not to startle the small human apparently raised by filthy Wolves. Her fearless Tigers hovered at the perimeter of her vision, their weapons trained on the small girl, but their eyes locked onto Fitz and his Wolves.

The Tiger recognized these creatures as some of the Wolf/human hybrids she had encountered before. That hadn't worked out so well for anyone, but this time she had the upper hand. Her team significantly outnumbered the Wolves.

Last time, it had taken bad luck and three Wolves to kill a single one of her Tigers—but now even if they could, killing one would still leave six more angry Tigerkin. Queen Malgato liked those odds. She continued to stare at the kitten, waiting for the small one to answer.

"My name is Rachel, and I am a Wolf in Trey's pack. Did you take my packmate from us? Did you kill my Ten?" Rachel asked with a deadly patience.

"How nice of you to bring us an appetizer, however… small," the Queen observed to Fitz, sweeping Rachel's torso with a merciless gaze. "She is spunky, isn't she?" the Major added.

Fitz was literally quivering with frustration and couldn't rein in his growling. But he also knew that if he gave in and attacked the damn cats, the Wolves' cub would be the first casualty of battle. Effective leadership demanded that he protect his pack, and that meant not fighting back right now. The whole situation was infuriating. His pack-mates were equally enraged but followed his lead.

Fitz glared at the Tiger queen for a few seconds, and then lowered his eyes. He didn't do this out of fear of starting a deadly chain of events; he lowered his eyes so that the damn cat wouldn't see how furious he was. Fitz would find a way to free his young charge and get her home unharmed. He just didn't know how he was going to do all that yet.

"No child, I am not the one. When I first entered this barbaric land of yours, my team numbered fourteen. Now we are seven, myself and my team. The one you speak of was killed at Bangor-Kitsap Naval base three weeks ago by Navy SEALs. His name was Yu Kui. But I was his superior, and that means I am responsible for my team's actions. So, if you have a blood feud, that would make me the logical target. And _that_ means I would be proactive if I ate you right here and now. What do you think about that, kitten? Are we going to have a problem?" The Queen snarled faintly, almost affectionately.

Rachel held herself motionless as she thought faster than she ever had. Then she knew—Wolf logic! Keeping her gaze unbroken with the massive Tiger, she growled, "I am pleased he is dead and can't hurt anyone else." Then she shut up.

Queen Malgato wasn't concerned with a kitten's opinion of a Tiger in her prime. She stretched her back, pleased at the kitten's response. The little one had already begun to surpass the immense disadvantage of being adopted by doggies.

This kit had promise.

"Our story has just begun, kitten. Don't be impatient for a finish. You might not like it," the Tiger Queen rumbled. Then she focused on Fitz, and flashed tooth.

"Lay down your weapons on the ground and step back. You may keep your knives. They are only pale imitations of a Tiger's natural weapons. Do this now and the kitten lives," Major Malgato ordered coldly.

Rachel turned to glance at Fitz as she abruptly realized that her pack was being blackmailed with her safety. She was the reason nobody was fighting the Tigers' demands. It was her fault.

Then she started to get angry.

"We Wolves need to leave right now. Get out of our way!" Fitz snarled loudly.

"You could, but your weapons and kitten stay here with us. All your rations," the queen of the Tigers demanded. That seemed strange to Rachel. *Would the Tigers even be able to eat Grandma's chili?* Then the Tiger lowered her massive head closer to Rachel and slowly licked her chops. *Oh.* Rachel gulped. Tigers eat *all kinds* of meat. Then she began to get even angrier.

Fitz threw back his head and howled in frustration. He slowly bent forward to lay his weapons down in the snow and took a step back. Something about this seemed to amuse the Tigers. Rachel could tell this made Fitz even madder because he got all quiet.

The ranking Wolf's head sunk dangerously low, and he continued to glare at the Tiger queen. After a moment, one of the other Tigers darted close enough to smack Fitz's head down in respect. Fitz blurred and then spit out two black fingers topped by long ebony claws. Wolves are fast.

The wounded Tiger screamed briefly and cursed in a foreign language, but her other captors seemed amused by the whole thing. Maybe now they would think twice about threatening a Wolfkin's young. Sami and Eddie also laid down their weapons and showed their teeth to the Tigers with the guns trained on Rachel. The Tigers flashed significant tooth back, unimpressed. Rachel looked down at the severed claws on the ground and dropped a wolf-smile.

The Tigers didn't like that one bit.

"Pick one of your Wolves to go back to this 'Alpha' of yours and make arrangements for us to meet here, face to face in the morning. If things go well, perhaps your kitten and you can return to your primitive forest camp tomorrow," the Major commanded her captives.

"Can't do that," Fitz answered. The Queen immediately drew her side piece and shot off half of Fitz's right paw. Fitz was really mad now but couldn't do anything about it. He ignored the pain and glared at the Major. He could already feel his nanites beginning repairs, but it still hurt like hell. Fitz looked over at the Tiger he'd bitten. Her fingers were already regrowing as well.

Damn. Fitz had forgotten about that.

"Why can't you do that?" asked Queen Malgato firmly. Her pistol was already pointed at Fitz's other paw—which was still a damn sight better than pointed at the cub.

"He's not there. Alpha went to Oregon in a fishing boat. He won't be back for at least two or three more days," Rachel said quickly. She unbuckled her harness and got down, moving quickly to Fitz's side where she began gently wrapping his injured paw in a white cloth she'd pulled from somewhere. Fitz raised his good paw to cover his mouth in the sign for 'silent walking'. Rachel nodded in respect. Fitz let out a deep breath he didn't know he'd been holding. Sami moved to lightly lean against Rachel's left side and Eddie put a paw on her back to let her know he was there, as well.

"Then I insist you all come back to my place for a visit until your alpha returns. Don't worry. It is uphill from here, but we can reach it before dark. And we have satellite TV!" the Major said drolly. The she snarled a command in a foreign language, and everyone began moving out, climbing the high trail. One of the Tigers attempted to urge Rachel to walk faster with his rifle barrel, but Eddie blocked the movement and got a rifle butt in the head for it. Rachel snarled and glared at the Tiger with contempt before swinging up into her harness on Fitz's back. Eddie got back up and patted her reassuringly as Sami secured her in place, and then walked closely beside them as the captive Wolves hiked up the snow-covered slope of the mountain.

It was a long way up.

Chapter 27

BATTEN DOWN THE HATCHES

The storms had begun to fall close enough together that Captain Marc Christensen worried about them merging into one continuous, unending snowstorm. At the current rate, his people had maybe three days while they could still work outside. Of course, a SEAL's definition of bad weather was quite a bit different than most people's.

It was their small air force that he was worried about.

Their mobile fighting force, his Seahawks and CH-53 Super Stallion helicopters, were their primary advantage in the hostile environment this post-apocalyptic world had become. His air cavalry became a force multiplier when paired with those most dangerous and innovative of fighting men and women, Navy SEALs. (With a few badass marines liberally salted in).

Unfortunately, that was two nations ago, but SEALs always remained true to their own, remaining SEAL clan despite their recent resignation-in-mass and walking away from a megalomanic tyrant with a huge chip on his shoulder and a massive arsenal that included all sorts of flavors in nuclear weapons. Definitely not someone you wanted mad at you, but Commander Elwha of Elwha Nation was a sadistic, angry native son, and nobody under his power was safe. The Commander was happy to punish family for the sins of the fathers, and not surprisingly, these white fathers had a lot of sin to make up for.

Regardless, fighting aircraft you cannot use because everything including the fuel lines is frozen solid are worthless. This was not an acceptable outcome. That was what the upcoming meeting was regarding. He glanced at his smartwatch. Two minutes to the meeting. The captain stretched in place for almost a minute before he pulled on his fur lined hat and started for the first-level open room where his senior staff met every morning. He arrived thirty-seconds before start time. Marc believed in fighting the good fight, structured days for his soldiers, and always being on time.

Well, he also believed in rye whiskey, but that was running out, and has become a thing to be savored on the rare occasions when the work is finally done.

Unfortunately, it always seemed like the work never ended. *I guess Shine would have to suffice until the troop's craft distillers could come up with oak barrels to produce real whiskey,* Marc thought to himself. He looked over expectantly at his second-in-command.

"The four mini-hangers will be two stories each, one level underground, and a camouflaged dome on top that will conceal the aircraft. The dome's hinged edge will raise to allow the domes to rise up to ninety degrees, which would permit our helicopters to be rolled forward onto the meadow to take off. We think that with practice, we can launch very quickly. This is imperative," Sergeant Liam Redcap said. His men straighten their posture in respect. Not all language is noisy.

The captain studied the map and proposed locations. The hangerettes were spread along the tree line at the back of the plateau that overlooked Lake Quinault. Made sense. He looked around the table at his team.

"What is the purpose of the lower level?" he asked.

The sergeant looked over at his tech specialist Annie and inclined his head two centimeters.

"Multipurpose. Because it is earth sheltered, the interior temperature will not drop below sixty-four degrees, just like a wine cellar," said Annie.

"Unlike a wine cellar, we will have a stone fireplace. The upper section's floor will be made of heavy beams to support our aircraft and will have deliberate gaps in the flooring that will conduct warm air upstairs. This should allow us to maintain a minimum of forty-degree-Fahrenheit air-blanket upstairs around our helicopters despite the outside weather," he stated.

"The lower level will also be storage for all the spare parts and equipment necessary to run our modest air base," Sergeant Liam added.

"How big a hole do we need to dig for the underground level? Ground is frozen on top. Is blasting a good option? I don't think our Bobcat can do it all in under three days," the captain mused.

"A combination of both, I think. And the lower level does not need to be as wide as the dome to begin with. We can duct warm air through the flooring across the entire dome area," the sergeant replied.

"Good. Start with simple gel explosives to carve out an outer wall for the lower level. Diameter is to be calibrated by the helicopter it will be protecting. Depth is to be four meters. We need to figure out where to put the fireplace to get the most heat distribution. Update me in two hours," the captain ordered. Where was he going to come up with a bunch of strong, lightweight beams and shell material for these domes?

He needed data.

"I think that it is time to take a quick, airborne survey of nearby abandoned or damaged structures that could be mined for aged lumber and nails. We could really use some PVC pipe for our sewage system too. That little tourist village around Quinault Lodge looked abandoned when we first came through, but hiding is probably a survival trait these days. For all we know, there could be scavengers, or pirates from Ocean Shores, or even little old ladies with large cleavers held behind their backs. I want Seahawks in the air in forty-five, info on my desk before it gets dark," he ordered.

Chapter 28

MISSING

The powerful scent mélange of home is richly textured. Wolves instantly know the physical position of everyone within twenty meters when they enter a room. *And this scent-picture had a few holes in it,* Ella thought to herself as she climbed up to the central area of the Treehouse with Tosh and Witboy.

It had been a long day. Ella loved working with stone, but by this time of day she was a little tired and ready for a chance to sit down.

"Where is the rest of the pack?" Tosh asked her curiously as they climbed up to the central area of the Treehouse together after a long day of cutting stone. Ella immediately noticed that Bookworm was sitting close beside by Ona, looking a little worried. Ona had an arm around him, comforting the cub while watching Ella as she climbed into view. Even the other humans were unusually quiet. Grandma was also watching her as she stirred a big pot on the woodburning stove. It smelled heavenly, but nobody seemed hungry.

That never happens.

Ella scanned the room in a sniff and a glance, then turned back to face Ona. "My stonemasons are home now. Why aren't Fitz and the rest of your team back yet?" she growled suspiciously.

Ella had a sinking feeling in her belly that something was wrong, very wrong. Grandma and Tosh shared one of those mysterious human-looks that she could never figure out. Then they both simultaneously turned their heads back to look up at Ella, the dominate Wolf in the room. Ella headed straight for them, quickly walking over to the large woodburning stove that was the social center of the Treehouse.

"You don't know where Fitz is, Ella?" Grandma asked soberly.

She shook her head 'no' and watched as concern filled Grandma's eyes. *Why? Fitz could handle himself.* She was about to say that when it hit her.

Where was Rachel?

Their pack's cubs had lost everything once before, and finally had a place in the world where they were loved and protected. A home. The whole pack had fought too hard for this new life in paradise to let their young lose everything again.

Not this time, Ella vowed. She came fully alert, her blink-away-from-battle body language automatically shifting her Wolves into hyper-alertness as well.

"Gear up!" Ella snarled, "Snowsuits, sniper rifles, explosives, Gustaf missiles. We are going to hunt down our missing cub and the rest of our pack! Leave in three minutes. Move!" Her Wolves blurred into motion.

In less than two minutes, the Wolves of the Stonemason team were neatly lined up in strict Wolf hierarchal order at the beehive's lower door, ready to go to war.

Ella looked over her troops. There were four extra heads, and three of them were not even Wolves.

Ella walked over to Bookworm and placed a paw supportively on his back. She looked at Grandma, Tosh, and Witboy with warmth. The tribal bond, the familial bond of pack and tribe are incredibly powerful. The hearts of Wolves are brave and fearless. They cherish their cubs and would never allow them to be hurt. She studied the Fisher clan humans in front of her. They cherished the young of the tribe as strongly as Wolves did, cubs included.

Tribe means family.

"We want to help, to come with you," Tosh explained calmly, "More of us means a better chance to find Rachel and the others. Fisher clan always pulls its weight," the young mother said firmly.

Ella shared an understanding look with Grandma, and the other humans watching quieted down so they could hear better. On one hand, they did not want to risk losing their matriarch, but the tribe also loved their children more than their own lives. The quiet grew as deep as still waters until Ella touched a paw to Tosh's shoulder and spoke sidewise to Grandma.

"I wish that we could all go after our missing ones together, but we must think strategically. What if this is a ruse to divide our numbers so that whoever is responsible for this can attack a poorly defended home base? Divide and conquer is a strategy well known to Wolves," Ella explained.

"Here's what we should do," she said.

"First, we must secure the den and our remaining family, then we need to track down our missing Wolves to find out what has happened to them. We need to keep the tracking team small and mobile. Wolves are the best choice. We can move faster over rough terrain. The rest of us need to prepare our ground base for defense, and further conceal all approaches to our beehive home in the sky. Keep all the cubs and people up there, out of the reach of any intruders. Also, the Alpha and his team will be returning home very soon. They will need accurate info waiting for them when they get here. Then Trey will know what to do," Ella said.

"Most importantly, I need Grandma and Tosh to prepare the family home for defense, and Henry to coordinate with the Viking Dudes in quickly building a few defensive nests to guard our ground base," Ella added quietly but firmly.

Grandma, Tosh, and Witboy exchanged looks with each other for a moment, then reached some mysterious accord and looked back at Ella. She was almost trembling in her anxiousness to be out the door searching for her lost Wolves, but she tried not to let anyone see her anxiety. Maybe a few of the humans didn't notice, but Wolves are not well-practiced at deceit.

"Of course," Grandma said, nodding her head. "We understand. Know that Fisher clan will be well prepared to defend you when you return, even if hell is close on your tail. Our clan always pulls its weight and we are Tribe. We will be waiting," she said.

Ona hugged Bookworm and gently guided him in Grandma's direction. The cub looked at Ella intently for a moment before dropping his eyes respectfully. Ella stepped over to give Bookworm a quick hug and watched as Grandma turned to lead their family back up into the warmth of the second floor.

Ella waited a moment in respect to the matriarch, then spun and was out the door in a flash with Ona, Sigrid, Tinker, and Theo glued to her side.

The scent-trail of Fitz and his team was multilayered and rich in nuance. Rachel's scent-print was much fainter and spread wider than her foot was capable of stretching. It was obvious that Fitz was carrying her, leaving her scent to mingle and slide to the outside of the Wolves' tracks. His prints in the snow were also deeper than the other Wolves, a dead giveaway. There were no fear or anger markers; from all appearances the Wolves were having a good time and not in any particular hurry. The trail was a good four hours old, though.

"They are too far ahead of us. We must catch up. We are faster on four legs than two. Move!" she ordered, and everyone dropped to all fours. This was a bit embarrassing, because it reminded them of when they were the Commander's slave-Dogs, but the moment of shame reluctantly faded after a moment.

Wolves have been well-bathed in the waters of Lethe, their weaknesses and memories washed away, leaving pure stainless-steel warriors relentlessly devoted to completing the mission.

They loped tirelessly up the broken trail through the snow and darkening shadows of the approaching forest night. The Wolves ran away from the sunset and into the moonrise. Often the sky above them was only a suggestion, trickling down through the mammoth trees surrounding them. Sometimes the trail would come to an open place and the steady falling snow gleamed ivory under the half-moon's cloud-disguised passing. Then they were back under the forest giants and running the dark snow-covered, pine needle trail. It was profoundly beautiful but none of them could enjoy the passage, not while their lost Wolves remained unfound.

Then they found it. There was no mistaking the place where it all happened. Ella roared, rising to her hindlegs, "Cats! I smell those damn Tigers everywhere!"

Nose-diving into the jumbled mélange of Tiger scent and Wolves, they found plenty of anger and fear sign. The team locked their gaze on Ella, intently waiting for her orders.

"Cover the entire area. Search out each scent and pawprint. Build a picture of what happened here," Ella ordered, snapping a chemical light stick to activate it. No detail was going to be lost to the dark and snow, no matter how good their night vision was. She was aware that light in the night might attract feline attention, but that was a good thing in the Wolves' eyes right now.

Sigrid and Ona began carefully following the trail uphill while Theo and Tinker spread out to work the perimeter of the forest glen. Ella took the center and started spiraling outward. What looked like a crushed snow mishmash was actually a time map if you knew how to read it.

Her Wolves did.

The initial attack had been from downhill, with two Tigers moving up to intercept Fitz and his team. After a brief moment the Wolves began a charge against one of the other Tigers, Fitz carrying Rachel in his back-rig, but then froze for some reason and looked back up the hillside they were descending. Another smelly Tiger, larger and heavier than the others, stood still for a moment there, facing downhill looking at the Wolves. Nobody moved for a moment, then four more Tiger tracks appeared out of nowhere, surrounding Rachel and her Wolves.

The snow started falling more heavily at this point. It was slowly filling in the traces, but to a Wolf it was as plain as day. "Here!" called Tinker, pointing out locations where impressions of the pack's M-4's had been temporarily laid down in the snow.

Ella's blood ran cold. Only one thing would cause her pack to lay their weapons on the ground and step back, to disarm in the face of the enemy.

Now the sequences and positioning of the thickly layered odors and pawprints in the trampled snow around Rachel's position made sense. The Tigers had threatened the pack's cub! Ella had to stuff her terrible anger into a back closet of her mind and think logically, like a Wolf should. It wasn't as easy as she expected.

Damned closet door kept creeping open.

"Okay" Ella said. "The reality is that the Tigers have taken our cub and family. They have forced our packmates to submit as if they were slave-Dogs again. This is not acceptable! We are free Wolves and must never bow to anyone again! This is the very essence of Wolf Haven," Ella said, looking into each of her team's eyes before continuing.

"We know the cub is still unhurt—no blood, Wolf bodies, or dead Tigers. Our packmates are still together, but they have been disarmed and forced to go with the damned cats. We can work with this." Ella snarled.

Her team's furious growls and snarls rose up into the forest canopy, frightening the birds overhead into flight. It was just as well that the humans were not there to hear it. Angry Wolfkin are already pretty scary, even before you add in those kinds of angry howls.

Ella deployed Theo and Ona as scouts and brought the rest of her team into fighting formation. Everyone re-checked their weapons, making sure that there was one in the chamber.

Now it was all about waiting for intelligence. Despite her desperate need to get going and save their cub, Ella's went to a dark place where she repeatedly played out scenarios in her mind until the scout finally reported back.

"They went up the mountain, on an old trail. Two Tiger in front, then Fitz, with Rachel on his back, Sami and Eddie in the middle, and four heavy Tigers rear-guard. I suspect that we have cut their lead in half, they are only a few hours ahead," Theo reported.

Theo's skill sets made him an ideal scout.

There are all sorts of Wolves. Some are relentlessly aggressive, some are simply unwilling to go against a powerful opponent and just hope not to get noticed, and there are a few that immediately roll over and bare neck submissively to a more dominate Wolf.

Theo was the middle kind. He didn't struggle to achieve pack dominance or higher rank, he was impossible to bait, and his strategic skills were extremely well developed. He could have easily been a big bad Wolf, but that simply wasn't his way.

He was also the second sneakiest Wolf in the pack after Twist. Very hard to see him coming until he was at your throat, and by then it was too late. Ella fully respected his skillset, despite his being a very different kind of Wolf than she was. There was room for all kinds of family in the tribe.

She straightened her posture to her full height and shook her furry head until droplets of melted snow flew everywhere. Time to bring her mind fully to the task at heart. Ella thought for a moment before speaking.

"Tinker, take point," she finally ordered, "and we'll follow you up the trail to the mountain. Slow down as we grow closer. When we finally reach them, we will NOT charge in firing wildly like we all want to. Instead, we will seek intel and figure out the best way to regain our packmates alive. We will recover our lost Wolves one way or the other. THEN, we kill all those damned Tigers. Let's go!"

The low, gravelly rumble of a mountain avalanche and angry Wolves on the hunt are surprisingly similar to the ear. Or maybe Wolves on the warpath are only a different kind of avalanche, one far more deadly than only snow and rocks. The only real give-away was that traditional avalanches don't normally flow uphill.

This one did.

Ella's team had left the tree line behind fifteen minutes earlier and were following the wide trail through snow-heaped brush and alpine meadows of purest white. An occasional moonbeam gleamed across the pristine snow fields on the belly of the mountain. It was almost enough to tempt Ella to pull out her sunglasses, but she was wary of missing a visual clue and so merely squinted as they loped up the sometimes-moonlit trail.

It didn't seem long before the tracks grew fresher, then completely disappeared. She slowed and then came to a full stop.

Sigrid, Theo, Ona, and Tinker placed themselves strategically around Ella, and settled into static poses. Everyone stared at the vista before them, eyes trying to pierce the pools of deepest shadow. There was a lot of shadow.

That much rock could not help but create dark places everywhere. The field of massive boulders, most at least the size of a small house, stretched on for almost a kilometer before apparently reaching the towering cliff wall of Tiger Mountain. Ella tried again to see between the nearest boulders, but the stone maze was visually impenetrable from here. She didn't like the look of it one bit. The close quarters were perfectly designed for ambush, and visibility in there was only a few meters. It left a bad feeling in her belly. Her pack slowed their panting for breath after a moment. It had been quite a climb.

Ella cracked her neck, racking her brain for an alternative. That was when a large snow owl glided over a few of the boulders before stooping into the dark between rocks. A small shriek was followed by the slow beating wings of the owl, as it resurfaced out of the shadow with a struggling rodent in its claws. It turned west and flew into the looming cloud bank creeping uphill behind the Wolves.

There was something about that owl…. the prey never saw it coming because the owl was flying over the boulder maze before dropping to attack. What if Wolves could do that? Of course, Ella knew that Wolves couldn't fly, but that didn't mean they couldn't travel *over* the huge stones instead of braving the dark maze below!

Was there that much difference between jumping from tree trunk to tree trunk in the rain forest and from the top of one big rock to another on the mountain heights?

Well, yes, it turned out, but Tinker made it anyway. Ella raised her right paw and gestured in sign language. "Cross the tops of the boulders, find a safe path for us. Don't get too far ahead – stay in sight," she signed. Then snarled "follow me" to Sigrid and Theo and turned to run at the nearest big rock at full speed.

Ella hit the stone face of the boulder hard and used her inertia to propel herself halfway up the side. The weathered rock felt wet and slick but was full of irregularities that allowed a Wolf to hook talon and climb the rest of the way. In a few seconds, Sigrid and Theo joined her and the three Wolves began following Tinker in great leaps from one of the snow-topped boulders to the next.

Twice, Ella almost slipped off from a bad landing, but managed to regain her balance and continue.

Ella was continually conscious of being silhouetted against the sky, a perfect target for a sniper, but all she could do was take deep nose-breathes to detect any sign of the enemy and keep going. At about halfway across the rock maze, she froze and growled low enough that only her pack would hear it. She smelled Tiger, down in the maze ahead of her. Ella paw-signed the others to lay down on their rocks and peek down below them into the stone maze.

Several of the Tigers had deliberately urinated on a log with a tattered coat covering it. It sort of a looked like an unconscious body. It was obviously a lure for angry Wolves. So where were the jaws that bite? And there had to be a mechanism to spring the trap, too.

"Go back two boulders, then slide down into the maze. We are going to close on the trap very carefully without tripping it. I doubt it has a live Tiger waiting to set it off, so look for tripwires, anything that looks odd. Move out!" Ella ordered before climbing down. She slipped and fell the last meter, then broke out another chemical light stick and activated it. It was pretty dark down here even for Wolves. The team moved forward centimeter by centimeter, examining everything. It took precious time, but they would eventually figure it out.

"We should just toss a rock in there and set it off, so the rest of our pack doesn't stumble into this trap," suggested Tinker.

Ella shook her head side to side like a human. "No, then they'll hear it go off and know exactly how close we are. Let's return the damn cat's gift. Preferably use it to open their front door, but I'm flexible," Ella said, with Ona, Tinker, and Theo growling in agreement.

They found two sets of claymore mines concealed along the path to the log dummy dressed in a smelly human coat. Looking down at them, Ella carefully removed the explosives and passed one mine to each of her team to carry. She wrapped the blasting caps individually in rags and passed them out too, tucking hers in an inside pocket of her long coat.

"Move out," she ordered, and the Wolves resumed their relentless boulder top journey, examining every meter of ground with noses and eyes that were hundreds of times more sensitive than ordinary humans.

Wolves at war don't miss much.

with noses and eyes that were hundreds of times more sensitive than ordinary humans.

Wolves at war don't miss much.

Chapter 29

THANK YOU, BUCKMINSTER FULLER

The captain's airmen searched the ground between the Cave and the main street of what was left of Quinault with the finest military drones on the continent.

Their first significant find was a barn roof lodged into a vicious mud pile at least twenty meters across. There were many wood splinters twice as tall as Captain Marc Christensen himself. The hundreds of wood spears thrust thickly out of mud chunks the size of a Dodge Ram. Drunkenly lodged across the top of the hill of splinter mud balls was the once-red roof of a large barn. It was huge, and not easy to get to.

But it contained exactly what they needed; aged two-by-fours that could be cut into short sections and nailed into triangles. Then the triangles would be joined together into a geodesic dome, one of the strongest structures they could build. Domes would protect their Seahawks and Super Stallion from the terrible weather that was coming, while also allowing them to be deployed quickly at any time.

"Sergeant, send Teams Five, Three, and Seven to salvage that thing. Use a Seahawk to get there, and to lift loads back to where we are building the domes," Marc ordered.

"The rest of you start getting those holes dug. Remember, each site will also require a place for the dome's counterweight to rise and fall. Those tops will be too heavy to lift if we don't get it right.

I know you will get it right. Dismissed!" Captain Marc Christensen ordered. He looked at his watch. Fifty-six hours until the first big storm was supposed to hit, and all outside work would have to be abandoned.

The first load of lumber came in within two hours. The captain helped break everything down, but it demanded a meticulous approach. The lumber had rusty nails poking out all over and that made it hazardous. Then you had to cut it into one-meter lengths. The aged wood was hard as iron, so once you removed the old rusty nails and angle cut the ends, it still took some bicep to drive each new nail through it. Wooden Geodesic dome frames have a lot of nails holding everything together.

Marc did not need to check his watch. They were not going to make the looming weather deadline like this. He could see that the lag was in production. But Marc had <u>all</u> his active forces busy doing important things. Active forces…What about inactive?

"Sergeant! Call up the families. See who would be willing to help us put these things together. No pressure, or pay, except for bragging rights and a couple of bottles of Shine. Come to think of it, our men have not been paid lately either, so they get a bottle too, if we make it. All we can do it our best. At least nobody goes to bed hungry," the captain mused to Sergeant Liam Redcap over the private command channel.

"On it," the Sergeant replied. Liam was a man of few words but was very effective in expressing his expectations.

The Seal Clan had thirty-seven adult Navy folk that were not active; they were a tight-knit community—family. Husbands and wives, aunts and uncles, grandmas and grandpas, all dedicated to keeping the small wheels of civilization going. They could teach classes and take care of the kids. And some of the old-guy chefs were already celebrities in their tiny microcosm.

People like to stay busy and eat well. Sometimes these simple truths are the most potent.

Within fifteen minutes, twenty-five volunteers showed up and quietly got to work. The captain cracked a stealth grin. Now they were back on track!

The four underground silos were being excavated by separate small teams. The logic was that you can always dig deeper underground later, just so long as the protective top part is finished. This was another place experience-rich old-guys were worth their weight in gold, even if they couldn't dig as fast as the young guys.

And blowing up things just never gets old for some people.

By the time nightfall fell, the silos were roughly shaped out, but still needed to be dug a lot deeper. The first geodesic dome for one of the Seahawks was fully built; it still needed an exterior cover and interior one too, for insulation purposes. However, the counterweight shafts were still only dents in the frozen ground and the actual counterweight boulders themselves were missing, as were the weight-balance mechanisms.

That night after dinner, everyone who could joined the sewing circle by the cave's central firepit as parachutes were frankensteined into eight Geodesic dome exterior and interior covers. They were not pretty, but they were well put together.

The impromptu sewing team got better with each cover. By midnight, they had two down, six to go in the next forty-five hours. Marc regularly sipped a little Shine stashed in his coat pocket as he stitched, finding he didn't mind the drudgery at all after a bit. He was discreet of course; despite being off duty, he simply didn't want people knowing how much he drank. No addict wants to be outed by his habit, yet it always seems to end that way.

There wouldn't be many secrets in the cavern. That is mostly a good thing, if a bit inconvenient, but people get along better when they're not cramped up together in a big room. How would they make it work? Marc let his mind wander. A whole village blossomed in his imagination. Restaurants, tiny apartments, childcare, schools, and last but not least, a few eclectic bars, and of course, a hand-crafted bowling alley would be nice. That was a home worth dreaming about. The clan mindset was already there. One hundred clan people of all ages that were used to staying busy are capable of amazing things. The Seal Clan…he liked the sound of that.

And you could do worse than a Seal Clan Cavern to ride out an ice age winter.

Chapter 30

TIGER TRAIL

Eventually, the snow-drenched rock field ended eighty meters short of a towering ice cliff, soaring far above them. It was the open field in front that concerned Ella and her Wolves.

It appeared to be a 'killing field', an open defensive area with multiple overlapping fields of fire and no shelter for attackers. There *were* a few scattered boulders offering concealment, but after finding the Wolf trap, Ella didn't trust the obvious approach route. This was a Tiger's lair. The obvious route of approach was just too easy. These Tigers had to be dug into fortified positions; they were too competent not to be. So…

"Okay" Ella said, "Team, spread out and take a good look at this place. It looks like there are several entrances and maybe a bunker dug into that ice cliff. The entrances appear to be fortified but not manned. Examine the footprint traffic and gun placements but stay back from that killing field and those rock piles out there!"

Ella leaned over the edge of her boulder, studying the entrances, and thinking about what it took to defend a fortified base. She wasn't used to thinking about stationary defenses, but the Tigerkin had to know that what remained of the pack would follow their trail. Yet, there were no obvious guards or sentries, no Tigers with machine guns guarding the front door. In fact, there appeared to be nothing to stop her from just walking up to the main door and kicking it in.

Right. Ella snorted. Rachel was probably the bait in another Wolf trap. So, if the Wolves were expected to follow, then that meant the Tigers knew their visitors would halt at the edge of the killing field for intel, then sneak in closer, moving from rock pile to rock pile until they could attack the main entrance.

That meant this was the <u>last</u> thing the Wolves should do.

"Fall back. Wolves fall back and drop down out of sight within the maze immediately," Ella ordered as she deliberately tumbled off her boulder to land perfectly on her paws in the dark shadows of the maze. What else would she do if she were in the Tiger's position? Probably lay proximity mines along the main access route, Ella thought. She would have explosives planted in the rock piles and at least two snipers up in that ice cliff. Fortified defenses at the actual entrance to the Tiger's den that could be manned without betraying the Tiger's presence. Plus, multiple back doors… everybody knows cats never stick around when things go bad.

Ella crept forward until she could see out of the maze while remaining concealed within the safety of the shadows. She took out her binoculars and held one lens to her right eye. They had been designed for humans and didn't really fit her face, but she could use one side perfectly. Her monocular showed three dark recesses in the ice wall at about the right height for sharpshooters. She scanned back to the rightmost cave. Something had flashed, something very much like a sniper scope lens. There it was again. *Confirmed.* She put her binoculars back in their pouch.

This was going to take some planning. Ella growled low to her Wolves and pulled back into the shelter of the boulder field.

"Theo, Tinker: go left along the open field's edge. Find us a temporary base location to rest and get warm while we figure this out. Someplace concealed that can't be seen by Tigers or drones above. Sigrid: you and I will go right. Meet back here in twenty minutes," Ella ordered. Tinker cocked their head at Ella questioningly. "Move out," Ella ordered. Tinker liked things spelled out, having little faith in their own ability to read other's intent. Ella suspected that this also avoided actually having to think much, but she was confident in Tinker. The Wolfkin would grow surer of themselves in time.

Wolves regularly rise and fall in rank; the hierarchy of the pack is a mutable thing. *This is a good thing.*

Ella just growled a little and her Wolves immediately dashed off on mission. She overtook Sigrid in five strides and passed her, taking lead; dominate Wolf and all that. Nobody had to talk about it like humans. Wolves just knew what to do and coordinated wordlessly. And Ella was the dominate Wolf until Trey arrived back here. Everyone one knew that as well, just as they knew precisely their own status in the pack, or any subset of it. It's good to be Wolfkin. Makes some things simpler.

Ella and Sigrid stayed close to the perimeter where the boulders ended and the field began. They tirelessly crawled to the south for at least ten minutes before they found what they were looking for. Three of the huge boulders rested against each other, creating a small cave. Closer examination found that the soil under one of the boulders wasn't completely frozen and could be easily dug out. No one would be able to see the entrance to an underground den without entering the small cave, which was virtually invisible from above. This was about as good as they were going to find.

"Sigrid: begin laying out the den while I go meet the others. When we get back all of us should make short work of this," Ella ordered.

By the time the Wolves returned, Sigrid had everything staked out and took over directing operations. It wasn't long before they had a wind-proof den carpeted with soft pine boughs and even a corner firepit that had a makeshift chimney. The Wolves all collapsed on the pine boughs, but Ella also had prepared a schedule of watches to carry them through the night, so Theo had to go back out in the cold while the rest of them helped get the fire going. The Wolves spent the next few hours piled in front of the small fire, discussing all the challenges they faced in recovering their lost packmates, and how they were going to overcome the Tigers. The second conversation was much shorter than the first.

It eventually grew quiet, late even for Wolves, as her Stonemasons slowly nodded in the warm darkness. No reason to keep talking once you've said what you intended to. The fire gradually transformed from flames to glowing coals, scarlet in the night.

Ella had second watch.

The night was turbulent, with shrieking winds and snowflakes hard as iron. The was no sign of the moon now, only rippling shades of black velvet in the sky. It was freezing, and some of the fur on Ella's nose was coated in ice. She was neatly tucked high into a nook on the side of a particularly large boulder. Ella could see both the den and the fortified entrance to the Tiger's base from her raised position. She had wrapped herself loosely in a moth-eaten wool blanket they had found somewhere, with only the tip of her nose and eyes uncovered to the storm. She was partially out of the wind, and sat cross-legged and motionless under her wool tent, watching for the enemy, and covering the stonemason's redoubt. The snow soon covered most of her blanket tent and Ella became indistinguishable from the rest of the snow-covered boulder. Wolves are patient hunters and know how to lie in wait.

A slow diesel motor chugged noisily in a small lit area of the Tiger's base only eighty meters away. It was a tempting target, but she knew better. The Tigers had to know the Wolves were here by now. But Ella's eyes were constantly drawn back to the electric light, a blatant reminder of the world from before everything changed. It was a powerful symbol, a potent sign of power in the wilderness. She stretched her neck slowly so she wouldn't dislodge any of her cold white camouflage and took a deep breath through her nose.

The uphill wind brought the forest close, the air fecund and rich with bruised fir, spruce, and rain on stone. She smelled her beloved forest, the wet moss and incense cedar's clean scent. Sitka firs. Fiddleheads. Mushrooms and deer scat and decomposing logs. It was lovely and Ella savored the taste of home, up here in her stone-boulder world. Suddenly she sat up a little taller and leaned forward to drink the night in through her nose again.

She certainly hadn't expected to smell Viking Dudes in battle leathers and Henry Chin's clean scent on the wind! And from the way their scent was growing stronger, the humans were close and getting closer. It wasn't long before she heard them too—Humans are almost incapable of silence no matter how hard they try.

They slowly trickled into view through the fog and drizzle, almost as if they'd always been there and she was just now noticing them. The Viking dudes were a little spooky sometimes.

But Ella hadn't seen *anything* yet.

She growled a polite greeting and the small group instantly clumped together facing outwards, searching for the messenger with their slow-arcing weapons pointed into the night like so many swaying charmed serpents.

"I'm up here," Ella said, standing and shaking snow from her wool blanket. Every eye snapped to her tall figure, leaning out from a fissure high on one of the larger stones. They all lowered their weapons back down simultaneously with the kind of discipline you only find in long-term elite soldiers and Wolfkin packs.

Or apparently, Viking dudes.

"We're here to help. Where do you need us?" asked Thorsten. Ella briefly lowered her head in respect and then sprang outward into the snowy night. She gracefully touched down in a roll from which she emerged striding forward until she came to a halt, quite close to Thorsten, the leader of the Viking dudes.

He looked affectionally at the dangerous Wolf and lightly slapped her powerful right arm. She took a subtle step back so he didn't hug her. Viking dudes were prone to such public displays of affection. You never quite knew what they'd do next, so it was better to be safe.

"What's the plan?" he asked happily. Ella looked at him. She didn't understand this human's thoughts at all, but she did respect a good fighter, and she had a feeling she hadn't seen anything yet.

"Welcome. We can use your help. Come on back to our forward bunker and get warm. We'll work on a plan of attack once you've dried off and had something to eat and drink," Ella said. She'd been watching Grandma of the Fisher clan and had noticed what seemed to work well with getting humans calmed down and able to think better.

Sit them down, feed them, and they chill out quickly.

She was still surprised that it worked so well.

Ella spread her motheaten horse blanket over her lower half and a few of the nearest Wolves, then leaned back against somebody and studied their visitors. Henry Chin appeared to be nodding, but the Wolfkind could sense his awareness. She returned her attention to the Viking dudes.

There were seventeen of them, all fully armed, armored and quite hairy to boot. The Viking dudes currently took up most of the underground den, but that was only because the Wolves were being polite. The aromatic combination of wet fur, human sweat and damp leather was stifling to a Wolf's nose, but their guests were being polite too, so nobody bit anybody.

"What do you bring to the table?" asked Ella.

Thorsten spoke up with neither hesitation nor eagerness. His long black beard was damp, glistening in the firelight as if he had tiny jewels woven in. He had removed his helmet and wore his long course hair in war-braids. Most soldiers favor short hair so that no one can grab them by their long hair with one hand and slit their throat with the other.

Viking war-braids dare you to try it.

"We came from a land of ice and snow, far across the Atlantic Ocean, to make a new home for ourselves on the Olympic peninsula. We know the Nordic forests of old, but the Hoh Rain Forest is magnificent! We love it here and it has become our new home. The Viking dudes are now part of this post-apocalyptic world's natural biosphere," Thorsten said, pausing to take a great draught from his stainless-steel growler. He wiped his overgrown mustache with the back of an armored forearm and continued.

"We are warriors born and bred for a thousand years. We know the old ways; the berserker is a rare and dreaded warrior by all who know of such things. We are your support force to aim as you please. We have snipers and a smattering of missiles, but our true strength is that we are melee fighters without peers. We always fight as teams, and we almost always achieve our objective," Thorsten summed up, then took another great swallow of his barley elixir. Ella nodded approvingly.

"Here's what we have so far…" she said, going on to explain everything that the Stonemasons had observed. Afterwards, Thorsten's people asked quite good questions, which required more intel, which meant somebody had to go outside into the snow and cold of the storm again. Over the next hour, they hammered together a plan that should work, while still being adaptable to changing conditions in the field. They hoped.

"Anything else?" Ella asked after the humans finally ran out of talk.

"Oh, I almost forgot to tell you. We gave some of our friends a call for help getting your cub back, but it's going to take them a while to get here," Thorsten said, chugging the last of his growler.

She didn't even ask. No Wolf was going to wait around for some mysterious human to rescue their people. Wolves take care of their own. And every minute counted. So, she relegated the low-priority statement to the back of her mind where she seldom went.

Ella intended to launch the attack just before false dawn, in the hour of the Cat, when humans and Tigers sleep their deepest sleep.

Chapter 31

HOMEWARD BOUND

The main part of the storm rolled out of the west, spreading out in a line almost parallel to the Washington coast as it hit shallower water. Luckily, between the shore and storm front lay a narrow channel, one in the direction we wanted to go—north, to the Bogachiel River mouth. Then upriver, deep into the magnificence of the Hoh Rain Forest.

Home. I could almost taste it.

I looked over at old Fisherman. The blind captain had his head cocked to the weather and his nose to the shore. This required an open window or hatch, things that normally keep the rain and wind out. Lenny stood to the captain's right, covered in orange rain gear, feeding visual data to the captain, and automatically ducking to avoid the more aggressive splashes.

The surging seas were at three-meters, which meant the gap between bottom and crest of the wave was double that—these were six-meter-tall waves. But I wasn't worried, the *Becky* is a tough-as-iron fishing boat that sneers at bad weather. She is captained by a blind prophet, piloted by a brilliant first mate, and crewed by Wolves. Takes more than a little rough water to stop us.

The storm did slow us down, though. Progress was methodical, if occasionally glacial. The *Becky's Reward* steadily chugged forward a meter at a time, threading the needle-thin northern passage, surprisingly graceful for a commercial fishing boat towing a heavily loaded barge.

Graceful maybe, but not fast enough—pirates are faster. That was on my mind.

What if that third pirate boat we wounded earlier in the drowned forest was able to radio their base or make it back to the pirate colony we had heard about in Ocean Shores?

The disgraced pirate captain we had taken at the windfarm told us all about their base, and I didn't much care for what I heard. Ocean Shores had become a chaotic, violent place, completely dominated by Chinese and Malaysian criminal clans. The pirate captain said that less than twenty percent of the original population had survived.

Ocean Shores is thirty-five kilometers below Wolf Haven's southern border. That is way too close.

I know that we are going to have to help the original residents, those that managed to survive under this brutal regime of Tong gangsters.

Henry says these Tong are nothing but pirates, and pirates are reavers, violently taking slaves and slaughtering anyone they can't profit from. After despoiling the prisoners first, of course. And now they had a permanent base—a captured ocean-side village with two sheltered harbors. Repair facilities. Slave labor. Wild streets where anything goes. Wicked things, too often.

We _are_ going to do something about this.

Unfortunately, that day is not today. I felt rage at the atrocities committed on innocent tourists and seaport year-rounders in what was once a sleepy beach town on the Pacific. Now, everything stank of death there. The disgraced pirate captain told us that the powerful scent of an abattoir was all you could smell for kilometers in all directions. The streets were almost empty during the day, but at night they filled with dangerous, intoxicated pirates looking for fun in all the wrong places.

There was no doubt in my mind that we going to have problems with this once-beautiful seaside resort—and they were the kind of problems that ended up chasing you down and trying to kill you. That was okay, they'd just need to stand in line. Wolf Haven has no shortage of enemies.

But the Commander tops the list.

The truth was that I just wanted to get home. I missed my pack and our beehive home in the sky.

Of course we would protect the Hoh Rain Forest, and our pack from these vicious raiders! There was no way that I would sail home to our beautiful home concealed in the upper canopy of ancient trees, dragging trouble in my wake. We protect the den.

I thought hard. Wolves are pack creatures, and function best as a team. This included problem solving. So, I explained the mission to my packmates and then looked at Twist, the next most dominate Wolf in the pilothouse. He lowered his eyes, growled politely, and spoke.

"First, we get the *Becky* successfully upriver and deliver all the wind generator stuff to our ground camp. We have to do this without leading any pirates back to our den and cubs. Second, we need to do this before the Bogachiel River freezes over completely. Third, we have to accomplish this without drawing the Commander's deadly attention. Oh, and we have to survive the coming winter," Twist summed up.

Right! No problem. I groaned, considering the possibilities.

I looked at Twist, but he just shrugged. Felix shook his head, and the White Wolf Nina just growled real low. Well, that was helpful. But I'm the Alpha, so I just kept moving forward.

"Lenny, how many navigable rivers empty into the Pacific between us and our Bogachiel River?" I asked. We may need to evade enemy at any moment, and we had to have someplace to run to, so this information was critical. The pilot didn't hesitate.

"Three main rivers as we go north. First one leads to a big lake named Quinault with its own rain forest, the second climbs up into rough mountain terrain and fades out, and the third, the Hoh River, leads deep into the southern part of our Hoh Rain Forest and may even loop north to merge with our Bogachiel River these days.

"The Olympic Island rivers have all enlarged since the world changed. It's possible that we may have a backway out that leads to the Pacific. Unfortunately, we haven't been able to get up there and see yet, so we just don't know for sure," Lenny explained.

"Storm's getting worse," said the captain, head cocked to hear things outside in the wild weather. I looked out the windows in the front of the wide bridge. The deck sloped at an angle engineered to quickly drain seawater, but the noise and sheer violence of the storm's fury had definitely notched it up.

"How fast are we going, and will we make it to the Bogachiel River before it gets a much worse?" I asked. The blind captain cocked his head, thinking for a moment.

"We need to get there before the full force of the main storm smashes into us, which I give less than two hours." The captain said. "We need to stay far enough from shore to avoid the rocks and surf but close enough in to slide by the main storm before it hits shoreside. We can actually pick up speed if we ride the waves right. And we need to—it will be very hard to get into the Bogachiel River without getting shoved into shore by the storm once it hits. The surf will beat us to death if we crash," the blind fisherman said.

Two hours. *We could do it.* Even if we didn't succeed in making it past the mouth of the Bogachiel, nothing would change. Wolves don't give up and bare neck easily. We try our hardest, regardless of potential failure. Wolf logic. Fisherman logic, too. I patted the blind prophet's shoulder with my right paw. A lot to like about that man. He never showed fear or shied from doing the right thing.

Never lied, even if he was a human.

We almost got sucked into the last river before our Bogachiel, but somehow managed to escape the tidal current and pull back out into the narrow sweet-spot of the northbound channel. We were getting close, and the good news was that no sane captain would willingly enter this maelstrom, so we didn't need to worry about pirates following us home anymore. I just held on to something solid as the *Becky* skillfully rode the wild waves, fearlessly chugging forward, homeward bound with her crew and stuffed with treasure.

The full fury of the storm rolled over the shore just as we reached the mouth of the Bogachiel and began to tack starboard into the river. The *Becky's Reward* pulled for everything she was worth, but surf was pushing us into the rocky northern side of the entrance to the Bogachiel. It was so close that I thought we lost the barge for one terrible moment.

But our sweet *Becky* managed to drag us back out into the center of the river where we had a little room. The barge was intact and now we were slowly making our way upriver through a half-frozen river of slush blanketed in an odd grey-white landscape of twilight snow. The wind still howled, but the deeper we traveled into the rain forest, the less impact it had.

Here the massive firs and spruce and hemlock soared high, chocolate straws seven-meters-wide topped by snowcaps and pierced by minty green needles. Incense cedar and Sitka pine perfumed the air, threading through the glorious mélange of scent we call the Hoh Rain Forest.

Home.

The snow and ice crystals still tore through the river air, but the violence was easing. We passed by the wreck of the Coast Guardian's plundered craft. The sight left me angry, but we Wolves would never forget our promise to the fallen. None of us spoke until we'd passed around the river bend and moved out of sight of the tragic boat. Out of sight but not mind.

The river's shore crept by painfully slow until several hours later when we finally spotted our home dock, half frozen and more beautiful than we could have imagined. As we drew closer Lenny cut the engine and we drifted perfectly into the small channel we'd prepared ahead of time. Home at last! Our mission was complete!

Tails might have wagged.

After tying up and securing the boat and barge, we grabbed our packs and forged through the waist-high snow to the base ground-camp, where a bonfire blazed in welcome. We dumped our packs against the sitting logs and drew close to the flames, holding out paws that we never thought could be fully warm again. Then I turned to see Grandma, Tosh, and Witboy silently approaching us from the cook tent. Those three never stopped talking when together.

Something was wrong.

My jubilant feelings immediately wilted as I read their body language and grim expressions. I momentarily stilled, slowly turning to face the Fisher clan trio, waiting to hear the terrible news.

"The Tigerkind have taken Fitz and his team prisoner," Grandma said, laying a warm hand on my right forearm. "And Rachel was with them," she said, fully aware of what kind of emotional impact this was likely to have on a Wolf. Grandma never messed around when cubs were involved, but an angry Wolfkin didn't scare her one bit. (I'm not sure what *could* actually scare her, Grandma was kind but tough as nails).

I didn't try to restrain the snarl that rumbled within me, way down in the sub-woofer range. I didn't want to frighten the humans, but a hot rage had descended over me.

I was not alone in my anger, either. Nina the White Wolf was shaking in unexpressed fury. After a moment, we calmed down enough to hear Grandma out, because she obviously wasn't finished.

"Ella and her stone masons are holed up in a newly-dug hidden base high in the mountains, not far from the Tiger base where our Wolves and Rachael are being held captive," she continued, still fearlessly patting my forearm.

"They have been joined in the last hour by Henry and the Viking dudes and are figuring out a battle plan to free our people," Grandma said, adding, "As far as we know, everyone is still alive."

I managed not to glare at anyone, but my snarling still got louder. After a moment I was able to speak.

"Fisher clan," I said turning to Old Fisher and Lenny, "please unload and stash our wind turbines in the ground camp. Don't touch the wind blades, they are worn razor sharp by the sea wind and storms. Securely cover the remaining cargo with tarps. After that go home to the Treehouse. Secure the den. Then hit the mattresses. The next few days are going to be long and difficult."

They nodded soberly.

"Wolves, we go to join Ella and our pack," I ordered. Gruff barks gave assent.

"And we'll need trail rations, long guns, and a lot of ammo," I said, turning to Grandma and Tosh. "Where… how far…"

"We've already got you ready, Trey," Tosh said. "We've been waiting for you with weapons and provisions. Let's go to the Treehouse to arm you all up, then you can get back our people," she said simply.

I nodded. We are pack.

Raising nose to air, I began to sniff deeply, searching for my missing Wolves' scents. Then I stopped suddenly.

"Viking Dudes?"

Chapter 32

IN THE QUEEN'S LAIR

Rachel watched the Tiger queen through slitted eyes, studying her huge captor for any sign of weakness. Queen Malgato reclined on a long green velvet couch situated to the left of the Wolves, directly in front of the blazing fireplace. She was half-buried in silk pillows and staring into the fire, lost in thought.

The wind outside screamed in frustrated high notes. The distant chugging of a diesel generator explained the dim electrical lighting and the big screen television currently showing a Chinese nature show of some kind with the sound turned down. The magic screen tugged at the edges of Rachel's attention, but she refused to give in and take her attention away from the wicked Tiger queen. Television was from her first life, not this one. Wolves stay focused, not distracted, she knew. And Rachel was a good Wolf to the core. But it wasn't easy. The old world was addictive.

She and her packmates were confined to a large soft pillow patch, in the corner of the main chamber of what appeared to be an extensive bunker system. Rachel scooted until her back was straighter and crossed her legs yoga style. The mound of pillows was admittedly comfy, but such pleasures are not high on a Wolf's priority list.

What *was* high priority were the two Tigerkin keeping Rachel and her defensive pile of wolves targeted with their assault rifles. Rachel ignored them, but Fitz couldn't refrain from growling so low and mean that they felt more than heard it. One of the other

Tigerkin 'growled' back mockingly and all the Tigers burst into deadly giggles. Well, all except for the two keeping Rachel in their cross-hairs—they never moved or showed any awareness of such humor. Discipline is ever the Tiger way.

Rachel thought the big cats were just plain mean, but still carefully remembered what she had been taught by her pack: to smell and paint a scent picture. To listen and paint a soundscape. To look and understand.

She exhaled slowly, like Ella had been teaching her, and slowly drew in a great breath. Damp Wolf and Tiger. *Duhh!* she thought. Oiled leather and a fire burning in an open hearth. Old blood and meat and cat musk. Ice… from where? She remembered hearing a strangely familiar squeak from around the time they were so rudely deposited here. Which direction was colder? She inhaled and sought the delicate scent of ice. Rachel gradually turned in a circle, her cheeks and nose seeking out the coldest quarter, where the sliding glass door must be.

The exit.

Most of the time, Rachel wished she had an enhanced body like the grownups in her pack. She hated feeling puny, but for once the sensitivity of her weak human flesh was coming in handy. She could actually feel the chill on her cheeks and tell which way the draft blew. Finding a strength in her human body was completely unexpected; it was the first time she could remember noticing an advantage to her weak, human side.

While Rachel couldn't wait to be a real Wolfkin someday, right now wasn't that day. It was getting-the-heck-out-of-here day. And the clock was ticking, because the Alpha was going to show up sometime soon, and then there were going to be *reckonings*. The kind of reckonings that leave a lot of Tiger and Wolf parts all over the place. Rachel knew that the Alpha would do whatever it took to protect his pack, and heaven help the Tigers, because Trey wasn't going to leave any threats to his pack alive.

She just wanted to be out of here before that happened. The pack could balance accounts later, from a position of strength. There was no need for any of her pack to endanger themselves needlessly just for her. Rachel knew she would feel terrible if anything happened to one of her Wolves. But she also knew Trey was coming for her—for all of them—and nothing was going to be able to stop the Alpha. This she knew without any doubts. That's why she wasn't scared one bit, despite the deadly threat of Tigers.

It's good to be pack. The hierarchal structure of a pack has many benefits. Knowing exactly where you stand in the pack hierarchy is time-freeing, allowing Wolves to focus on the important things and work with a coordination that is almost miraculous. Without dominance struggles, communication is greatly enhanced, and action becomes almost instantaneous.

The bonus of always knowing your family is coming for you, no matter what, was both rare and wonderous to Rachel, but that's simply what a pack did… and kick ass when they got there.

Once she was sure of the sliding glass door's direction, she gently poked Fitz with her index finger. He automatically snarled and turned to face her instead of glaring at the Tigers with the drawn weapons like he had been the entire time they'd been here.

"Fitz," she said quietly, "I think that through that room with the com-center is a sliding glass door to outside. It's the only way out I can find." Rachel suddenly felt a sense of relief because a burden shared weights half as much.

Adults mostly had all the answers, and she was turning the matter over to a wiser wolf who would know what to do. Rachel actually felt her shoulders relax when she hadn't even known they were tense. Leaning back into the pillow mound, she continued studying the Tiger queen through squinted eyes. After a moment, she shifted her gaze back to the senior Wolf in the room, Fitz. She was impatient but trying not to let it show.

Unfortunately, Wolves are not well-practiced in deceit. She didn't fool anyone.

And she simply couldn't let it go. She needed to be part of the *answer*, not just the cub who asked the question. Rachel was pretty sure she was going to have to help save them from captivity, but it wasn't her place to boss grown Wolves around. All she knew was that waiting sucked. She stared rudely at her superior in the pack, willing him to act.

Fitz was acutely aware of the weapons aimed at their cub and continued to tremble minutely in a frustrated fury that was just aching to erupt. The desire to throw himself at the damned cats threating his pack's young was almost overpowering. But only 'almost'. Even the thought of harming a cub had been unimaginable until Tigerkind made it real. The world has not become a better place because of it, that was for sure.

Fitz slowly turned his head to face Rachel, knowing his Wolves would be watching and listening. There are many ways of talking and they are not all noisy or obvious. Slave-Dogs under the Commander's yoke had known some of these well.

Fitz allowed his eyes to lose focus slightly, in order to perceive any peripheral movement sooner. This also served the purpose of not triggering the automatic, 'Yes, Boss!' response from a lower ranking pack member that a direct gaze would have. Fitz needed both Rachel's attention and quick intelligence, not a rote, ritualized mindset.

Fitz raised his paw to cover his mouth in the sign for 'quiet walking'.

Rachel's head perked up. Sami and Eddie casually moved to stand between the Tigers pointing rifles and the cub's sign-language-exchange with Fitz. The Tigerkin did not care for their change of position and moved clockwise to cover the cub again. Eddie kind of shrugged back into the Tiger line of sight as Fitz quickly signed to the cub.

"Make ready to go. We go in formation. Stay in center. You don't have nanites, and we do. Go in three, two, run on one..." paw-spoke Fitz. He rested his gaze in the area over Rachel's head until she signed back.

"Ready," gestured the cub.

Fitz held up three fingers. Then two. Then the lights went out and all hell broke loose.

Chapter 33

EVERYTHING LOOKS WHITE IN A BLIZZARD

My team had tracked our pack for hours to this dark maze of huge boulders and stunted trees. The wind whistled eerily and we were losing the trail as the wind whipped the snow across the frozen ground, erasing what remained of the tracks, and almost all traces of scent.

Besides the faint traces of scent, all we had to guide us was our training at the hands of the monster, Commander Elwha. We were very young back then and took everything they said at face value. We didn't understand that humans lie a lot. But they drilled fight tactics into us until they became second nature. I knew what my Wolves were doing because it was what I would have done. And that made me angry—that the Commander's shadow was still telling us what to do.

We were already dangerous warriors before they mind-wiped us, loaded us with Timber Wolf genes and cooked us up in giant techno eggs. We were genetically redesigned to be the Navy's personal biological killing-machines.

I guess they never expected us to begin thinking for ourselves, much less disobeying our extensive conditioning. And now here we were still following our early training! I snarled in frustration. Were we ever to be free of our terrible childhood?

I knew that eventually all cubs grow up, and become something different than their parents expected, even if those parents were as deadly as the Commander and our cold scientist mothers. I think we beat the odds and became something *more*. But the monster still whispered in our heads.

Yes, our biology and training mase us downright lethal, quick death to those who oppose us in battle. And sometimes when things become intense, it was difficult to differentiate between friend and foe. That could be a problem.

We were learning as fast as we could.

Fifteen minutes later, we crossed the top of yet another huge boulder and saw a small clearing below us ahead. Despite the silent falling snow, we could see the clearing was mottled in silver moonlight and too many black depthless shadows.

Then a magnificent Wolf slid out of the black, striding into the moonlight in full-battle-mode. She was obviously on a journey that was not going to end well for those who took our packmates.

The Wolf was Ella.

She was accompanied by her team. Everyone was fully geared up for battle, and they were single-mindedly raging. I could literally smell the bloodlust pouring off them.

We had fought together many times, but this was the first time I had seen how Ella looked to outsiders. She was very beautiful and looked incredibly dangerous.

She wasn't alone either; four of my Wolves and Henry were with her. Henry wasn't the only human, either. Outsiders, sporting a lot of hair and weapons.

I returned my gaze to Ella.

Taking a deep breath, I stood up fully. She immediately scented me. Her response was not promising. She bared significant tooth and snarled but didn't slow or show any sign of recognition.

Not good.

We needed to join up and plan this out. Not lose more Wolves. I was going to have to stop her. I just hoped she broke out of her battle-trance and listened to her Alpha.

I lightly jumped down to block Ella's path.

I knew her outraged roar and instinctive go-for-my-throat reaction was not a thought-out plan. I just needed to reawaken her mind. I needed her to acknowledge her Alpha.

I snapped my throat backwards out of her jaws before they could close. I continued with a twist to the right, pushing her left shoulder up between her teeth and my head. I reversed my momentum and rolled to my left while avoiding the fighting knife in her right paw. It was close. Ella is a deadly fighter.

But so am I.

It's significantly more difficult to immobilize somebody without damaging them than it is to kill them. I was going to need every bit of my fighting skills to pull this off. I sucked in my belly to avoid another knife slash intended to gut me. I responded by catching her upper arm in my teeth and diving, using her body weight to try flipping her. She instinctively countered, which played right into my true plan.

I snapped my head up under her arm to seize her throat in my jaws before she could cut me with her blade.

She froze. I was growling so low that I knew she could feel my teeth vibrating in her throat as they held her immobile.

I guess sometimes you have to use the old ways to get through to people. Still didn't make me feel any better about it.

Within seconds her struggles ceased, and Ella's eyes focused on me.

Recognition bloomed on her face and I could see the weight coming off her powerful shoulders as I took command.

I also saw shame in her eyes and in that moment, I hated the Commander even more, if that were possible. I pulled her to her feet as she looked around her as if seeing the world for the first time.

On the other hand, good things happened as well. I got to see Ella as I never had before, and in that moment realized that I loved her, loved her fierce independence and fighting spirit. *Huh...*

"Report" I ordered, giving Ella the comfort of formality, and a way forward without things getting all awkward like humans were prone to.

"The Tigers ambushed Fitz on patrol and took our cub," Ella said with a low growl. "They're alive—we can smell them, but

Fitz, Sami, and Eddie must have been disarmed when our cub was threatened. It was either that or die and leave Rachel surrounded by hungry Tigers."

"I got that from the scent and tracks at the ambush site. Where are our lost Wolves now?" I asked.

In a low voice, Ella reeled off the facts she and her Wolves had collected in their scouting, her words growing louder as she wrapped up. "They are dug into that glacier's ice cliff a half kilometer uphill from here. In between lies a broad killing field, a no-man's land we need to cross to get to the fortified entrance of the Tigerkin's bunker. Then we have to break through and navigate the Queen's Lair to find our stolen packmates," she said. She paused for a second before continuing, as if caught in the memory of a nightmare.

"We haven't been able to figure out how to do that without the damn Tigers noticing, so we ended up deciding on a two-pronged frontal attack in conjunction with our new allies, the Viking dudes." Her eyes rolled to the left where Henry and a bunch of hairy tattooed barbarians with too many guns waited silently, watching our exchange.

Of course, I had noticed them.

The night snow silently fell in the small area between the massive boulders, quickly settling on Wolf and human alike. The wind wasn't as bad in this sheltered oasis, but I knew we were upwind of the ice cliff, and the Tigerkin most likely were already aware of our presence.

They were expecting our attack; that's what this was all about. To draw us out of our territory, and into an arena Tigers controlled. Why else take our cub and Wolves, if not to draw us in?

If you know it is a trap, do you go in anyway?

Wolves do, but there was no room for error here.

I nodded at Henry and turned to scan the hairy humans, as they studied me back. Nina eased up to cover their right flank and almost all of their eyes followed the White Wolf, but nobody so much as twitched in reaction. Their assault rifles remained pointed at the ground. Good discipline. That brought them up in my estimation.

The one that didn't take his eyes off of me had to be the alpha of this deadly pack. I stepped closer, towering over him, waiting to see how he would react. Most humans don't care for this and instinctively step back.

He just showed me his teeth.

Didn't see that one coming, so I showed him mine back, drawing my lips back menacingly. He didn't cringe and his mouth spread wider—it was friendly though, not quite submissive.

He sure didn't seem like the kind of leader to take such dangerous liberties, so that meant that he was comfortable enough in the company of Wolves to show his teeth to us.

"Thorsten Baldurson," he barked gruffly.

He spoke a little nonverbal Wolf as well as Pacific Northwest English. Just who had this hairy human been hanging out with? I turned to look at Ella questioningly.

Ella just looked upwards into the gently falling snow, not meeting my eyes. I looked at Twist, but he remained completely focused on the Viking dude alpha to the exclusion of everything else. He knew where any trouble was going to be coming from.

Of course, Nina coughed a low note of amusement at me, and Ella dropped a silent Wolf laugh on top of everything.

Yeah, being the Alpha doesn't protect you from the humor of Wolves. Still, I found myself calming a bit. Peace had already been made between these Viking dudes and my people, and that was good enough for me. I trusted my pack, so I tucked away my snarl and looked down at the human alpha.

"New plan time," I stated.

Thorsten simply nodded in agreement and all his dudes relaxed around him.

Ella led us back into a concealed underground den. Inside, the fire's coals were still brightly glowing. Theo and Tinker began building the fire back up as everyone gathered around. Wolves don't need a lot of personal space, but humans are consistent and always want more. It was a little tight, so I stood up to run my paw across the giant boulder that made up the ceiling. Then I turned to look around at the others in the room.

Wolves, Vikings Dudes, Stonemasons, Henry. All met my eyes without hesitation, then dropped their gaze before it became a challenge. The recently-excavated chamber was silent except for the crackle of the newly fueled flames. The gold hues of firelight flickered hungrily across the gleaming stone ceiling.

"We are Wolves! We will never allow cubs to be harmed. Never! Wolves will always stand between children and danger. And we are not alone.

"Tonight, we are fighting as one family, one tribe, one pack, despite being different species. We all cherish our young. We will get our little Wolf and our packmates back, but it won't be easy. It is obvious what needs to be accomplished, but how to go about it successfully seems less than clear," I said, my gaze sweeping the gathered. Everyone's attention was laser-focused on me, and some of my Wolves were leaking growls here and there. I raised chin in sync with my people's emotions and continued.

"The enemy is dug in and fortified. The approach to the Tiger's den is well laid with explosives and probably tricks we don't even know about yet. Cats are sneaky," I stated. The growling got louder and not all of them were from Wolves. Sneaky is awfully close to lying. Anyway, nobody trusts a cat.

"They have at least two sniper nests tucked up under the lip of the glacier ice wall, each with a sweeping field of fire." Ella spoke up and quickly lowered her eyes. I nodded.

"Once we've got past the snipers and through the open field, we have to break in—and the main entrance appears to be well-fortified despite the apparent absence of Tigers," I said, pausing for a beat before continuing.

"This whole time our cub has been in danger of being harmed or killed by the damned Tigers." My head lowered, trembling minutely in fury. I was not alone, we were deeply united in our anger, each and every one of us.

"It doesn't matter what they've planned! We *will* rescue our cub and lost Wolves, make no mistake!" I roared. I waited for the excited yipping, growling and a strange, penetrating hum of approval from the Viking Dudes, to die down before continuing.

"A full-frontal assault isn't going to work," I said, bring quiet to the room again, "They would react too quickly and while we could win that battle, we would still lose people. We need to be smart about this. So, I guess the question we have to ask is why did the Tigerkin take our packmates prisoner instead of simply killing them?" The very concept hurt my head. I willed myself to relax, and deliberately cracked my neck before continuing.

"These are terrible times, and the unthinkable—that our cub could be hurt—must now be considered. We will do what is necessary to rescue our people alive," I continued, gazing across the crowded room, seeking an answer.

"They want something" Henry Chin said quietly, but Wolves have very good hearing. Viking dudes too. "They took one of our children hostage and are now waiting for us to open negotiations. If we don't respond quickly enough, they will hurt our kid to encourage us," he added in a winter-cold voice. We all remembered how he lost his little daughter Lily, and I knew he shared our fierce protectiveness of children.

"Yes. Tigers are vicious, but not completely insane. They want something. But what?" I asked. If we could figure that out, I'd have something to chew on, something to leverage our cub's survival. Everyone was thinking furiously, but the room remained quiet for several moments.

Then Thorsten Baldurson, leader of the Viking dudes, spoke. "That diesel generator looked pretty big. They must go through a lot of fuel over time, and we have the long Fimbulvetr winter ahead of us. Can't be a ton of diesel still around after Ragnarök destroyed the world. Maybe they want to trade child for generator fuel?" he suggested.

I stared at Thorsten in shock—it made sense! Could it really be that simple?

Well, one way to find out. I snarled and the room quieted.

"Nina and Ella, in a few minutes I will need you to position yourselves on top of some of those big rocks and sight in your Robar-C50s. Tinker, you spot for the snipers and launch drones. Primary observation targets are the two enemy sniper nests and that generator. We're going to have to neutralize them before we cross that open field. Send the drones high enough to escape notice, but low enough to give us a good look at our targets. Take no action until I say.

"The rest of you, make your way to the edge of the field and find observation points, but no one steps foot out there until I give the word. Ella, get your team back here after we take down those snipers!" I ordered, looking around to make sure I was understood. Yep, I was.

"Move out," I commanded, and everyone abandoned the warmth of our underground shelter to enter the ice storm. It was very cold for humans, but we Wolves run at a hotter internal temperature. Within fifteen minutes we were all hidden, spread out along the edge of the dangerous open field. Between the swirling snow, brush, and rock falls there was plenty of cover.

I looked around. Couldn't help but notice that each of the Viking Dudes were passing around and ritually eating large mushrooms with red tops and little white specks. Of course, humans eat every chance they get, so I dismissed it as ordinary hunger, despite the odd ceremonial feel to the whole thing. I turned back to watch the shadowed nook where the Tiger base's generator sullenly stroked without ceasing. The wind sang loudly up here, reminding me of the Hu's Mongol heavy metal music we found on YouTube before the fall. There was definitely a storm coming hard.

I turned my head to the right where Ella was stretched out in a shooting stance, cradling a Robar antimaterial rifle she had obtained from Twist. She was aiming into the concealed side entrance where the chugging generator squatted. Ella could wait like that for days, if need be, until she received the signal. She is a magnificent Wolf, and I can't imagine a world without her.

I leaned closer and spoke. "Prepare to kill the generator but leave the spotlight intact. I want to see if there is a back-up generator. On my order..." I commanded. Then I clicked once on my headset and spoke to my troops concealed all along the edge of the boulder field.

"Ella, Nina, Tinker: make those Robar's happy. Give them what they love. Fire!" I ordered.

The first shot tore a hole straight through the generator's engine and the second one followed almost immediately after, blowing up the fuel tank with a crack that was very dramatic. Lots of flames and dirty-looking smoke. At about the same time, a long body fell from somewhere above on the ice cliff to smash snow by the disabled diesel generator. The spotlight high overhead flickered and went out.

"Target one down," Nina breathed.

Target two winged, no kill," Tinker whispered into the headset.

Ella's work spoke for itself.

The Plan was working so far, now we were waiting to see if a backup generator was going to automatically kick in. Wolf Haven had found it very difficult to run a pack, much less a small country, without sophisticated communications and computers. There were just too many threats out there. Information and the ability to interpret it is vital. The problem we've encountered is that all this sophisticated tech requires a reliable source of electricity.

Of course, we had our own answer to this problem waiting down at our dock: salvaged wind generators. But Thorsten was probably right about the fuel needs of a diesel generator like that. I was also pretty sure no one was importing diesel fuel in bulk to our newborn island of Olympia. Everyone in the southwest states of America were too busy keeping the massive FEMA refugee camps running down in Sonoma and Calistoga. The local radio station claims the camps are only thirty-six hours from being completely out of food. Nine-million angry Americans next door is not something to sneer at. That kind of pressure can lead politicians to take unpleasant steps.

So, then where would they find more fuel? How many stranded big rig's fuel tanks would the Tigerkin need to drain a month to keep up with their power needs? Just how many big rigs got stuck on the new-born island of Olympia after the Apocalypse? "Twenty? Fifty? Hundreds?" Certainly not enough to power Tigertown for very long. Not a long-term option. These Tigers needed power sources in the worst way.

I still had no idea how many Tigers there were, but the last time we had encountered them there were around a dozen, and this time we had only found tracks of six different Tigers. That didn't seem like enough Tigers to accomplish anything that labor intensive, much less to have enough spare time left over to mess with a nation of Wolves next door. And anyway, cats never struck me as particularly high-energy.

After sixty-seconds we had our answer. The Tigers were presently only running one big generator and we had disabled it. It would be pitch black inside those cat burrows right now.

Chaos to the enemy.

Now the Tigers were going to have to fumble around in the dark to drag out any backup generators they had on hand. And they probably wouldn't be as powerful as the big one we took out. Ventilation, power cords, light to see what they were doing. Takes time to get everything right.

It's too bad they didn't know anyone with access to a stash of wind turbines that generated electricity in the megawatt range. I looked around me again, watching the increasing violence of the snowstorm rolling up from the coast. It sure is windy up here in the Olympic mountains once you get above the tree line.

A bad storm was hurtling toward us. I could see it easily, a towering roiling black wall, shedding white as it swept out of the lowlands, swallowing everything in its path. It was coming our way quickly. We needed to move across that field to the underground Tiger base *fast*. I estimated we had less than five minutes before the storm got here.

Then I had a thought. Maybe we should catch a ride? It sounded crazy—the fury of the maelstrom could tear our bodies to pieces if it caught us wrong. A cat would never risk it.

But we are not cats, afraid of a little wet and cold. I decided that we were going to move across the field under the cover of the storm just as it hit.

With any luck, they would never see us coming.

I gave the orders and settled back into an icy stone crevice to watch the dark rumbling storm front close on us. In that peculiar moment as we waited for battle and the storm, an almost savage quiet stole across the Viking Dudes. It was weird. The overall change of mood was actually a little spooky, very unexpected for humans. They glared into the darkness as if they could see things in the storm that I couldn't. A few had started to hum in a low, threatening key. These Vikings dudes were turning out to have a grim side.

The forward edge of the storm rolled up in sound and fury, and we welcomed it with open arms. I clicked my headset to get everyone's attention as the blizzard began to rage across us.

"Stonemasons, I need the front and rear doors open as quickly as possible. Blow the hinges if you can, the entire door if you can't. Henry, Twist, Nina, Felix, and Henry: gain entry through the back door behind the dead generator. Viking dudes, secure both our exits from the Tiger's lair, then follow us in. Everyone, avoid the rockpiles. I'll accompany the front door team. Ready?" I asked.

They were.

"Attack!" I snarled.

With the clouds we came to Tigertown.

Chapter 34

UNTO THE BREECH, ONCE AGAIN

Up here in the mountains, storms hit hard. The shrieking blizzard could rip warmth from your core in minutes. It was deadly out there, but Captain Marc Christensen wasn't worried one bit.

"Lower the last dome into place and lock it down. Then move downstairs below the flight deck and help build up the initial fires. We need to warm the upstairs air around our fleet," Captain Marc Christensen ordered.

Later that evening, he took a casual walk to check out how everything was going downstairs below his small air fleet. It was quiet in the tunnels beneath the shrieking blizzard. The hastily dug walls were still damp and cold, but the burgeoning fire in the centrally located fireplaces was throwing warmth with a purpose. The harsh, blue-tinged overheads had been shut down, and only the flickering gold and crimson of the fire laid bare their surroundings.

Marc had just walked around the curve of the third underground installation when he became aware of two people wrapped up together in the cozy bunk nook carved in the wall directly across from the fireplace. It didn't sound like they were sleeping, either. He almost smiled. The Seal Cavern was fine, but everyone living on top of each other… privacy was going to be scarce and valuable. He had a feeling this would be a popular posting as the ice-age winter dragged on. He made a point of not noticing anything as he walked by studying the fire instead of the couple behind him. It got noisy again before he was out of earshot, but the new policy was set now. Maybe he and his wife Laura could arrange a fire watch some night too.

The next morning the captain and Sergeant Liam headed to the hangers to see if the warmth from below was enough to keep his Seahawks in a state of readiness. There were a lot of soldiers crawling all over his helicopters and checking everything twice. Or more.

Apparently, there wasn't a lot to do now that they were snowed in. You could either work on painstakingly expanding the Cavern with pick and explosives, or you could jog the cavern loop, constantly circling past the same non-active SEAL families; the children, grandfolk, and civilian parents of the clan. The center section of Seal Cavern was getting a little noisy these days but that was okay. The sounds of innocent play don't bother you once you've known the horrible hymn of war. It becomes like cold water in the desert.

The place was packed with competent men and women, all looking for something to do. Preferably something important, or at least interesting. They needed something, anything to keep them occupied. And the captain was all too aware of the kinds of trouble soldiers could get into when they were bored and went looking for fun in all the wrong places. He wasn't about to let *that* happen in this new post-apocalyptic world.

Drills are when you find most of the real problems, which is the whole idea of the thing. Reality too often screws up your best plans, despite your best intentions. That's why smart people war-game it. Much better odds.

He turned to his Sergeant. Liam looked back, waiting patiently to hear what his captain had to say.

"Sergeant, we need to find more ways to keep all these good soldiers too busy to get bored. I think it's time we began training in the effective use of force with what we have on hand. Let's start ready drills, too. Top four performers get a night of fire duty, a private isolated evening to share or not share, as they choose," the captain ordered. He could detect quiet smiles as his people considered the romantic refuge they had already started calling

'Firewatch'. Competition was about to go through the ceiling. Marc almost smiled but killed it at the last moment out of habit. Sometimes he forgot that he and his men were no longer Tier-Two American Special Forces.

The problem facing them was the unexpected weight of constantly-deepening snow covering the parachute-clothed geodesic dome over each helicopter. Who could have predicted an ice-age winter and ash-choked skies overhead? The snow never stopped falling and eventually the geodesic lids simply wouldn't be able to move upwards under all that weight.

And initial reports were that we simply didn't have the tools required to do the job properly. No snowblowers or sleds, there hadn't been room on board during their exodus into the wilderness.

But there was always a way. Captain Marc decided they needed to go low tech.

"Topside teams are to assemble twig brooms, so that we can manually sweep the snow off the geodesic dome, hopefully quickly. Consult the grandmas. We need to find an efficient way to quickly remove enough weight to raise dome. Break into teams and report back what works best. SEALs, I can't afford to lose a single family member, so don't stay out in the blizzard long enough to go hypothermic. I need you in working conditions," Captain Marc Christensen ordered.

It turned out that some of the civilians were quite skilled in crafting and made quick work of designing efficient twig brooms. They worked quite well although the SEALs had to go over each section at least three times to reduce the weight enough for the dome to lift. Everyone took turns snow-sweeping so no one got dangerously cold.

Unfortunately, the first time took forty-seven minutes.

Yeah, that wasn't going to work. Captain Marc swore.

"Practice it until we can go from first alert to in-the-air in under four minutes. One day our lives will depend on this, so get it right," the captain ordered.

After the eighth time through, the captain figured out something they could change. "This time, everyone concentrates on the CH-53 Super Stallion's lid. It's the largest we have, so if we can get our times down on it, we'll do fine on the smaller ones.

Ready? Go!" he ordered, and snow flew into the air so thickly that it became as if a clumpy fog had arrived and set up shop.

Three hours later they had it down to under seven minutes.

"Okay, everyone, grab some food and catch some shuteye. We're going to do it again tomorrow, but I'm proud of you tonight. Sleep well" Captain Marc Christensen said. His team seemed to straighten, and walk a little taller, if only for a bit.

Then the satellite phone rang—which never happens. Everyone froze and turned back to watch Captain Christensen pick up. He listened for a moment, said "Thirty minutes," and hung up. Marc turned to face everyone.

"Battle stations for mission. First wave. Two seahawks, fully-loaded, go in low. Expect to encounter hostile forces. We've located some old friends of ours, the Viking dudes, and it turns out those damned Tigers are messing with them. The very-same Tigers we fought in Kitsap/Bangor. Seems they've gone to ground less than sixty kilometers from our new home here in the Quinault. We have unfinished business," he said, in the kind of quiet voice you never want to let down.

"Second wave. Third Seahawk closely follows our first team's position, twenty seconds behind them. I will be aboard third craft with command staff. We will carry a Class M special weapon, so make sure you give us a little more room than we've been training for. First team secures ground, second team hits them in the jaw really hard. Launch in twenty minutes. Load up with as many smart missiles as you can. Snow teams go now," he ordered. Then Marc turned to rush to his quarters to gear up properly and grab the prototype railgun from the armory before they took off into the blizzard, barreling into the good fight as fast as they could. From bored to War in ten seconds. Marc loved it. These were the moments that made him feel fully alive.

Certainty nothing wrong with helping out a new neighbor, and maybe even turning them into allies. Worst case acceptable would be to find a friendly border state, Marc thought to himself. Seal Clan would do well with a friend or two in this new world born of the ashes of the old. And he knew the Wolfkind's history too, he had seen them when they were slave-Dogs of the Commander. This was back before they escaped Commander Elwha's military base at Indian Island, before the slave-Dogs broke free and found their way into this strange new world. The Wolves had always been known as exceptional fighters, and maybe now that they were free of the Commander's shock-collars, Marc hoped they could evolve into something…more.

Besides, somebody had to keep an eye on the Tigers. Wolf Haven was closer. Captain Mac Christensen just wanted to shoot them into a thousand pieces. But he wasn't about to declare war on a neighbor, either. So, he would owe the Wolves a favor, if Wolf Haven decided to step in.

The captain was just lending a hand to a neighbor. Unless it accelerated in the wrong direction and then the captain was going to have a warm chat with the Tigers. Very warm.

Twenty-one minutes later Captain Christensen was in the air, on his way to meet the free Wolves for the first time, in the middle of battle from what the Viking dude Thorston had explained. Marc began unpacking the equipment and strapping up with the massive railgun armor as well as the power-pack that fuels everything. The steel needles it fired weighed almost nothing in comparison, but the rest was very heavy. It took two of them to strap him up. Railguns were normally built ship-size for a reason. This was just inside a human's strength boundaries, but he could do it. Marc would do *whatever* it took to ensure his clan's survival in this new land, in this ice-age winter. Making new friends increases everyone's survival.

Plus, everyone was starting to get tired of talking to the same people every day in the Seal Clan Cavern. You've heard all their stories too often and you can't even escape outside because…blizzard. You're in command, but…trapped. Then the phone rings and you have a mission! Now everyone is running around efficiently wearing smiles. I mean, how often do you get a chance to go outside and shoot Tigers? Yeah.

Volunteers far outnumbered the available slots.

Chapter 35

CAT FIGHT

The terrible winds shrieked so loudly that normal speech was impossible. We moved at full speed across the snow-covered field under the forward edge of the terrible storm, leaping from spot to spot to avoid wading through pockets of waist-high snow or triggering the landmines I was sure were there.

Behind us the storm lifted everything into shredding whirlwinds. I sped up even faster and didn't look back.

The angry wind-gusts ahead of us could knock us down if we weren't nimble enough, but that didn't matter. We could only keep leaping forward because to fall backwards into that chaos was not an option. We were fully committed to this path forward.

Of course, it was easier for Wolves; our humans were beginning to fall dangerously behind.

The storm's crest was filled with splintered bush limbs and ice hail as large as a young human's fist, all roiling in the chaos at the front, just before us. We stayed barely behind the deadly forward edge, bounding through the open field like maddened mongooses in a den of spitting Cobras—we saw that once back in our YouTube days—glancing off the top of the snow without triggering any detonations. The precise landings of our paws minimized contact with landmines because many booby traps are reliant on tripping obstacles to set off explosions. Such static defenses only respond to forward movement, and our movements were precisely laid out to avoid that.

My Wolves were arrayed tactically around me when, a blink later, we slammed into the Tigerkin bunker's fortified entrance. The hatch door barred our way to the den where the Tiger queen lurked with her faithful followers, holding our lost cub and packmates within arm's reach. I could almost smell it.

My Stonemasons positioned themselves at the heavily armored doors in front and at the back entrance, quickly chiseling holes in the ice and stone around their edges. They moved fluidly, with a relaxed synchronicity that was beautiful to watch.

After a moment, homemade plastique was packed into the fresh-cut grooves and covered with improvised steel plates paw-bent precisely to direct the force of the explosive inward. Blasting caps were quickly inserted in the proper spots, and then wires were connected to a cell phone.

We fell back and I turned my gaze to Ella.

She held up three fingers, then two, then tapped a button on the satellite phone she had pulled from a pocket in her battle harness.

There was a boom only slightly louder than the howling wind, and the metal doors abruptly flew out into the howling maelstrom. One of them almost took Theo with it, but luckily Wolfkin are quick on their paws.

I clicked on my headset. "Front door open, entering," I stated.

"Back door open," Twist reported.

"Entering," said Nina.

And then we were in, down among the Tigers, deep in their underground compound.

Our surroundings were pitch black, and we knew that there were bad cats all around us. I snarled in challenge and was answered in a low percussive cough from somewhere ahead. It was not the only thing back there moving in the black of deepest night, either. That's okay.

Wolves have no reason to fear the dark.

I raised my nose to read the warm air flowing past me, as it was sucked out into the storm behind me. A burning green-wood fire, raw meat, old blood, and unwashed feline... the Cub! As well as my missing three packmates! All alive, but definitely not happy. I felt my shoulders relax slightly—I hadn't even realized they were tense.

Facing into the current of warm air I…

…phase into Flux.

The black world around me shudders to a snail's crawl and I am liberated from the burden of language. My mind turns over all that processing power to the fight-tasks of fine motor control and peripheral awareness. It feels as if we Wolves are the only living creatures in this molasses world everyone calls base reality.

I step forward into the moist, warm air crawling up through the entry passageway. My eyes can make out nothing in the absolute blackness.

Not a problem, because our ears hear everything, and our noses paint the night in fine detail. We can literally feel the pressure of nearby movement with our very fur. We were designed at a genetic level for battle.

We may have risen above our deadly roots, but combat continues to feel very satisfying in the depths of our souls. I find that I am savoring the looming battle. I want to punish the kidnappers and rescue our packmates. My family.

I find that I am glad none of the humans have caught up yet— the first thing they do in the dark is turn on flashlights and wave them around.

Wolves don't like to call attention to themselves until it's the moment to strike. Darkness is our ally, if sometimes a fickle one.

I step forward again, inhaling the scent trails laying all over the place.

The sound of something large breathing through its nose almost inaudibly, is slightly off to my left about four meters ahead. It has a slight cold, and the ragged inhale was as loud to me as a shout. It is very large. And tall. I silently breathe deeply, readying myself.

The overhead lights abruptly flickered back into life, revealing a huge Tiger well loaded with armament, moving effortlessly forward in a stealthy creep, stalking me. Our eyes meet. The Tiger stares at me with an alien, cold look as it freezes in the sudden light.

It wasn't that she was scared, I could tell.

There is no guilt, no weakness in this lack of motion—only a quick study of the new situation, and an underlying confidence that it is dinner time and I am on the menu.

I still myself as well.

I consider my whole-body impression of this dangerous Tiger. This is going to become a serious fight in less than an eyeblink.

Sliding forward in a spiral curve, I hear a few garbled snarls in a foreign language, no doubt cursing the generator's timing. They had that feel even though I couldn't understand the words.

Meanwhile, Ella steps closer to me and opens up with a shotgun well-stuffed with lead slugs. The Tiger in front of me is slow-motion blown sideways into a wall. She takes forever to hit the carved stone of the corridor wall.

Ella continues to slide past and partially in front of me, jacking slugs into her shotgun and rapid-firing at the Tiger's right knee until it is gone, then moving to its other knee. The big cat only now begins to crumple to the ground with molasses speed.

I re-assess my surroundings.

Primary target—down. I shift focus to my secondary goal, the female Tiger six meters to my right and closing.

She is huge. The hulking Tigerkin strides my direction, bringing a full-auto machine gun up to point at in my direction.

She covers a surprising amount of distance in a short time, closing rapidly with me. As she draws nearer, I can see that she outweighs me by at least fifty kilos and has a much longer reach than a Wolf does. The Tigerkin warrior slings a firehose of fifty-cal projectiles in my general direction. They move with gelatin speed in base reality.

Luckily, we Wolves are quick and hard to hit. We are extremely agile, so maybe the big gun is not as much of an advantage as the Tiger believes.

Besides, this is exactly what shotguns are for.

My bullpup twelve-gage is loaded with powerful incendiary rounds that Henry came up with. (For such a quiet human, Henry has a surprising knowledge of the instruments of violence).

I crack my neck as I bring my weapon to shoulder. My shotgun is much more efficient than chomping down and biting an enemy's head off, if not as viscerally satisfying.

Or maybe I just want to completely annihilate anyone who had a part in stealing our cub. It *is* the only way to make sure it never happens again.

And I am very angry.

The rounds leave a gaping hole through its massive head, which is still sort of attached to the rest of it. There isn't much of a throat there anymore. Good armor though. The enemy can still run, but that won't save these damned Tigerkin from my pack's furious attention. We *will* recover our people.

I phase out of Flux, tumbling back into mundane reality.

Immediately I feel drained, exhausted as world started running normally again. The tiredness didn't matter. Wolves never stay down.

I scanned my left quadrant for the third Tiger Ella and Theo had rushed. Ella has switched to her M4, letting the searing barrel of her shotgun hang free on its tether under her right arm. She appeared to be continuing with her new tactics of crippling her enemies' lower body. I realize that Ella has decided to immobilize the enemy so we can deal with them at our leisure later, after we rescue our packmates. Lives before revenge—it's simple logic. Besides, it is obvious to me that Ella believes these monsters have forfeited any right to a quick death.

I agree.

Ankles and knees seemed to be her favorite targets; it appeared that the Chinese Tigers' body armor had a few built-in flaws. I follow Ellas' lead and focus on the weak points of the Tigerkin's body armor.

Of course, I had noticed Ella and the chef from Wudang Mountain talking intensely earlier, when we left the giant boulders shielding our forward base.

Henry is a very knowledgeable human. An exceptional soldier from the birthplace of true Taichi, Wudang Mountain, he has the true heart of a Wolf. Henry says that's what twenty years in the People's Liberation Army does to a man. I think he is being very modest or humorous, but I can't tell which.

Henry was rapidly becoming one of my favorite humans. He didn't talk much, but that's a bonus in my eye.

I scanned the entrance chamber one last time. It was full of looted locker-room benches, raised on raw pine platforms, and tons of cast-off winter snowsuits and skis, there was even a pile of huge boots that I didn't think any of my Wolves were large enough to wear.

I was pretty sure that professional soldiers would take better care of their gear than this. But everything else about these Tigers spoke of highly-disciplined soldiers. It just didn't make sense to me. I growled in frustration.

We *were* making progress though. Twenty seconds in, we had one sniper down with the other disabled, and two Tigers incapacitated, at least for the moment.

Unfortunately, that left at least four Tigerkin and perhaps as many as eight more that we hadn't run into yet.

Let them come.

I strode forward out of the mud room with my Wolves around me, entering a large corridor leading deeper into the Tigers' den.

Tigers think weird, but I'm guessing they are superb tacticians, at least as long as they're winning. These underground tunnels had been built in deliberate bind spots and long stretches ending in hardened bubbles that could hold some of the bigger weapons. The whole layout was designed to wear down large numbers of attackers, leaving a weakened, diminished, and tired opponent for them to play with before they ate them.

Yeah, we have no illusions about Tigers, I thought, but then wondered if it all might be a little more complex than that? I stretched my shoulders, shrugging off the burden of second-guessing myself while at war. These kinds of thoughts could wait until after the action. We needed to figure out exactly where we were going.

Tigerkind has widened our world, and not in a good way. My Wolves all agreed that the most terrible place we could think of for the enemy to position itself was where they could quickly punish an attacker by hurting or killing their child, preferably in front of them.

We Wolves found this whole concept abhorrent. This ruthless strategy was carried out on the innocents, for the profit of the wicked!

I felt a hot anger growing brighter and fiercer in my heart. These Tigers were an aggressive blend of cold pragmatism and cruelty. We were all meat or toys to them, and they liked to play with their food. Wolves were not food!

It was time to get our people back.

I raised my shotgun to shoulder and growled low and mean into the dark before us.

Chapter 36

DOWNTOWN TIGERTOWN

We ran downwards at first, and then the four-meter-wide tunnel began to rise, climbing up into the ancient glacier we had studied earlier. We quickly passed a series of open storage rooms filled with split wood, drums of reeking diesel fuel, and boxes of assorted salvaged junk. Diesel kills our sense of smell after a few seconds, so we didn't linger. Well, most of us; Theo and Twist kept breaking off to plant explosives behind the fuel drums, but they caught up fast. This was just a last resort tactic that we didn't intend to use. Unless we had to.

The choice wasn't always up to us.

The icy tunnel was poorly lit by long strands of low-wattage bulbs. There was just enough light for us to get to the next patch, and we Wolves don't need much to see by. Henry and the Viking dudes had high-intensity lights attached to their rifles; they ended up turning them on in a few spots.

We came to a new, heavily trampled tunnel that broke off to the right of the main one. It had plastic walk-in refrigerator curtains, puffing out slightly into the corridor. I paused, lowered my body to four legs, and pushed my head through to breathe in the warm draft flowing our way.

I smelled Tiger.

And our cub and missing Wolves! Gun oil and wood fires and damp velvet. Hours-old human blood. Wolf blood, too.

I snarled. Anger is a potent stimulant, maybe a little habit-forming, but this was a whole level up—a thing called Fury—and all bets were off.

I touch my deer-horn Bagua blades (a gift from Henry) in their holster at the small of my back. That was good enough for now. We moved up the passageway as one, quickly as we could. We were closing in on our missing packmates, but I was keenly aware that it had been almost two minutes since we blew up the Tiger queen's front door. A lot can happen in that time.

Of course, we continued storming the Queen's lair, but suddenly everyone could hear all hell breaking loose up ahead. Abruptly, I could smell fresh pack blood in the air.

Howling in fury, I...

...phase into Flux.

The world around me turns to syrup.

I drink the world around in scent and sight even as my legs propel me upwards to the large room I am just beginning to perceive ahead. I jam sensory data into tight bundles that I digest whole, instantly. Mundane linear thought just can't compete at times like these.

I am completely aware of everything around me, without focusing on any one thing. My rage has become something cold instead of the burning fury of the everyday world. This somehow makes me faster, as I stride another step closer to the Queen's lair.

We all know it's a trap.

And one I fully intend to trip, once we've gotten past it, of course.

Three steps from the steel ship's hatch set into the ice tunnel's end, I see that someone conveniently left it cracked open. I sneer.

Yeah. Trap.

Leaping forward without hesitation, I burst through hatch door.

I am fully aware that my momentum will soon land me in the middle of an unseen battle site where Tigers are waiting to kill me.

Unless, of course...

I hit the hatch door hinges with my lower-paws while grabbing ahold of the side of the door frame with my uppers. I swing the rest of the way around to the right wall, let go, and started running down the wall until I hit the floor.

As I slip through the molasses world of base reality, I assess my surroundings with unfocused vision that will quickly alert me to any movement. I will have plenty of time to focus then.

Slipping my deer-horn blades from their quick-release sheaths at the small of my back, I charge at my still-unseen enemy at the speed of Flux. I don't need to see them; soundscapes are all-telling and my nose paints flamboyant scenes. I barrel at speed into the room, whipping my Bagua blades in a flowing infinity-loop overhead.

I sense Ella come in behind me, turn to see her land on the chamber floor. Ella balances effortlessly atop a pile of treacherous fluffy pillows. She doesn't look like she is in the mood for fluffy, so I am not surprised when she snarls, kicks free of the nasty soft things and raises her M4 to her right shoulder.

We study the chamber intensely…and I find myself dropping out of Flux, only for a moment, to take in the surroundings better.

There were a few pillow piles tucked into low-lit nooks and crannies of the large room. The chamber was dominated by a large-screen television and a crackling fire in a polished black stone fireplace. It was large enough to roast a pig in, if you liked your meat that way.

A huge emerald-green Victorian couch was neatly placed in front of the TV, and to the side of the blazing fireplace. This didn't look like the den of a monstrous dictator with a taste for human flesh. It looked…comfy.

Three Tigers stood gathered in front of the fireplace with that deceptive look of relaxed aristocracy. It didn't fool any of us—everyone knows that a relaxed muscle is much faster than a tensed one—and these Tigerkin were relaxed in the worst of ways.

I suddenly remembered a YouTube vid we had watched on the deadliness of notorious human crime queens. Pretty sure any queen in that kind of hybrid body was all kinds of dangerous. Great. However, while I certainly wasn't underestimating this cladder of Tigers in front of me, I also wasn't particularly concerned with them at this precise moment.

At first, I had been focused on the two Tigers waiting on either side of the chamber door as we leapt into the room. Of course, I had immediately known that they were there; I could smell the rancid gun oil from their heavy machine guns cradled in their oversized paws. Somebody had run out of machine oil!

This is way things are in these early days on the recently-created Olympic Island, where tech is already rare and expensive, and critter fat fills a multiple of second tier roles. Unfortunately, this has not been a historically successful approach, but then you do what you must in order to insure the survival of your people, your pack and tribe.

Luckily base reality runs at a faster pace than the mundane world—and I phase back effortlessly. That's why the first two Tigerkin killers are still aiming at the door we just came through. Mired in the gelatin world of mundane reality, they haven't yet realized that not only has their sector been penetrated, but the enemy is not where they expected.

I maintain an elevated sense of awareness of all Tigerkin in the room, but now I am focused with deadly intent on the three Tigers in front of the fireplace. There is no questioning that they are the predominant threat in the room.

I step closer.

At first, the Tigerkind were barely aware of, and even seemed amused at my entrance. This was entirely the wrong thing to be thinking about.

I held my fury under control, glaring at Queen Malgato, but it bounced off her without effect, because she was not even fully aware of us in the room with her and her Tigers yet. Downside of base reality, I sometimes forget about.

I abruptly notice the huge male at the queen's right is slowly raising something in his paw overhead. I look closer. The Tiger clutches the severed left foot of a Wolfkin, dripping a dark red blood that reeks of pack.

My head explodes outwards into a new, deadlier shape that I don't recognize.

The world around me shivers into even slower motion as I Flux-tear a hole through still air, aimed precisely at the center-mass of the only male Tiger we have encountered so far. He looms over us in ignorant arrogance, overconfident in his disdain.

A flash thought pops up.

"What if this is the only male left of her species? How valuable does that make him to the queen Tiger? Could he be the key to the future of Tigerkind?" I wonder as I wield my high-carbon-steel double-crescent knives as easily and naturally as I breath.

I am aware of a dawning horror in the Tiger queen's huge eyes as I snap past on her right, too fast for even the Queen to focus on. But she doesn't need to see me to know where I'm going.

"Se-e-ergeannt Ti-i-im-i-ing!" Her roar rumbles over my head interminably as I leap.

I hit the huge male Tiger at full speed, head-butting him in the gut as my twin fighting knives slice up his inner thighs in search of an artery. But his massive legs are covered in layers of thick muscle and I can't find a bleeder before I am peeled off like a thirsty swamp-leech in search of a drink. His cuts are healing as I watch. So are mine.

I curl out of the male Tiger's clawed grip only by leaving a little Wolf meat behind. I continue my roll until I am on my feet, almost close enough to touch the queen. Sergeant Timing freezes motionless behind me, watching his queen closely for instruction. He knows better than to swat at his queen's mouse. Surprisingly, I am oddly safe at that moment, at least from his corner of the room.

The towering Tiger queen stands close to three-meters high, with a massive head that is only slightly human and a long, silky-furred torso balanced on legs bred for pouncing. She wears a heavy war harness stuffed with lethal blades, spikes, grenades, and garrotes. And that was just what I could see from here.

Cats are sneaky.

I fix my focus on her, holding still; she has a Gatling mini-gun tucked behind her right shoulder, but what really holds my attention is the barely glimpsed auto-crossbow stuffed with black quarrels dripping with something that stunk of death. She holds it almost out of sight with her left paw but I can still see and smell it. I drift into fighting stance slowly enough not to trigger the feline's chase instincts. The Tiger queen glares intently at me as she takes another step closer. She leans forward to tower over me, baring her very-impressive teeth in an alpha-predator's unmistakable challenge.

That's when something changes, and she goes all still and deadly, not because me. I quickly look around, but I don't see what has changed…

But something has… something important.

Her left arm holding the crossbow begins, ever so slowly, to rise, but it isn't pointed at any of us or even where she is looking. Her weapon is beginning to aim further to her left, where abruptly I can just make out my missing Wolves as they emerge from behind the Tiger queen, running as fast as they can with our cub Rachel protectively nestled between them! Our cub doesn't have nanites like most of the pack does, so they shield Rachel with their own, unarmored bodies.

Just because my fleeing Wolves are unarmed doesn't mean they're helpless. Their powerful bodies are all they have to offer in this fight, and they give it without hesitation. We cherish our young.

I howl furiously as I leap to snap my jaws at the Tiger Queen's upper left arm and miss. I don't think she was expecting that though, because she also misses her shot and fires past me.

Then the massive Tigerkin hits me like a freight train, hurling that heavy elongated body into my right side, forcing me to choose between guarding my neck from those huge jaws or protecting my already bruised ribs. Her teeth certainly look huge, up this close and personal. Her breath is hot and smells of decaying flesh.

I twist downwards to my left and hopefully out of range of those fangs. The ribs, not so much.

But yes, Tigers hit hard. Effectively. And they weigh a lot.

The downside of moving all that mass of muscle and teeth is that they get tired fast.

Tigerkind simply aren't built for the long chase or extended combat. Wolves, on the other hand, are. This is what we Wolves call a weakness, and its where we attack when we're out-massed and out-fanged. Like now.

The Tiger Queen and I whirl and bite and slash, clawing at each other for what seems like forever, but our wounds stop bleeding in seconds, and we both heal almost immediately. We are closely matched in this kind of fight, so I know I need to change the battle. And my nanites simply aren't going to be able to keep up with all the damage much longer.

I abruptly phased out of Flux *against my will*. Bad time to find out that you could only maintain yourself in base reality for so long before it dumped you. *Ouch.*

The sudden exhaustion I experienced upon reentering the mundane world was sharper than usual, which didn't help much in staying ahead of those snapping teeth and terrible claws. Maybe it was a good thing we couldn't stay too long in Flux.

I found myself teetering on the edge of slowing to mundane speed. And that wasn't good, because then I would become fresh meat for Tigers. And Wolves aren't food. So, I fought harder than I realized I could and for longer than I believed was possible.

We broke apart to land in separate messy piles. We were both panting heavily now, our fur stained crimson in the darker hues. My head was splitting and the rest of me was very unhappy. I was in no hurry to continue this ground-fight and by the Tiger's motionless position and loud panting, neither was she.

Next time, I decided, I would just have to shoot her a bunch with my biggest gun.

Chapter 37

THE ART OF BATTLE

As my breathing finally slowed down, I looked around me to take note of my surroundings. Ella, Tinker, and Sigrid were methodically defeating their adversaries and the rest of my team was busy chasing the remaining machine-gun toting Tigers, who in turn were vindictively pursuing the Wolf-cub express.

Everybody disappeared into another room to my right, the one that seemed better lit than the one we were currently in. My guys were in dedicated pursuit of our escaping pack members in order to render aid and deal damage to anyone attempting to stop us, in equal measures.

I returned my gaze to my main opponent, the big female Tiger. She was back on her feet now as well, but stayed where she was for the moment. She still hadn't caught her breath. Her male sergeant loomed quietly at her back showing me his teeth over her wide shoulder when she wasn't looking. They were truly impressive teeth, but I gave no sign that I even noticed *him*. That didn't go down so well, but he stayed where he was. The queen Tiger extruded a dollop of professional disdain almost slight enough to miss, but only almost. This level of precision communication skills in an alpha predator was not a good thing by any measure.

"We are Queen Malgato of Tiger Mountain Kingdom," the Tiger queen purred. "You have trespassed on my lands, wandering across my country's borders without acknowledgment or respect.

You will cease. Trespassing on imperial lands is traditionally rewarded with a slow and painful death. You are lucky—we have decided to accept your Wolf Haven as a vassal border-state, one that pays hefty taxes to their Tiger superiors and follows their wishes in all matters. If you have problems understanding this, we will try to use simpler words," she sneered.

Right. I don't know what she expected, but it was obviously not what happened next. All the Wolves in the room were immediately infuriated, howling and snarling in anger at her words. It got pretty noisy for a moment. Then the towering Sergeant Timing roared back.

"Shut up! Now we own your filthy dog asses!" the Tiger mocked us. His sneer infuriated me, cold icing on a cake made of our worst memories.

Once we were slave-Dogs of the Commander, to use and kill as wastefully as he wished. We were fed swill in rusty troughs like animals and killed the enemy without mercy, because we had never known mercy ourselves. Then one day we woke up. We fought all the way to the promised land, the Hoh rain forest, where we have made a new home, a nation for all species—Wolf Haven.

We have risen far above our ignoble birth and will <u>never</u> be slaves again! But that was what the damned Cats wanted! Our complete subjugation! I felt my head lowering and my teeth showing more than usual.

Growling way down in the sub-woofer range, I could feel my pack's rage burning hot all around me. I took a deep breath to calm myself, then leaned forward and snarled real low as I chambered a special shell into my bullpup twelve-gage's chamber. This ammo had been specifically loaded for Siberian Tigerkind by a vengeful Henry Chin. He assured me that his ammo would drop a bull elephant at ten paces. Tigers too.

"Make no mistake. Ours is a nation established by Wolves, with room for every kind of people or species. Maybe even Tigers. But we are nobody's slaves anymore. There will never be **any** slavery in Wolf Haven. We don't give a damn what Tigers think," I said bluntly.

Would the queen reach out to claw my face or would she consider my words?

"I see," she purred dangerously, her voice rising gradually to a roar. "Let me use little words even you can understand, Pooch. You are our property, you will come when we whistle, and lick our boots when they need that extra polish. If you defy us, we will punish you until you break, and are pathetically grateful for any rancid tidbits we toss your way. Now, down little doggies, on your filthy bellies! Crawl!"

I looked over at Ella and snarled, "Henry is here. Now!"

Then I was done with words and phased into Flux.

Chapter 38

WUDANG COMES TO TIGERTOWN

Henry can hear them long before he sees them.

Somewhere behind him in this icy labyrinth, the Viking dudes are stomping in sync as they low-volume croon a savage tune, all in some arcane language he has never heard before.

Henry can feel the distant music in his *Dantien* more than actually hear it. Despite the lack of volume, it remained not a little creepy, and while Henry has faced many dangerous situations in his life, it generally takes a lot to creep him out.

But this is different.

These are no longer the same men and women he pleasantly shared a fire with last night.

Tonight, in a little over an hour, he had watched them transform into something else. Something strange and very deadly. After a moment, Henry mentally shrugged—he was deadly himself when necessary, so who was he to look a gift ally in the teeth? In this place and time, 'deadly' was a desirable trait. And three of those massive Tigerkin could be a handful for a single fighter, even a man with his highly-trained skills and knowledge.

Henry learned long ago that everything goes better with a little help and he knew exactly where to find that help. Just listen for the scary humming.

The man from Wudang Mountain reached the translucent walk-in curtains at the end of the tunnel and burst into the main corridor, making a hard turn to his left. The White Wolf Nina floated silently in his wake with her M4 locked to her shoulder.

Henry Chin gently bounced off the next corner but lost no speed as he made the turn. The tunnel began to slope downwards and he had covered maybe twelve-meters when the next set of almost-clear plastic curtains were violently torn free and a bunch of angry Tigerkin spilled out into the passageway in front of him.

These Tigers were spitting mad and even noisier than the Viking dudes, which was very good. He didn't want the enemy to notice his fast-approaching reinforcements. He hoped the Viking dudes fought as well as they sang scary music. Henry had a feeling that this impending battle was less than certain in outcome.

He was going to have to move very fast to live through the next hour and accomplish the mission. Henry never forgot that he still had a ship to kill. A family to avenge.

Then he could finally rest.

Sifu Henry sinks his chi down below his navel and….

…shifts smoothly into Zen mode, just as hundreds of his ancestors on Wudang Mountain have over the last thirteen-centuries. The ordinary concerns of his life fade away as his muscles loosen in preparation for Battle. The world around him comes slows drastically down. Henry stops processing most sound, leaving the world around him on the edge of silent. He is peripherally aware of all movement around him.

He stretches his next stride longer, reducing his total steps by a fraction. Henry is in an all-out sprint, and only four meters from the storeroom entrance where some of the Viking dudes wait in rhythmic stomp. He knows that the other seven Viking dudes are spread out in the blizzard, covering both entrances to the underground bunker and this passageway.

Henry can sense the massive Tiger queen drawing closer to him, a molasses roar vibrating out from behind her saber teeth and a white-hot fury burning in her gut. The intensity of her anger is muted in base reality, allowing Henry the sensory insulation necessary to rise above it all.

It's still going to be close. Henry reaches deeper inside himself and somehow finds the extra speed he need. He reaches the storage room entrance and passes it.

The Tigers are not so lucky.

The Viking dudes hit them from the side, smashing bone and rib as they sandwich the bad cats between the wall and old-school Viking berserkers.

The Dudes tear into the Tigerkin in lockstep like a buzzsaw factory, laying waste to everything before them in savage song, expertly wielding close quarter weapons—blade and shotgun. These are hands-on kind of people.

But that's a lot of angry Tiger to lay hands on. The damage is going both ways.

The difference is that the Tigers are healing as they fight, their nanites on overdrive. Viking dudes don't have nanites. Their wounds don't heal in minutes and tend to slowly degrade the body's ability to fight once they start leaking red stuff.

The deadly Tiger claws and fangs aren't slowing down the northern barbarians yet, though, Henry notes. Then the moment reaches fullness and it's time.

Henry T-steps and is suddenly facing the way he came, whipping his twin deer-horn blades in perfect arcs over his head and shoulders in Autumn-Wind-Sweeps-Leaves, sliding closer and closer to the furious Queen Malgato. His Bagua crescent moon knives grow warm in the air-cutting spin, building fury for the moment of contact.

For his next step.

The massive fang-filled jaws of an enraged Tiger slow-snap a few centimeters over Henry's blade-filled hands as he dips and then rises in Monkey-Picks-Grapes. He automatically adjusts the angle of his whirling high-carbon steel and begins to slice into the reinforced leather collar around the hulking Tigerkin's throat as his right leg simultaneously snaps out to pierce the Tigerkind's solar plexus. She staggers back.

Now she *sees* the mouse from Wudang.

The queen gelatin-slaps several razor-filled paws at Henry's face but he is never there when the blow arrives. The Tiger queen has stretched tall to bite and claw down at him, so Henry T-steps and spins low around the Tigerkin's right side, slashing the unarmored part of the Tiger's belly open like unzipping a purse. Before the queen can focus on him Henry T-steps again, reversing his circle around the massive Tigerkind, cutting as he goes. Intestines make a brief appearance and the queen quickly clutches one paw to her belly, intent on keeping her insides inside until the damage can be reversed by her frenzied nanites.

In the meantime, this momentarily gives her only one arm to fight with and everyone around her realizes it at the same time. Sergeant Timing roars in outrage and fury, but Henry isn't listening.

Circling an angry one-armed Tigerkin is easy—you just stay on their injured side. Henry continued doing as much damage as possible, spinning around the angry queen, going for the joints or her throat whenever an opening appears. So far, his strikes have been too shallow, the tough feline muscles and tendons are like steel wire and difficult to slice through in a single cut. He needs more time and a heavier blade. Wudang steel would be perfect.

But there *isn't* any more time. Henry senses something huge about to tear into him on his right side. It is moving like warm pancake syrup on a cold morning and closing on him with all the inevitability of an avalanche. Henry isn't going to be able to avoid contact this time.

Sergeant Timing's hulk strides closer, leaning over towards him, spraying projectiles from an enormous machine gun he has butted up against his right hip. His damaged arm is holding down the trigger, and the torrent of lead is slowly swinging Henry's direction. Mired in the agonizingly-slow world of mundane reality, the Tigerkind gradually brings his bullet firehose to spray where Henry used to be, a blink ago.

Henry is now behind the queen, who has begun activating fragmentation grenades and throwing them further down the tunnel ahead of her. That only takes one arm, and is surprisingly effective, if you don't care much about your ability to hear things. She dashes down the tunnel as the first blast finishes, already throwing the next grenade down-tunnel. She tosses one back in Henry's direction without even looking, just for good measure.

It bounces twice on the tunnel floor and clatters into the storeroom where the Viking dudes were concealed a few seconds ago. The same storeroom with the drums of diesel fuel in which Twist had concealed the Wolves' homemade plastique.

It seemed like a good idea at the time, because you never know when you'll need to burn the enemy's base to cinders. The Wolves didn't expect to have to use it, but also didn't take anything off the table when it came to the safety of the pack.

Unfortunately, it turns out that Chinese fragmentation grenades make exceptional blasting caps.

It's not possible to outrun an explosion, even in Flux.

But sometimes you do have time to duck and cover. Henry goes full out, leaping for the freezer-curtains that now hung in shreds at the entrance to the tunnel leading back to the queen's lair. The only problem with putting everything you have into running in a straight line is that now the furious Sargant Timing has more time to shoot you, at least if he's not paying close attention to his surroundings. He still misses.

When the blast wave hits, even hulking Tigers tend to char. And Tigerkin are a much larger target than a compact human like Henry, and therefore take significantly more damage. Henry makes it around the corner, but the blast-furnace hot air and the unholy reek of singed feline fur and burnt flesh makes him breathe in short, shallow breaths. This was automatic; soldiers experience and smell many terrible things in war. You learn to adapt and try to forget, but your body knows, no matter how long it has been or how hard you try not to remember.

Suddenly, the ice ceiling overhead shatters like crystal into a jagged falling mass, crashing to the floor and burying everything under it. The Tigers were lucky—they managed to be on the far side of the cave-in when the ceiling collapsed. Henry Chin survived as well but didn't consider himself lucky at all, because he viewed honorable death in battle as an opportunity to rejoin his beloved first family in heaven.

Henry ignored the unpleasant aftereffects of rapidly phasing back into mundane reality and climbed to his feet. He dusted himself off and then stepped closer to the tunnel blockage, trying to see a way through the cascading barrier of broken glacier ice and the occasional boulder.

It appeared that the way forward was completely blocked, cutting off all access to the main entrance to the Tiger's underground bunker from this side. He thought about Queen

Malgato and her Tigers escaping out through the main entrance and immediately spun in the direction of the back door he originally entered through. By the time he got there the way out would probably be clear, due to the Tiger's fondness for grenades. The Viking dudes guarding the door would be either dead or fled. And then there would be nothing left to stop the Tigers from escaping and reacquiring Rachel and the other escaping Wolves outside the complex. Henry shared a look with the white wolf Nina. This was simply not acceptable.

Henry exhales in exasperation, and they begin running up the entrance tunnel to the queen's lair. They were going to have to take the long way around, back the way he had originally come. Henry regulated his breathing and changed his gait to match Nina's as they burst into Queen Malgato's now-empty pillow palace. Nina led the way to a door standing ajar at the other end of the room. Nothing was going to stop him until all his people were safe and home. Henry wasn't about to lose one of his new family's children. People rarely got a second chance in life, and Henry was not a man to undervalue that. Losing one family in a lifetime was far too much to bear.

Two was unthinkable.

Chapter 39

THE WORLD IS BLEACHED AND I MUST SEE

…I phase into Flux and the universe around me stutters to a crawl. Both the ability and desire to use language falls from me in a brilliant white light that never hurts my eyes. I balance in the moment between heartbeats, studying the world around me with eyes that see things as they truly are, without all that comfortable illusion. Base reality is like that. It's not for everyone.

But I think I was born to it.

Ella has phased into Flux with me. A meter away the Tiger Queen Malgato stands in frozen mid-snarl, moving so slowly that I can barely perceive her movement. Of course, it is me who has sped up, but in base reality this seems like an illusion. We dash through the syrup world around us, following the curve of the left wall, leading the Tiger queen and her soldiers to where we want them.

Suddenly Queen Malgato freezes, her eyes riveted on Henry Chin. It is obvious that she forgot all about Ella and me for the moment, not realizing that we are no longer where we stood a split second ago.

Ella and I attain full-flux-speed just as we enter the room that our missing Wolves and enemy Tigerkin disappeared into. Abruptly, I find myself losing traction on the slick floor, power-sliding into the doorway much harder than I intended.

I kick off the doorframe and enter a brighter lit room, one stuffed with large potted plants and a wide frosted window. There is even a long fancy desk, but not a pillow pile in sight! Guess this wasn't a place you relaxed in. War room maybe? My missing Wolves are nowhere to be seen. Ella spots another door leading onto a balcony of sorts. I actually bend the doorframe as I tear my way out in mad pursuit.

The blizzard outside has reached one of those odd, calm moments, when the wind drops like it does in the eye of a great storm. The moonlight has a strange hue to it and the snow continues to fall in heavy flakes. For an uncounted moment, there is an eldritch hush laying across the mountain.

I screech to a stop at a chest-high ice balcony overlooking the kill zone—the no-man's land we so recently crossed. Ella appears beside me and we gaze over the edge together. The ice is severely scraped up on top of the balcony. This is where they went over.

Below us a lies a white blanket of open ground. It is ten meters below us and wildly disturbed, far beyond the constant snowfall's ability to conceal. Ella and I raise our heads and howl into the night our determination to find our missing pack.

I leap over the edge and fall to the snowy field far below. I hit the ground running and Ella lands at the same time. We rip through thick drifts of ivory, bleeding off our inertia until we come to a full stop. The cold snow feels good and numbs our minor injuries as our nanites heal us.

I study the ground before us. The disturbances in the snow that our people left behind are obvious. Ella and I immediately take off to follow the broken trail in perfect symmetry. Visibility is less than fifteen-meters in the thickly falling snow and I can't see them yet, but my missing pack's scent saturates the broken trail and very air we blast through. We are so close, but I can't quite tell by how much.

I check my bullpup twelve-gauge to make sure there is a shell in the breech and a full load of cat slugs for the third time, then push myself to move even faster through the waist-high snow, glued to the crumpled trail leading to my people. I am gaining on them; we should be catching up pretty fast.

That's when I see the Tiger.

She stands motionless in mottled silver moonlight, her powerful hybrid body tall in the falling snow. She is at the edge of sight, where the world dissolves into bleached white. The Tigerkin holds a heavy machine gun with both arms, the weapon's stock pushed against her left shoulder. She is looking down her trail in our direction with an unfocused stare designed to catch movement instead of detail.

She hasn't seen us yet. But she will.

I fall to all fours and veer left into the unbroken snow drifts. My speed immediately drops alarmingly. Ella's and my heads are below the snow level of the no-mans-land around us, leaving us invisible to the enemy at this distance. We rapidly crawl forward through the snowdrifts with predator grace, packing down virgin snow and closing on the enemy Tiger standing lone watch.

After we have gone about ten-meters, I pop my head up out of our snow trench to take a quick look around. Then I drop back down before I can be seen, close my eyes, and visualize the ground around us I had seen it.

The huge Tiger is now gone, faded into the swirling white snowstorm.

She was acting like a rearguard of a squad moving through hostile territory. That meant we weren't tracking just a single Tigerkin now. This meant that there was more than one Tiger hunting my people. Ella reads my realization and angrily snarls in harmony to my own roar of fury.

Never stand between me and my people. You have taken my packmates, and hell's fury has now come 'a hunting you. The Alpha is here, and your remaining moments of life are measured on one paw... if we decide to grant you the release of a quick death.

Depends on what we find.

Ella leaps forward gracefully, following the roadmap written in packed snow and broken branches. We come to a narrow, deep ravine and she leaps over the untrampled snow below and lands, blurring as she breaks into motion in an unbroken forward stride, relentlessly following the trail of our packmates and at least two Tigers. I am at her side within two steps, as together we tracked down our missing people, who were in turn being hunted by Tigers.

There wasn't much time left to save our kidnapped family members. As we ran, I studied the signs left behind in the disturbed snow. We never paused, hurling through the harlequin night in furious pursuit of our missing pack. I knew that we were being reckless, but my heart was full of worry and anger all mixed up together. It didn't matter, though. I bent my muzzle closer to the ground. Fitz and Rachel and the others were still in the lead, but that was dwindling. The new blood spots I spotted in the snow weren't decreasing in size and disappearing the way they should, if a Wolfkind's nanite system were working properly. I didn't like the smell of this. There was only one thing I could think of to explain that—it meant my Wolves were being repeatedly reinjured–that they were being shot over and over as they fled.

I knew Fury in that moment and it fully possessed me for the next few minutes. I somehow moved even faster. But the scent-picture painted by their tracks didn't get any prettier.

Two Tigerkin were about forty-meters behind our missing Wolves. Ella and I were less than thirty-meters behind them, and rapidly closing the distance between us. Everyone was paralleling the ice cliff. I just hoped the sniper we wounded coming in wasn't still up there on his perch drawing a bead on us right now. We ran full out across the broken snow, intent on catching up while hopefully not getting blown to pieces.

Then a number of things happened all at once.

First, Ella and I closed the gap to ten-meters between us and the rearmost Tigerkin.

Second, as we passed the front door to the Tigers' bunker that had been reduced to rubble on our way in, suddenly, the hole in the cliff wall belched out billowing smoke and brimstone, bruising our ears as only multiple detonating fragmentation grenades can—even at this distance.

Third, the Tigers we were chasing finally closed the gap between themselves and our missing pack members. They were close enough to smack.

And lastly, the Tiger queen and two of her Tigers burst out of the front door of Tigertown on the side of the ice cliff, in full attack-mode. They were only twenty meters from our fleeing packmates, who were actually running *in their direction* at that moment.

All I could do was focus on the objective—to keep our packmates alive until my remaining forces could get there. Everything else was secondary. This included smiting of Tigers, which was very disappointing for some of us. Most of us. Well, actually all of us were looking forward to teaching the enemy a lesson they won't forget. But Wolves at war are nothing if not disciplined. The hostages came first.

The rest could wait.

Our experience with Tigerkind was that Tigers always initiate hostilities quickly, usually in a machine-gun hail of lead followed by a powerful pounce. This pattern differs very little from situation to situation. And this wasn't the first time I had fought this Tiger queen either, so I knew a little about what to expect.

It didn't make any difference; I didn't like what I saw one bit.

The Tigers were now physically closer to our fleeing Tribe than we were to the pursuing Tigerkin. Ella and I simply weren't going to be able to reach them in time. It was a terrible realization, but my Wolves have been through the anvils of hell and emerged burned free of impurities. We are high-carbon steel now, and we will slice our way through any enemy that stands between us and our pack.

I didn't waste energy on howling or gnashing my teeth. If it all went bad, I would need every bit of anger I had to be able to stand over my fallen and punish the guilty until there was nothing left of them larger than a toe.

My eyes burned strangely, but I ignore this sensation like I am everything not important to the mission. I'm phasing in and out of Flux, unable to remain in that state but pressing myself beyond the limit, to get as high a speed as I can. Ella, just slightly faster, moves ahead of me… That's when I realize the sound of helicopters has been gradually increasing in volume in the background, unnoticed in the fury of battle.

Then the sky opened up above us and the terrible thunder of Navy Seahawk's heavy machineguns fell between us like acid rain.

The hard crack of what later turned out to be an experimental rail gun punctuated the machinegun's metallic scream and my ears hurt every time it fired. There was only one person this unseen force could belong to.

Commander Elwha, our former master. And now the sadistic monster has found us, his runaway mutts!

I shudder involuntarily as I remember what the Commander does to bad Dogs. Then I shake my head and remember that we are nobody's Dogs anymore. We are free Wolves!

We can't be enslaved, because we no longer fear the Master. We would rather die than put on the shock collars again.

So be it.

I lift my head and snarl my defiance at the Seahawk overhead, as it continues dropping closer and closer to us. Ella touches my shoulder with her left paw and I know that I am never alone, that my mate will fight to the death to protect her pack, same as me. Pack is pack. I sling a quick look of raw emotion at Ella, before turning to search for my target on one of the two hovering Seahawk helicopters.

I have decided that I will sink my sharp teeth into our former Master, Commander Elwha, before I go down.

It is very difficult to stop a furious Wolf on a mission when they aren't concerned with an exit strategy. Any person who doesn't care if they live out the day can be an almost unstoppable force if they apply themselves properly.

I am numb now but my mind grows crystal-clear in a strange state of grace, as I crouch, preparing to leap high and close with my enemy, our hated former Master. The Seahawk helicopter is slowly dropping down out of the storm right on top of us. The Commander's forces are here to punish us for running away, to discipline his bad Dogs. Ella and I are leaking growls nonstop.

The Commander is about to get a big surprise. I'm not his half-starved "slave-Dog Three" anymore. Now I am the Alpha Wolf Trey and I'm about to bite the Commander's little round head clean off.

I was on the edge of leaping upwards to savage the Commander when the unholy scream of a railguns hyper-speed needle stream tears a meter-wide trench in the frozen ground. A trench that separates Queen Malgato's team from my lost Wolves. The screaming needle storm has separated the two parties in a deadly barrier none will brave. When the terrible weapon stopped firing, the ringing silence that followed was shocking, broken only by a few loud ticks like cooling metal.

"What?" I snarled in confusion, somehow back in the mundane world. Why were Ella and I still alive and free? Why did the Commander ignore us and interfere with the Tiger queen's capture of my packmates? Did he want to capture both the Tigers and his runaway mutts too? Or did he just want the pleasure of killing us himself?

Why wasn't anybody fighting?

A panting Henry appeared out of nowhere and dashed forward to join Ella and me, as we blankly stared upwards at the two hovering Seahawks in confusion. Thorsten was right behind him. The Viking dude was actually waving his arm back and forth like humans do when they see a packmate. How would the Viking dudes know Commander Elwha? Ella and I turned to study Thorsten suspiciously.

"These are the friends I called for help, Captain Marc Christensen and his SEALs. They're your southern neighbors from Quinault. Don't you remember?" he asked in a tone that said he clearly knows I didn't. I turned to Ella. Her posture was beginning to relax.

"What's happening and why aren't we fighting anybody?" I demanded.

"I think we won!" she answered, her eyes bright.

I didn't have any time to think about it because Rachel and Fitz and the other lost Wolves were upon us, out of breath, big-eyed and mostly intact.

Rachel. She was crushing my neck in her arms before I could register what was happening—but my heart knew. All I could do was grunt and blink a lot, but she understood. Then all the Wolves converged in a group hug, huffing as if, well, as if to hide tears or something. Quickly, we broke apart, back to business.

A few tails may have wagged.

Ella held on to her though and gazed at me intently. I raised chin. We were pack...more than pack...I huffed to cover my confusion. She gave me a silent Wolf laugh and I returned a wide Wolf grin. *Huh.*

I was still figuring it all out as Ella leaned against my side. Together we studied the fuming captive Tigerkin. The second Seahawk landed behind us while the first continued to hover overhead, their fat machine guns tightly focused on the Tigers. The gun barrels must have been still hot because they were smoking in the falling snow.

I turned to face the SEAL's alpha as he lightly leapt to the snow-covered ground behind us. I didn't think that a human that powerfully built and carrying so much equipment could do anything lightly, so he had my full attention.

Thorsten had joined the SEAL group and was talking fast, patting the SEAL Alpha's arm. I think there may have been a little mushroom still in his system, but at least no one was shooting anybody or singing. After sharing a look with his second in command, the SEAL leader stepped close enough to be able to speak to Ella and me over the roar of the Seahawks. We shook hands and both of us pretended not to notice how my paw was swallowed up in his huge hand. At least I was a head taller.

"Thorsten said he needed our help, so here we are! You must be Commander Elwha's runaway albatross, the one he can't shut up about. Three.

"I'm Captain Christensen, former US Navy SEAL, and former Kitsap-Bangor base defender for Commander Elwha." He grinned. "We resigned from that crazy bastard's military junta. Then we found a place to settle as far away from the megalomaniac lunatic as we could, in the Quinault Rain Forest. When Thorsten called for assistance, I decided that it would be a good idea to help out our new northern neighbor!" he shouted over the fast-rising storm and throb of helicopter blades, but Wolves; hearing, you know.

"Right, uh, thanks. My name is Trey now," I said.

We didn't hug.

But the enemy of my enemy would be a good ally on the day the Commander finally tracked down his missing mutts.

Captain Marc, the Seal Clan alpha, was turning out to be a pretty good guy for someone who had once worked for the Commander. He wasn't always loud-talking or doing the dominance thing, so we should get along just fine.

Somebody started a bonfire, and about then the rest of the Viking dudes showed up with a fresh keg of IPA. Thank heaven nobody was scary-singing anymore, just the occasional robust humming now that they weren't busy mauling Tigers. The rest of my tribe showed up too, the blind fisherman even waved at me.

How does he do that?

Chapter 40

PEACE TALKS

Thorston even offered the glowering Tigerkin some beer, but they just looked up at the hovering Seahawk with its heavy machine guns aimed their way and showed the Viking dude their teeth. Thorston snorted, and returned to where most of us were gathering on the other side of the helicopter's landing spot. It was pretty noisy over there.

I guess my people had to be loud as they compared stories above the scream of the wind and two Seahawks, but that was not where my attention was focused. Cats are sneaky. While we had carefully disarmed them, they were superb weapons all by themselves. I think Captain Marc's team felt the same, because they never took their eyes off of the captive Tigers either. This raised the SEALs in my estimation because they recognized where true danger lay. And still-smoking Gatling guns were a hell of a persuading tool. Maybe a negotiating tool as well, I needed all the help I could get to forge a treaty this day.

The Tiger queen was very unhappy. When we disarmed the Tigers under the captain's intent scrutiny, for some reason Fitz had insisted that the Tigerkin lay their firearms down in the snow and back away slowly. This had both angered and embarrassed the Tigers, but I had no idea why. I would have to ask my second-in-command later.

I caught Captain Marc's eye and he joined me on the rise overlooking the captive Tigers. He brought his second, Sergeant

Liam with him. I nodded for Thorston to join us too, as well as Ella and Henry.

For a moment we just studied the captives, then I began to talk about the peace I—uh…Ella and I—envisioned.

"None of us are strong enough by ourselves to stop the Commander in a conventional battle," I began, "He has enough firepower to destroy the world many times over. Henry says we are going to need to fight like resistance forces do. He knows what he's talking about." Captain Marc and Sergeant Liam hadn't paid much attention to the quiet man from Wudang Mountain but studied him now. Liam's eyes widened after a few seconds and Captain Marc straightened. A small smile might have flashed across Henry's face, but he just nodded, a gesture that was returned respectfully. Not all language is loud.

"We think that a new nation made up of three different independent states will be strong enough to stand up to Commander Elwha's forces. The problem is that we are all very different and have a bloody history with each other," I stated, meeting Captain Marc's eyes briefly before continuing.

"Different genes, different lives, but different skill sets too. Together, we can do much, but we need more than that to get us to work together. As one nation, we gain the ability to survive the ice-age winter descending upon us. Wolf Haven can do that for everyone. We are going to make the Tigers and SEALs an offer they can't refuse without risking a cold winter death," I said.

I had everyone's attention with that statement. I paused for a moment before looking directly at Captain Marc.

"How are you situated for power to run your operations, to heat your people's homes, to follow the info trails broadcast by some of the surviving weather stations in the US and Europe? They say we may not have a spring, that we may not even see the sun before next summer at the earliest. Are you confident you have everything you need to survive?" I asked. I didn't need to hear the answer, I could see it in their eyes.

"My people," I said, "have just acquired some commercial wind generators capable of producing electricity in the megawatt range. One generator will exceed all of my people's power needs for at least three years. A single wind turbine can easily power all of Seal Clan's needs. Tiger Mountain has been using diesel generators, but we unexpectedly blew up their fuel reserves along with half of their base. The Tigers desperately need this. This is the glue that will hold us together through the hard times coming."

Then I shut up and listened.

"Okay, you're right. We all need this. But gift horses..." Captain Marc said. I exchanged questioning looks with my team, then turned back to the SEAL alpha.

"Old reference to conqueror's tricks," Captain Marc explained, "What do the Wolves want in return? Are you going to tell us how to run our lives, or collect excessive tribute, or insist that we foster our children in your homes? There is a long history of people using this kind of thing to control others. It rarely turns out well for the receiver of gifts."

I shook my head as if that would help to somehow shed these ugly ideas.

"No. All I want is for you to show up when it's time to fight, as we will show up when you need help. I don't know if you're aware, but we discovered a pirate colony in Ocean Shores, a little south of you. Henry says that it is very difficult to remove them once they gain a foothold and they've definitely settled in," I said. Henry nodded in agreement as did Sergeant Liam.

"I would also like untaxed trade between our states, and to patrol our combined borders, but that's only to our mutual benefit," I said, glad that Grandma had explained these things to us.

"That's it? No surprises?" the captain asked.

"That's it. Same for the Tigerkin," I answered. The captain nodded politely and withdrew to discuss it with his people. Fifteen minutes later he returned and stuck out his big hand. We shook, and I saw what a smile looked like on the SEAL alpha for the first time.

Now for the hard one.

I gave Queen Malgato the same pitch I had given the Seal Clan and it was no surprise when she kept interrupting, denying everything I said, and uttering threats. After we'd been at it for an hour, the queen and I, and it didn't feel as if we were gaining much ground. I could tell that my humans were angry, and my Wolves were livid, but this was important. Besides, if we couldn't make the deal, I could always shoot her with my biggest gun. I think this is what Lenny called "win-win". It's all this talking that was exhausting me.

"Will you listen now instead of threatening me?" I asked Queen Malgato of Tiger Mountain. The big male standing behind her wouldn't stop glaring and making shooting motions at me, but then she abruptly stopped arguing and studied us. Progress?

I sighed and leaned forward.

Someone had made a new bonfire right there in front of the blasted front door to Tigertown, and then dragged a few of the surviving couches out of the bunker, and up to the fire. Now at least we could be snowed on in comfort. Queen Malgato managed to take up a whole couch—I was pretty sure she wasn't very good at sharing things.

Well, she was just going to have to learn. Playing well with others is a learned skill for some. Wolves have it down. Humans are not very good at it. Tigerkin make humans look competent. I looked up into the sky.

The snowstorm was behaving for once, slow-motion dropping big fat flakes that silently fell on us all. I had a shoulder leaning against Ella in warm comfort, one arm holding my shotgun pointed in the general direction of Queen Malgato's feet, and Rachel snuggled at her other side. The pack takes great comfort in non-verbal languages of love and support. I remembered right then that Wolves mate for life. Of course, there will always be some Wolves who never mate and are fine with it, but all of us need simple physical contact with those who love us. As Grandma said, "Wolves need hugs, too." I don't know; maybe everyone does.

I studied the massive Tigerkin as these thoughts flew by.

Eventually the queen met my eyes, with a surprising trepidation, indicating her rare familiarity with the concept of not getting her own way. Then she abruptly nodded and sat up on her couch, oddly silent for such a dominant leader.

About time. Finally, we could get started on the nation building part. Now, the question was whether I needed to make her say it out loud? Or just go with the flow and assume both of us meant the same thing? Right. Not letting the cat out of this bag; so

I leaned forward and asked, "What are your electrical power needs to get through this terrible winter descending upon us?"

I used my peripheral vision to assess the others quickly, but I never actually took my eyes off of the powerful Tiger queen, and she was completely aware of the fact. Of course, the shotgun helped a little, but Captain Marc's Seahawks were probably the deciding factor. After a moment of thought, the huge Tiger queen spoke.

"We need at least a continuous half-megawatt to run our supplemental heating systems and full communications—and now you have destroyed our only large-scale electrical generator. Are you going to turn us out of our own homes and loot them too or simply leave us outside to freeze to death?" snarled the Tiger queen.

I almost smiled. I had wondered how long her contrite mood would last. Now we had the true queen speaking. This was better. No deal can be sealed if the two sides can't be trusted to speak a little truth. We would see, but I was hopeful.

"Is it windy like this just the last few days, or is it like this all the time up here?" I asked calmly. Queen Malgato gave me a contemptuous look implying I was crazy, then shrugged and said, "Yes. All the time."

I looked around the fire once more. Her defeated Tiger pack lay around in obvious exhaustion, grooming as their nanites healed their wounds, their stomachs growling from what must be a ravenous hunger—but they waited patiently and watched their queen with a devotion I found extreme, but then I wasn't a Tiger, so maybe I wasn't in a place to judge. I just knew that we couldn't survive what was coming in the spring on our own. The Commander and the Pirate Tongs and even the bad boys out of Beijing would be coming our way. We were going to need a cohesive nation of different species, including the bloody Tigerkind. It was going to take all of us working together just to survive.

"Here's the deal, I said, "We have just salvaged a few commercial wind turbines and towers cut up into sections for transport. Together we can build you a secure power source that will meet all your present needs. We can also add any additional equipment as your Tiger kingdom grows and your requirements increase.

"In return, your mountain kingdom will become an independent state of our Lands of Haven, with dual assistance treaties and a demonstrated respect for each other's cultures. We have no intention of intruding upon your Majesty's ways and means. The mountain kingdom of Tigerkind will still be its own, as it is now."

Queen Malgato leaned back in her seat and blinked several times. She certainly wasn't expecting that! I turned my head to the right. I think Captain Marc was waiting for me to look his way because he immediately raised chin in allegiance. I raised chin back in thanks. My Wolves followed suit.

The SEAL was a man of few words for a human and we had already forged an agreement during the time we spent waiting for the Tigers to calm down enough to talk. Now we just had to work out the details. I looked back at the Tiger queen and continued.

"The Seal Clan Haven lands are to be the Quinault Rain Forest and mountains south of the Hoh River, all the way west to the sea. Their battle skills and firepower will secure the southern border of Wolf Haven from the pirates of Ocean Shores.

"The Tiger Haven extends from the tree line above the Hoh Rain Forest to the high mountains, and all the way to the eastern Olympic Mountain slopes. That's enough room territory for a hundred generations of Tigers. Your presence will protect our eastern border from the Commander and his navy.

"The Wolves are stewards of the Hoh Rain Forest, north all the way to the straits of Juan del Fuca, west to the Pacific Ocean, and bordered by the Tiger Haven on the east and the Seal Clan Haven to the south," I said, pausing for a beat before continuing.

"However, Wolf Haven includes all of this, all of us, and by banding together we will control almost seventy percent of the land on Olympic Island!" I said resolutely. "We will all belong to these lands of Haven—to Havenlands!"

I glanced over at the Viking berserkers, but they were still coming down off their mushroom-fueled battle trance, and an alcohol hangover looked pale in comparison. I shook my head. Humans and their toxins.

"Together, we are going to build three wind-power generator stations, focusing on the Tiger Haven first, followed by the Seal Clan Haven's cavern, and then the Wolves' rainforest last. We will have a joint defense treaty, we will all come to the defense of each other when called and share untaxed trade with free passage between us. Do you agree to these terms of surrender Queen Malgato?" I asked formally. It was a really good offer. But the Tiger queen stuck her nose in the air as if she smelled something nasty and refused to look my way. Some much for the carrot. Time for the stick.

"Or should we just take your *only* male hostage? That could hinder your plans for building a kingdom," I added after a moment of silence.

Both Seahawks had landed beside us by now but their gunners were still tightly focused on the six Tigerkin. My mixed tribe of Wolves and Humans stood still in a silence broken only by the banshee howl of the wind. Our weapons were pointed at the ground, for now. The damned cats were disarmed and trapped in their own kill zone! What was there to even think about? Time crawled but everyone was hyper-aware of the SEALs deadly weapons aimed this way. Not all language is verbal. Sometimes it gets pretty loud anyway.

After a long pause, Queen Malgato glared at me and snarled "We will allow you to exist and we will tolerate your treaty on one condition. I must be allowed to train this young cub according to her potential." Her eyes practically flamed with ferocity as she said that. She added under her breath, inaudible to humans, but of course, I heard, "No *dogs* should be left to educate such a Tiger-hearted kit."

I wasn't surprised; our cub deserved the respect of the Tigers. And with a quick unspoken glance, Ella and I decided it would probably be the best way of building trust between the tribes. So, I nodded.

A chorus of Tiger growls rose above the storm, which didn't personally bother me. Tigers have a very high opinion of themselves, and don't give up ground easily. They sounded angry, but I think they were actually pleased.

"We agree," the queen finally snarled. I raised my face to the sky and bellowed "Havenlands" into the evening sky. "Havenlands!" every one of us present roared back, except the Tigers, although Queen Malgato made a sarcastic sound that could have been interpreted as agreement. After things quieted down Captain Marc cleared his throat and spoke.

"While we all agree in theory to come to each other's aid in a fight, our individual forces are quite different, each with our own way of doing things and command structures that don't mesh. There have been so many examples in history of military forces not knowing their allies' strengths and weaknesses, leading to defeat. We can't afford to lose a single battle, so we definitely need to train as a joint military force," Captain Marc explained.

"Your military 'history' only goes back three or four hundred years," the Tiger queen declared, "China has a five-thousand-year track record. But you are correct, we must know how to work together to win our battles. The solution is to send your fighters to Tiger Mountain, and I will form them into a proper fighting force under my command."

Right. Trust the Tigers.

"I think it is a better idea to start small, experiment with mixed teams to learn each other's ways, before we can know how to best utilize each other's skill sets. Then we can scale it up," I suggested. Queen Malgato snarled but didn't actually disagree with me. The problem was that I simply didn't know how I was going to make this happen! Then Thorston of the Viking dudes stood up.

"We have experienced this when we worked with NATO forces a decade ago. Troops from fifty countries with widely varying abilities, some with purchased rank and a habit of ignoring collateral damage to get the job done. My team believes in the precision application of force, not cutting down an entire village because it's easier than sorting out the bad guys," he said, shaking his head.

"We know it is absolutely imperative that we patrol our borders. We have many enemies. Instead of each of us being responsible for our own territory's borders, I propose we form a mixed squad to patrol our entire nation's borders. The team would consist of a single Tiger, a couple of Seal clan soldiers, a Wolf or two, and several Viking dudes. This patrol would be out in the field for weeks, and there is no better way to know your allies than being cramped up together while fighting the weather and looking for signs of invaders," Thorston explained.

"Of course, one Tiger is worth many mice, I mean, humans and Wolves, but this also addresses our different population sizes. I like this idea, but only if a Tiger is in command," the Tiger queen said.

Not going to happen, but I didn't say anything right now. We have achieved the impossible this day. There would be time to sort out the details.

There was still one more problem to address though.

I looked up to study Fitz as he approached me with his head hung low and eyes downcast. I could tell he was miserable; his tail was curled up between his legs. It was obvious he had been shot up pretty badly, but his nanites were on it. Unfortunately, nanites don't assign pain a high priority. Fitz came to a weary stop before me and bowed quite low to his Alpha. He was very respectful. I motioned him to proceed.

"I have failed to protect our cub and pack and allowed us to be captured by Tigers on my watch. I am very ashamed. Punish me as you will," he requested. I just studied him. He wouldn't meet my eyes directly.

Huh. It seemed Fitz had learned wisdom, if at a terrifying cost. I raised chin for him to continue.

"I remember when my name was 'Dog Five'. I remember when Grandma said "Five" was my name of bondage, one given to me by our former masters once they had stolen my original one and buried it where I can never find it. Then I didn't want to be Dog Five anymore. And I will never be a slave-Dog again!" he said with a little of the old fire.

"Then my name was Fitz and I liked that. But I don't know who I am anymore. I was arrogant in my ignorance of the world. I endangered our cub and pack. But I am no longer that Wolf either. Is my name still Fitz?" he asked, the pain oozing through the spaces left behind by his words. I reached out and pulled him closer into the comfort of pack arms. The Wolves not pointing guns at the Tigers gathered close, everyone leaning against or touching our hurting Wolf.

"Fitz is still your name, and you are never alone. You are a loved and respected Wolf in my pack. Pack will always be there with you," I said, comforting him as best I could. It seemed to help a little. I heard a feline snort, but when I looked back at the Tigers, they pretended not to be paying attention.

"And you are still my second-in-command, Fitz," I said, but he wouldn't raise his eyes even for a moment. He just hung his head and turned away.

I rose to my feet, leaned my shotgun against the couch I was sitting on and nodded at Captain Marc. He nodded back, made a hand gesture, and his people immediately began readying themselves to leave.

"Want a ride home in a Seahawk?" he asked.

Tails might have wagged.

Chapter 41

PLAYING IN THE MUD

The howling wind and monotone days dragged on, night and day sometimes being only a matter of opinion, with only the grinding monotony a constant. At least she had snow duty, Ella thought. Unlike most of the humans, she and the Wolves could go outside every day if they wanted.

She looked over at Sifu Henry from where she was smoothing the side of a basalt block with a chisel and mallet. He was sitting near the campfire, playing in the mud, as far as she could tell. She sighed. The extended time confined indoors due to the snowstorms was making all the humans a little batty, but she hadn't expected Henry to fall prey to it. Of course, it must be warm over there, tucked inside the quarry cave.

He looked up to see her watching him.

"We need to do something with all this clay we've collected," Henry explained. He got up and walked over to place the final fire-roasted brick into the kiln he had built into the quarry's wall and lit a small fire inside it. When he saw that no one got what he was doing, he explained further.

"There are a lot of us now and that means a lot of bowls and plates and cups are needed. We are going to shape this cleaned clay from our quarry into dishes, and fire them until they glow red. When they cool down, we will have stoneware dishes. One of my aunties on Wudang mountain was a potter and sometimes my mother traded her for dishes," Henry said with an inward smile.

He found himself thinking of those olden times from his youth when his most pressing decision was which book to read next. Maybe these thoughts were connecting to teaching skills from his long-ago youth? Henry felt a strange link forming to the time from before his world ended, before the death of his wife and young daughter.

At least these days he got to teach, and his students learned quickly. The Wolves were young enough to embrace multiple disciplines. Time for them to learn a new one.

"Why don't you join me, Ella? I want to show you something," he said to his Stonemason student. He picked up a round slice of wood one of the Viking dudes had cut for serving platters and a flat smooth stone from the river someone had brought in, and walked over to sit down beside the tub of mud he'd been playing in when Ella had gotten a concerned look in her eyes.

The huge Wolfkin gently sat down beside her teacher as he set the wood slice on top of the flat rock and spun it. It fell off the rock in a few rotations. Ella looked at her teacher out of the corner of her eyes. Henry wasn't a man much given to explaining things, but she was going to need something here pretty soon. Her teacher began examining the river rock and turned it over. Ella reached over to pick up the wood platter and placed it gently on top of the rock once again. Henry smiled at her without showing teeth and spun the wood disc with a finger. This time it didn't fall over. He smiled again. Ella considered the possibility that he had recently hit his head or been sampling toxins with the Viking dudes but stayed silent. You can't hear very well if you're busy talking.

Then Henry reached into the tub full of mud and glopped a double handful onto the piece of wood. Ella looked around to see who was watching and realized all the Wolves had stopped what they were doing to watch. Great...

Her teacher scooted forward, close to the mess he was making, and spun the wood piece again, but this time he put both hands around the glob of clay and gently squeezed. The mud grew taller and smooth on the outside. Ella started to get excited. When the wood stopped turning, Henry reached down to spin it again and stuck his thumbs into the center of the clay, then slowly moved them up and out. A crude bowl took form! Her breath caught in her throat.

This time Ella reached down to spin the wood so he didn't have to stop. Henry put one hand on the inside of the spinning bowl, and the other outside it and kind of pulled the clay upwards. The shallow bowl became a cup, and then almost an urn! Ella trembled with the need to create something, to make the mud obey her paws, but just kept spinning the disc until the urn collapsed back into a lump of clay. She let out a breath of disappointment.

"We keep working on it until it's what we want, then stop. If we work with the clay too much it sulks and collapses. Then we just start again. Clay is very forgiving," Henry said gently. Ella was trembling in excitement. Her teacher made a sound that was somewhere between a laugh and a smile.

"Would you like to try it?" he asked.

"Oh yes, Sifu. Very much!" she answered. Who would have thought that a rock, a piece of wood, and mud could come together to create a thing of beauty? Ella moved around until she was across from Henry, right in front of the wood that spun. Her teacher gave it a spin so that she could use both paws.

Ella's first bowl was lopsided and heavy. But Wolves learn fast and she loved the feel of the wet clay spinning between her paws as she turned it into something of use and maybe even beauty someday, although that day was not today.

Henry leaned forward to slow Ella's spinning wheel of clay. He had been working with Wolves for a while now, and they all seemed to think that faster was better. That was not the case in all things, and it was a good time learn that lesson, especially with how much time everyone had on their hands now that they couldn't go outside and play. The Wolves needed to learn how to slow down and savor the experience. Henry almost smiled when he realized how much he sounded like his grandfather, Grand Master Chin of the Wudang Mountain School of Tai Chi.

Ella continued to improve, and Henry was pleased at her progress.

His student was coming along nicely, especially in the modified Tibetan Charging White Crane fighting style he was teaching her and the rest of the Wolves. It suited her hybrid body.

Henry's spec-op team had operated out of Tibet for three years and there's not a lot to do there between missions besides gamble, or frequent low places, so he had eagerly taken the opportunity to study another art of fighting in a nearby Tibetan monastery. Even the cloistered monks there had heard of Wudang Mountain and its famous fighting styles. He ended up doing as much teaching as learning by the time he left, but it kept him out of any of the troubles soldiers are prone to, in such distant reaches of the People's Republic.

Soon, all the Wolves were spinning wood and throwing pots as if they had been born to it and the quarry became their favorite hangout spot.

A few days later the Fisher clan kids showed up with Grandma and Tosh, eager to exchange the stuffy air of their beehive high above for a warm baby cavern where they actually had room to run around. The snowstorm madness of this eternal winter was getting very old. They were welcomed with open arms, especially when the Wolves scented their beloved Cioppino, in a large steaming pot Tosh was lugging.

For the humans, moving between the beehive and the cavern-quarry could only be done during the infrequent calmer moments of the storm. When children were involved, the trips were prepared for with the kind of intensity normally only found in mountain climbing expeditions. Or maybe there just wasn't enough to do, so everyone got involved—Ella didn't know or really care why. Wolves approach the safety of their cubs with a single-minded devotion that completely understands such an approach on a gut level.

After an impromptu feast, smoked trout cioppino served in huge, slightly irregular stoneware bowls, the Wolves got back to work. Towers didn't build themselves.

The children spent the afternoon fascinated with watching half of the stonemasons spinning mud and making pottery, while the other half split stone with big hammers and chisels. It sure beat studying, jammed into a stuffy room filled with everyone while trying not to get irritable and maybe bite someone.

Of course, the quarry cave was completely irresistible to the bored human youth. The large warm fire didn't hurt any, either. It wasn't very long before their hands got muddy as well. This was a very "pack" way of doing things, working together. The Wolves thoroughly enjoyed themselves teaching the cubs about stone and spinning potter's wheels.

Tosh decided to call it 'art class' and got thoroughly muddy as well. Meanwhile Grandma chatted with Henry, eventually requesting stoneware jars large enough to store dried beans or grain and round-bottomed mixing bowls. The needs of a low-tech kitchen that feeds over eighty people are substantial. You can't just run down to the corner store for something you're out of, either.

Suddenly, pottery making was becoming very popular and regular classes had to be held once all the adults got involved. It was very exciting, and exuberant potter styles began to emerge from the friendly competition common to humans.

Within a week, people were beginning to produce stoneware pots that finally had tight fitting lids! All you needed was a ring of leather for a good seal, and if there was one thing that they were awash in, it was leather scraps. Lots of meat-eaters here.

The informal 'school' system of moving between their beehive in the sky or the Cavern-quarry every three or four days for classes was working out well, as that was about how often there was a break in the snowstorm's ceaseless tantrums. For the middle of an ice-age winter everything was going pretty well. Except maybe the weight loss.

The problem was that the Wolves were burning more calories than they were consuming. The demands of a Wolfkin body are much higher than an unaltered human. They simply needed more protein to operate than an unenhanced human did. But everyone got served the same amounts, and the Wolves understood this. But it still wasn't enough to meet a Wolf's needs.

Until now, Ella had no idea how much thought went into feeding a large group of people. Wolves hunted together and then gorged or starved as a pack. Ella was amazed that Grandma and Tosh had figured to the calorie per person what they could do with what they had and knew exactly how many days we had before we ran out of food. They had to, they explained, because in an ice-age winter there's very little new food coming in. This also turned out to be why we always had stew or soup for dinner these days.

Stretching the protein further kept our stomachs, if not full, then not empty either.

Apparently, despite a smokehouse half full of salmon and trout, a large tin can collection, and the venison cold storage, our larder was only going to take us so far, and it wasn't far enough. Grandma and Tosh had to put everyone on a seventeen-hundred-calorie diet to stretch it that far. The humans did okay, but Wolves needed more food to thrive. Then there was also the fact that the Commander had kept his slave-Dogs protein starved to be easier to control, and this felt like that, even if everyone knew it wasn't. But some ghosts never die.

"Fitz, we need to go hunting. Even in this weather," Ella said to the formerly carefree Wolfkin. He still didn't meet her eyes, giving her dominance. But he listened silently and waited for Ella to continue. Fitz said more with less these days.

"I know all the game is burrowed in and waiting for the storm to pass, but it never passes. The deer and rabbits are just as thirsty and hungry as we are, and they are going to brave the weather rather than starve. Are you a rabbit? No! You are a Wolf, the Alpha's second in command!" Ella growled bluntly. She had already tried repeatedly to get Fitz out of his depression but Wolves do what is necessary, even if you feel bad later. And she did. At least it worked, a little.

"We'll need to hunt down more than a solitary deer or mountain goat. Deer nest in small groups for warmth. We're going to need all our Wolves out there, split into teams large enough to catch two or three deer at a time. There won't be much prey out though, so we will need to spread out our coverage and then converge for the kills," Fitz said without meeting her gaze.

Ella waited for him to continue, but he didn't immediately assign teams as a pack leader would. That was a little disappointing, but some wounds can't be fixed by nanites, and take a long time to heal. She would carry the burden. She had grown used to calling the shots and surprisingly found it quite satisfying.

"Fitz, you lead a team up the south shore of the Bogachiel River. Twist, go with him. I'll take the north side, going upriver across from you. Felix, you take the south shore, headed downstream, then return upriver on the north side. The rest of you

Wolves chose which team you want to hunt with and be ready to go in ten minutes. It's dangerously cold out there so I want everyone suited up in the white snow gear the Fisher clan sewed for us. Bring your rifles, snow boards and sleeping bags, we may be out for several days," Ella ordered.

Then she stood up and made her way across the crowded middle floor of their Beehive-in-the-sky to join Grandma and Tosh, who were waiting for her by the wood burning stove. The women had developed very good hearing for humans and looked at her expectingly.

"Would you mind making up some packets of smoked fish and those biscuit things leftover from last night? I don't know how long we'll be gone, but we will need to eat on the move. We're not coming back empty-handed," Ella requested. Grandma glanced at Tosh and she immediately peeled away, gathering a few kids to help pack the trail-meals as she walked away. Grandma smiled at Ella without showing any teeth, and Ella got it. Now it was just two alpha females with no young ears listening. Straight talking time.

"You need to leave the cubs with us. It's just too cold for their young bodies. Somebody could die. I know you travel everywhere as a pack, but sometimes we have to make sacrifices. Leave a Wolf behind to keep them company. You can spare someone for that. I know they won't be happy, but children get over such things with time," Grandma suggested. Then Grandma reached out to pat Ella's shoulder in some mysterious human gesture that was supposed to mean something, but Ella had no idea what.

She tried to keep herself from growling, but a little slipped out anyway. Grandma knew this was pack business.

Ella didn't interfere when the humans punished a cub by making them hand-wash everyone's dirty socks and the mud towels. That was because it was Fisher clan business. Ella didn't see the connection, but it wasn't Wolf business so she butted out. Now, Grandma was breaking one of the unspoken agreements between pack and clan. She was worried about Rachel and Bookworm enough to risk screwing things up. *Hmm.*

Would she do the same if she was worried enough about one of the Fisher clan kids? But that wouldn't happen because the

Fisher clan wouldn't knowingly put their cubs in danger! But what if they didn't *know* about a danger? Yes, Ella would point it out so they would know to avoid endangering their cubs. So… maybe Grandma was only pointing out a danger too.

Ella looked over at the Wolves listening in from the other side of the room. Theo was quietly repeating the conversation to Rachel and Bookworm. Both cubs were intently watching her without being disrespectful by staring. Sigrid nodded her head minutely when Ella looked her way. Fitz's opinion was obvious—he'd already come too close to losing a pup once. He wanted nothing to do with endangering them again. Ella turned back to Grandma.

"The cubs will stay home," Ella said.

Ten minutes later the Wolves were gone, except for Theo and the cubs. Rachel and Bookworm were not happy, but Wolves don't much care for drama, so the cubs kept it mostly to themselves. They wanted to be good Wolves, but they just wanted to be with the rest of their pack. Ella decided to take them both outside as soon as the deadly freezing weather had passed.

It was very cold outside. The bitter wind lashed them ceaselessly with snow and frozen bits of ice. Even a Wolf couldn't see farther than ten meters. Ella's team slowly worked their way upriver along the Bogachiel's banks, wading through the heavy snow and thick brush because they were going uphill and snowboards didn't work that way. It was slow going even wearing snowshoes but Wolves are very patient. Especially when the payoff is dinner. Ella figured that the deer wouldn't be far from a water source and would leave sign when they went down to the river to break the ice and drink. By paralleling the river, they should intersect any game trails, and then follow the tracks back to their nest.

Fitz's team had quickly crossed the frozen river and were presently working their way north, directly across the Bogachiel from Ella and Sigrid. Felix's hunting party was already out of scent range going downriver. She rewrapped her scarf across her nose and mouth, so that only a slit of her eyes was exposed to the snowstorm and increased their pace a little. Ella knew that a Wolfkin's metabolism runs hotter than a human's, but the candle burnt at both ends lasts half as long. Her Wolves desperately needed protein; this hunt *had* to succeed.

Ella and Sigrid found their first game trail to the river in less than twenty minutes. Rabbits. They were tiny compared to a buck, but there were a lot of them in the burrow Ella and her team dug up. The meat was quickly field-dressed and each Wolf snacked on one, but the remaining meat barely covered the caloric debt they incurred with all that digging. The Wolves hit the riverbank again after stringing up their catch in a Sitka fir for retrieval on the way home.

The next time they were luckier. Ella and Sigrid followed a game trail with fresh scat, which lead to three deer. They released the female as usual, but this still left two bucks. Her Wolves didn't have enough time to enjoy the traditional hunt, so they settled for shooting each deer through the heart, field dressing it, and stashing their kill up in another fir. Wolve are born to hunt, and this method wasn't anywhere near satisfying. But this was okay, they were on a mission, and that was all that counted.

Still felt like kind of a waste of a good chase, though. Such things were rarer than they liked.

Twenty minutes later they got all the excitement they wanted.

Ella and her team were silently ghosting through the forest when they abruptly smelled raw bacon on the hoof. The Wolves crept closer to a feral pig band rooting around in the roots of some trees that had lost all their leaves. The wild pigs made little excited grunting sounds as they dug up clusters of stinky little black puffy things. Something about one of the boar's colors made Fitz think that these might be formerly domesticated apocalypse survivors. These pigs were not very hairy and one of them was kind of pink where the mud had been scraped off. Their tusks were a little small too.

They were plenty mean though, and glared at Ella the same way she looked at a deer when she was hungry. Which was all the time, lately. Meat-eaters then. The largest feral pigs massed at least one-hundred-kilos of tough muscle and hide, and they outnumbered the Wolves almost three-to-one. Ella met Sigrid's eyes and they both dropped a silent wolf-smile.

The two Wolves phased into Flux.

The burden of language falls from her mind... and she saw the world as it really is. She raises her right foot and shifts her weight forward as if she has all the time in the world. And she does—the space between the heartbeats is plenty big enough to do anything you want.

Ella and Sigrid take another, more powerful step, propelling them forward through the syrup world of Flux. They are three meters from the closest charging boar, who has his tusks low and his hate high, and is charging directly at her with mundane speed. But to Ella and Sigrid the hateful boar is barely crawling at the speed of a lush after happy hour ends and the bill is due.

Her next step is at a forty-five-degree angle left, and this set her up to extend her other leg ninety-degrees right. Her fists punch out in opposite directions as her hips snap into position, imparting a whip to the fist just now coming into contact with the angry beast's throat. Her hips twist again and the choking red-eyed pig trips over her speeding foot, face planting in the snow as it slides an impressive distance. Ella slides her big bowie knife free and effortlessly slits the homicidal pig's throat as she moves forward into the next wild boar's personal space and slips her blade through the fourth and fifth rib to pierce the heart that she can actually hear beating. Then a hard right, a slice and twist, then back to intercept a truly massive hog with filthy tusks as it tries to gut her. She dodges without effort, turning to scan for her team.

Sigrid has efficiently dropped two feral pigs as well and is bouncing around a third with fluid grace before she lunges and snaps her teeth. Suddenly the hog doesn't have a throat anymore. Sigrid never breaks stride, her gray muzzle stained crimson as she moves to her next target. That's when Tinker and Ona arrive, and immediately bring down the last two feral pigs.

Ella looks around with satisfaction and drops out of Flux into the mundane world. The usual temporary exhaustion took over as Ella and her team admired their kills, panting for breath. Eight hogs, two deer, and a bunch of rabbits—that was at least five-hundred-kilos of meat and bone! Definitely time to wind things up and drag home their battle spoils. Any more kills and they wouldn't be able to carry everything. They'd have to come back for it the next day, and who knew how that would go?

She raised a paw in a small circle, then pointed at herself. Her Wolves were suddenly around her, waiting for orders.

"Hang and drain the hog's blood for fifteen minutes, then cut them down, rope the carcasses together in pairs. When I give the signal, we'll begin dragging our kills home on the river ice" she ordered.

"If any of the other teams have had our luck, then we'll make it through this damn winter just fine!" Ella added, feeling as if an enormous weight she hadn't been aware of was suddenly lifted from her shoulders. If she'd been human, she would have grinned.

Ella hefted a pig up by its feet and tied it overhead. The crimson splashes draining onto the white snow were shocking in their vivid color after a long day in the monochrome snow globe of the rainforest in winter. The scarlet color was beautiful, because it signified that her people would have enough to eat, at least for a while.

She locked the visuals in her mind, wondering if any of the glazes Henry had been talking about might turn out that color. She'd like to sign her dishes with the color of success and full belly's, she decided. A crimson splash on the pale stoneware would be beautiful in more than one way! She hardly noticed all the hard work dragging everything home—her mind was busy painting crimson pools on pots and plates that didn't even exist yet.

But they would.

Chapter 42

ON PATROL

It was three weeks before Havenland's border patrol was ready for its first journey. The Viking dudes had a really good map, which made planning simple.

Or so we thought.

I made sure I was part of the team, along with Nina the White Wolf, Thorsten of the Viking dudes and his brother-in-law Tore, Joe of the Seal clan, and—of course—Lao Zi of Queen Malgato's Tiger Haven.

My team had talked the whole thing over late into the night around the wood-burning stove in our arboreal home in the sky. Sometimes things got a little chaotic, with all the helpful suggestions from, well, everybody. Of course, everyone agreed in principle that patrols were a great idea, but everyone wanted input. Took longer than I expected to put together, but we finally thought we had worked the bugs out. Our finalized route was well-marked on Thorston's map, and we figured it would take us less than two weeks to get to the Seal clan's base over on Finley Mountain.

If the bad weather conditions remained as they were.

So, there we were, Wolves, Tigers, and Humans marching single-file through waist-high snow, eyeing each other suspiciously, dedicated to figuring out each other's strengths and weaknesses. The problem with getting to know someone under these conditions is that it is always a mixed bag. Hopefully you'll find more good things than things you don't care for. But that's only a part of it. There really **is** something about battling the elements together, walking the borders of your own lands, and fighting for survival every day that clears the vision, and allows you to see your teammates for who they are. And what kind of team we are, what kind of team we can become.

We knew that Tigerkind were deadly predators that eat just about anybody and like to play with their food. Surprisingly, they also had a razor wit and a dry sense of humor, something we Wolves never suspected. They were smart and highly disciplined, but also bullies and comfort-loving sociopaths.

No surprises there.

Wolves are former runaway slave-Dogs who rebuilt themselves into apex predators in the Hoh Rain Forest, and now live high up in the old-growth trees in a giant beehive. We are lethal, bioengineered fighters and pack hunters who work together seamlessly to achieve the mission. Of course, the mission was usually dinner these days. Everybody's always of one mind there.

As for the Humans, they're just "please don't try to eat me or I'll turn up the music and feed you shotgun shooters, all night long." The threat of music was always enough—**nobody** wanted to hear the Viking dudes sing again.

Halfway through day three, we hurriedly made camp in a small clearing made by falling trees. The blizzard was kicking into high gear. Fifteen minutes later, we were all jammed in together with our supplies, in a tent designed for a half-dozen small humans at most. Our tent was quickly buried beneath a meter of snow in the howling snowstorm, the kind of blizzard that strips body heat like the way Tigers eat, quick and messy.

We weren't going anywhere for a while.

We were piled on top of each other, of course; Wolves, Humans, and Tigers alike in one big heap. When body-heat becomes a valuable commodity, distaste mostly evaporates and everyone just tries to stay warm. You really need a fire to combat this kind of cold, but it's neither safe nor simple to maintain a fire in a buried tent, so we just had to do without.

It was the smell that you had to get used to.

Apparently, Tigers aren't partial to bathing, and despite being heavily clad in newly-sewed snowsuits, the powerful scent of pungent big cat was all you could smell. In this tiny air-bubble tent buried beneath the snow, it could be very difficult to continue to be polite even as Mother Nature wrought havoc noisily outside. That's because having an excellent sense of smell is usually a good thing. Not here though, with hour after hour of inhaling Tiger fur and Human sweat. I swear, humans sweat even when it's freezing! As far as Wolf smells, well…our own scent never irritated any of us Wolves, although Lao Zi did make sarcastic remarks about wet dog fur a little too often to be chance. So maybe we're all at fault, but please! Take a bath in the next mountain stream!

On the other hand, once we *were* on the move again, and the snow wasn't bleaching out the world, we had developed quite an efficient way to patrol, one that worked for every one of us. Each of us had their own role in each scenario. Lao Zi immediately took command when we spot prey; the big Tigerkin was hyper-alert, far beyond mundane senses once she had shifted into the Stream.

Tigerkind excel at the hunt, we learned, even before you factor in their human intellect. What we Wolves have in Flux, apparently, they get in a very different, but no less potent, reality-interface they call the Stream. The Stream is all about the hunt, and nobody can hunt like the Tigerkind when they're in the Stream.

So, our best hunter led every hunt, and we all had our roles in this, too.

I led the rest of the time. Thorston took rearguard, while Joe and Tore kept us oriented in the proper direction. The White Wolf covered our left flank, while Lao Zi guarded our right.

I've come to believe that the team is strongest when we are guided by our strongest, in each's area of expertise. Reeds aren't strong until they're woven together to make a basket. Henry showed us that too.

We learned to travel as one creature instead of many, completely in tune with our surroundings. We slid through the snow-bound rainforest as ethereal as ghosts at twilight. Our Patrol team learned to not to fight the land, but to move in sync with it. That took a while.

We silently swept through the unending snowfall on our way to the warmth and hearth of the Seal's Clan Cavern. It was hidden high on Finley Mountain, overlooking the Quinault Rain Forest and lake. All the maps say so.

Our patrol quickly adapted to snowboards, skis, and snowshoes as needed. During the day we never stopped moving forward or watching for game sign, as we quietly skied and snowboarded through the heavy snowfall and white-drenched forests. Our only rule was that we never backtracked, and nobody ate until we made camp in the evening and everyone did. Some dinners were fat with spit-roasted venison, and some were simple soups made from dried meat and vegetables. Food became very important at times like these.

On good nights, we sat around the fire after dinner and told stories. Some were hilarious—Tigers have a droll sense of humor with a highly caustic finish. Some were just plain bizarre, but none were boring. I mean, what else was there to do in the last hour before going to bed only so you can wake up to do it all over again? It wasn't like we had Netflix on the satellite phone. I'm not even sure there is a Netflix anymore. Why can I remember Netflix but not my former name or who I once loved?

As the days pass, we slowly grew to respect each other. To know how far we can count on each other. Or not.

Tigers don't think like Wolves and it would be a mistake to turn your back on a hungry Tigerkin when you don't have someone *watching* your back. Nothing about this journey was easy, so in working with Tigers, we've had to be satisfied with baby steps. Safer all round that way.

Well, as safe as traveling with a hungry Tiger can be.

Looking back, I believe that this is where Havenland was truly forged. But it didn't seem like anything monumental or historic at the time – just long and too often unpleasant or irritating. But this *was* where we first learned how different species could work together, like a good fire squad comes to rely on each other in combat. This was where we laid the foundations for eventually going to war with our enemies. But we weren't thinking about that right then. All we wanted was a warm fire, a not-empty belly, and a good night's sleep, hopefully free of pungent body odors and sour-scent nightmares.

Anyway, why not dream of paradise? It costs the same as being miserable, doesn't it?

Good times.

The ice-age winter grew worse by the day until there was little difference between night and the weak light of day. The never-ceasing snowfall continued to lay down meters of the white stuff, and after a while game began to grow scarce. Our snowboards didn't care how deep the snow was, though, and we were able to make good time, at least when our path was downhill.

The forest was never completely empty of life, even if it looked that way at first. All creatures need water, even if they're burrowed underground for the winter and are living off their stored fat from a glorious summer. They still had to come up where we could track them, sooner or later. The problem was with the 'later' part.

There were some nights that only a couple of rabbits went into the soup pot, to stretch between six hungry people. We all quickly lost any fat we had left as our muscles turned lean and wiry. It was the Tiger who had it the worst, though. They carry too much muscle for the caloric numbers we were forced to survive on. Lao Zi's skin was beginning to hang a little loose on her. We all needed meat in the worst way.

It was late in the afternoon of our eighth day on patrol when we came across the bighorn sheep.

They were arrogant and aggressive.

We were hungry.

There were eleven of them, massing as much as a deer and buried in fleece so thick you could have concealed a small human in it. They stood looking down on us as if guarding the ridgetop that we were methodically climbing so we could snowboard down the other side.

Lao Zi appeared to barely be moving, but somehow still covered a lot of ground, smoothly climbing up the ridge's slope like water flowing uphill. The biggest of the shaggy sheep glared down on us from a small boulder jutting over the edge where he'd staked his ground. He would shake his enormous curled-horns at us every so often, his foggy breath spraying warm-air clouds in the cold mountain air.

Our Tiger quickly gave us our marching orders and began her approach center-right, laser focused on the bighorn sheep. I moved forward to cover our left flank, and the humans followed behind Lao Zi on my right. Meanwhile, Nina climbed a stunted tree to make sure no one was sneaking up behind us while we were busy hunting. She always kept one paw on her beloved Robar C-50 antimaterial sniper rifle.

I had four bighorns clustered in my path on the snow-covered slope of the no-name ravine. Now, we were separated by less than ten meters, all uphill. They appeared to be standing their ground rather than attacking us, a tactically superior position in the short term. The bighorns were making us come to them, on their home ground.

Whatever. They're still sheep and we were big bad Wolves with a hungry Tiger along for the ride. We were happy to accept the invitation.

I phased into Flux… and my mind clears wonderfully now that it's not groaning under the burden of language and structured speech. The world around me changes, slowing to a snail's pace and I am changed too. I experience little emotion in base reality, and that speeds up things considerably. I drink in the world around me in unfiltered draughts, digesting what I see whole instead of running it through the normal linguistic filters. I see the world as it is at times like this, and it is good.

Especially moments like now.

I continue moving forward and up, climbing the slick slope without trouble now that everything around me has turned to cold syrup. We are five meters from contact with the enemy, aka mutton chops for dinner.

Thorsten, Tore, and Joe are remarkable fighters, but they don't know Flux and are mired in mundane reality, slow and ponderous. Despite their best efforts, the three humans are quickly left behind.

The Tiger and I come over the ridgetop simultaneously. I veer right and hit the lead bighorn's side hard enough to pulverize ribs, while Lao Zi goes for the back of its neck. It bleats, dodges a severed spine, and then gets really angry; the ram's eyes are actually red with anger and popped capillaries. Our Tiger spits out a mouthful of wool with contempt.

The Bighorn ram lowers its head and charges us on the ridge—all I can see is a lot of horns coming at me like a bolt of lightning. They must have been moving almost sixty kilometers an hour, with heavy horns almost a meter wide!

Big and lightning fast, but not nearly fast enough for a Wolf in Flux.

Blood on snow is shocking in its scarlet brilliance. The snow is the purest of white canvases, painted with a badass bighorn's lifeblood in bold swatches and arterial spray. All the rest of our snow globe world is shades of gray and chromium white. The bright red splashes are all you really see. Then you taste it—the prey's coppery blood in your mouth as you sweep your head and ripping teeth in a hard right.

I continue to spin, coming around the long way to tear at the prey's neck. He is only one of eleven, but this is the alpha bighorn, and taking him down fast will leave the others in confusion for a moment.

We are so hungry and the smell of blood in the air is like a hammer to our olfactory awareness, but nobody breaks discipline. We are Havenland Patrol, and do not stoop to such things.

I look over at our hunting chief. Lao Zi is the master of the hunt and does not even consider the possibility of the mouthwatering scent of fresh blood having any effect on her or her team's actions. I have drawn first blood and now it is stage two of the hunt. A hunt is never over until the Tiger in charge says it is. And Lao Zi says this is just the middle part.

The best is yet to come.

She inclines her head to me, and I continue my spin to separate the big ram's head from its shaggy neck. Its massive horned head flies out to wetly smack the ground and then begins to bounce downhill in dull thunks. By now the humans have caught up. I turn my gaze back to Lao Zi.

She raises a paw to chest height and briefly clenches it in a fist. Nina, the humans, and I nod in acknowledgment, and immediately raise our rifles to begin thinning the herd.

The females are spared. They are already pregnant with the next generation, and inviolate to intelligent predators. No harm will come to the mothers.

The seven males, on the other hand, are steak tartar that hasn't been harvested yet. The angry, red-eyed bighorns intend to go down fighting, and charge hopelessly downhill at us. They are as slow as a mudslide and never even get close. We bring down the big horn rams quickly, and move to the next stage of the hunt, harvesting the kills. A ringing silence in the wind descends upon us as we work. Everyone pitches in to help gather the shaggy wool coats stuffed with delicious smelling meat inside.

Now that the hunt is concluded, I drop out of Flux and command automatically returned to me.

We've come so far in only a few weeks. I can't even imagine where we'll be a year from now, should we actually survive this ice age winter the Viking dudes call Fimbulvetr.

I picked up a smelly wool bundle weighing almost as much as I did, draped it over my shoulders, and began snowboarding down the other side of the ridge we had climbed so dramatically. There was a nice, tree-sheltered ravine a little way down the slope. We would make camp there, and finally sink our teeth into as much fresh meat as we can eat.

And Wolves can eat a lot. But have you ever seen a starving Tiger tear into a haunch of fresh meat?

Yeah. Not something you're likely to forget.

Ever.

Chapter 43

BAD DOG REDUX

Dog Fifty-seven discretely watched the Commander strut across the snow-covered parade ground, inspecting his latest batch of slave-Dogs as they lay shivering in the good-dog position, paws out straight in front of them, eyes lowered. He dangled his Shiny from his left hand, but none of his Dogs dared to glance at it, or him. "Excellent! Finally!" he muttered. Commander Elwha seemed to be wondering how much extra voltage he could apply before he completely fried their brains. It was the only method he had of successfully wiping their memories of any previous disobedience. Otherwise, they continued to rebel and he was forced to put them down, which was expensive, because then he had to start all over again.

He never saw the glare Fifty-seven threw at his back. He didn't suspect that she was Awake, or he would have immediately burned the self-knowledge out of her brain like a cancer. In order to survive, the slave-Dog had learned to be sneaky as a cat. At first, she hated this, but it was the only way. Fifty-seven found herself waiting with murderous patience for the chance to kill the masters, or at least their frightened sailors. Her time would come—and after that—the master's time would be over.

Slave-Dogs were already 'Waking Up' again. But this time Fifty-seven, the ranking member of the Awakened in the pack, insisted on hiding their new-born sentient awareness from the Commander and his pack. She knew they needed to try to stop the endless cycle of electro-shock punishment long enough for their minds to fully clear. That meant her pack had to pretend to be good Dogs. Everyone understood this now. The pack was of one mind.

That night, Fifty-seven briefly pressed her forehead against the forehead of Dog Sixty-four, the male alpha of her pack. She willed him to wake up, then quickly moved away before the guards saw her. Her pack was lost without him, but he'd been badly hurt in the most recent punishment. Fifty-seven always bounced back first, and she was just going to have to handle things as much as possible until her alpha Awakened to lead them to freedom. This time, things would be different. This time, they would finally be able to successfully throw off their chains of slavery and kill the masters. This time, her poor brain-damaged pack was going to outsmart the humans, until there weren't any humans left to outsmart.

To the outside world, she patiently lay in good-Dog position, her eyes hooded. Inside, her mind dreamed richly of bloody slaughter without end.

Meanwhile, one-hundred-twenty meters below her, Commander Elwha poured two fingers of Teeling Irish Whiskey into his coffee mug and picked up his phone to call Kitsap-Bangor Naval Base again. No answer. The Commander sighed and refreshed his coffee. He ordered his adjunct to get SEAL Team leader Captain Christiansen on the line, but the answer was always the same. Nobody knew where they were, all they knew was that the captain and his teams were somewhere out in the field, in the Olympic Mountain range on the Commanders mission—searching for his run-away bad Dogs. Captain Christensen hadn't reported in for over two weeks and this was beginning to really irritate him. He might need to cull the SEAL ranks soon; they were becoming as unreliable as slave-Dogs.

Operations insisted that Bangor-Kitsap remained secure and stood ready to repel all intruders. No outsiders had attempted to approach the base, with the exception of a random criminal gang in search of munitions and anything else they could steal. In the ensuing fight, most of the intruders were killed or had fled, but at least they had taken the leader captive. All they had been able to get out of him so far was his name, Riley and that he went everywhere on this newborn island of Olympia on his "business".

Riley was currently locked up in the stockade, awaiting Captain Christiansen's return for further interrogation. Everything else was quiet.

In the underground bunker beneath Indian Island Naval Magazine, it was shift change and the staff were keeping as quiet as they could, hoping to avoid the Commander's attention. They already knew the warning signs. Besides, he could hear everything in the spacious command room, and nobody wanted to be the person the Commander focused on when he was in a *mood*. The remaining staff had learned that quickly; the slow learners weren't around anymore.

"Call number five from the Pentagon. Do you wish to take it Commander?" his adjunct asked by phone. Commander Elwha blew out his breath and casually lit a cigar, despite the 'No Smoking' signs posted everywhere. Nobody so much as looked in his direction, RHIP.

"Yes, put it through," he instructed.

"Commander Elwha, this is the assistant to the Assistant Secretary of the Navy. You haven't responded to the supply requests we've sent you, and now management is involved. You'd best have a damn good excuse, because in this time of national difficulty we have the right to requisition anything we damn well please! Now get me those inventories and start preparing for shipping out in quantity. Do you understand me, boy?" demanded the faceless bureaucrat.

"Who exactly is this again?" the Commander growled, "I want to be able to direct your superior's wrath where it belongs when they want to know who screwed up the initial diplomatic contact with a sovereign nation. The United States abandoned us by social media, and nobody gives a damn about our losses! You just want to chew our bones like vultures!" the Commander shouted into the phone. Then he took a deep breath and spoke again.

"We are the newborn nation of Elwha, and we are the only thing standing between the United States mainland and the Chinese People's Fast Attack Fleet. We control extensive stocks of hydrogen and neutron payloads and have multiple Trident submarines to fire them. I can deliver a surprise to Beijing in thirty-one minutes or Washington D.C. in sixteen. The next call I'll take from your government will be from the Secretary of State. Do you understand me, <u>boy</u>?" the Commander replied and slammed down the phone. Damn bureaucrats! A Native American had to fight for every break he got in life. But now things were changing! "Boy!" he snorted in disgust. Stinking white racists! He was a grown man in his prime. He was nobody's "boy"! He was a damn emperor in training!

That evening, the Commander pulled out a rare bottle of Tallisker eighteen-year single malt and slowly got smashed. He assumed his Dogs were sleeping; it was way past lights-out. Most of his soldiers were also asleep or busy drinking too much in the officers' club. The night was almost peaceful, down here in the secret facility beneath Indian Island.

It was not exactly peaceful upstairs. The Awakened weren't about to waste their only unmonitored hours locked behind iron bars. Slave-Dog Fifty-seven had way too much to do now that it was dark. Her Dogs called it the Hour of the Cat. Sneaking time.

She listened carefully, but nobody seemed to be actively eavesdropping; the hidden mics in their cages weren't emitting the faint hum a Dog could hear when they were active. There were still the cameras up high in the corners, but that didn't matter if you faced away and spoke very softly. Slave-Dogs had very good hearing. And if they moved slowly enough, no motion caught the camera's attention. She growled softly to get the packs attention, and nudged Sixty-four with her cold nose, but their alpha leader was still lost in white static. She raised her chin and her pack came alert. Fifty-seven was taking command.

"How many Awakened do we have?" she whispered, knowing that the only answers would come from self-aware Dogs.

"Eight," came the soft reply from Forty-nine. She eyed him and he lowered his gaze, acknowledging. He was now her second in command.

"During the day continue to study the enemy and pretend to be stupid. Watch everything. Remember everything. We will find the path soon," Fifty-seven said. She looked at her handpicked squad, and the three slave-Dogs immediately inched their way over and spun loose one of the cage's bars to the squad room. Then the Awakened were free, passing undetected through the room and squeezing out a window high up on the wall, breathing the sweet night air of freedom.

Once they'd climbed the rest of the way to the roof as they did every night, her Dogs faded into the mottled shadows cast across the sloped metal roof by the nearby trees. Then it was decision time. If you wanted to be safe, the good Dogs stayed right there on the top of their prison, enjoying the brief taste of fresh air.

Fifty-seven and her bad Dogs went hunting. It didn't take many nights until they were all bad Dogs.

At first, they only chased deer through the forests of Indian Island. The pack learned where the surveillance areas were and were careful to never cross one. It was so easy to get excited in the hunt and forget to be careful. The hunt had been the most exciting thing Fifty-seven had ever been a part of. When she buried her nose in steaming venison and hot blood, well that was even better. She reveled in the gore of terrible wounds and savored the salty-copper of hot blood on her palate. Nights like this were the only time she felt fully alive.

Of course, before they went back to bed, all the bad-Dogs sponge-bathed in the industrial sinks of the prison head and made sure to clean away all signs of blood from their late-night dinner. The masters didn't even notice the wet floor after their slave-Dogs mopped.

Humans just weren't very observant at all.

Dog Fifty-seven decided that the masters had that in common with deer; neither noticed the slave-Dogs extracurricular activities until it was too late and were stupidly careless with their personal security. It became obvious to Dog Fifty-seven that the Sailors with guns and keys were not predators at all, but rather prey. Their fearsome masters were actually deer waiting to be run down and gloried in.

Fifty-seven fell asleep wondering what the masters' hot blood would taste like when she eventually ripped their throats out. It was an idea she never grew tired of thinking about, late at night. As always, sleep took her to bad places that night, but they were no worse than what she awoke to every day. As the unchanging weeks passed, she continued to pretend to be a good Dog during the day, but she was waking to her true nature. She was a bad-Dog by night, and she liked it that way.

It wouldn't be long before she could be bad all the time.

Chapter 44

BLUE GLACIER

We lightly grilled the left-over mutton so that it was warm and bloody in the middle and ate our dinner in unhurried pleasure. The hunger's edge of yesterday had grown dull and blunt. Last night, we feasted on fresh meat after a long drought, until our stomachs bulged and we were sated. Tonight's dinner was delicious as well, if slower paced. After eating, we kicked back around our cozy campfire to tell stories.

The wayward pine makes an excellent shelter in heavy snow. The constant snowfall has completely covered and insulated the pine's branches, leaving it a forty-meter-tall, upended snow cone in a winter wonderland of thousands just like it.

But when you dig through the tree's snow-coat, it opens up inside, hollow almost all the way up to the top. It was like a dim hidden sanctuary, and you could build a campfire in there without getting smoked out or showing any exterior sign someone can track. The storm howled outside, but inside the air was almost still.

I was warm, my stomach didn't hurt, and the crackling fire soothed me as I stared into the glowing blaze. Tore had just finished telling an exciting story about hunting down some Neo-Nazi terrorists in Brussels, which turned out not to be a round green vegetable, when our Tiger Lao Zi straightened up a bit and spoke.

"In China, feral Tigers hold huge hunting territories, and are quite serious in protecting unharvested meat. This is why the Tigers despise the bears," Lao Zi explained.

"The bears steal the Tiger's dinner. They are very touchy. When they are upset, bears simply slaughter anyone around. They have no, you will say, finesse, to difference from… differentiate from innocent, the meat, and the competitor. Also, in addition, they are messy, always making big mess. Humans are all stirred up. Not good for anybody.

"This is why our grandfathers, the non-sentient Siberian Tigers of northern China, develop a method to reducing bear population. I think is something only old-world Tiger can come up with, because in our days everyone has *some thing* they will not do. This is that category. It is weakness—such drama over simple thing. But some fade when the wind changes….

"Anyway, when the Tiger on its mountain becomes aware of bear infestation, it waits until the darkest hour of night and conceals itself on low-hanging limb over game path. Then it cries.

"Siberian Tiger mimics young bear cub who is scared out of its wits and in danger. The Tiger continues to cry and make panic cub sounds until mama bear gets angry. She charges out to the night to rescue helpless infant.

"When the bear passes under limb where Tiger waits, Tiger drops down to break mother bear's back. It is paralyzed, and helpless to defend itself.

"This is old-school Tigers dinner and entertainment. These days, we Tigerkind rise far above our common roots and have given up such simple pleasures," she said, with an elegant shrug. "Most of them," she adds quietly.

"Those were old days. Now Queen Malgato believes that hunting down and paralyzing the prey—Commander Elwha and also General Sun of the People's Republic is much more fun than tricking stupid bears in dark. We will figure out best way to break their backs," the lounging Tigerkin finished.

Huh. You never knew what you're going to hear around the campfire! Tigers were definitely crazy, but in an almost likeable way on rare occasions. I mean, they were still dangerous, cruel, and narcissistic, but I wanted to get along with anyone who intended to bring down the Commander as strongly as we Wolves did.

The important thing was to not turn my back on a Tiger without a firm grip on my shotgun, no matter how much we had in common when it came to enemies. I dropped a silent Wolf laugh on the team. The Commander may have a large navy, but now Havenland had Tigers! The possibilities… I pulled my mind back to the matters at hand.

"Okay—yes—killing the Commander and General Sun is good," I said, "but more important, we need to survive the ice-age winter before getting into things like that. Nobody is moving around out there in the snowstorm except us, and we just need to get to the Seal's Colony Cave so we can warm up, eat, and rest before we turn around and go back home."

"Then we can break backs," I added.

Lao Zi cocked her head and her ear tugged down to accent a grin that disappeared so fast I wasn't entirely sure I saw it. "Working for me," is all she said, but she rumbled a little when she spoke. I took that to be a happy sound, but with Tigerkin, who really knew?

I mean, Tigers sure were master hunters, but they were still a little too bloodthirsty for a Wolf. Admittedly, I wasn't above tearing out throats and dropping enemy bodies when the situation demanded it. I just didn't think of it as fun.

I guess I am in no position to judge though, this post-apocalyptic world is not as gentle as the one that preceded it. A world more suited to Tigerkind perhaps, but this is still a world created by the Fisher God for Wolfkind—and all kinds. The blind Fisherman told us that, so it must be true.

We have brought balance to the forest for the first time in over a century. When we arrived and first walked through our treasured forest, I saw massive stumps scattered throughout the beautiful old-growth trees and wondered how anyone could do that to something so magnificent. Humans have decimated the rain forest, cut down the biggest trees for money, and slaughtered the wildlife until only a few scattered deer and rabbits survive. Even the salmon have become as scarce as diesel fuel. Invasive species such as bighorn sheep, wild boars, and even coyotes have begun to move in, tearing up the soil and over-hunting or grazing beyond the lands ability to heal. The ecosystem was barely holding on when the apocalypse slaughtered millions of humans and isolated the newborn island that used to be the Olympic peninsula from a completely self-absorbed United States of America.

Now Wolves have returned to the Hoh Rain Forest for the first time in over a hundred years. Humans slaughtered the last of our kind for a five-dollar bounty per skin.

I sleepily looked around. Our snow-covered tree shelter was warm and dark except for the glowing coals of our fire. I fell asleep wondering how long it would take for our forest to be fully restored. I dreamed of thousand-dollar bounties on humans, but only the other humans would hunt them down for the money. Wolves are above such things, at least, in the world of dreams.

The next afternoon, we stared across Blue Glacier, in the brief clearing of the air when the snow slowed for a few moments before dropping heavier and harder than before. On the map, it didn't look very big, but all we could see was a treacherous snow-covered ice plateau stretching for kilometers. I looked up into the angry gray sky to gauge how long we had before sundown. I didn't want to get caught out there on the ice at nighttime.

"Lao Zi, looks like we have at least three hours to cross before it gets dark. What do you think?" I asked our Tiger.

"We can do it," she replied in a tone that implied *Tigers* could make it, anyway.

I unconsciously bared my teeth at the implication and she flashed a toothy grin that disappeared as fast as it showed up. Thorsten made a fishhook-in-the-cheek gesture and chuckles broke out all over. Yeah, Wolves are kind of easy to bait sometimes, but we prefer that to lying, even in jest.

"Single file this time. Snowshoes. Lao Zi, take point, you're the heaviest. Nina after me with the Robar C-50 ready. Tore and Joe next, with Thorsten bringing up the rear, as usual. Walk lightly. Move out," I commanded and we began to cross the glacier.

We were scoured by a brutal freezing wind throwing snow all over the place, but all of us had confidence in our teammate's snowcraft and situational awareness. Wasn't our first time outdoors. We lowered our well-wrapped heads into the powerful wind and strode forward onto the ice field gambling that we wouldn't fall into a concealed ice crevice. I had the Tigerkin leading the way for a reason, despite her bossiness and acidic sense of humor. She didn't hurry and would veer sideways for reasons she never felt a need to explain. Lao Zi carried a long staff she'd trimmed last night around the fire. She used it both as a walking staff and to test the ground ahead of us. She must have been doing it right because none of us fell to our icy death. Anyway, I figured that as lean as the Tigerkin had grown, she still massively outweighed me—and if she could make it across, then I knew that the rest of us could.

I just made sure to step in her footprints.

We made it across Blue Glacier with an hour to spare, and only one injury. Human, of course, the rest of us have nanites to take care of such things. Tore didn't break an ankle, but he came close. This was rough country, with very few flat areas on the map and none close enough for us tonight. I didn't like the choices we had for making camp somewhere out of the wind and snowfall, but it was almost dark and the temperature was rapidly falling. We were running out of time.

Tomorrow, we would locate a better place to make camp, but tonight we all needed rest. It had been a hard twelve days since we embarked on patrol.

Tonight, we would have to make do with a fire and a stone overhang that we could all just fit under if nobody got claustrophobic. It wasn't really sleep, but it was rest. Sometimes that's all what you get. Really made me miss our beehive-in-the-sky, though.

And Ella.

The next day dawned slowly and was heralded by heavy snow. The fire had gone out sometime during the long restless night. I stepped out from under the dubious shelter of the stone overhang and pulled my wool scarf tighter around my neck. Snow was falling heavily, big flakes that didn't melt on my shoulders and floppy knit hat.

"Move out in five minutes. We need to find a good place to ride out this storm and give us a chance to heal up and sleep. The map shows a small valley to our left, down a way. Sure to be heavily wooded. Might just be the spot," I said as my teammates crawled out from beneath the ledge and rose to stand beside me in the heavy snowfall.

"Tore, Joe, that valley is our goal. Shouldn't take too long to get there," I said, pointing to a location on the map. What I didn't say was, "If it takes too long, we'll freeze to death in this snowstorm."

Some things don't need saying.

Lao Zi grasped her staff and I moved to take point. We fell into our usual spots and began a painfully slow trudge down to the little valley. We had no shelter from the biting wind and snow so it was lucky we were going downhill. The visibility was too poor to snowboard, or, in the case of our Tiger, ski, so it was the snowshoes.

None of us liked wearing snowshoes, but in certain terrains they were the only things that make sense. They were just so slow! And tiring after a while because we are using different muscles than we normally do. Wolves are practical though—we don't complain about the things we can't change. Tigers, however, have no problem complaining.

They're quite good at it, in fact.

"Why are we patrolling route no one would traverse in this weather? Since you Wolves are so practical, please you can explain why we wasting our time getting wet and cold. We are protecting border that no one even knows, from who? What? Oh yes, I now remember—is because you think this construct good relations for our peoples. How is this working? I am start to hate a little on Wolves... and Humans," Loa Zi complained without looking back once. Tigers take hostile situations extremely seriously, but that doesn't mean they can't bitch about it.

It turns out that when the Tiger in your team isn't happy, nobody is.

They simply wouldn't dare.

I ignored the discomfort of the snow and cutting wind just as I ignored the verbal clawing we were enduring. But I couldn't wait until we got there and the big cat shut up. Nina's C-50 crept upwards in the direction of the Tiger's skull more than once, but I shoved the barrel back down each time. It was going to take all of us to get out of this one. Even Tigers on a mean rant had survival value.

The tiny vale was much steeper than I had expected. Massive Hemlock, Incense Cedar and Sitka Spruce filled up the slope enough that we had to dig through the snow-coat of the outer trees to reach the sheltered part of the tiny valley. Under our paws, the broken ground existed in its rough natural state, one normally very difficult for anyone to cross on foot, or paw—and forget about your snowboard.

From inside the upside-down snow cones, it was a bit like climbing from room to room in a giant's dimly lit playhouse, as we dug through white walls to the hollow spaces under each snow-covered tree. We had to clamber onto and across some of the thick lower branches inside just to make it over to the next tree. The whole thing was a slow, painstaking process but we eventually made it to the deepest part of the vale and settled on a home tree. We were so tired, and we could hear the wind howling like a banshee outside, but we couldn't just sit down and rest yet. The ground was so broken that we needed to construct a level floor where we could build a fire pit and spend a day resting up on. We were kilometers away from any flat ground so we made our own.

First, we laid fifteen poles we cut side by side, across three tree limbs that were at about the same height. We used strips of fresh bark to secure them in place. Then we cut thinner, more flexible branches and wove them in and out between the poles. My frozen paws were too clumsy at this point, but the humans came in very handy here. Once we couldn't fit any more in, we built another smaller platform below the first. Then Nina and I went to another nearby tree and began cutting huge armfuls of green pine fronds. Thorsten and Tore ran them back and forth as Joe, Nina, and I cut more fresh pine boughs.

Lao Zi assembled the thick bed of pine with insulation in mind, but when you patrol together you notice things. Like when someone really likes pillows and soft comfy beds. She was definitely the right Tiger for the job.

The finished bed was very thick; both soft and comfy, and smelled good too. That was a relief after so many nights in cramped circumstances. I'm not saying you couldn't pick up a whiff of ripe cat, but the clean piney scent dominated, making it a little easier to ignore the other, more pungent nuances. We were getting pretty good at ignoring unpleasant details by now. I just hoped I didn't need an intact sense of smell anytime soon.

Okay. Now we just needed a fire. For that we needed a flat rock as a firepit base, and some other smaller stone pieces to contain the fire. Plus, semi-dry firewood and a little dried moss to use as a fire starter. We already had all the green, wet wood we needed overhead, but someone was going to have to climb up and trim deadwood from our sheltering cedar.

That was okay, Wolves excel at climbing and jumping between big trees. It felt very much like our natural habitat, even if we were creatures new to the world. The truth is, just because there had never been a tree-hopping Timber Wolf/Human hybrid warrior before, didn't mean the Hoh rainforest wasn't our natural habitat. All things have a source and beginning. This was ours.

"Nina, Thorsten, help me pry hearth stones from that jagged ridge we saw, about thirty meters uphill from here. Lao Zi, Tore, Joe, I need you to clear and prepare the area where we are going to make our firepit. I want it to be someplace naturally downwind of our bed, so that the warmth of the fire is blown upwards, ensuring a nice currant of hot air under our pine needle bed through the night." Then I said, "Let's go," and tired or not, we scrambled for the jagged ridge.

It was not easy going, and the deepening storm threatened all kinds of mayhem, but so far, we had been lucky. We could still see where we were going.

Nina got there first, with me a step or two behind her and our human a distant third. Nina and I tried pulling together at the layers, but it remained a frozen block of old stone, pushed out of the earth by ancient tectonic plate shifts. The rock was hard and almost brittle, layered partially-crystalized sheets of black slate-like stone. Then Thorsten showed up and pulled out a compact tool-grade-steel pry bar and a hammer. I had to shake my head – the Viking dudes were a constant surprise to me. In a good way, that is. I stepped back to give him room.

Thorsten was wearing a white snowsuit crisscrossed with belts and pockets holding ammunition and weapons in every conceivable nook and cranny. I mean, how many people find room to carry a big hammer and prybar with them, just in case? But that's Thorsten. To the Viking dudes, a hammer is not just a hammer, it's a symbol of their faith. Viking dudes are efficient, funny, and terrifying all, depending on the situation. Sometimes, they are all of those at the same time. Still, you could do a lot worse in a teammate. Just don't let them start singing, trust me. At least not when they're facing you or even glancing in your direction. And if they start eating those red-topped mushrooms again—run!

It took a number of tries before we got a sheet of rock big enough for our new hearth. I couldn't feel my paws by then but took my turn whaling on the prybar and splitting off pieces of stone just like everyone else.

I couldn't feel my feet either, by the time we got enough stone on to a tough piece of canvas and began dragging the improvised sled back to our tree. It was really cold up there, exposed to the blizzard. I was very glad we didn't have to stay out there any longer than we did.

The rest of our team was glad to see us, and Lao Zi immediately picked up the big hearth stone and placed it precisely on the second, smaller platform we had built. It was positioned slightly below our comfy pine-bough bed.

The fire was glorious. My paws began to tingle in an unpleasant manner as circulation improved and I started to warm up, but I didn't care. It was a long time before I felt comfortable though.

We strung the rain tarp from our little tent over the bed and fire at an angle so that the hot air would flow across our shared bed. Joe filled a collapsible bucket with snow and set it on the hearth to melt. We popped the tent open and tied it over the bed so we could still trap body heat when we slept in soft comfort.

Now we had shelter, heat, and melting water. That just left food.

Tore started a stew with the meltwater and some dried stuff, while Joe began skinning a rabbit we'd startled on our way down here. When Tore began to unwrap some of our mutton and cutting chunks to drop in the stew, Lao Zi mumbled something in Mandarin. We were sitting around the fire watching and I was kind of glad Henry wasn't here, because I was pretty sure I wouldn't be very happy if I understood what she had said.

The cooking meat smelled wonderful, and Lao Zi's eyes were locked onto it as Tore worked. My eyes met Nina's, and she scooted a little back from the fire to lay her antimaterial rifle across her lap and start wiping it down to remove any moisture. It just happened to be pointing in the Tiger's general direction as she worked.

A Tigerkin's growl is much different than a Wolf's, but we had no problem understanding it. Nina slid her Robar's safety off and stood, raising her rifle to her shoulder, and abandoning any attempt to be diplomatic. Lao Zi slowly stood to tower over the White Wolf, her eyes furious as she showed Nina her teeth. Big mistake—the Tigerkin took her eyes off the rest of us, who had risen as well.

I deliberately jacked a cat-slug into my shotgun to get the Tigerkin's attention. Her body turned to present a narrower profile, but she never took her eyes off of Nina. Joe and the Viking dudes automatically separated to cover the angry Tiger with their assault rifles, and then Thorsten started humming a little.

Everyone froze. Lao Zi turned her massive head to face me.

"My need is greatest. Give me the meat. You can eat soup with the mice!" she demanded.

Okay, talking is better than fighting, but you never back down from bullies, it only encourages them.

"Soup spreads out the meat so that everyone can have a little. We all need protein. You can have two bowls of stew when it's ready because your bigger body needs more. But you can't have all the meat. Or, we can shoot you to pieces, butcher your body, and then everyone will have enough to eat," I said, wincing inside at the thought of eating Tigerkin meat. Wolves don't eat sentient people.

But Lao Zi didn't know that.

The hulking Tiger suddenly roared into the tree overhead in frustration and anger, then sat back down as if nothing had happened. She only growled, "hurry up," to Tore and stared into the fire.

We all sat back down too, some of us quicker than others. The soup came out a little bland, but Lao Zi didn't complain. That didn't mean she was happy about it, but I'd take it. I don't think any of us slept easily that night except the Tiger, but at least there were still six of us come morning.

Baby steps.

Chapter 45

THE INDIGO TOWER

Fimbulvetr was in full blown tantrum-mode across the Hoh Rain Forest and showed little sign of calming down anytime soon. The blizzard's lethal cold prevented anyone from going outside, it wasn't even possible to do a full perimeter check of the ground camp and surrounding trees. Sigrid said that no matter how many coats and hats the humans put on, they probably weren't going to be coming back if they stayed out there for more than five minutes.

Henry Chin, Ella, and the rest of the apprentice stone masons were holed up in the Cavern-quarry during this never-ending snowstorm. When the fledgling Stonemasons first started cutting basalt blocks a month ago, the place had been a little cramped for everyone. Not anymore! Now there was plenty of room, at least for Wolves, but then they do sleep in a pile and don't really need all that extra personal space like humans do.

The entrance to the Cavern-quarry was well-concealed. Inside, the most noticeable thing was the broad stone ceiling, with a gray clay layer still showing at the back of the chamber. To the right was a large fireplace with a glowing pottery kiln built into the left side of the fireplace. To the left were a dozen undressed stone blocks in various states of finish. Straight ahead was the constantly receding basalt seam being harvested for the Indigo Tower. The room was warm, especially when the kiln was in action. It was large enough to relieve the pressure of being cramped up in the

Treehouse, knee to knee, with dozens of humans and Wolves all day long.

Wolves like to stay busy. Each morning started with several of the Stonemasons painstakingly chiseling out rectangular blocks of iridescent basalt from the bedrock. Another team dragged each crude stone block to the work area, where they were chiseled smooth with steel tools and iron mallets, which the Stonemasons were wielding with increasing skill and speed. The Wolves had not only grown passionate about stonemasonry, but it was rapidly becoming something more for them, an art. How do you know when something is art? When no one wants to stop at the end of the day.

Once each indigo basalt block was painstakingly finished, it was transported, one at a time, to the building site where the five-story defensive tower was beginning to come together.

Transported. It sounds so simple.

In the old world, technology made this kind of thing a breeze. In this new, post-apocalyptic world, it is anything but.

First each stone block was dragged out the hidden quarry door, rolling on small logs that had to be constantly picked up from behind and placed in front as you went. Nanites repaired a few pinched paws and flattened feet before the Stonemason team got the hang of this process.

Once the building blocks emerged into the storm-lashed air of the blizzard, they had to be carefully loaded onto a Wolf-powered sledge the Viking dudes had built. That was the easiest part of the process.

Walking up the path to the ridge when they first arrived didn't seem to take long at all. Dragging a sturdy sled loaded with sixty kilograms of rock uphill through the frigid chaos of the snowstorm was quite different. Realistically, the journey took about forty minutes, but it seemed much longer to the Wolf pulling the sledge.

Once they arrived at the building site, another freezing Wolf waited for them with a well-tended fire that kept the mortar fluid. The sled was immediately abandoned for the fire until everyone could feel their paws and feet again.

Next, it took two to heft the stone block up into its place and mortar it securely in the tower's growing walls. Without the pullytripod, they wouldn't have been able to raise the stone blocks off of the ground high enough. The Fisher clan's 'pully thing' had a surprising range of advantages. Sigrid, the treehouse-in-the-sky architect, was a natural at it, and the Viking dudes could build anything Sigrid could dream up.

Then it was time to turn around and go back for the Wolf who had tended the mortar pot fire. Their job was to drag the empty sled back downhill to the warmth of the Cavern-quarry. This part always went much faster. The Wolf that had just pulled the loaded sledge up to the building site stayed behind to keep the fire under the mortar pot alive, and rest until their replacement arrived, dragging a new block of Indigo basalt behind them.

Lately, Ella felt like it took her at least twenty-minutes to warm up and stop shivering after a Tower run, but she didn't complain. She always felt ravenous after getting back to the Cavern-quarry and headed straight for the small kitchen tucked into the corner by the pottery kiln. She was quickly joined by the other members of her pack, being dominant Wolf and all.

Ella was just savoring the warmth of the kiln next to her, glowing fiercely in the dim, warm air of the Cavern-quarry. Ona ladled a big bowl full of smoked salmon stew for her from the brick stove bult into the side of the kiln. Then she passed Ella one of Tosh's home-ground-whole-grain baguettes, to dunk in the high-protein salmon chowder. Everyone else got a bowl of stew as well, so Ella grabbed a pitcher of spring water to sit down and dine with her pack around the fire. Everything was absolutely delicious, and she could tell that this was just what her body craved.

Ella was glad that there were four other Stonemason Wolves capable of making the Tower run, so her duty only came twice a day. She had plenty of time to get warm and work on her stoneware jars in the meantime. The Viking dudes had built a new potter's wheel for her, and she absolutely loved working with it. She was able to finish a stoneware jar and a soup bowl before it was her turn to make the last Tower run of the day.

Ella and Sigrid were able to mortar the first block of the Indigo Tower's third story into place, and it felt wonderful to see everything coming together. The downhill trip home seemed to go much faster when you weren't alone. The Cavern-quarry's warmth was heavenly, and her team had big bowls of chowder waiting for them when they finally got back from the building site. The workday was finally done for today.

Her eyes were drawn to the other side of the cavern where fresh-hewn blocks of basalt were being finished. This particular basalt stone shimmered with indigo glitter in the right light, but only if you had enhanced-spectrum eyesight like all of the non-humans did. Even the Tigers could see it. The Wolves found it quite beautiful, but unaltered humans were blind to its beauty. Sigrid said that they were just too primitive, like the Neanderthal before them. That this new world belonged to the Hybrid races, but only a handful of unaltered Humans were even aware of their existence, which they outnumbered millions-to-one.

Funny, Ella pondered, how a genetic upgrade that was originally designed to enhance our battle prowess now only showed beauty, of a sort not everyone could see. It seemed almost like fate might be playing a hand, at least to Ella. But then she didn't think she believed in fate.

Ella half-dozed, her fur glowing in the warm fireplace light, wondering how the Alpha and his mixed-bag-of-species was doing out there in the frozen wilderness. Maybe the wind wouldn't be too bad up in the foothills of the Olympic mountains? The rainforest old growth should spare them some of the wind's fury. But if she'd learned one thing on her Tower runs, it was that it's much harder to conserve heat while you're exposed to the storm. Out there the wind cuts like a sharp blade—you don't really feel it at first, and then it burns cold.

Ella didn't like that part of her pack was out there in the storms, day after day, traveling to someplace they'd never been before. Oh, she was sure they were okay—the Alpha was smart and tough as nails. Trey had pack watching over him, so he was as safe as anyone…traveling with a Tiger and some Humans would be…piece of cake... Ella sat up gnashing her teeth. It wasn't that she lacked faith in her people, she just missed Trey. The world was simply a colder place when he wasn't around.

And it was cold enough already.

Chapter 46

FOUND MY PARADISE

I could feel my strength slowly leeching away into the wind's unforgiving cold. We had relentlessly forged through the screaming whiteout, intent on getting back home before our bodies gave out. I intentionally kept the starving Tiger in front of me as we hiked through the ice-sheathed forest, for obvious reasons.

The Seal Clan's hidden cave was three weeks ago, and they saved our lives. I had considered the possibility of the Seals giving us a hard time, maybe throwing their weight around, like humans are wont to do. I was wrong—they were delighted to see Joe and the Viking dudes. They gave us Wolves and our Tiger a sort of automatic acceptance, just because we were traveling with Joe and two Viking dudes. This was something I had never experienced before, and it felt nice. Most humans either felt immediately threatened by our differences and size or embraced us with cioppino and hot baguettes. Not a lot of middle ground in my experience, although it's only been a pawful of months since I woke up, so… maybe not an expert in how this new world works.

I did know that threatened humans far outnumber the welcoming ones, so we just ignored the haters and enjoyed the company of a few good men and women of different species. The blind fisherman says life is something beautiful you make with what you have. Our life was indeed beautiful in his eyes. Well, his eyes don't work anymore but he insists that his Fisher god has made him see.

Yeah, I don't get it either, but he sure gets around well for a blind man.

The Seal colony cavern was truly amazing, like nothing I had ever seen before.

The immense cavern sloped upwards in a basalt dome at least thirty-meters high in the center. All along the perimeter of most of the cavern were pine-wood scaffolding, filled with apartments or bars or quiet book-corners with soft lighting, going all the way back into the cavern walls. Rough ladders provided quick access to the different levels, of which I counted five. The gentle light of amber LED bulbs dotted the great framework walls in thousands of small golden lights. The impact was stunning—both deliciously warm and beautiful to boot. We could smell marvelous food cooking. This place was like water in the desert to me, if you could call anything in this white hell of Fimbulvetr a desert.

Pretty sure that made this Seal colony's cave an oasis in the wilderness, like the kind the blind fisherman told stories about on nights when maybe he'd had an extra whiskey or two.

I decided I liked oases. I looked down into the immense chamber. In the center of the cavern's main floor was a great firepit, complete with a huge beef thigh slow-roasting in goat-powered rotisserie splendor on the nearest corners of the central fire pit. The smell was heavenly—so I immediately turned to focus on Lao Zi. For a Tiger, this was temptation most foul. It was, however, the lesser of evils.

Tonight's beef haunch could either be dinner for close to eighty people, or it could sate a starving Tigerkin on something that was already dead, instead of slaughtering dozens of living humans in a mad feeding frenzy.

Pretty simple math to me.

Although we couldn't help but notice how well armed the Seal Clan people were. The Seals were also sharp enough to not only recognize the dangerous force they had brought into their home, but secure enough in their own power to deliberately loose our Tiger companion on an innocent steamboat round of very rare beef.

I did notice that there were no humans between us and the roasting meat. In fact, everyone was on the other side of the cavern at least three stories up, watching us intently. Every one of them held a firearm pointed our way, too. They *were* unusually quiet for humans in a group, but I was beginning to realize that our Seal Clan was anything but ordinary.

Earlier, I had made sure that Thorston let the Seals know that once a Tiger has fed, it would revert to the cold-reasoning mind of a sentient Tigerkin. Admittedly, Tigerkin were sadistic meat-eaters with a loose definition of meat, but Tigers were also capable of reason and logic once they weren't really hungry.

Really, they are highly-intelligent people. Monsters, yes, but intelligent ones in full control of themselves, capable of both logic and sociopathic hierarchy competition, just so long as they weren't too hungry. Despite the obvious threat Tigerkind represents, we Wolves never forget that we have been painted with the same brush, and we are all monsters to most humans who come across us. It doesn't matter how nice we are, many humans are initially terrified of us until they actually get to know a Wolfkin, and that unreasoning fear is very dangerous for anyone different. After all, humankind has slaughter millions upon millions of their fellow men and women, simply over minor differences like skin color or religion or political opinions.

And we are an entirely different species. Doesn't look too promising in the long term.

However, *my* Wolves have risen far above our gene-engineered parameters, and are determined to be honorable monsters, instead of the primitive killing machines humans designed us to be.

"Go—feast on warm meat!" I commanded our Tigerkind. She bared her teeth in a happy way and spun to do so. Lao Zi was at the firepit in seconds, roaring with both triumph and ferocious hunger. I hoped that any small children watching looked away in time. The almost-three-meter-tall Tigerkin slashed the massive haunch of rare roast beef once with each paw, and then fell upon the helpless meat in a ravenous feeding frenzy that was frightening enough to maybe reappear in a few nightmares later tonight.

"How do you feel about grilled sausages and barbequed goat?" Captain Marc asked me, "Have you ever had Sevilla goat barbeque? It's wonderful, but a little greasy. We serve it in fresh tortillas, but you need a lot of beer to balance the grease out. Jacob will help you out there, he has keys to the liquor lockboxes. Now come on over here and leave the Tiger to play with its food. When's the lasty time you had a full meal?" My stomach growled loudly in answer and smiles broke out all over. Seal Clan sure does know how to take care of a post-battle warrior, be they Wolf, Tiger, or Human.

Food. Beer (for humans). Sleep.

Despite everything, I wouldn't trade places with a human for all the meat in the world. I love being a Wolf. Things are a lot simpler for a Wolf than a human, too. We mate for life, and I already knew who my beloved was. Didn't matter how far apart physically we were, Ella and I knew. Like I said, simpler.

We ate in shifts, children first, then mothers, warriors (including my team), and single females and males last. After dinner I curiously watched the Seals break down everything with military precision. It was all very organized and felt comfortable to Nina and me. Everyone slid smoothly into the routine of their evening like pieces in a giant clockwork. It was very impressive because of the scale and gave me a few ideas as well for my guys.

I looked around. My team were the only people who didn't have a routine in this place, unless patting our full bellies and fighting off sleep counted. So, I was intrigued when Captain Marc came by and invited me for a tour.

"I think I can see everything in the cavern from here, did you want to go outside?" I asked, reaching for my snow gear.

"It's deliberately not possible to see *everything* from here. That would be lousy security. Come on, I think you'll enjoy this," he said with a smile. I shrugged my shoulders. "Sure!" I answered. What else was there for an Alpha Wolf to do around here, anyway? At least we were full-bellied and warm!

We wound our way around the glowing firepit, veering between groups of SEALs doing PT and older cubs learning how to disassemble and put back together weapons of all kinds on long tables. I can't remember learning how to do that, but my paws remember just fine.

We approached the fresh pinewood scaffolding that rose six stories above us. The captain and his staff flowed up the ladders without pause, until they reached the third story, where they settled next to the ladder as I joined them.

I looked around curiously. We were on a wide three-meter-wide walkway, with packed compartments on one side and open air on the other. To our left was a bar with translucent plastic walls that showed movement without detail. I could tell it was a bar because of the yeasty scents mixed with human sweat and sawdust. The music and raucous laughter helped too.

In front of us was some kind of medic's office run by a hard-eyed human female who appeared to completely ignore us. She had as many wrinkles as the Cat-lady back on Marrowstone Island. Captain Marc walked up to and past her without pause as the she typed something into her computer. I heard a metallic click, and the wall behind her swung open. The captain walked right in.

Good security indeed!

Huh. I wonder what needs this level of protection?

I gave the wrinkled female plenty of room as I followed Captain Marc into the wall. She kind of gave me the creeps. Couldn't help but notice that she kept her right hand out of sight the whole time. I had a feeling that that was part of her job too, so I didn't take it personally. Still didn't take my eyes off of her.

We walked down a short curving tunnel, through another salvaged metal ship's hatch, and then into a big room. The large chamber was carved out of solid rock in a roughly oval shape with a mostly-level floor. The rugs helped. Bundles of wires seemed to run everywhere, but our path was well lit and clear of trip-hazards. There were large monitor screens on three of the walls and a cluster of individual workstations in the left half of the room. All the chairs were full of busy people. The other side of the room just had a fancy lit-up table with several higher-ranking SEALs studying it. Everyone in the room only briefly looked up as we entered before returning to tapping their keyboards, and for the first time I realized that my Wolves and Lao Zi must have been under observation all day. Why else would no one be surprised to see a Wolfkin stroll into this kind of high-security intelligence center? I was definitely expected.

Well, I didn't have anything to hide, so I didn't let it bother me. As these new neighbors of ours got to know us, they would come to realize that Wolves are not sneaky. I guess there are worse things than having a non-hostile neighbor keeping an eye on your place.

We walked over to the lit-up table.

The officers that had been studying it drifted back to both give us room and flank us. My eyes met Captain Marc's and he might have been about to smile but didn't. He shrugged minutely and I had to drop a silent Wolf-laugh. Well-trained people are worth their weight in platinum, Henry always says. "It's the amateurs that you worry about. You never know what they're going to do next."

Yeah. These Seals were the complete opposite of amateur. Some of their warriors were as highly-trained as we Wolves once were. When skills are equal, it comes down to a matter of speed and power, an arena where Wolves seldom lose. But these guys were very good, I could just tell from the way they held themselves.

"Here is where we are" he said, pointing down near the center on the glowing table. The detail was amazing, and then Captain Marc did something with his hands, and the area blew up, focused on the mountainside trail we took on our way to here. I recognized it. I turned to look at Captain Marc and raised my chin in respect.

"You have a satellite!" I growled happily. He shrugged and I thought I saw his face move for a second. Then it was back to its normal, stone-like mask of a Seal ranking officer on duty.

"You'd be shocked to know how many satellites were lost or misplaced after the apocalypse. We were the only ones who went looking. We adopted some we liked and gave them a new home orbit," he said. "One of them is yours now," he added as if it were nothing important.

"Some?" I asked. He nodded. "What? One is ours?" He nodded again. I was a little stunned. I wanted Captain Marc to know that this wasn't something small to us. I leaned forward to speak.

"From our first week in this life, Wolves have always valued good communication. We developed a hand-sign language under the brutal hand of Commander Elwha's Sailors in our third week of slavery. We painfully learned to speak again, but never where any humans could hear. We practiced late at night. After we gained our freedom, we discovered YouTube and the internet. We hungered to fill the places in our heads where memories used to go. That's how we discovered our paradise, the Hoh Rain Forest.

"Now we hunger for the kind of access this satellite gives us. Havenlands needs to move forward in the world, not look backwards. This gives us what we need to survive the coming war, when the Commander's sailors come armed with electro-shock collars, looking for their runaway Dogs. Now we can be better prepared. Thank you, Seal Clan," I said. Captain Marc's professional face is one carved in granite. I know that. He prides himself on running a professional operation, and never smiles.

But he did this time.

"You gave us refuge and a huge wind-powered generator that takes care of all our electronic needs and more. Seal Clan will always come when you call. We know that you will come when we call. We are of one tribe. We are Seal Clan Haven, a part of Havenlands," he said and everyone in the room snapped to attention. This startled me, but I knew they didn't mean any harm, so I pretended that I hadn't jumped a little. Alphas in command don't show signs of weakness in public if they can help it.

"We will also send some techs and new equipment to that beautiful tower you are building in the spring. We need to sync communications and install computers systems that will allow us to talk with each other in seconds. We'll also do a deep dive into your entire electronic network to make sure it is fully state of our art. The Tigers are next after we finish with your needs," he added.

"That would be great!" I said. "Just have your people defer to our Wolves, Sigrid and Tinker, during the upgrade," I added just to make sure everyone knew where they ranked in today's flexible pack hierarchy.

Captain Marc nodded, saying, "just as you will defer to my people when you are here on my base."

"We will," I agreed, "but we won't be staying very long; just enough to get a good night's sleep, reprovision, and then we'll head home by way of the lower elevations," I added. I sure was glad we were done with the mountainous part of the route. Just big foothills and forest and frozen rivers from here on out.

Piece of cake.

"Stay as long as you need. Jacob?" he said into the air. A powerfully built young human appeared at the captain's side.

"Please escort our guests to the liquor lockboxes and find them something to drink. Then show them and the Tiger to the quarters we have ready for them," Captain Marc Christensen ordered.

"Instead of intoxicants, can we just give the Tiger her own room? Preferably the humans as well?" I requested of our host. Everyone in the room looked at the captain.

"Find them all a shower and a room to themselves. Fully provision them. The next time one of our Seahawks has to get out and stretch its legs, do a resupply drop for the homeward-bound Wolf patrol. Enjoy your stay Trey, need to go now," Captain Marc said politely and turned to join a small cluster of people who were all waiting to talk to him.

I really enjoyed my hot shower and not sleeping with my nose tucked into a human's armpit.

Hot water is a beautiful thing.

Now, plodding through the bitter wind, I sighed through the scarves wrapping my face, protecting it from frostbite, and found myself wondering what Ella was doing. The blizzard shrieked its defiance in pitches known only to elementals. I couldn't feel my ears or feet, which is never a good sign. However, it was Lao Zi who had it the worst. Her large body was a natural target for the mean wind screaming in my ears. Her heat loss was greater with her larger frame, no matter how withered and skinny her once muscular body was becoming. The problem was that we hadn't had any fresh meat in five days. That's a long time for a Tiger in the field. Bone soup just wasn't cutting it anymore. The hulking Tigerkin's survival instincts battled with her intellect constantly, and it didn't look like intellect would be winning the day for much longer.

Tigers are always dangerous to be around. We all knew that, but a starving Tigerkin was lightyears worse. Tigers have never had the same firm definition of "edible" as humans or even Wolves to start with. And everyone knows that a Tiger will eat anyone under the right circumstances, and the circumstances weren't looking too good for any of the rest of us these last few days.

Yes, we could tell she was fighting her ancestral instincts, but all of us knew that the longer this starvation diet went on, the closer a bloody end for the rest of us came. Lao Zi needed meat badly. And it was going to take more than one of us before she would be able to stop chomping people as fast as she could swallow.

We needed our Tiger alive. I really didn't want to have to kill her. "Halt. Take five out of the wind. I need to study the map," I said. I was almost surprised everyone heard me, but they all collapsed into the dubious shelter of stone outcroppings or tree trunks. After a moment, Nina and Tore stumbled over to my side to study our Topo map. We were very close to home.

Everyone gave the Tiger plenty of room.

Lao Zi ignored the rest of us, drinking meltwater from a steel canteen. I was good with that; I had no desire to be the subject of her hungry gaze. She knew better than to start something she couldn't finish anyway, but there would come a point at which this would no longer carry weight. Starving Tigers were terrible to behold.

I kind of liked Lao Zi, but she wouldn't be the first Tigerkin to meet her end at the clamping of my jaws. Better all round for her to pretend disinterest. Tigers are very smart; I have no doubt that she had already considered all of the variables. It doesn't always take a weather satellite to tell which way the wind blows.

We were meters away from the frozen Bogachiel River when we surprised two deer. Lao Zi took command immediately, and we were soon found ourselves with two piles of venison so fresh that they were steaming in the frozen air.

Lao Zi remained disciplined for the second it took me to tell her to take one of the deer. Then she was glorying in the fresh meat, noisily crushing bones with those impressive teeth and inhaling globs of bloody protein. The rest of us ate more slowly, but we were equally famished. After five minutes Lao Zi wrapped the remains of her meal in the deer's raw hide, stood tall, and turned without a word to climb the slope to our right, headed home to her mountain haven. I had to smile.

Cats never waste time saying goodbye when it's time to go.

We Wolves were normally patient people, but all I could think about as we finally crossed the frozen Bogachiel River, was grabbing my pack and cubs and Ella and squeezing them tight.

My Patrol team had evolved into something powerful and deadly over the past seven weeks. The hardships of traveling through the forests, traversing mountains and glaciers, of walking forever in a snow globe somebody shook really hard, has left us lean and with an innate knowledge of our companions, and ourselves.

I'm normally not prone to introspection, but out here in the snowstorms we live simultaneously in two realities. The first one is the simple physical awareness and tactical coordination with your teammates as we silently move through the foothills of mountains.

In the other reality, we're left alone with our own thoughts, starved for the real-world sensory bandwidth we are used to. Our minds are neither terribly sophisticated nor complex—we've only been sentient for a little over half a year. Not a ton to work with there, so we found ourselves reexamining the few memories we've built so far. Wolves are acutely aware of the holes in our heads where memories used to go, but we can't focus too much on our losses without becoming bitter and who wants to be that guy?

So, you trudge through the screaming whiteout, repeatedly replaying your favorites in your mind. These often turn out to be small moments of triumph or simple physical contact with your pack. Moments you often took for granted.

But now they keep you warm in the cold.

We crossed the frozen river and hurried in the direction of our ground camp, where we could see a bonfire and smell some of our pack. Ella's sweet/spicy scent warmed my heart, but there was something new, something intoxicating about it. My heart beat faster, and I could feel the blood in my veins pulsing. I dismissed these things to wrap my arms around her and my packmates. I never wanted to let go.

Ella nuzzled me as I hugged her tightly. Then I leaned away a little and reached out to gather Rachel and Bookworm in as closely as I could. The pack closed in around us again, taking comfort in the scent and touch of pack come home. Eventually we physically broke apart to hug and say hi to the others of our tribe. That was when I noticed how bony Ella and the other adults were.

"You are so thin. Are you and our pack okay? What happened?" I asked, although I was pretty sure I knew.

"Our food stores are low and we've been rationing," she said, and I knew that meant the Wolves had been getting the same amount as the humans were; maybe insisting on it. "Don't worry! We will be alright as soon as the snow lets up a little and we can hunt again. Then we can eat our fill of fresh venison and rabbit," Ella added a little wistfully. I nuzzled her again.

"Come on!" Rachel yelled, waving an arm toward home, "We've got a whole party planned!" Cheers and laughter burst out all around. Except from Ella. She growled in the most bad attitude way I had ever heard from her.

"Oh, she has been SO crabby!" Lenny said, rolling his eyes. "We've learned to just stay out of her way. Come on, let's go!" And the whole crowd happily moved toward the Treehouse.

Except Ella. She looked distressed somehow. She grabbed my arm but I pulled her along, anxious to get home and enjoy the pack.

"No, Trey," she hissed in my ear as we trudged the final steps. "We can't go to the Treehouse tonight…"

I looked at her in confusion. "What are you talking about? Everyone wants to hear about our journey!"

She snarled with a scowl…or more of a cute frown, maybe? I couldn't think straight. My head was spinning from my mate's closeness and her oddly delicious scent.

"The old fisherman and Lenny and Grandma…" I said.

"Grandma is the one who helped me figure out what was happening…I wasn't sure…" Ella whispered. Then she added the bombshell.

"I'm in heat," she said softly.

Suddenly silence fell. I stared at her in amazement; so did the rest of the pack. Wolves have very good hearing. Even the Viking dudes shut up to listen.

"Heat?" I repeated just as softly—but everyone could hear. Somebody mumbled, "That explains a lot…"

She nodded. "You are my forever mate and will be the father of my cubs," she said, gazing into my eyes.

I tipped my head up, nose to the sky, and howled, louder than I ever had before. Rachel whooped and Bookworm dropped a head-splitting Wolf grin on us. And it got kind of noisy for a while. I raised my eyes to the sky, noticing that the snowfall had turned to a freezing rain. Maybe the long winter was finally coming to an end?

"Give your love to the tribe, but then we need to get going," Ella said and tugged on my paw. I did, and she led me away into the rainforest. She had a private little shelter up there, set up in one of the lower levels of the tower.

Long ago, there had been someone and some cubs, I think. Before the Apocalypse. Before I was remade into a weapon. Someone and something that had been torn from me forever. It had seemed like a hole that could never be filled.

Not anymore.

Sure, it was the most amazing night of my life, but that wasn't the best part. I had a future now; a way to make new memories to fill those gaping holes.

Memories to keep us warm through the coldest of times.

**Watch for the third book in the series, "Bad Bear, Good Wolf"!

Spring is coming and with it, all the Wolves enemies are gearing up for payback. And the Commander isn't the only one looking for revenge. World forces are zeroing in on the thorn in their side and the Havenlands just might be the only point of resistance.

About the Author

Eric Little lives in the Pacific Northwest, drawn by his love of the mountains and rainforests. He slings wine by day and writes science fiction by night. He has a lifelong background in the martial arts with Sun Tai Chi, Lu Bagua, and Xing-Yi being his preferred styles.
Eric is working on several different sci-fi series and has published short stories in several NIWA anthologies, OPA anthologies, as well as Varida P&R anthology, "No Way Out".

The Good Wolf Series includes "Bad Dog, Good Wolf" and "Bad Cat, Good Wolf". Watch for the third book in the series, "Bad Bear, Good Wolf" coming out soon.
Follow Eric on Twitter: @Yipman44

www.ingramcontent.com/pod-product-compliance
Lightning Source LLC
Chambersburg PA
CBHW071132180726
48291CB00007B/2153